THE YARD GIRL

by

Eugenie Laverne Mitchell

Thanks and appreciation:

To God for His constant presence, loving care, tender mercies and divine leading
and inspiration
To family for constant support, listening ears and firm shoulders
To friends and love ones for encouragement and just being there - just being you

Cover art by David Bernard

TABLE OF CONTENTS

Chapter 1

April 2015

"You liar - you Jezebel - you wicked ungrateful girl", the words slapped Sienna across the face like a large open hand. This was not the reaction she had expected.

"How dare you stand there in my own house and tell me lies a...a..about my wonderful son - you liar - you viper". Sister Newson was a raging bull ready to charge as she stood, hands akimbo, spitting out the ugly insults.

"Or maybe I should use stronger terms - you *dutty* cheap wretch - I thought you were decent that's why I allowed you to come and live in my house, but now I realise you are about as innocent as the devil's PA". The hurtful words were spewed out as though they were hot coals burning the inside of Sister Newson's mouth. She began to gesticulate wildly with her arms, intensifying her rant. This person acting like a crazy fool was not the sweet holy spirit-filled church warden that Sienna had come to know over the past four years - surely her soul had been possessed by a belligerent spirit.

As she continued to demean, degrade and debase, Sister Newson became short of breath and Sienna fretted that the exertion might trigger a heart attack or stroke in the frail older woman. "Please calm down Sister Newson", she implored, but the exhortation went unheeded, apparently serving only the unintended purpose of spurring to higher heights of fury and deeper depths of wrath. Sister Newson got up close and personal, trespassing into Sienna's personal space, as she poised to launch a further verbal onslaught.

"The audacity, the impudence, the effrontery.....de...de cheek", Sister Newson fluctuated between the Queen's English and Jamaican patois, as saliva escorted her words.

Eyes of burning coals pierced through Sienna's fragile persona and penetrated to her nervous system, causing her to shiver with fear at being accosted by this crazy being. She shrunk away from her verbal attacker, endeavouring to dodge the assault - and the spit, and turned her eyes up towards heaven in a silent prayer for the blitz to cease, as she regretted that she had sought Sister Newson's intervention into the situation.

"Look at me when I'm talking to you". Sienna involuntarily obeyed the command.

"Impertinent". Sister Newson spat suddenly, while simultaneously throwing both arms into the air, causing Sienna to jump as the threat that she might cause serious damage with her inch long fingernails made itself felt.

"After all that I have done for you - you ungrateful little tramp - the only way you saw fit to repay me is by casting aspersion upon my poor innocent son - you frustrated trash-bag". Sister Newson paused to take several shallow breaths then continued, "As if my son would even give a second glance to a cheap dragged up urchin like you".

Sienna bowed her head as the words cast shame over her spirit. Tears stung the back of her eyes. She felt acutely alone and vulnerable as she appreciated her position.

"I said look at me when I am speaking to you - you s**g-bag". A sudden surge of strength from somewhere deep within prompted Sienna to disobey this order. The power from within also assisted her struggle against an overwhelming desire to release pent up tears.

Sister Newson - whom Sienna once viewed as her saviour, had turned against her so abruptly and so completely. This customarily mild mannered, pious Angel who never missed Sunday morning praise and worship at Born Again Church of God, whose mouth and tongue customarily sang and shouted God's praises, now apparently possessed by a demon, was using the same mouth and tongue to spew out unrighteousness, smiting Sienna's fragile ego as though with an unyielding cat a nine tails.

"Look at you - which gentleman would look at a bedraggled stray like you".
"Take a good look at yourself Sienna - go on - LOOK".

Sienna looked down at her arms, acknowledging the cheap material of the polyester dress that she had purchased at the local market with money given to her by Sister Newson, funds that she was informed were from the elder woman's own pocket, over and above the bursary paid each month. Her eyes travelled down her body and alighted upon the plimsolls that adorned her feet. They too had been a gift from Sister Newson - one she had accepted gratefully and with humility, in the same manner that she had accepted all of Sister Newson's other gifts to her, including the purple plastic handbag which she carried daily regardless of the fact that the colour, more often than not, clashed with the rest of her attire. Sienna knew how to be appreciative - she had been brought up in a home where poverty had taken up residence as a non-paying tenant and had been groomed by her family's circumstances. They were among the poorest in the small village where she was born and bred, so Sienna was well seasoned in the art of showing gratitude for the kindness of others. The opportunity to put that experience to good use had arisen most days over the past four years whilst living in Sister Newson's home, for she was constantly reminded by the older woman of the "sacrifices" made to accommodate her and each time she said "thank you", or bowed in subservience.

Suddenly Sienna was overcome by a strong surge of indignation, accompanied by a raging torrent of pride which she was not previously aware inhabited the depth of her soul. The combined emotions rose up within her and seized control of her mind, forcing her to acknowledge that she had been grateful to a fault. She became acutely aware of her adornment - the distinct tastelessness of the cheap polyester salmon coloured dress, the less than comely bargain basement purple plastic handbag and the black plimsolls that no other pupil at her university would be seen dead in. The overwhelming flood washed over her, prompting her to kick off the plimsolls, to begin to free herself of the scourge of pitiful charity. She listened to the previously silent voice of her self-esteem that now shouted that she would not continue to be an object of Sister Newson's arrogant sympathy - that she would rather walk bare-footed and sleep with dignity upon frost covered pavements.

"What you doing?" Sister Newson shouted. "You wan' fe fight me now?" "Why you kick off you' shoes dem?", she stepped back, head cocked, anticipating Sienna's next move. But Sienna just hung her head in frustration, and satisfied that there was no impending threat from the younger woman Sister Newson resumed her rant.
"You have been living with me for four years now - practically for free". "You come and go as you please - do as you like in my house and you pay me back by maligning my son".

Sister Newson was overlooking the numerous commandments, including an on-going curfew, that Sienna was obliged to observe whilst living under her roof. The voice of her conscience did not speak to remind her of the fact that Sienna more than paid her way by doing all of the household chores, including washing her clothes, most of the cooking and all of the gardening, which obviated the need for her to employ a home help or gardener. Sister Newson's needs invariably ranked above Sienna's studies, which meant extra hard work at university to keep up with the curriculum, but she never grumbled - not even once.

"Your parents sent you to London to study in order to better yourself but all you see fit to do is follow men".

"Who me? Not me?" "I don't follow men... I have never even had a boyfriend", Sienna broke her silence as tears gave last warning. Sister Newson sniggered - she had hit a home run with that unjust statement. She gathered momentum from Sienna's reaction.

"All these bwoys that I see you wid walking 'pon street..,.. you tink I don't know what you getting up to wid dem". Jamaican parlance framed the lies that flowed freely from Sister Newson's lips, calculated to inflict harm. She had seen Sienna twice in the company of two boys and on both occasions the plausible explanation provided was that they had walked her home from late study sessions. Why on earth would she bring up these encounters now, Sienna wondered, even as she opened her mouth to remonstrate.

"Me... boys - no - you haven't seen me with any boys". "You have only seen me with Carlton and Melvin..... dem is me class mates .... we study together", tear-muffled words tumbled from Sienna's lips.

"We study together" Sister Newson mimicked then continued. "Who are you kidding - certainly not me - I know how your type operate - s**g". "I know what you are giving dem boys, you can't fool me - you have no home training - just like a *leggo beast"*. The slur against her virtue did not affect Sienna nearly as much as that against her upbringing, which proved too much for her to tolerate and she sobbed loudly in retaliation before murmuring indecipherable words.

"Not one bit of home training you don't have". "Whoever brought you up must be just as cheap and nasty as you", Sister Newson rubbed salt into the open wound now festering within Sienna's heart, obliterating any gratitude that had once resided there.

"Don't you ever insult me madda and fadda .... you .... you ... old obeah ooman", Sienna shouted uncharacteristically, before turning and running towards the safety of her bedroom.

Unaffected by Sienna's retaliatory outburst, Sister Newson followed hot on her heels, huffing and puffing.

"In my own house..... oh no you don't young lady .... not in my own house." The volume and pitch of her voice was just below glass shattering range as she clambered up the stairs faster than her arthritic joints had ever allowed. She rapped at the pine bedroom door so hard that her hand ached, but she ignored the excruciating pain. "What do you think you doing?" "How dare you lock this door". "How dare you insult me in my own house". "Open this door right now - open it - you little tramp." Then, after pausing to take several breaths, she concluded. "You better look for some other mug to mooch off of". Her tone was resolute. After another series of breaths she further proclaimed. "You are no longer welcome in this house - you hear me - you hear me - you have to go .... you must get out". "This is your last night in this house". The final sentence was shouted loud and clear and Sienna understood the message very well - she had overstayed her welcome and it was time to leave.

Chapter 2

April 2015

After a full hour of sobbing in the dark Sienna had no more tears. The drying up of her tears coincided with the beginning of Sister Newson's snores. For the first time since she had come to live with the older woman Sienna appreciated the sound, which was reminiscent of a horse's neigh. Tonight they had begun suddenly - one moment there were curses resounding through the dividing wall between the bedrooms and the next there was snoring.

Reaching over to the bedside table Sienna switched on the lamp. She looked around her, and pondered her surroundings. The room reminded her of one she had seen in an old movie, set post second world war. It was apparent the last time it was decorated predated the passing away of Sister Newson's husband. The brown and beige floral wallpaper was peeling at the edges. There were several small patches of damp in corners, as there were throughout the house, which contributed a rancid odour to the general degeneration of the dwelling. The red and green patterned carpet which must have been the rage back in 1988 when it was purchased, now had moth eaten sections, and the blue, red and green floral curtains defeated uniformity, and did nothing to lift the ambience. The room was at its very best dull and drab, and at its worst, stomach-churning. There were no choice antiques here. The furniture was just old. Both the wardrobe and dressing table bore heavy scrawls and scratches all over them. They may once have been grand, but had clearly seen better days a very long time ago.

Rolling over flat onto her back, Sienna stared up at the ceiling and mused over the circumstances that had led to Sister Newson's outburst. That afternoon, she had been working on an assignment in the university library and was feeling mentally and physically exhausted. So instead of going to choir practice as she would usually do on a Wednesday evening, she had come straight home, intending to have an early night.

****

"Good evening Sister Newson", Sienna called out in her usual manner. There was no reply. "Sister Newson - hello - are you in?" With a concerned expression Sienna mused that this was unusual. Sister Newson would usually be sitting in her favourite armchair watching TV on a Wednesday evening. Sienna was about to head upstairs to check if her host was okay, when she suddenly recalled that a meeting of the Women's Department had been announced at church last Sunday. "Oh yeah - the women are meeting tonight", she muttered as she veered towards the kitchen instead, the low rumble in her stomach reminding her that she was not only exhausted but also famished. A pleasant surprise awaited her on opening up the refrigerator - there she found her favourite, freshly prepared red peas stew. Her mouth watered in anticipation of the sumptuous meal. She hummed a favoured tune "cos I'm happy" as she spooned a generous helping into a bowl. Her salivary glands danced and filled her mouth with water as she placed the full bowl into the microwave to reheat, squeezing her thighs together at the same time - she needed to go to the loo too. Sienna hummed the happy tune, now more to keep her mind off the fact that she needed to pee than anything else. She stopped briefly in her tracks half way up the stairs - was that a noise that she heard?
"Hello - Sister Newson - is that you?" Sienna called out. She walked slowly now, reaching the top of the stairs. There was no reply. The only sound was the distant whirl of the microwave in motion - her mind must have been playing tricks.

Now pressed to empty her bladder Sienna rushed into the bathroom, narrowly avoiding an accidental spill.

"Wow, I was bursting", she gushed. She sat for a moment, savouring the relief.

"Well, well - what have we here". Shock etched its expression upon Sienna's face. She gasped as her eyes almost popped out of their sockets - Jonathan, Sister Newson's son was standing just inside the door wearing a lecherous expression.

"What - what - what do you think you're doing in here Jonathan?" "Can't you see that I'm using the toilet". Sudden dread did not defeat Sienna's will to speak but rather emboldened it. She attempted to pull up her underwear as she stood up.

Jonathan's leer was direct and penetrating.

"Well, well - I can see you very, very well Sienna", he prowled closer to her as he spoke.

"Have you no manners?" clearly he did not. He stood like a brick, towering in the way of Sienna's escape, watching her insolently, menacingly. She attempted to go past him but he shifted his bulk to prevent her.

"Get out of my way, please", Sienna's voice cracked as fear gripped her heart.

"Well I don't really want to do that Sienna - I'm having so much fun".

"Just move will you? she shouted manically in spite of the terror she felt.

"Make me - make me move", Jonathan boomed then chuckled as he moved forward.

Sienna stepped backwards. "You better leave me alone...."

"Or what - what if I don't leave you alone", another chuckle.

The next scene played out in Sienna's mind like a bad dream. To her disbelief Jonathan grabbed her left breast and squeezed it hard. She raised both arms across her chest into a protective stance to try to fend him off, but to no avail.

"These are so very tempting - you don't expect to keep them all to yourself, do you", his tone was easy as he groped her. He acted as though what he was doing was perfectly normal.

"I have a right to everything under my mother's roof".

"Not my body - leave me alone Jonathan", Sienna scratched at Jonathans large crusty hands as she voiced the cross between a plea and a command. Jonathan disobeyed, brazenly reaching to grasp Sienna's other breast, and a full struggle ensued. Large arms overcame a feeble frame - no David and Goliath scenario here.

Like a rag doll Sienna was pushed to the floor. Jonathan was a ravenous wolf - he grabbed and groped her private property as she fought to defend her virtue by any means necessary. She kicked, scratched and bit but he easily overcame her efforts. Then as he forced his hand beneath her underwear and trespassed fully upon her intimate parts she winced and prayed for divine deliverance. Pinning her to the floor with his right hand, he used his left to unzip his jeans. Squirming beneath his powerful grasp, Sienna resisted, even as she felt all hope of breaking free was lost. Still she fought scratching, biting and kicking. If he violated her further, it would be over her dead body. As Jonathan eased back to facilitate easy removal of his trousers, Sienna's right hand broke free - as fast as lightning she reached out, grabbed and twisted the object of ultimate violation.

"Ouch - you stupid little cow", Jonathan shouted and as he let go of her to attend to his affliction, Sienna scrambled to her feet and aimed a round house kick that landed on target. As Jonathan howled in pain she tried to make her escape. But he recovered sufficiently to reach out and pull her back into the room.

"Let me go you monster", she said between gritted teeth.

Moments passed as the captive wrestled her captor, then the front door slammed - a welcome sound to Sienna which spelt defeat for Jonathan. He reluctantly loosened his grip on her.

"Good evening Sienna", Sister Newson's voice had never sounded so sweet to the ear.

"Yeesss - yes maam - goood evening", Sienna called back. She tried to straighten her clothes as she bolted from the bathroom.

"Are you okay?

"Yeesss, yes I'm - I'm coming Sister Newson", Sienna bounded down the stairs. She rushed into the living room where her host was removing her coat. "Are you okay, Sienna - you seem out of breath and flustered, and why you look so dishevelled".

"Yees maam - aa..a..I'm okay", Sienna said as she tried to regulate her breathing.

"How come you're breathing so heavily - are you sure you're okay? "And how come you are home so early - why didn't you go to choir practice?"

"Oh - I...I was very tired - I have been working on this big assignment, so I came straight home..... and... I was..... I.... was.....in the toilet and ... Jonathan.... Jonathan....."

"Jonathan? "What about Jonathan?"

"Jonathan...."

Just then Jonathan entered the room "Mum.... Jonathan is in the house", he announced then breezed confidently over to his mother and placed his large arms about her shoulders in an uncharacteristic embrace.

"Oh Jonathan - you're here", Sister Newson said as a wide smile brightened her countenance.

"And how is my favourite girl", he smiled back charmingly.

"I'm fine - Jonathan - when did you come?"

"Mum I was in the neighbourhood and thought I would pass by and see you - something smells glorious", he steered the conversation towards food. A compliment about her cooking was all it ever took to get his mother eating out of his hands.

"I cooked your favourite red peas stew - come let me heat some up fe you". She ambled off into the kitchen and he followed closely behind. Sienna felt nauseous as she watched him - then she headed upstairs to her bedroom.

"Sienna - your food is in the microwave - come and eat it before it gets cold", Sister Newson called after her.

"Oh - no maam - I'll eat it later - I just lost my appetite".

"I'll have it mum", Jonathan obliged.

"Well she said she is not hungry so of course you can have it all", Sister Newson said with a casual shrug and no second thought.

When he had eaten all the red peas stew, which was more than enough for two people, Jonathan promptly said goodbye and left. Sienna heard the front door slam, followed by the stirring of his old jalopy which drove away with a "bang".

After Jonathan left Sienna returned to the living room where Sister Newson sat watching the late news. Propping herself on the opposite end of the sofa, Sienna wondered how she would broach the difficult subject that needed to be addressed. She decided to simply say what was on her mind. It had been going on for far too long now, and had gotten way out of hand. So she took a deep breath.

"Sister Newson, Jonathan tried to trouble me", she said and awaited a response.

"Trouble you - how do you mean trouble you?", Sister Newson asked.

"Trouble me - you know ... you know - molest me", Sienna clarified.

"Do you mean what I think you are saying, Sienna?"

"Yes maam.... Jonathan tried to rape me"

"WHAT - what..........", and Sister Newson had exploded. There had then followed the most unforeseen response that Sienna could have imagined. Now she lay awake contemplating what to do.

Propped up on her left elbow Sienna viewed her reflection in the cracked mirror on the dresser. She directed her mind to ponder the options open to her - there were just three.

Chapter 3

April 2015

Option number 1 - she could apologise to Sister Newson in the morning, tell her that she had lied about Jonathan's attempts to molest her and beg for forgiveness for her folly. While considering this option Sienna cast her mind back in time - it had been two years since the pestering begun. It was soon after Jonathan had visited his mother and discovered that she was living there. After that first time his visits had become increasingly frequent and his behaviour towards her progressively more inappropriate.

Prior to that first visit Sister Newson had not seen her son for over four years. Sienna paused to recall how happy she had been living with the older lady back then. She had even joined Sister Newson in praying for her wayward son to be reconciled to her, but now she fully regretted that their prayers had been answered.

Sienna shook her head - not only would she never admit to lying when she had not in fact done so, but Jonathan's attempts at molestation had become brazen. She was no longer safe in Sister Newson's home. Indeed she feared that the next time he found her alone in the house, she would join the statistics of women raped daily by those they knew. She had taken the decision to tell Sister Newson, hoping that as a woman she would be understanding, had hoped that as his mother Sister Newson would admonish her son, that he would have taken heed to his mother's reprimand. But Sienna saw now that she had been mistaken. And in light of Sister Newson's reaction to her divulgence, she feared that Jonathan would have his mother's blessings to take her most prized possession by any means necessary.

As Sienna recalled the brazen assault and the coldness behind Jonathan's smile, she shivered. And the memory of the inflexibility of his grasp and the intensity in his eyes flashed upon the front page of her psyche and remained there. She hugged herself tightly, overcome by a sudden fear that Jonathan was so fixated upon her that he could perhaps commit the ultimate crime in order to satiate his dark desires. Another shudder, "I'm far too young - I'm not yet ready to die".

And anyway her newly encountered pride would not allow her to stay in Sister Newson's house for another day - no-one degraded her parents and got away with it. Now that her self esteem had been stirred up, nothing could ever be like it was before.

So Sienna affirmed with a shake of her head, that the first option was not a choice that she would take.

****

Option number 2 - she could go to see the Bishop of their church, Bishop Gooden - to ask that he intervene in the situation, hopefully by arranging for someone else to take her in. It immediately occurred to Sienna that Bishop and Mrs Gooden had known Sister Newson for over twenty years and were quite close, so she surmised that they might doubt her account of the incident, if not disbelieve her outright. But whatever they believed, she knew that both the Goodens would try to placate Sister Newson by reminding her of the Christian virtue of forgiveness and Sienna just did not want to deal with that scenario at all. And anyway, how would she even begin to tell them the full details - she would be far too embarrassed to discuss such a subject with the

Goodens. So shaking her head, Sienna decided that the second option was not a choice at all.

****

Option number 3 - this was by far the most palatable option and her only choice. Sienna had been blessed to meet Carlton and Melvin on the very first day of the Legal Practice Course, when they were grouped together in a "getting to know you" session. At the end of the lesson they had exchanged contact details and the bond of friendship forged that day had grown stronger as the days, weeks and months passed by until they were now practically inseparable.

All three of them also shared a special bond due to the fact that they were from needy backgrounds.

Sienna was studying at the prestigious University of Law because she was fortunate enough to have won a Scholarship, Carlton was lucky enough to have been partly sponsored by a distant relative and Melvin was there only because his tuition fees had been largely subsidised by a bursary from a charity associated with the University. Melvin's living expenses were also subsidised - he paid only a nominal rent of £200 per month for a two-bedroomed flat. And he had magnanimously opened his door to Carlton when his friend's landlord had raised his rent so high that he could no longer afford to pay it, even though he worked all the hours that he could in order to keep up. Now the two of them lived together in Eden Park, a couple of miles away from Sister Newson's home. They shared the nominal rent and all seemed to work out well between them.

Sienna was accustomed to spending many hours each day with Carlton and Melvin, either studying or just hanging out. At their flat she felt at home, nurtured and protected by her two brothers, for that was how she had come to regard them. Due to Sister Newson's strict curfew she had never stayed overnight there, but she instinctively knew that it would not be a problem should she decide to do so - she knew that she would be welcomed by Carlton and Melvin however long she should wish to stay, although she would do her best not to out-stay her welcome. Sienna nodded in silent concurrence with her thoughts.

"But it will have to be only on a temporary basis", the whispered soliloquy left Sienna pondering more questions about the future but she shooed them aside - they would have to be addressed at another time.

Aware that she must protect her reputation, Sienna avowed that no one could find out why she had left Sister Newson's home. She would simply say that she and Sister Newson had fallen out - that she was asked to leave.

No one could find out that she would be living with Carlton and Melvin either. A good reputation meant everything to Sienna - her mother had taught her to preserve her good name as a priority. So Carlton and Melvin must be sworn into her secret. People would never believe that she was not romantically or sexually involved with either of them - that they were simply her two best friends. People would rather believe the sordid to be true.

That she loved both Carlton and Melvin there was no doubt, but it was a pure and untainted love. Sienna had never thought of either of them in a romantic sense and she was certain that they felt the same way about her. She trusted them absolutely with her life - she would trust them with her virtue and reputation too.

The previously evaded questions nibbled at the fringes of Sienna's mind - what, where, when, how? She did not have any of the answers. What she would do to move on from Carlton and Melvin's place she did not know. How long would it take for her to do so? When..... where? Sienna took a deep breath and pushed the questions to a corner of her mind a second time although she was aware that they would not be reined in indefinitely.

There was no family for her to turn to in London - no other friends that she could rely upon. In fact she had no family in the whole of the UK - not even in Europe. All her relatives were in Jamaica. But by far the biggest problem that Sienna faced was that she had no money. Apart from the paltry allowance that she received monthly from the scholarship that she had been granted, which allowed her to live and study in London, she had no other means of support whatsoever and with no job, she did not anticipate earning any money.

Ever since Sienna came to London the scholarship funds had been paid directly into the Sister Newson's bank account. Her parents had sanctioned that arrangement because they felt that at eighteen, she was not old enough to handle money responsibly. Sienna was not aware exactly how much the monthly allowance was but she believed it to be around £250, because each month Sister Newson would murmur - *"You're living here practically for free - of the little money that they send I still have to give you half of it...".*

The £125 that Sister Newson gave her each month covered Sienna's travelling and other living expenses. She would certainly need to keep receiving that money in order to survive and she would have to work out what to do about changing the payment arrangement as soon as possible.

Try as she did, Sienna had not succeeded in finding a suitable part-time job to fit in with her studies. Due to the fact that her guardian had imposed a curfew and forbade her from entering the house after 9 pm, evening work had also been out of the question. Once she had applied for and was offered a very good evening job in a fast food restaurant. However the job finished at 9 pm. She had accepted it in the hope that Sister Newson would relax the curfew to allow her to enter the house after 9 pm. But when she had explained that it would mean her getting home at around 9.45 pm two nights a week, the older woman had reaffirmed, "That is after 9 o'clock - no decent young lady should be seen walking the streets after 9 o'clock at night and no such person will be seen entering this house". So Sienna had withdrawn her acceptance of the job offer. Thereafter she had refrained from the fruitless exercise of applying for any similar vacancies.

"At least now I can try to get an evening job", Sienna said quietly, even as she doubted that any evening job would pay enough to enable her to rent a room of her own.

****

Sienna awoke pre-dawn, long before Sister Newson's usual rousing hour of 7.00 am. She had packed her meagre belongings, which consisted mainly of books and study materials, into her suitcase, a rucksack and two large carrier bags, before falling into a fitful 3-hour nap. All the clothing, shoes and other items that Sister Newson had gifted to her were to be left behind. This meant that Sienna had just two complete outfits. And she vowed that never again would she allow herself to be treated as a charity case. "Sienna Miller - you will never again accept charity", she whispered with conviction. Her going to stay with Melvin and Carlton did not feel like charity, somehow.

Whilst struggling to carry the large suitcase, rucksack and bags down the stairs one at a time by the light from her mobile, Sienna had tread as quietly as possible, missing out the creaky stairs, so as not to awaken Sister Newson. She had agreed with Carlton hours earlier that he would call her when he arrived with the taxi so she waited in the hallway for her 'phone to vibrate. At 5.30 am precisely she felt the faint buzz and made her way out the door.

Carlton helped her with her luggage and moments later Sienna sat in the back of an Uber taxi speeding away from Sister Newson's house for good. She looked back at the place she had called home for the past four years and as tears welled up in her eyes, contemplated the uncertainty of her future.

Chapter 4

October 2015

"Brrrrr", Sienna reacted to the cold as she stepped outside the front door. The cold snap was forecast to get even worse later in the day - last night the weatherman had warned gravely "don't leave home tomorrow unless it is absolutely necessary". The travel news this morning had been even bleaker. Apparently the services on the mainline trains that served her home station, Eden Park, were severely affected by the adverse weather conditions and Sienna knew from experience what that meant - disruption to the already less than efficient service, and even more cancellations than usual.

She stood upright for a beat as though frozen in time, then suddenly jerked into motion, pulling her shoulders up into a protective stance, braced to face the elements. Any hopes that the weather report could have been wrong were well and truly dashed as she looked towards the sky. The day was dark and gloomy. Heavy clouds, pregnant with precipitation, were suspended overhead, casting their weight over Sienna's already melancholic mood and causing her to feel degrees lower than the freezing temperature. And as the clouds began to deliver the first snow, Sienna whispered a prayer, "Lord help me to be strong".

Beginning to trek the 5-minute journey to the bus stop, Sienna mused - she needed to be strong today - she could not let a little thing like the weather distort her vision. So like a determined soldier preparing to face a deadly battle, she pushed her chest upwards and outwards, took a deep breath and focused. The dank air rushed into her lungs, shocking her to full alertness and causing her nose to tingle. She became fully aware of how bitter it truly was as a deep chill penetrated to her core, and as though to add insult to injury, an offensive wind smacked her across the side of her face then proceeded to blow her calf length A-line skirt up way too high, revealing her thigh and cheeks and reminding her that she was not dressed appropriately for this cold snap. Luckily no-one was around to witness her disgrace. Sienna sighed with relief and turned her mind towards contemplation. She only had a few pieces of warm clothing to defend her against the cold. Stupidly she had washed most of them yesterday, including both pairs of jeans. She was wearing a warm top and cardigan and the skirt was by no means flimsy, but evidently not warm enough to ward off this punishing cold.

As another wind-tossed assault threatened, Sienna scrambled to retain her modesty and dropped her bag in the process. "Sugar", the alternative expletive revealed her frustration.

Bending down, Sienna retrieved and rearranged the books in her bag and checked to see that her purse was securely zipped into the side compartment. As she resumed her journey, she returned to her cogitation.

It was only the first week of October and Winter had announced its arrival. A late Summer this year had lasted but two short months and Autumn only one month it seemed.

"Why do I even have to go out today - why couldn't I have just stayed snuggled and cosseted in the warmth of my bed". The errant thought was quickly banished. Sienna recalled that it was not her bed after all, but Carlton's. He had given it up in order to secure her comfort, to sleep every night on the sofa in the lounge in the face of continuous remonstration from her, as she offered to swap places with him, fretting that he was missing the comfort of his room and bed.

As Sienna thought about Carlton and Melvin, she imagined halos suspended above the heads of her surrogate brothers. They were truly her guardian Angels. She had been lodging with them for the past 6 months and she felt just as secure today as on the first day of her arrival. Not even an inkling of a thought that she may have outstayed her welcome or that they wished her gone had ever presented itself in her mind. If anything, they both encouraged her not to even think about leaving until after she had passed all of her final exams and secured suitable employment to enable her to rent decent accommodation.

****

Carlton would not heed Sienna's bleating and he never tired of reassuring her that it was his pleasure to sacrifice his comfort for hers. From time to time Melvin switched places with Carlton, giving up his bed for a night or two. And both insisted that Sienna always had a bed to sleep in.

Having passed all modules of their examination with flying colours first time, Melvin and Carlton were shocked and dismayed when Sienna had failed two of hers and now lent their shoulders as rocks for her to lean upon. They were aware that the upheaval in her life was responsible for the under-performance in her exams. She had always been amongst the brightest of pupils in their class and they were sad to see circumstances deal their friend such a harsh hand. So nothing was too much for her to ask of them.

****

As she walked on Sienna allowed her thoughts to regress to her last visit to the Newson home. It was two weeks after she had moved out. She had gone there to ask for the grant money to be transferred directly to her, a request which had been flatly denied. Since then Sienna had remained at the mercy of her friends mostly, although she had been able to obtain casual work from time to time, stocking supermarket shelves during the holiday periods. The little pay that she received did little to better her circumstances, but did keep hope alive and kicking.

From meagre Trainee Solicitors' salaries, Carlton and Melvin paid all the bills, bought most of the food and even gave her pocket money when she wasn't earning. She accepted their kindness gratefully, for now repaying them by cooking the most delicious well balanced meals that they could afford, and always with the proviso, "One day when I get on my feet I will pay you two back double - God knows". And she meant to keep that promise. Her new-found self-esteem would never allow her to rest unless and until she did so.

With the benefit of hindsight, Sienna realised that the main reason for failing her exams was due to the fact that she had been stressing herself out trying to find better paid work. She wanted to be independent. Upon learning of her failed heads both Carlton and Melvin had made her promise to stop worrying, to shake off the anxiety about finding a job and to concentrate solely upon passing her exams.
"Look, I don't like what you are doing to yourself - you need to concentrate on your exams". "Stop stressing about finding a job - it's not worth it - remember that you have been studying for these exams for too many years to

mess them up now", Melvin had stated upon finding numerous copy job applications on his laptop.

"But I need to pay my way - I can't just keep on depending on you and Carlton - it's not fair".

"What is not fair is what has happened to you - you should never have had to go through this upheaval, especially at such a crucial stage in your studies - so just chill, right", Melvin's tone was resolute.

"Yes Sienna - please stop worrying yourself - we are all for one and one for all - as long as we have food you will eat and as long as we have electricity you will have light and heat - as long as we have money to share with you when you are broke, you will cover your travel and other expenses - so please take a chill pill", Carlton had sealed the debate.

"Okay... okay - I love you guys - always remember that".

"Yeah - yeah - right back at you Sister", Carlton sounded sincere.

"You know it, man", Melvin concurred.

And following that tete-a-tete, the miasma clouding Sienna's mind had dispersed and was replaced by a firm assurance that her brothers had her back.

The dream had come true for both Carlton and Melvin so far. They had both secured "Articles" to train as Solicitors in prominent City firms. Sienna was happy as she had fretted that they would not remain in London following their studies. She was glad that they would stay close instead of returning to their family homes - Carlton to Leeds and Melvin to Dudley. She could not bear the thought of losing her two brothers - they were like family to her now, not to mention that she would have nowhere to live.

"Thank you God for my friends and brothers", became Sienna's daily prayer of gratitude. The final law exams were an awesome challenge on their own without the added concerns or stresses with which she had been faced, but God's contingency plan had been put in place on the very first day of term when she had been grouped together with Carlton Haines and Melvin Kean.

****

"No, man - I will never understand the English weather", Sienna grumbled as another wind attacked her. She pulled the zipper right to the top of her puffer jacket and wished that she could afford to buy a full length winter coat. She hiked Carlton's scarf up over her nose so that it warmed her next deep breath then pulled Melvin's leather satchel to her chest in an attempt to ward off the ferocity of the wind, as another delinquent thought nibbled at the fringes of her mind *"why did she ever leave the tropical climes of Jamaica and the warmth of her family to come and suffer in the unyieldingly harsh British weather far away from those that she loved?"*

"Because opportunity knocked", Sienna smiled in spite of her discomfort, bolstered by the intrusion of the sobering voice into her psyche, as she was reminded of just how lucky she was to be here - to be taking advantage of this opportunity of a lifetime. A chance that most, if not all, poverty stricken Jamaican school children would die for. A chance to study to become a Lawyer in London - to fulfil her ambition to qualify, find a good job and lift her family out of the doldrums of destitution. So, even if a more vicious life threatening blizzard had been blowing she would have soldiered through it this morning.

Sienna willed her heavy legs to carry her along. And reluctantly at first they heeded her mental command, then they willingly succumbed to breakneck speed as she wafted away on the wings of a dream. Daydreaming was her tried and trusted mode of survival.

In Sienna's imagination, the grey London morning gave way to a bright Jamaican day as she was catapulted back in time to one of her favoured memories. In the twinkling of an eye she was in Soursop Bay, with her girlfriends at a "Jerk Out" and reggae music on the beach.

It was the last time she had gotten together with all her friends in Jamaica. The four of them had arranged the frolic to celebrate the end of term and success in their exams. But on arrival at Lebert's Jerk Shack, Sienna found that there were a lot of unexpected attendees of both sexes. No one knew how the other twenty or so had found out about the "Jerk Out", but all fingers pointed to Catey. Everybody in their exclusive sect loved Catey for her naturally affable qualities, but being a flamboyant extrovert meant that she had many other friends outside of their exclusive circle, and the downside to her personality was that she talked far too much - her tongue had a life of its own - one completely independent of her brain. But no-one in their clique could maintain malice against Catey for very long because they knew that she possessed a heart of pure gold - she did not deliberately divulge secrets - she just couldn't help talking too much. Many people outside their clique referred to her as "labber mout Catey" behind her back, whilst smiling to her face. Her outgoing personality kept her affiliated to their exclusive circle in spite of the fact that she was loquacious to a fault.

A warm smile graced her features as Sienna reminisced about her friends - she missed them all so very much. Her "besty", Takema and her two "maties" were all so special to her in their own ways - Takema was like the sister that she never had - they were playmates born just days apart, who lived next door to each other all their lives until Sienna had left for London. As toddlers they played together every day, and as teenagers they had been inseparable. Then there was Catey - she was always the life and soul - such fun but far too popular for her own good. And Jessica who was like a second mother. Sienna could always rely upon Jessica's wisdom to guide her and to pray for her. Sienna said another "thank you God", this time for Facebook, Twitter and Whatsap as her smile broadened and she resolved that she had put off trying out Skype for far too long. Then Sienna returned to her reverie.

She had taken time with her appearance on the day of the Jerk Out, her newly pressed hair piled high into a chignon atop her head - her signature style, which added to her 5' 5' statute, making her look 5' 10" tall. Sienna's parents' standing rule of no make-up meant that her sun-kissed face was naked, giving full exposure to pure features: the wide slanted eyes complimenting her small bulb of a nose, which fitted perfectly into its reserved space; her full and even, smooth textured dark cherry lips shimmering under a film of Vaseline; the smooth slightly raised forehead and baby like dimpled cheeks which completed the content of her oval face, all composed to set Sienna apart as a classic natural beauty in the eyes of many, if not most people. And her slender yet curvaceous form was wrapped all over in a cinnamon glow.

That dreamy day almost 5 years ago, Sienna (then aged 17) had worn her favourite loose fitting cullotte knee length shorts and a tee-shirt - all afternoon, unlike her friends who had all changed into swimwear at the beach. More worldly-wise than she, they knew all the latest beats and had danced confidently, busting moves that bordered upon outrageous in Sienna's eyes, as she sat quietly observing the shenanigans. She had refused all requests to dance with one or other young man and in general shied away from the opposite sex, unlike her friends who had a growing interest in boys and romance and flirted openly. It was evident that she had led a sheltered life and due to her Christian upbringing she embraced sobriety. Her mother had inspected her attire before she left home, to ensure that she did not have any change of clothes hidden in her bag. Sienna did not mind though. She appreciated that her parents knew best and was happy to abide by their house rules. Her ready submissiveness was borne of experience, for she had not always been so readily amenable. Experience had taught her well because once before she had disobeyed her parents and the hint of a bitter taste left by the less than pleasant lesson remained in her mouth.

It was the Summer when she had turned 16. Sienna had given in to Takema's constant cajoling to attend a beach party, and on the pretence of going to visit her elderly grandfather, Langford Miller that Saturday afternoon, she had been let off accompanying her mother to sell their farm produce at the local market. Sienna did in truth drop by to visit her grandfather, but had sneaked away early to join her friends at Cane Gully beach. With further coaxing she had changed into a bathing suit loaned to her by Takema. But as soon as she put on the swimsuit Sienna had regretted doing so. She felt naked and vulnerable, but that was not the worst thing that happened - the costume had apparently fitted her so well that two of the village boys had gotten into fisticuffs to decide which of them should win the prize of wooing her. That brawl brought a sudden and unexpected end to the party as attendees grabbed their belongings and put their legs into top gear, running as fast as possible in various directions toward their individual homes. Fighting was a taboo in their small village and no one wanted their names to be associated with such irresponsible activity.

If only either of the two combatants was worth a second glance, Siena might not have minded quite so much. But had she been given the choice between buck teeth Ronald, and the chicken pox and acne scarred-faced Hilton, she would have chosen to "pass". However, it turned out that her opinion was not taken into consideration which both infuriated and discomfited her.

Shaking her head gently from side to side Sienna sighed as she recollected.

The rumour that she was the object of the duel had spread like wildfire throughout the locality, mostly due to Catey's unbridled tongue. She had been grounded for a month from going out without either of her parents' chaperoning her. However her punishment had not ended there because the apparent winner of the contest had surreptitiously stalked her and, having discovered where she lived, had taken to waylaying her outside her home and accosting her each time she went out alone. After trying to deal with the situation by herself for the third month, Sienna had had no choice but to seek her father's intervention. It was quite a task to get her parents to believe that she had not encouraged Hilton and that there was nothing going on between them as far as she was concerned. Her father Alexander had warned Hilton off gravely and also made a complaint to his family.

Hilton Bayliss was a stubborn ass of a boy who barely heeding Alexander's warning, had merely changed his vantage point to a position further down the road from Sienna's home, and continued to make his presence known to her every time she went out alone. So Sienna had voluntarily grounded herself, never leaving home without an escort until Hilton's interest had eventually waned and strayed to a new subject.

****

Sienna gave a sigh of exasperation as she continued to reminisce about her encounters with Hilton Bayliss. Then her thoughts returned again to her parents and friends and she sighed once more - this time with longing.

How she missed Soursop Bay, the simple sea caressed village where she was born. There she had known much happiness in spite of her family's impoverished existence. There the sun had been her friend - it had never hidden it's face from view for too long but would come out to greet her with a smile each day. Even its harsh unforgiving, crop destroying rays had been swiftly and easily forgiven, for there the love of family, friends and the local people compassed the atmosphere, overshadowing all else.

There the breezes were never unkind but warm and comforting, soothing the depth of the soul and endowing the spirit with wings.

Even the rain was an inestimable treasure there, its light spray or drizzle a welcome respite from the sun - its heavy pounding downpours like medication inducing deep and restful slumber, healing the sun-ravaged earth and bringing the promise of a bountiful harvest to anxious tillers of the soil and planters of seeds, grain and root crops. There the rain had never seemed deliberately harsh and unfriendly sometimes, as here - as now.

It seemed that adversity had worked to secure the greater good there, for untold joy would be ushered in by the ceasing of a hurricane or other natural disaster, and would remain, empowered and emboldened by the unyielding smiles of the village folk - a bliss ushered in by the passing of hard times, its intensity far overreaching that of any pain or any depth of sorrow.

****

Sienna shivered, as she was jolted back to reality by the beating icy rain that had hijacked the brief snowfall. She extracted her umbrella from her bag and sighed longingly as she fully closed her mind's memory page and began to focus upon her quest for the day ahead.

Chapter 5

October 2015

Today marked the beginning of the end of Sienna's long journey - the study of the law. She was about to re-sit the first of two failed heads of her final legal exams and she was determined to pass them. Her nerves were frayed due to excess studying, her mind was a-clutter with principles, precedents, cases, acts and rules and she only hoped that the jumbled information would be digested and settle into its rightful place in her mind, in time for today's exam - she had invested everything possible and her sacrifices had to pay off

.

Having swotted and sweated for four years, giving of her time and of her flesh (more often than not depriving herself of sleep and her mind and soul of ease), Sienna was disappointed when she had failed two heads. Yet she could have done no better - she had given her all.

Recollection of the previous failures caused anxiety which created a bubble in the pit of Sienna's stomach. She swallowed hard to try and dislodge it but the bubble seemed to rise up her windpipe, into the back of her throat - she felt nauseous. Soon the nausea subsided but the bubble seemed to mutate into a stiffness in the back of her neck which rose up into the back of her head. Then it made its way to her forehead where it mutated again into a tight band of tension, spreading itself and settling there, it remained firmly lodged, tightening more with each passing minute. Sienna massaged her brow to dislodge the deposit but found no relief. *"Breathe deeply in and out"*, she recalled the guidance of her class tutor. As she concurred, the tension slowly eased and released its band about her head and she felt her body relaxing more with each exhaled breath.

"Well I'll just have to do my best", Sienna mumbled. *"When you have done your best even Angels cannot do any more than that"*, she recalled the old adage that her mother used to recite and smiled.

As Sienna neared the bus stop she was tempted to wait there. But a glance at her mobile warned that she must be cautious - time might become a factor. Commonsense dictated that although all she could realistically afford to do was to travel by bus, she would more than likely arrive late for her exam if she did, especially due to the harsh weather conditions. Although the trains would apparently be severely affected, that was still the better option, since as long as a train arrived within 20 minutes, even if it travelled at a moderate pace, she would get to her exam venue with a little time to spare. So Sienna walked past the bus stop and headed toward the train station, quickening her step to a brisk canter - she would give herself every possible chance to arrive on time.

Sienna had not worked for a while and her finances consisted of meagre handouts from Melvin and to a lesser extent, Carlton - it was all they could afford to give her and she was really struggling. For weeks now she had been totally reliant upon her friends for support and they too were surviving on miniscule salaries. Melvyn was by far the better off among them. He had been permitted to remain living at the flat at the subsidized rate until his Training Contract came to an end and he gained well paid employment. He was also granted an allowance from the same Charity that had awarded him the bursary, which he shared freely with his friends. But in spite of this concession the ends were still not meeting.

Sienna shouldn't be getting the train at all but she could not risk being late or worse still not arriving at all for her retakes - she would get there on time by hook or by crook. "*If you wan good, you belly haf fe bun*", Sienna mumbled under her breath (another old Jamaica adage which provided strength to her frail morale), shooing away the thoughts that she would have to forego lunch if she took the train.

"If you want good you belly haf fe bun", the words resounded in her psyche and Sienna's countenance brightened as she arrived at the station and hurried into its inviting warmth.

"Single to Old Street, please", Sienna proffered the ten pound note, the only money that she had in the world, to the cashier who exchanged it for smaller change and a ticket. "Here you are young lady - you have a nice day now", the man reminded her of her father - his smile was radiant, just like sunshine. "Thank you - you too", her smile dazzled back in spite of her true mood.

****

The last thing Sienna wanted was to be squeezed onto an overcrowded commuter train. Five minutes later the last thing that she desired rattled into the crowded station The doors opened and a flood of passengers oozed out of them. The exodus continued for a full minute which seemed much longer to those waiting to board. Sienna was among the first to enter the still overcrowded carriage. She looked frantically to see if there were any seats available but noted with dismay that there was definitely standing room only. It occurred to her to wait for the next train, but that idea was quickly banished. It could not be taken for granted that the later train would arrive on time, or that it would arrive at all. So she squeezed herself into a better position within the packed sardine tin. Any hope of going over her spider charts were dashed.

The train travelled quicker than expected, soon arriving at the next station. As bodies eased out of the carriage, Sienna was able to shift about more freely. She fumbled in her bag for her spider charts, managed to extract both of them and held them up above the heads of the nearby commuters Then she proceeded to read first the ones on Civil Litigation. "Order of Statements of Case", Sienna mumbled to the curious glances of fellow passengers, "Claim form - Part 7, Particulars of Claim, Defence and Counterclaim, Reply and Defence to Counterclaim", she could care less what the scoffers around her thought - she needed to refresh her memory and found it more beneficial to recite aloud from her spider charts and memory cards. "Practice rules for statements of case..... state facts......relevant facts". Stares and sneers of consternation increased to the point that Sienna began to feel uneasy but not uncomfortable enough to abandon last minute cramming. She closed her mind to her surroundings and entered her own personal cocoon, oblivious to the eyes that surveyed her, adjudging her crazy as she struggled to change sheets and opened her mind wider to take in the information on her memory cards on Contract Law. "Invitation to treat", she announced then fell quiet as she contemplated the rule. "Offer", "acceptance", "intention", "consideration", "form", Sienna spoke without apprehension, ignoring an obnoxious young lady that snorted at her every utterance.

At the next stop several people, including the snorter, got off leaving a little more room. Sienna noted from the clock on the platform that she was on track to arrive 15 minutes before the start of her exam. Mild confidence flowed through her as she thought about today's exams. It was one of her favourite subjects - Civil Litigation. Briefly she wondered how on earth she could have failed both the Civil Lit and Contract exams the first time around, and concluded that for one her mind must surely have been in the wrong place then, and secondly because she might have been overly confident. She must have thought that she knew the subjects very well, so well that she may not have devoted enough time to revising them. When she received her results she had been inconsolable for days.

"Why me?" became her mantra in the days following and Sienna's misery was compounded by the fact that both Melvin and Carlton had passed all heads convincingly. Although they did all they could to console her, it did not really put Sienna's mind at ease. She had a lot to worry about - homeless and jobless without kith or kin she sunk into a funk. Melvin and Carlton constantly encouraged her with positive words, reminding her every day that they were her brothers for life and that she had a home with them indefinitely and need not worry about looking for a job or another place to live until she had passed her exams. And eventually the message had sunk in, so much so that now she had to persistently remind herself that she was a mere guest.

"I have put in the work for these exams and I must do well", Sienna soliloquised. She had to believe in herself. But though she was relatively confident, she was still nervous and waves of anxiety flowed and ebbed over her mind.

Added pressure was brought to bear by the fact that it was imperative that Sienna passed this time around because her bursary would not cover more tuition fees or any further retakes. Another deluge of anxiety flowed over Sienna's soul as she contemplated this. Quickly she endeavoured to seize back control, *"I'm breathing in relaxation - I'm breathing out tension"*, Sienna mentally replayed the recitation taught her by her class tutor as she breathed in and out and found relief. *"I'm breathing in relaxation - I'm breathing out tension"*. *"Breathing in relaxation..... breathing out tension..."*.

As her mind returned to near normality, Sienna ran through the main principles again and found that she could easily recall the sub-headings and finite details of each provision that she had learnt and revised. She felt better *"I'm breathing in relaxation - I'm breathing out tension"*. Realising that it was best not to cram anymore Sienna directed her mind to prayer, thanksgiving and praise. She had put in the work and she would be okay when it mattered - in the examination room.

"Lord I'm depending upon You to see me through this exam today - please help me to remember all that I have revised and to apply the knowledge appropriately", she whispered. Then she quietly hummed a new tune. *"I bless You Lord for all that you have done"*. *"I bless You"*. She repeated this refrain over and over again. Then she gave thanks to God for the privilege to be studying in London. After a few minutes she found herself in a pleasant place - she was ready to roll.

Chapter 6

October 2015

As the train hurtled towards the next station Sienna allowed her mind to regress once again, this time back to June 2011 when opportunity had knocked loudly, when least expected.

It had been nothing short of a miracle that Sienna was chosen to receive the prestigious prize above 29 other high school students who had entered the competition. She was by no means the brightest star amongst them. There were at least 2 others that she felt should have been selected above her and many people were, understandably, up in arms about the decision. Mr Stennett, the Principal of Coble High School had announced her as the winner, in the face of protestations. He had called together an assembly of the parents and pupils who were aggrieved, and explained that the decision to award the scholarship to Sienna was not taken by him but by the Governors of Wensley Grammar School for Girls (Mill Hill), the London college with which they were twinned, which organisation had created the scholarship. They had made the determination using their own criteria, he had pointed out, and that it was out of his hands. He also presented documentary proof to the aggrieved to allay their anger.

The Governors of Wensley Grammar School wanted to give the chance for one pupil in the twinned Jamaican School to have a privileged education, similar to that of most, if not all, the students who studied within their prestigious gates and later moved on to pursue further education. They had also compiled the test, had marked the papers and they had more or less had total control over the process.

The scholarship came with full board for a year at the college of North East London, and thereafter, covered lodgement at the university that she would be attending in London, the world renown University of Legal Studies.

Praises had rung high up to God Almighty for His supreme blessing when the prize was announced in church that Sunday. But following the jubilation, doubt and fear had set in. Alexander and Myra, Sienna's parents were concerned that she was too young to travel abroad and live alone so far from home and they had begun to give serious thought to forfeiting the prize. Sienna consulted their Pastor, beseeching that he intervene to save the day, for though she too was encountering a good degree of trepidation, she longed to spread her wings. She had never been further than 20 miles away from the small village where she was born and she longed to discover new and exciting places, none more enticing than London. Pastor Minot had contacted a Bishop friend that he knew in London to request that he and his wife find a suitable place for Sienna to live while she was in London, and to look out for her welfare generally. His friend, Bishop Gooden, had agreed unreservedly to do so. The promise had been put into writing and relayed to Alexander and Myra personally.

And so it was that Sienna had arrived in London in August 2011. Bishop and Mrs Gooden met her at the airport and their warm welcome had made her feel immediately at ease. At the request of her parents the Goodens' had arranged for Sienna to lodge with a trusted member of their church. And so she went to live with Sister Newson. A retired Nurse aged 75, Sister Newson was also a widow who lived alone and longed for some company.

Tears of joy had flowed from Sister Newson's eyes as she welcomed Sienna into her home. A widow for decades, she had reared her two children from teenagers to adulthood single-handedly. Both her daughter and her son had left home in their early twenties. A couple of years later her infant grandson had come to live with her and she had also nurtured him to adulthood. But he too had flown the coop, leaving her all alone. As the years passed Sister Newson had grown increasingly lonely and due to a problem with arthritis, her mobility was limited. Her drivers' licence had been confiscated due to a problem with her eyesight caused by cataracts. As a consequence she could not get around as much as she would like to which contributed to her isolation.

Before Sienna's arrival, apart from the twice weekly visitor/volunteer from the church who did her shopping, undertook various errands and stayed to chat with her for a few minutes, Sister Newson saw no-one from Monday to Sunday most weeks. For many days, weeks and months after Sienna's arrival, Sister Newson could be overheard giving thanks to God for the helper that had come to aid and comfort her.

"Thank God that he has brought you to live with me my dear - it is something I have been praying about for a very long time - God is faithful", Sister Newson had repeated at least 4 times that first day of Sienna's arrival. Being brought up to be polite, Sienna had nodded enthusiastically each time, as though she had heard the statement for the very first time.

That first night of Sienna's arrival Sister Newson had kept her up talking into the wee small hours. She talked as though she had been storing up conversation for many years, only to utter them on this night alone.

Sienna listened and learned that Sister Newson's daughter lived in America and her son, just a few miles away in South London. Sister Newson spoke fondly of her daughter and granddaughter.

"My daughter Sarah is 44 - but she doesn't look a day over 25 - she takes after her father, you know, my beloved husband Leonard". "He passed on 29 years ago (God rest his dear soul)", a pause to reminisce then she continued. "He was 49 when he died - cancer took him - what a cruel disease". "He was tall and handsome - he didn't look a day over 35", another pause, "That was until the diagnosis, then within 3 months he aged a full 30 years", another pause, "And then suddenly he was gone". Tears were dabbed away from Sister Newson's misty eyes with dexterity.
"Never mind", Sienna had empathised as memories of the recent passing of her grandmother Beryl came flooding to the surface of her psyche.

"Sarah is married to a Yankie who she met while they were at university here in London". Sister Newson returned to the original subject matter unexpectedly. "At the end of their studies, he proposed, she accepted and he whisked her off to his mansion in Florida". "Oooh you should see their house...... it has four separate apartments in the one house". "Each apartment has its own living quarters and bathroom". "There is a swimming pool, jacuzzzi and sauna - dem really living large". "And they only have one daughter at that - just three of them in that big, big house".

Sister Newson continuously checked Sienna's response for interest. In spite of the on-set of jet lag Sienna enthused with oohs and ahhs, and blinding smiles, giving the impression of alertness instead of fatigue. Her demeanour was one of exaggerated humility that could only come from one acquainted with destitution. She listened with genuine wonderment in spite of her tired *state, and her imagination found wings, catapulting her to the palace of Cinderella's Prince Charming as Sister Newson's narrative brought the fairy tale to life within her mind.*

When Sister Newson informed that "They come to visit me every two years or so and I go to visit them once a year", Sienna wished that Sister Newson would become her Fairy Godmother and whisk her to the palace with her when she next visited. But that dream was never to be realised. In the four years that she lived with Sister Newson, the older woman had visited her daughter twice and on both occasions Sienna had gone to stay with Bishop and Mrs Gooden. Sarah never visited her mother in the four years that Sienna lived with her.

Sister Newson bragged about her granddaughter a lot too, moreso on that first night. "Her name is Marva - she reminds me of you a lot - she is about the same age as you", Sienna felt a stir of emotions as she listened to Sister Newson's first account of her granddaughter.

Both Sienna's grandmothers had died, her father's mother had passed away just a few months earlier and her mother's mother had died years before she was born. She had only one grandparent still alive, her paternal grandfather, Langford Miller who was now 91.
"I don't have any grandmothers - they both died", Sienna had confided.

Sister Newson had smiled sweetly, "Never mind sweetie". She had consoled dismissively before changing the subject.

When Sister Newson travelled to her family in America Sienna had to stay with the Goodens. They were good people, but Sienna felt far too imperfect to live with veritable angels with no visible flaws. They were even stricter and more pious than her parents. The weight of unworthiness that came to bear upon her when she stayed with the Goodens' was too heavy. Although she wished she could aspire to their lofty heights of holiness, Sienna consistently failed. The Goodens had a morning devotion together for about half an hour each day and spent at least an hour in personal prayer within their separate bedrooms. They also had Bible reading and meditation sessions, in the same way that other people might perhaps watch a daily soap opera. Sienna went through the motions as was incumbent upon her to do when staying with the Goodens'. However, instead of praying, her mind would often drift away somewhere and frolic, and instead of spending time in the word, she involuntarily found her mobile 'phone far too enticing to resist. Each time her stay with the Goodens' came to end Sienna would sigh with relief. Then she would repent within her heart, "Sorry that I'm not as holy as I ought to be Lord", was the prayer that she breathed first thing in the mornings and last thing at nights.

After a few days back at Sister Newson's home Sienna's conscience would revert to its ease. For Sister Newson was far less than perfect, spending much of her time watching TV and very little time praying; she was also far more likely to devour a good thriller or romance novel than to read her Bible; sometimes borderline or mild cuss words would be uttered; a tipple of brandy or wine "for her health and strength" was far too regular an indulgence; and more often than a few times Sienna had caught Sister Newson in a blatant lie.

******

The rest of that first night's "getting to know you" conversation was devoted almost entirely to Sister Newson's verbose account of her son Jonathan. It became apparent to Sienna, from her incessant chatter about him, that Sister Newson loved Jonathan very much. But in time Sienna became aware that there was an issue of denied affection on Jonathan's part. She learned that Sister Newson did not know his whereabouts and the truth was that he had not visited her in nearly two years, a fact concealed by Sister Newson as she made various excuses for him that first night.

"He usually makes sure that he visits me at Christmas".

Once a year? Sienna said nothing but her body language must have conveyed her surprise due to the senior's reaction.

"He is very, very busy, you know with work and so on", a dubious expression upon Sienna's face prompted Sister Newson to elucidate.

"He used to come on Mothers' Day or on my birthday but his work is so demanding that he could not make it last year, she defended.

"But he telephoned me though", she smiled but Sienna sensed a deep sadness within her host as she droned on - her voice a melancholic monotone.

"Oh, what does he do for a living?" Sienna enquired.

"He.... he.... I.... he was working with the bus company - yes - yes I believe he is still working there", Sister Newson stuttered, her voice tinged with doubt.

"Oh - I see". "Is South London far from here?" was Sienna's next curious question.

"Well it's not that far really.....bu....but... it takes time to travel around London these days, you know". Sister Newson had then changed the subject. She went on to tell Sienna about her grandson Damien, whom she had brought up from since he was two weeks old.

Damien was Jonathan's illegitimate son. Jonathan had brought the child and left him with his mother when he was just two weeks old, stating that his girlfriend had left him without taking the baby with her. A promise to come back for his son the following week was not kept and various assurances to come and collect him were continually broken for over a year.

"It was hard for him you know - trying to hold down a job with a baby to look after", Sister Newson had explained, as a frown had inadvertently crossed Sienna's face. How could he go without seeing his son for a year after leaving him at two weeks old? The question hung in her mind where it lingered unanswered.

Sister Newson bonded with the child, and after a year could not bear to be parted from him, and so she agreed to keep him. And she had reared him singlehanded.

Sister Newson spoke of Damien in fond terms that first night, but what Sienna gleaned from living with her was that neither Jonathan nor Damien cared much about their mother and grandmother. Now in his early twenties, Damian, much like his father had all but abandoned her. Although Sister Newson had never admitted it, Sienna was to learn that Damien had grown into a rather confused young man, probably due to the fact that he had never met his mother and had had little input into his upbringing from his father.

Sienna recalled Damien visiting only four times while she was living at the house. He always brought a huge bunch of flowers. The flowers were always absolutely beautiful and the smell would linger throughout the house for up to two weeks after Damien had visited. That was the only reason why Sienna liked his visits. She recalled how he would manipulate his grandmother with one sob story after the other, cajoling her to part with money, always promising to repay. However, Sienna could not recall a time during any of Damian's visits where he gave Sister Newson any money. She recalled only that Sister Newson kept on giving and never asked for the return of any funds previously loaned to him.

On his last visit a year and a half ago, Damian had failed to get any money from Sister Newson.

"Sorry son - I just don't have it", Sienna had overheard her say.

"Well no wonder you don't have any money - you can take in strays yet you can't help your own flesh and blood, innit grandma", Damian had stated

"Son - nothing like that, I just don't have any money at the moment because I made a loan to your father last week". "Sienna is a great help to me and I am blessed to have her here with me". "And she does not stay here for nothing - that is what you need to understand", Sister Newson had set the record straight.

"Okay - so why you giving money to that man", Damian always referred to his father in derogatory terms.

"Well he is my son for one and if he needs help I cannot just ignore him - who else is he to turn to but me?" Sister Newson had explained.

"Okay", Damian had apparently accepted then added. "But I spent over £50 on petrol to come and visit you so who is going to pay for that?" And Sienna recalled Sister Newson emptying her purse and pockets to provide Damian with £41.36 pence as reimbursement for his petrol money.

"And what about the flowers - they cost me another tenner", Damian had said before heading towards the front door, "Bye Gran - you know you should stop giving that big man your money - see you again in a while, Gran", Damian had said before exiting the front door without hugging his grandmother as he customarily did when she doled out cash to him in the past.

After that visit, Damian never came again during Sienna's time at Sister Newson's. When his girlfriend gave birth to a daughter he had telephoned to let his grandmother know and thereafter his baby daughter had become his main excuse for not finding time to visit. Sienna recalled Sister Newson's pride in her new great-granddaughter, bragging to all who lent her an ear about the child's beauty. Of a truth the infant was a stunner - Sienna could tell from the two photos that Damian sent, taken when she was just a week old, that she would perhaps grow up to be a classic beauty. Sister Newson dubbed her "my beauty" and sent Damian a very large cheque to purchase a crib and other items for the new born. He had promised to bring the infant to meet her, but had never done so, although he would telephone from time to time to make requests for further financial assistance which Sister Newson willingly acquiesced to. And Sister Newson talked incessantly about a great granddaughter to whom she was acquainted only through two pictures taken at one week old.

****

Sienna was jolted back to the present. A smile still graced her face - she had been thinking about happier times spent with Sister Newson. Soon her smile began to fade and a solitary tear traced its path from her left eye down her cheek - a melancholic spirit hovered about her mind but Sienna resisted it's landing by quickly turning her thoughts to her family and immediately her spirit sprouted wings again.

Although she missed them terribly it always cheered Sienna up to think about her family. The fact that they did not own a telephone had previously been a thing of regret to her but for the past six months that disadvantage had proved to be a blessing.   Due to lack of funds and resources her parents rarely telephoned her and to her relief had not done so since she had been living with Melvin and Carlton.   She sent them messages through her friends and was kept updated as to their welfare in the same way.

Sienna dreaded her parents' next call. She could not simply ignore their call, because that would only arouse their suspicion that something was amiss. Her mother Myra always knew when she was lying. She could sniff a lie out from thousands of paces away. It was obvious that word of her departure from the Newson home had not yet filtered through to her family in Jamaica or they would most certainly have begged, borrowed, if not stolen, in order to make a phone call to her in an effort to find out what had happened.

Chapter 7

October 2015

Alighting the train at her destination Sienna breathed deeply *"I'm breathing in relaxation - I'm breathing out tension"*. Holding her head high, she pulled her shoulders back and breathed in deeply again and spoke positivity - *"I can do all things through Christ Jesus that strengthens me"*.

Sienna made her way to the examination venue in good time. On arrival she visited the ladies room, freshened up then returned to organise the apparatus on her desk. She then joined all the other students pacing back and forth throughout the building, spider charts or memory cards in hand. Periodically she did her deep breathing exercises *(I'm breathing in relaxation - breathing out tension)*, to ward off stress and anxiety. Before the examination commenced Sienna whispered a prayer and then directed her mind towards the task ahead.

Ready, steady, go! Employing good examination technique Sienna read through each of the questions, making brief notes as she did so. Then she selected the four questions that she could best answer. Having made her selection she then proceeded to dissect the first of the chosen questions, breaking it down into sections before breaking it down further into sub and sub-subs. Only then did she begin to write, fleshing out her answer with facts, laws and principles and citing cases of precedent and persuasion.

Before she knew it the examination was nearly half way through and she had only finished one question. Tension threatened but Sienna grasped back control - *"I'm breathing in relaxation - I'm breathing out tension"*.

Sienna forced her mind not to panic - she wrapped up the first question and proceeded onto the next, repeating all the previous steps but much quicker than before. This question proved to be far bigger than anticipated. She had written five full pages and still there was more to add. There was so much more that she wanted to write in answer to this question but time was running out. So Sienna bullet pointed essential points and took the prudent decision to move on to the next question.

"You have 20 minutes until the end of the examination". announced the invigilator and Sienna went into overdrive. She blocked out everything around her, including those who had finished early and were leaving - she was running her own race and would not be distracted.

With just 7 minutes left, Sienna started the last question. Writing as quickly as possible, her hand writing became almost illegible. She fretted that it may not be understood, but persevered. Blockages began to close her mind, so Sienna said another prayer, closed her eyes and visualised herself doing what she needed to do. She breathed deeply *"breathing in relaxation - breathing out tension",* and in a few seconds her thoughts began to flow again. She did not have enough time to write all the information in order to answer the question efficiently, so she decided that she would bullet point the rest of her answer to demonstrate to the examiners that she had the requisite knowledge.

As the end of the examination approached Sienna began to feel ill with anxiety. There was a band of heat about her head and she felt as though she was losing touch with reality. She felt as if she was having an out of body moment as the invigilator announced.

"Please put your pens down - the examination is at an end".

Sienna fell backward, collapsing into the chair. Then she leaned forward and placed her forehead upon the desk. *"I'm breathing in relaxation - I'm breathing out tension", and repeat.... repeat......* After a few minutes she was herself again. She felt confidence flowing into her being and a winning smile spread across her face as the invigilator collected her paper.

Chapter 8

August to October 2015

Jonathan

Jonathan was a frequent visitor to his mother in the two months following Sienna's departure. In the first month he visited her almost every day. Sister Newson was in her element then. She had not been so happy in years - she was reminded of family life when her husband was alive and her children were infants, up to their teenage years, when Leonard was snatched from her by death. Unbeknownst to her, Jonathan's frequent visitation had nothing to do with affection or concern for her, but was solely due to his longing to encounter Sienna.

When Jonathan learned of the altercation culminating in Sienna's departure from his mother's home, he was furious and blamed his mother. He now harboured a secret grudge towards her - he could barely stand being near her. Eventually his visits fell off and declined to about once a month.

****

Sister Newson

It had been several months since Sienna's departure from her home. Sister Newson sat at her kitchen table with a steaming hot cup of tea and biscuits, musing over the circumstances.

Upon awakening to find Sienna gone she had initially felt triumphant. She had won the argument and her nemeses had gone packing. Soon she would no doubt return with her tail between her legs, begging for pardon. Surely she would, for she had no other family in London, and anyone that was currently harbouring her would no doubt become tired of doing so after a few days - one week at the most.

When Sienna had not returned after a week Sister Newson began to panic - what would she tell the Goodens if and when they found out that she was missing.

Then, two weeks after her departure Sienna had returned, but not to beg for clemency - on the contrary, she had come back to request for the bursary to be transferred and made payable directly to her. Imagine that - the girl's only concern was money. It was obvious that her greeting and enquiry as to Sister Newson's welfare was insincere - anyone could see that.

"I have no qualms whatsoever about refusing to transfer the bursary to that scamp's bank account", Sister Newson soliloquised. Then she nodded her affirmation - why should she be concerned? She had given the Goodens her word that Sienna could live in her house and as far as she was concerned, she was still living there. If the girl chose to sleep and spend her time elsewhere - probably with numerous men - there was nothing that she could do about that. As far as Sister Newson could tell, Sienna had no good home training and she was just too old and frail to try and correct other peoples mistakes in rearing their children - she had not signed up for that when she agreed for Sienna to come and live with her. Now Sister Newson knew that the girl had been pretending to be well behaved all the time - it was all an act - she is just a devil in disguise.

Sister Newson dunked one biscuit after the other into the hot liquid and popped each into her mouth. She savoured the warm substance as it slid easily down her throat and continued to reminisce.

It had put her to great inconvenience having that girl living in her home, so much so that she viewed the continued payment to her of the bursary as mere compensation and it could never be enough to repay her for the humiliation that she had suffered. The insults heaped upon her son by that ungrateful girl, for example, no amount of money could ever compensate for that.

The last conversation with Sienna, when she had come two weeks after her departure to ask for the bursary sprung to the forefront of Sister Newson's mind and she mulled over the encounter. Sienna had not wasted any time in asking for the money.

"Sister Newson, now that I am no longer living with you, I would like to arrange for the bursary to be paid directly into my personal bank account, please".
"Are you serious? Do you realise how much inconvenience you have caused me by my allowing you to live here?"
"No... no - I can't ... I don't..".
"Well the little money that they pay for scholarship can never provide me with sufficient compensation so the answer is "no" - I will not agree for it to be transferred to you".
"But I am no longer living here and I need it.... and remember that I did pull my weight while I was living here".
"What do you mean by that - take a good look around you - my home is spotless". "I don't and have never needed you here". "And I am certainly not going to take any order from you, young lady". "I made a promise to the

Goodens and your parents and I intend to keep it". "That room is vacant for you". "Do you realise how expensive rent is nowadays?"

"No... no.. nno - I guess I don't, but Sister Newson you do not need to keep the room vacant for me because I'm not coming back".

"You ungrateful scamp - is that all you can say". "So you want the money paid to you so that you can go gallivanting with different men like a woman of ill repute - I know what you are - young lady".

"I am not a prostitute - how dare you infer that I am".

"Only prostitutes behave the way that you are - your room is here yet you choose to stay outside - you think I don't know what you are getting up to?"

"Okay - you know what, please don't bother Sister Newson - please just forget that I asked"

"I had no intention of "bothering" young lady". "You can come and go as you please - no-one asked you to leave and you can still come back any time that you want to".

"You asked me to leave, remember".

"I obviously did not mean it, if I did say it."

"You asked me to leave when I told you about Jonathan - remember?".

"Oh that - well what did you expect me to say Sienna?" "What did you honestly think I would say to such baseless allegations". "You are cruel Sienna - evil, that's what you are".

"Ahh!" "You know what -

"You wicked girl - why would you hold a word spoken in anger against me - and you profess to be a Christian".

Sister Newson recalled that Sienna had then given her a look that could kill. Sister Newson knew what she was thinking - either that she was going senile or lying, but she couldn't care less what Sienna thought.

"Okay you keep the money but it won't make you happy - I guarantee that because you are effectively stealing from me". "I'm going now - goodbye Sister Newson".

Sister Newson recalled calling after her.
"You can always come back - no-one asked you to leave".

Following that encounter, Sister Newson, felt no pang of conscience in not signing over the bursary to Sienna and any occasional niggles at its fringes were swiftly allayed with the premise that she had been inconvenienced by taking in a stranger and should be fully compensated for her trouble.

Now as she sat at her kitchen table contemplating, her third mug of tea growing lukewarm, she soliloquised, "How many people would open their doors to have a total stranger living with them - how many people would do such an act of charity - not many that I know of".

****

It had come as a surprise to Sister Newson that the poverty stricken scamp, Sienna, had not come running back with her begging bowl since that last visit. And she affirmed within her heart that Sienna was living off a man, or men for that matter - who knew? She voiced her summation as she pondered.

"I bet she has found some man to scrounge off of". "I suppose she might as well use her good looks to her advantage, after all, she will never amount to anyone of substance", and with that Sister Newson chuckled. The illicit tag with which she had labelled Sienna on the fateful day of her departure was firmly imprinted upon her psyche, without evidence of its authenticity.

"It's probably married men - I bet", she compounded the slur then downed the dregs left in her cup.

Sister Newson's conscience mostly rested at ease as she sang daily her favourite song "It is well with my soul". But sometimes after listening to a sermon her conscience would be pricked ever so slightly and on those occasions she would talk it over with her god and her soul would quickly return to its ease - and as long as her god forgave her of any wrongdoing (not suggesting that she had done anything wrong of course) she had no further concerns. She continued, unperturbed, to receive the bursary every month.

If only the Goodens were not so inquisitive all would be fine, but they just never let things rest - always asking after Sienna. Sister Newson wanted to tell them to butt out - that Sienna was an adult now and no longer a child, and didn't need them vetting her whereabouts all the time. But she had not been able to muster up enough courage to "put them straight". Why should she alert the Goodens that Sienna was no longer coming home? After all, she was at liberty to come and go as she pleased. Sister Newson had often bitten her tongue to keep from giving them a piece of her mind about the issue and no more so than last Sunday when Sister Gooden had left the platform and apprehended her as she had attempted to leave the service early, informing her that they would be paying her a visit during the week. Sister Newson did not want them to come but how could she tell them that? She only hoped that when they came to visit they would not snoop around too much, and would keep on accepting her account of Sienna's whereabouts.

Some people might believe that Sister Newson wanted to keep the Goodens at bay in order to continue receiving the bursary payments unchallenged, but she knew differently. She was doing it to protect Sienna's reputation. But if the Goodens forced the issue, she would have no choice but to tell them the whole truth about Sienna's licentious lifestyle, of the fact that she had seen her with various men in the past and suspected that in truth she had gone to live with them.   She did not want to malign Sienna but if they pushed the issue she would have to 'fess' up because she was tired.   How could they expect her to keep the tramp on a rein.

It occurred to Sister Newson that she would have to do her best to see that the Goodens did not see the rascal's room, because then they would certainly begin to ask some serious questions for which she would have no viable answers.   A week after the rogue's departure, in anger, she had arranged for the disposal of all her clothing and other items.   Now she wished that she had not acted quite so impetuously.

Chapter 9

October 2015

Bishop Gooden was worried. He was concerned that Sienna had stopped coming to Sunday morning worship. Although he got word that she attended the Sunday afternoon youth service from time to time, her attendance had fallen off significantly in recent months. He himself had not seen her in church at all for many months now and he was worried about her welfare and apprehensive about her soul. It had been far too long since he last saw her attending Sunday morning church regularly like she used to do and although his congregation numbered in the thousands, he missed her smiling face amongst the throng as he ministered on Sundays, or in the middle row of the thirty-strong youth choir.

Week after week Bishop and Mrs Gooden grew more fretful about Sienna. As time passed their angst grew until Sister Newson's explanations, variously that Sienna had located distant relatives the other side of London with whom she had taken to spending much of her time, or that she was at home studying hard, or swotting at the library or with study mates, could no longer assuage the growing anxiety within their hearts.

So in order to put their minds at ease that all was well, they had paid a visit to the Newson home in the hope that they would encounter Sienna during their visit. Unfortunately, she was not at home when they dropped by, and this had only caused their concerns to gather new momentum. Sister Newson's final account that Sienna had "taken up" with strange boys with whom she now spent most of her time caused them more unease than ever before. Whilst they struggled against disbelieving Sister Newson's account, they did not wholeheartedly accept it because they had never before seen that side of

Sienna (if in truth it existed), and would not therefore judge her unknowingly.

During their visit, Sister Newson's son, Jonathan, had shown up. He was certainly not the same boy that Bishop Gooden had nurtured in Sunday School - he had changed considerably and definitely not for the better. His manner had been gruff - he had not properly acknowledged them, whom he had known from the days when as a teenager he attended church. Indeed they had been more like second parents during Jonathan's formative years. Jonathan had vaguely nodded in their direction before rudely pulling his mother into the kitchen, when they overheard him asking her for money. He had demonstrated no real concern for her, and displayed no true affection usually evident between mother and son.

This encounter left Bishop Gooden to wonder how Sienna was treated in Sister Newson's home and the question as to why she felt it necessary to spend the majority of her time away, presented in his spirit. So Bishop and Mrs Gooden became more troubled than ever before. He had given his word to Bishop Minot and to Sienna's parents that they would look out for her welfare here in London and he now realised that he had "gotten his eyes off the ball" somewhat. But he made an inner vow that he would redeem himself.

Upon leaving Sister Newson's home, Bishop Gooden voiced his concerns to his wife.
"I feel somewhat unsettled about Sienna's welfare, don't you?"
"Yes sweetheart, I know what you mean - it would have been good if she was at home today so that we could gauge how settled she really is there", Sister Gooden leaned over and stroked her husband's arm as he drove.

"I should have asked Sister Newson for Sienna's number", she stated. "I unfortunately lost her number when my 'phone was stolen", she lamented.

"Yes it is unfortunate - you know what I think I will try and contact her through the university - I need to have a talk with her to find out how she is doing", Bishop Gooden obeyed the prompting within his spirit.

"Yeah - that is a good idea because I checked with Sister Mena the choir director to find out if she had her telephone number but she said that it no longer works and she is no longer on Facebook either.

Bishop Gooden arose early the next morning. Having carried out his daily devotion he prayed, pulled on running gear and went for his customary jog. Returning home, he took a shower and ate a healthy muesli breakfast. At 9.05 am he telephoned the University of Legal Studies. He was informed that there was no one he could speak to as much of the University was closed because it was examinations week. So he left a message, requesting that Sienna Miller's class tutor give him a call back.

The next day Mr Morton, Sienna's class tutor telephoned Bishop Gooden.

"Hello may I speak to Bishop Gooden, please".

"Speaking...who's calling?"

Bishop Gooden, this is Brian Morton, Sienna Miller's class tutor - I understand that you wanted to speak with me about Sienna's progress".

"Mr Morton, thank you for your call - yes, my wife and I promised Sienna's parents that we would look out for her welfare while she is living here in London so we just wanted to make sure that she is attending classes and doing okay".

"Yes Sienna never misses a class", Brian chuckled and continued, "she is one of my star pupils".

"Oh - that's wonderful", Bishop Gooden's voice was laden with relief. "We're so glad she's doing well". "Do you happen to have her telephone number, Mr Morton, we'd like to give her a call, you know". "My wife had her number but her 'phone was stolen a while back and she lost it", Bishop Gooden explained.

"I can ask her to give you a call Bishop, but it's against University policy to give out the telephone numbers of pupils", Mr Morton replied, then added as an afterthought. "Come to think of it, Sienna did seem to be going through some issues a few months back - I had expected her to pass all her exams with distinction but she unexpectedly failed a couple of heads - I tried to find out whether there was anything I could do to assist but she reassured me that she had everything under control". "She seems to have settled down again and hopefully she will pass both heads this time around". "It's not unusual for pupils to fail a head or two, but Sienna is a cut above average --- it was a surprise to all of us when she failed....".

"Oh dear I do hope she is okay", Bishop Gooden sounded very concerned, prompting Brian to add.

"Anyway, as I say she seemed perfectly okay when I last saw her yesterday - I will ask her to give you a call".

"Thank you so much Mr Morton - please tell her its nothing to worry about, but just because we haven't seen her in church for a while and want to make sure she is okay".

"Sure, sure - I'll certainly ask her to give you a call", Brian replied

"Thank you - bye now".

"Bye.

As soon as Brian ended the call he searched his contact list for Sienna's number and called her.

"Hi Sienna - how's everything going?"

"Hello Mr Morton - all is going well - I had my Civil Litigation Law exam re-sit today - I feel really confident, although you never can tell", Sienna sounded upbeat.

"I have every confidence in you - Sienna - I am certain you did enough to secure a distinction", Mr Morton always made Sienna feel like a million dollars.

"Wow - I hope so, but I will just be happy to pass".

"Sienna - I spoke with a Bishop Gooden today - he was concerned about you and wants you to give him a call".

"Bishop Gooden?" "Okay, yeah, sure I will.... I will". Sienna stuttered.

"Is everything okay Sienna?" Nothing got past Mr Morton who had a keen sense of perception.

"Yeah, yeah sure - I'll give Bishop Gooden a call - I haven't been to church for a while that's probably why, but I'll call him - no problem", Sienna reassured.

"If you are concerned about anything, you know you can always discuss it with me in full confidence - don't you Sienna?".

"Yeah, sure, sure Mr Morton".

"Okay - Bishop Gooden gave me his number just in case you don't have it".

"I've got it thanks - I'll call him tomorrow after my Contract Law exam", Sienna promised.

"Okay Sienna - all the best with that tomorrow - I have every faith in you - bye now".

"Thanks Mr Morton - bye".

When the call ended Sienna sat deep in thought for a beat. She was wondering what she should say to Bishop Gooden. She knew she would have to call him back as she promised Mr Morton, and there was no way she could lie to Bishop Gooden - she would have to come clean and tell him that she was no longer living with Sister Newson. She thought of ways that she could colour the truth without actually lying. She would admit that she has been staying with friends but she could not divulge that those friends are men. She also wondered what she would say if Bishop Gooden asked why she had left Sister Newson's home. Should she tell him about Jonathan's attempted assault? A resounding "No" registered in Sienna's psyche. Then she pushed it all to the back of her mind - she would not permit anything to take up too much space in her mind today - after her exam tomorrow she would return to musing about this subject. She was currently in the library which was open until 8 pm and she had only four more hours to swot.

****

After replacing the receiver and ending his call with Brian Morton, Bishop Gooden engaged his wife in a prayer session - they prayed in earnest for Sienna - asking God to reveal to them whether she was facing any issues - they went further, asking for God to reveal to them what they could do to assist her and also asked for divine help in her exams.

That night Sister Gooden had a dream - she was in a boat with Sienna who fell overboard. She called out for help and two hands reached out and pulled her to safety back into the boat. Sister Gooden awoke shouting.
"Thank you Jesus".
"Amen", Bishop Gooden concurred. He had been meditating upon a Bible verse that said *"Cast your burden on the Lord and He shall sustain you. He shall never permit the righteous to be moved"*.
"I just had a dream about Sienna". Sister Gooden said. She then told her husband the details of the dream. He knew that the dream concurred with his revelation that Sienna had encountered some danger but that God by his

Angels was looking after her. And they agreed that it was imperative that they made sure that she was safe and well.

****

Next day when the Contract Law exam had ended, Sienna felt as though a heavy weight was lifted from off of her shoulders. She knew that she had done well today and felt that she had some divine help. She breathed easier than she had done in months. The tension in her forehead and neck loosened - she felt free - she felt at one - she wanted to laugh - she wanted to cry tears of pure joy.

Sienna hugged Marion then Mimi. Then they shared a group hug. "Hooray - it's all over", Marion shouted.

"Yes - thank God", Sienna concurred.

"Well - let's wait for the results before we start celebrating ", Mimi cautioned.

"I feel confident that I have passed this time", Marion chirped

"Yeah I think I've done okay too", said Sienna.

"Well - let's hope I've done enough", Mimi added.

"Oh I really hope so Mimi", Sienna engaged Mimi in a comfort hug.

"Yeah - you don't want to go through that again", Marion chimed in.

"Let's hope none of us do", Mimi sounded annoyed.

Sienna and Marion looked at each other but said nothing more.

"Anyway - I'll talk to you later", Mimi said "Say "hi" to Melvin for me - Gotta dash".

Mimi spoke in a girly, girly voice, reminding Sienna that she had a huge crush on Melvin.

"I will" - she called after the quickly departing Mimi.

"Wanna go for a coffee, Sienna", Marion asked - she was in celebratory mood.

"I'd love to but I can't I'm afraid - there is something very important that I need to do", Sienna

said - she knew she couldn't afford to buy even coffee but there was no way she was going to

admit that fact to Marion.

"Never mind - we must meet up soon though and celebrate - maybe at the weekend?"

"Maybe weekend", Sienna promised, knowing that she wouldn't be able to afford to go then either.

"Okay - walking to the tube?" Marion pulled on her coat as they walked.

"Oh....oh no - I'm not going straight home", Sienna said - she didn't have enough for the tube. She would have to get the bus home. It would take her nearly two hours to get home by bus instead of the 45 minutes or so that it usually took on the tube and train.

As they neared the bus stop Sienna slowed her gait, "I'm going this way", she stated with a smile.

"Okay, make sure you keep in touch Sienna".

"You too Marion".

The two friends hugged goodbye and parted company. Sienna felt as though she was walking on a cloud as she turned and walked down a side street. After a few minutes she turned back and walked to the bus stop. Her bus arrived within a minute. The early afternoon traffic was relatively light and the bus moved quickly. Sienna's mind was running almost as fast as the objects whizzing by her sight as she peered out of the side window. She was thinking about her future. Because she was a foreign student she could not simply get a job like her peers. She had to find a firm that would be willing to apply for a work permit in order to take her on. So far she had written tens, if not more than a hundred application letters but so far she had failed to garner any interest whatsoever.

"Maybe I should just attend in person", Sienna mumbled. The woman sitting next to her eyed her curiously. "Then again - maybe that wouldn't be such a good idea". The woman got up and changed seats. Sienna shrugged her shoulders nonchalantly. "Well more room for me to spread out", she thought and smiled widely. She was having a wonderful day.

As the school rush started the second bus progressed slowly but Sienna hardly noticed as she mused over her future. The long journey took its toll and when she alighted at her stop, Sienna felt drained. Her gait portrayed dejection and lethargy. She could do with a nice hot shower and a very early night.

When Sienna arrived home she was glad to find the flat empty. She fell into the sofa and looked up at the ceiling - the question "where do I go from here" hung in the air. Then she remembered that she had promised to give Bishop Gooden a call - now was as good a time as any. She made herself a hot cuppa, curled up on the sofa and dialled his number.

Bishop Gooden answered on the first ring. "Hello, Bishop Gooden speaking", he caught Sienna off guard.
"H...hello Bishop Gooden - ... iiits Sienna", she stuttered.

"Sienna - Sienna - how are you my dear - so good to hear from you"

"Yeah - thank you - nice to speak with you too Bishop .... how is Sister Gooden - and your family?"

"Oh they are absolutely fine my dear ", Bishop Gooden sounded grateful for Sienna's interest in his family's wellbeing.

"Okay - I'm glad to hear that". "Mr Morton said you wanted to speak to me - I know it's probably because you haven't seen me in church for a while b..b..but it's just that I've been really busy with exams", Sienna hoped to appease with this explanation.

"Yes I understand you had your last exam today - I hope it went okay". Bishop Gooden was excited about education - he had studied extensively himself although not many people were aware that he was a qualified doctor, and he liked to encourage young people to work hard to excel.

"It was okay - I just hope the results are good ".

"Fantastic - just great - we thank the Lord - I believe they should be - I know that you are a hard working young lady and as long as you do your best you will go far ".

"Thank you for your vote of confidence Bishop". Sienna felt encouraged. There followed a pause before Bishop Gooden spoke again.

"Sienna - I understand that you have been spending a lot of time with family recently - I hope everything is alright", there followed another pause as Bishop Gooden awaited a reply.

"Y...yes - well not exactly .. I've been staying with some friends - they are more like family though I guess".

"I hope everything is alright Sienna", Bishop Gooden said, putting her on the spot. What should she say?

"Yes - yes everything is fine.... thank you Bishop Gooden".

"I was just wondering whether all is still well at Sister Newson's", the question was loaded, putting Sienna on the spot.

"Well - as I said I've been staying with friends a lot so haven't seen Sister Newson for some time".

"So you haven't been staying at Sister Newsons then?" Sienna felt cornered. She would have to admit that she was not staying at Sister Newsons at all.

"No not for a while", she then fell silent, prepared for a lecture.

"What?" "You mean you moved away from Sister Newson without letting us know", Bishop Gooden's tone was chastising.

Sienna cringed and her breath quickened as she anticipated that this was just the beginning. "Sienna you do recall that we promised your parents that we would look after you". "Do you realise that if you have any problems we are here for you", Bishop Gooden's tone softened noticeably - he now sounded concerned and Sienna breathed normally again and relaxed. "So if you are no longer happy living with Sister Newson, we will find somewhere else for you to stay", he went straight to the point. "We made a promise to your parents to look out for you while you are here in London", he stressed and continued. "We trusted that you were safe and well living with Sister Newson ..... because we have known her for well over 20 years so we had no concerns about arranging for you to live with her". "But I am perturbed by the fact that you have moved out to live with friends". "We do not even know who those friends are, Sienna that is of great concern to us", Bishop Gooden rested his argument.

"Well they are friends I met at the University - they are good people - Melvie and Carlie", Sienna replied sheepishly, feminizing her male friends' names - how would she begin to explain that she was now in fact living with two men?

"It would be good if we could meet your friends - that would put our minds at ease, although I would prefer it if you were living with people that we know".

"Yes Bishop - I understand that". "I will invite Melvie and Carlie to church soon". But Bishop, I know that you are concerned about me, and I am grateful, but.... it's just that ..well.. I'm a lot older now Bishop and I think I want to be more independent", Sienna entreated.

"Well - yes I guess you are not the little girl you were four years ago when you arrived in London but you are not too old to receive guidance from us, are you Sienna?" the question hung in the air for a beat.

"Of course not Bishop - I would never think I am too old to be guided by you", Sienna reassured then continued, "I have the utmost love and respect for you and Sister Gooden, but please rest assured - among my peers most are living independently of parents or guardians". "Carlie and Melvie, are sensible young people with the right mindsets and attitudes - working hard to qualify well and find engagement in the meaningful profession of the law". "It is only a very few of those who embarked upon the same course as myself, that are living lives of debauchery and giving the rest a bad name", Sienna made a slight chuckle as did Bishop Gooden.

"I do appreciate that Sienna - I am not suggesting that you are living like a party animal or anything like that - I am merely concerned for your welfare because you do not have any close family around you or nearby". "I realise that you are now an adult and may wish to make your own decisions, but please do treat us like the family you don't have around you", Bishop Gooden implored.

Sienna was surprised by Bishop Gooden's reaction - he was speaking to her as an adult, not as the young naive girl that he had collected from the Airport. "Thank you Bishop", Sienna said.

Bishop Morton was about to bring the conversation to a close when it suddenly dawned upon Sienna that he should have the details of those behind her scholarship. He had arranged for the monthly payment to cover her bed and board to go to Sister Newson. Sienna needed to contact the Governors to ask that in future that money be paid directly to her - although there would only be three of four months of it remaining now. Even though it was a paltry sum, it would be better than the nothing that she had been surviving on.

"Bishop Gooden - do you think you could let me have the phone number and address for the head governor of the Wensley Grammar School"
"Oh of course - of course my dear". "I guess you wish to change the payment arrangements so that the scholarship boarding costs will go directly to you - Miss adult", Bishop Gooden teased.
"Yes - thank you Bishop", Sienna breathed a sigh as she appreciated Bishop Gooden's response.
"Hold on a minute dear..... you know what I will call you back with it in a while okay instead of keeping you on hold.
"Okay thank you again Bishop", Sienna said then cut the call.

Five minutes later Bishop Gooden rang her back with the details - a name, an address and a telephone number of the Governor in charge of the scholarship.
"Thank you very much, Bishop - I will try and make it to church soon - that is a promise", Sienna was sincere.
"Okay Sienna I look forward to seeing you - and remember that although you are an adult now, you will never be older than me and Sister Gooden and also remember that the main, if not the only advantage of age, is that it comes hand in hand with wisdom, so if you ever need a listening ear you are welcome to come and see us at any time", Bishop Gooden chuckled as he spoke.
"Yes Bishop - thank you so very much", Sienna chuckled back. She was grateful to hear his kind and genuine comments.

Chapter 10

October 2015

There was no reply when Sienna telephoned the number given to her by Bishop Gooden. She tried several times a day for a whole week but still received no response. This was the eighth day that she was trying the number, in between her active search for a job.

"I wonder whether this number is still in service?" she soliloquised - Melvin, in the bathroom getting ready for work, overheard her.

"Talking to yourself again Sienna", he teased and continued "What number do you mean?"

"The number for the Governor in charge of my scholarship"

"Oh right".

"I wonder if I should just go to the address instead of all this messing around".

Melvin walked into the living room, "Yeah - why don't you do that - I would go with you but as you can see I have to go to work".

Sienna nodded, "I guess I should just go there - if only I could afford to do that", she hinted, not wishing to ask Melvin outright for money.

"Where is it?"

"Barnet".

"That's only up the road - jump on the train - no the bus is better - get the no. 34", Melvin walked back into the bathroom where he stood in front of the mirror checking his appearance.

"Well I would if I had bus fare", Sienna stressed.

"You can have some bus fare if I can have a hug", Melvin made puppy dog eyes as he walked back into the living room.

Sienna reached out and engaged him in a platonic hug. "Come here you".

"Ok that's set me up for the day" Melvin smiled broadly as he pulled away from their embrace. He reached into his back pocket for his wallet, extracted a crisp £20 note and handed it to her.

"You are some Angel Melvie", Sienna hugged him again and gave him a peck on his left cheek.

"Yeah - me know", Melvin replied and puffed his pecks out playfully and flapped his two arms to imitate wings. He had warmed to the new version of his name that Sienna had taken to calling him suddenly - it was a term of endearment to his ears. Everything that Sienna did lately was charming to him, and he had even taken to speak with a slight Jamaican lilt just like she did on occasions.

"But seriously though Melvie - you are an Angel - you truly are", Sienna reaffirmed.

"Yeah, yeah - sure - see you later I'm off to work" Melvin replied before fluttering towards the front door.

"I haven't seen Carlton for a few days", Sienna called after him.

"Oh that's because he's met someone - he's always at her place"

"Ohh...oh really".

"Yeah - tell you more about it later - I'm running late now", then he was out the door.

After Melvin had left, Sienna stood still for a moment, thinking about Carlton. The revelation that he had found a girlfriend was having an unexpected effect upon her. Why, she wondered, did she feel so strange. After a few moments trying to analyse the emotion, she shrugged off the strange thoughts, took a deep breath and focused upon the task ahead. "I will have a successful and beneficial journey today - I will encounter many blessings on my way", she spoke positively, putting Bishop Gooden's teaching into action. Bishop always taught that you could determine how you wanted your day to turn out by simply speaking into it - that what you spoke into the day would come to pass.

After straightening up the flat, Sienna searched Google maps on Melvin's computer to find out exactly where she was going before setting off for the governor's address. Hoping that someone would be there when she arrived unexpectedly at her destination, she set off determinedly. The address was two bus rides away. The first bus journey was just a mile and as it was a mild day Sienna decided to walk to where she would catch the second bus and save herself some money.

Walking briskly with beats from Carlton's IPod throbbing in her ears, Sienna soon neared the no. 34 bus stop. From a distance she espied the next bus meandering in a long line of traffic. "I must catch that bus", she mumbled and began to run as fast as her legs would carry her. Moments later, to her dismay, the traffic began to move and the bus gathered pace. Running at speed Sienna willed the bus to slow down but to no avail. It arrived at the bus stop. All was not yet lost though - there was a long queue of people boarding so she kept up the pace. In her hurry she dropped her handbag and had to run back and retrieve it. She picked up pace again but the queue of passengers went down far too quickly and the bus moved away - she was just 5 steps or so away from catching it. "Oh doodoo - he could have waited - horrible man - I'm sure he must have seen me", she exclaimed. An irate woman, running just behind, sidled up to her and nodded her concurrence with Sienna's comment, then proceeded to greet the bus' departure by uttering a string of vile expletives. She gestured to Sienna who cringed and turned away, ignoring her outburst. *"I may be poor but I'm not common"*, she thought.   But misery loves company and Sienna felt better - at least she wasn't the only who had missed that bus.

Sienna took the only vacant seat at the bus stop and prepared for a long wait - there were only 4 number 34 buses every hour so it would be 15 minutes before the next one arrived.

"I see that you missed you bus", the deep bass voice startled Sienna. It belonged to the man seated next to her. She smiled and nodded slightly.

"I saw you running from across the road - it's a shame that you missed it though after you ran so fast and even dropped your bag", the uninvited conversant attempted to strike up rapport. This time Sienna did not respond - she was not in the mood for conversation at the moment "So *whappen* - you can't answer me?" the man asked gruffly. Sienna buried her nose in her book and continued to ignore him, but he did not take kindly to that.

"So you think you are nice, innit?".

"Please do you mind I am not really in the mood to talk", Sienna informed.

"A was only trying to be friendly that's all", said the conversationalist.

"Okay - thank you". A couple of minutes passed in silence before the man spoke again.

"So why are you so stuck up, anyway?" was the next uninvited comment.

"I'm not - I just don't feel like talking that's all".

"You mean you don't feel like talking to me".

"No - that's not the case".

"I can tell you are a stuck up ......".

"This is getting silly", Sienna mumbled and got up from her seat. She walked a few paces away and stuck her nose into the book. She did not look but imagined scathing glares from her unwanted admirer.

"Mr stupid is very good looking - he could get almost any woman - shame he doesn't have a brain", Sienna thought as she watched him board his bus 5 minutes later. He was 6' 1" tall, classically handsome, with a smooth dark chocolate complexion and unbelievably bright teeth and expressive eyes. She felt bad for having rebuffed him but she just wasn't in the mood to talk to a stranger who obviously wanted more from her than just casual conversation. Her priority at the moment was to sort her life out by getting a Training Contract, to help her family climb out of poverty and to find somewhere to live.

The number 34 arrived 15 minutes later - it was running 5 minutes late. The advantage to that was that the bus travelled faster than expected and within 30 minutes Sienna alighted at the stop she believed to be closest to the Governor's residence. Having asked for directions from a nearby flower vendor, Sienna walked leisurely towards her destination. The directions took her past a quaint row of shops consisting of a cafe that invited her to come in and have a welcoming cup of tea, coffee or whatever other refreshment her heart desired. She declined the invitation and set her sights ahead. A barber shop that looked as though it had flown off the pages of David Copperfield next caught her attention, as did a cobblers shop. The two shops standing adjacent looked as though they belonged in a bygone age as did their proprietors. The patrons though, were of this age. Sienna's interest waned and she moved on up the road.

Devey Road was a quiet turning off the main thoroughfare. It seemed out of place in Sienna's mind, as she observed the large imposing houses set back from the road, their frontages large enough to accommodate 4 to 6 cars. Most of the drives had at least 3 top of the range cars parked in them. As she arrived in front of number 28 she appreciated that it was even more imposing than the other houses. The grounds were larger by far and the house was more set back from the road. It looked to be two properties incorporated into one. In addition to the off street parking there was a large area to one side of the premises that was laid to lawn and immaculately cultivated, framed by an array of flowers, shrubs and tropical or exotic trees. There was a smaller area of greenery on the other side of the house which looked to be a secluded private garden. Tall leylandii trees grew from this area and imposed their heads above the housetop. The unusual scenery triggered Sienna to daydream and momentarily her thoughts regressed to Soursop Bay.

Sienna stood in front of the large wrought iron gates which were supported on either side by huge stone pillars. At the top of each pillar was the head of a lion. Each stone lion had a fierce expression etched upon its face. Between the lions' heads, at the top of the gates there was a plaque affixed, bearing the legend "High Trees". Sienna guessed the reason for the nameplate. There was a smaller iron door by the side of the gates and a bell upon the door. Taking a deep breath and saying a brief prayer for courage, Sienna pressed firmly upon the bell. She waited for what seemed like an age but which in reality was just 30 seconds and just as she became uncertain as to whether anyone would answer, she heard a voice over the intercom.
"Yes - may I help you", asked a well cultured English woman's voice.
"Hello", Sienna replied then a rogue cat bit her tongue and she was rendered momentarily speechless.
"How may I help you? asked the refined speaker"
"Well aam..... am.... my name is Sienna Miller". "I've been trying to call Mrs Miranda Addison for over a week but the number I was given is just ringing and ringing...."
"Miranda Addison did you say?"
"Yes - that is correct - Mrs Miranda Addison"

"And you are Sienna Miller?"

"Yes - that is correct", Sienna tried to emulate the posh speaker.

"Please wait a moment", Sienna obeyed. After two minutes or so the speaker returned.

"Will you please push the door on the right and walk through - and kindly ensure that you close it behind you then walk straight ahead and up the front stairs". "I will come to meet you there".

Thank you very much..."

Having entered the gate Sienna tentatively attended to closing it behind her. She then made her way across the drive, up the steps and stood by the front door, waiting to be let in. It surprised her that there were only two cars parked in the expansive drive - one a five year old Nissan and the other a Land Rover that was not a new model but which looked to have been excellently maintained.

"Miss Miller - please come inside", said the dark haired woman who opened the door to her.

"Thank you" Sienna said and stepped inside. The scene that greeted her caused her breath to catch in her throat. Never before had she encountered such grandeur.

"Follow me please - Mrs Addison will see you in her study". The marble floor gleamed impeccably, so much so that Sienna felt guilty for walking upon it, but she obeyed and followed the immaculately dressed woman. Their heels click clacking on the marble floor sounded like a cacophony of hollow drums as they echoed throughout the vast corridor.

In awe as she observed the ornate decor upon the walls or the hallway, Sienna's jaw fell open. Beautiful and no doubt expensive paintings in intricately designed frames, lined the walls. Sienna was tempted to linger, consider and admire each one, but she resisted the urge. She could not believe that she of such simple beginnings was here in such an impressive building - if only her parents and friends back in Jamaica could see her now. Looking up at the high ceiling she studied the artistic design of the bespoke edgings and the crystal chandeliers hanging from them and missed her step, almost tripping over.

"Are you okay?" a steadying hand reached out to assist her.

"Yes thank you", Sienna replied as she composed herself. Resuming her pace she looked around and observed that the doors leading off of the hall were all shut. She craved to open each one and look inside and she imagined how breathtaking each room would be.

Just as Sienna's imagination was going into overdrive the attendant came to an abrupt stop. "Please wait here", she said and smiled. Her smile helped Sienna to relax a little. While she waited, Sienna's nerves began to kick off again - what would she say - how would she be received seeing that she had no appointment. She did not have long to wonder.

"Please come in, Mrs Addison will see you now", another reassuring smile.

Chapter 11

October 2015

"Hello Sienna - so wonderful to meet you", the greeter spoke to Sienna as if they already knew each other.

"Aa-aahhh - oh - p-pleased to meet you too Mrs Addison", Sienna stuttered. Mrs Addison reminded her of Her Majesty the Queen and Sienna found herself curtsying involuntarily as she spoke.

"Please take a seat over there on the sofa - I'll be with you shortly", Mrs Addison indicated with her outstretched hand. The attendant also pointed toward the sofa as she stood by the door awaiting her next orders.

Miranda fussed with paperwork on her desk, putting them into neat piles - a daily routine of hers when finishing work for the day. Since her husband's illness and death she had been thrust into the role of overseeing their vast interests. She played only the role of a figurehead, however, checking through already prepared documentation and signing them off mostly. Andrew Lawson, her husband's business partner whom she trusted implicitly, really held the reigns. Most of her real work comprised the philanthropic ventures which she spearheaded from time to time.

"Sienna would you like some tea?" Miranda's voice startled, rousing Sienna from her state of wonderment.

"Oh - yes please - I'd like that", Sienna replied, her voice was louder than called for, betraying her nervousness.

"Please arrange some tea Linda - bring a variety - and some biscuits and cakes too", Miranda gestured to her assistant who nodded furiously before trotting off to carry through her command.

Sienna glanced surreptitiously at Mrs Addison. Although she knew that she had never met her in person before she felt that there was something familiar about her. And she loved her. She had loved the faceless Governors of Wensley High School since the moment she found out about the scholarship. Such benevolent souls as theirs, who had stretched out their hands to rescue her from a future that would most certainly have been plagued by poverty, deserved her unfailing love. Such was the history and legacy of her family, that she had expected nothing better from her future than to marry another poor soul and give birth to children with equally hopeless futures - that would have been her lot, despite the fact that she had always demonstrated an aptitude towards academe. But what use would aptitude have been if some good soul like Miranda Addison, from thousands of miles away here in her opulent palace, had not given a thought to those is penurious need, and reached out a hand of love, like a God-sent Angel, to offer the lifeline of a scholarship to one so lowly as she.

Looking now upon her munificent countenance Sienna knew that she owed all gratitude to Miranda Addison - she instinctively knew that she was truly the *"Governors of Wensley Grammar School"*. She studied her benefactor, putting her age at between 73 and 75 years, yet she still possessed captivating beauty. As Miranda arose from her seat Sienna observed that she was about 5' 8".

Miranda caught Sienna glancing at her and smiled. Her smile radiated compassion - her whole face, in fact, was benevolence personified. She looked as though she had stepped out of a bygone decade - the 1960s perhaps - she wore a teal woollen dress and cream and teal cardigan that would have been purchased in one of the more exclusive stores situated in Knightsbridge or along the Kings Road and her shoes were cream and teal brogues with kitten heels. Her creamy white complexion was complimented by fine strawberry blonde rinsed hair that was pulled back into a chignon and the only make-up she wore was a pale pink lipstick that barely coated her lips. Her embellishments consisted of small pearl earrings and a small string of pearls about her neck.

"Well it truly is wonderful to meet you Sienna - oh I've said that before, haven't I", Miranda said with a chuckle as she took a seat on the other side of the sofa.

"Yes you did - nice to meet you too", Sienna replied and joined in with an uncertain chortle.

"You are far more beautiful up close Sienna", Miranda complimented as Sienna's cheeks reddened under her dark hue.

"Oh - thank you very much".

"Yes my dear - you have the most beautiful eyes", Sienna looked away from Miranda's unwavering stare, turning her eyes downwards.

"Thank you - I take after my mum", she replied.

"Then your mother too must be an exceptionally beautiful woman - wonderful".

"Well .... yes my mum is", Sienna didn't know what else to say so said nothing but kept on smiling.

"Well I think I've embarrassed you enough for one day - so enough frivolity - what can I do for you, dear" "I'm sure you didn't come all the way here to listen to me yapping on", Miranda reached over and touched Sienna's arm affectionately.

"Ok - I don't mind", Sienna's smile was sincere.

"You may regret saying that." "So tell me dear - how were your exams?".

"I just finished the final two".

"That's right Civil Litigation and Contract - and how do you think you did?"

Sienna hesitated as she wondered how Miranda knew the subjects she had re-taken. "I feel confident - I think I passed them all now".

"Wonderful - I know you are wondering how I knew the subjects you had to retake", Miranda looked directly into Sienna's eyes as she spoke. She continued, "A condition of the scholarship is that we receive periodic reports on your progress, Sienna".

"I see", Sienna replied.

I have every faith that you have passed them all now", Miranda said reassuringly.

"Thank you".

"I saw you looking at me - you are also wondering where you have seen me before", Sienna nodded gently.

"Well, you may have glimpsed me at the University - I have visited there a few times to inspect the learning facilities and the like - I observed you at work and I know how well behaved and studious you have been", Miranda divulged.

"Really?" was all that Sienna could think to say. Then she recollected that she had indeed seen Miranda before in the University library on at least three occasion. She had stood out as a very mature student, Sienna had thought her to be.

"Yes my dear - your behaviour was just impeccable - wonderful".

Sienna decided that "wonderful" must be one of Miranda's favourite words.

"So Sienna - I assume you want to go on and practice as a Lawyer, am I right?"

"Oh yes maam - if only I could convince someone - anyone - to offer me a Training Contract", Sienna replied, her bright smile belying the dismay that clouded her heart with thoughts about the ever elusive Training Contract.

"I see - it must be very competitive".

"Yes maam - it's incredibly so, but I believe I will be able to secure one in the end". "Or else I will begin knocking on doors until someone gets fed up of me and offers me one", Sienna chuckled.

"Wonderful - that's the spirit - I think you have the answer Sienna - those who come out on top are the ones who are relentless, who refuse to give up or throw in the towel". "I am certain that you will get your heart's desire", Miranda said.

"I believe the main difficulty is that I am a foreign student and any firm that takes me on must also be prepared to apply for a work permit for me", Sienna sounded disheartened.

"Oh yes, of course", Miranda became pensive. "I wouldn't worry too much about finding a Training Contract Sienna". "I am sure that I can connect you with someone who can help you", she said after a moment's thought.

"Really maam - that would be so very kind of you", a tear sprung and sat in the corner of Sienna's right eye. She forbad it from advancing further and held others in check.

"Give me a couple of weeks or so and I'll get back to you on that".

"Yes maam - thank you - thank you very much - even if nothing comes of it, I must express my appreciation that you would think of trying to help me", then the tear broke away and rolled freely down her cheek.

Just then Linda returned with tea and snacks, providing some distraction and Sienna was able to wipe away the rogue tear without being noticed. After serving the pair, Linda left the room, and there was silence as tea was drunk and biscuits and cake sampled. Midway through her cup of tea Sienna broached the subject of the reason for her impromptu visit.

"Mrs Addison, I've been trying to call the number given to me by Bishop Gooden for over a week now but I could not get through and that is why I took it upon myself to come and see you in person maam", Sienna continued. "I do apologise if it is of any inconvenience to you".

"Oh not at all Sienna - it's perfectly proper for you to call in person since you could not get through on the telephone - I'm so glad that you did", Miranda looked meaningfully into Sienna's eyes before continuing, "What number have you been given?"

Upon checking the number Miranda ascertained that Sienna had taken down one digit incorrectly hence the reason why she could not get through.

"Oh but I'm so glad you came by Sienna - you are delightful company and it is an absolute joy to have met you in person at last", Miranda's countenance echoed her words.

"I reciprocate - I'm truly enjoying your company too - you're so easy to converse with", Sienna said, lapsing into a slight Jamaican twang as she did when she felt at ease.

"Anyway, the reason I needed to see you maam is because - well you know I was living with a lady who was recommended by my Bishop, well I'm no longer living there", Sienna hoped that this statement would not provoke too many questions.

"Oh - you're not living there - when did you move away - was it recently?"

"It was around 6 months ago, maam".

"Six months - really - they didn't tell me at the University". "And Bishop Gooden didn't let me know either". "I should really have been made aware of that fact Sienna" "Why did no-one inform me?" Miranda appeared to be horrified by this revelation.

"Sorry maam - I...I ... I didn't tell them at the University.... aannd .... Bishop Gooden didn't know either - sorry - I was not sure what I should do....."

"You didn't tell anyone?" "You really should not keep such information to yourself Sienna - you are all alone here in London". "It is imperative that you inform those looking over you of such circumstances", Miranda reprimanded, then continued. "Is everything alright Sienna - do you mind me asking where you are living now?"

"No maam - I don't mind - well... I...I'm staying with my friends Melvie and Carlie".

"Really - and is that a suitable arrangement for you?"

"They are really good friends but it's just a temporary arrangement, maam".

"Temporary huh", Miranda became thoughtful as she continued to speak. "Temporary ... huh?" "I assume the bursary is being paid to you by Mrs Newson?"

"Mrs Newson maam - ahh no maam - she refused to transfer it to me when I asked her to".

"Really", Miranda returned to her desk and did a computer search as Sienna tucked into the delicious fare".

"I can see that the bursary is still being paid to Mrs Newson even though you left there six months ago - well the first thing I'll do is to stop the standing order payments immediately and start paying the bursary directly to you Sienna".

"Yes maam - that is the main reason why I came to see you".

"But I believe there is only a further three months to go before the scholarship will lapse", Miranda stated.

"I'm not sure maam but I thought as much there wasn't long left as my course is at an end now, but it will still come in handy to me for three months", Sienna replied.

"We will extend the term if you need more time to secure Articles", Mrs Addison reassured.

"Oh - that is so very kind of you - I do hope to get a job soon, even if I have to take one stocking shelves again for the time being", Sienna smiled. *"Could this woman truly be an angel?"* she questioned within her heart.

"Sienna - you have been stocking shelves - oh no". "I would never have permitted that had I known". "You, stocking shelves again - God forbid - you are far too bright for that", Miranda balked. "It will never come to that Sienna - but we need to find you somewhere permanent to live".

"Well maam when I get a job I will find a room somewhere", Sienna sounded uncertain.

"Oh I see", Miranda replied absentmindedly - she seemed lost in thought.

After a few moments of silence Miranda spoke again, "Sienna do you know anything about gardening?"

"Gardening - ww...well I think so maam". "In Jamaica we call our gardens "yards" and from the age of 8 years I was the yard girl in my family". "That meant tending to the chickens and the flowers garden". "I also had to sweep up everywhere and make sure the whole yard was kept clean and tidy and I also had to prune the small fruit trees, cut and rake the lawn and so on and so forth", Sienna gave her verbal CV.

"Great - well we don't have any chickens to tend to here, but we do have two dogs, lots of flowers and a couple of lawns", Miranda chuckled between words. "We also have a very efficient gardener who is not as young as he used to be". "But he is the best, and will be continuing." "I've been trying to get him to slow down for years so if you want the job of assisting him then it's yours - you can be our *"yard"* girl Sienna", an unbridled laugh ushered from Miranda's mouth and she was joined by Sienna who laughed even as tears of joy sprung forth from her tear ducts.

After the laughter had subsided Miranda spoke again, "I can offer you room and board thrown in with the job - so what do you say?" she spoke so casually, oblivious to the fact that she had just spoken life changing words to the young lady sitting next to her.

"Waaaah ..I... I say yes maam" Sienna gushed - she did not need to think about it. "Thank you - if you are serious - I'd love to take that job - I'll work really hard - I'll give it 100% - you won't regret giving me this chance Mrs Addison - I promise you - you won't regret it at all", then Sienna burst fully into tears. And the unbelievable happened, the regal, almost royal, Miranda Addison, walked across the room and hugged her in the most genuine fashion.

"Don't cry my dear, don't cry - unless those are tears of joy", and then she laughed heartily, not haughtily, as she blinked to restrain tears from falling from her own eyes.

Miranda handed her a tissue and Sienna dabbed at her eyes, then she smiled as she contemplated the new beginnings that awaited her, and her heart overflowed with wonderful hope.

"So when would you like to start?"

"I can start straightaway if you like, maam".

"Well that won't be necessary but you can start work next Monday".

"Next Monday - that will be great - I can do with a few days to get myself together".

"But the flat will be ready for you to move into from tomorrow - I will ask the cleaners to prepare it for your arrival".

"Flat?" Sienna gasped.

"Yes dear - the job comes with a two bedroom flat which is situated at the back of the house", Miranda pointed out.

"Oh my goodness - *tank* you Jesus", Sienna exclaimed in Jamaican twang and turned her eyes towards the sky. "Oh - thank you sooo much maam - thank you", she reverted to textbook English as she turned to address Miranda.

"Don't mention it my dear", Miranda said as she rang for Linda to come and show Sienna the flat.

Chapter 12

October 2015

"It's a miracle", Sienna whispered for the umpteenth time as she arrived home. As she set about finishing the housework that she had started earlier in the day she sang a new song "It's a miracle. An awesome miracle. Gotta be a miracle. Nothing but a miracle", and she danced as she worked.

When she had finished cleaning, Sienna prepared a sumptuous meal for her friends. From the £20 gifted to her by Melvin that morning she had purchased chicken thighs. She applied her home made jerk marinade with a dash of honey and black pepper and rubbed the mixture into the chicken thighs then left them in the fridge for half an hour. Removing them from the fridge, she sprinkled the thighs with rape seed oil, covered them with foil and placed them into the pre-heated oven to cook. She had also bought oven ready seasonal vegetables (potatoes, sweet potatoes, swedes and carrots). When the chicken had been in oven for 40 minutes Sienna placed the vegetables on the bottom tray of the oven and moved the chicken to the top tray to brown. She prepared gravy from the drained chicken stock, onions, garlic, sweet and scotch bonnet peppers to which she added various spices to taste.

Sienna also cooked a small pot of rice and black eyed peas, as both Carlton and Melvin had apparently become addicted to it. They could not seem to eat a meal lately without the companion staple. And lastly Sienna prepared a green salad with olives.

This was to be a special celebratory meal to be eaten before she broke the good news to her friends. She wanted to feed them until they were fit to burst - her way of beginning to say thanks for their hospitality over the past six months.

At 5.35 pm Sienna rang Carlton to find out what time he would be home that evening.

"Hi Carlie"

"Please don't call me that - it sounds like a girl's name", Carlton said with a chuckle even though he was serious.

"Ok - hi Carlton", Sienna said then continued, "What time are you coming home this evening, or perhaps I should ask whether you are coming home this evening - I haven't seen you for a few days?"

"Well I wasn't planning to come home until tomorrow."

"Oh, please come home this evening, I've got a big surprise", Sienna whined.

"Okay - but can I bring someone along?" Carlton asked.

"Yeah sure - and who might that be?"

"Her name is Becky and she is my new ladeee".

"Wow - you kept that quiet".

"I was going to tell you soon - but it's early days - I haven't told a lot of people so don't feel no way", Carlton said. He was fast developing an Inner London accent and street speak from the clients that he had been dealing with on a daily basis in his work for the past few weeks. His chosen legal specialisation was Business and Commercial law, but he had to cover all areas of legal practice in his two years of training and was currently covering Criminal Law.

"Well congrats", was all that Sienna could muster.

"Thanks a lot - just hope it keeps going sweet".

"Yeah - she's really a lucky girl - you are an absolute gem, my brother", Sienna found her voice and complimented. She felt an unusual fluttering of her heart as she spoke.

"Thanks again - I'm blushing", Carlton said. She imagined how he looked the other end of the telephone line. He would be smiling as he spoke, in his own unique style, as his cheeks glowed red. Sienna mused that if she had not taken him for a brother, she might have found him romantically attractive. His oval shaped face, small aquiline nose, defined lips and strong jaw-line placed him in the definitely above average class and Sienna was in no doubt that Becky had been instantly captivated by his bad boy young Brad Pitt with extra attitude persona. With his semi casual way of dressing, he didn't fit the mode of a conventional Solicitor, but she knew that his integrity was impeccable.

Melvin arrived home first - "Wow - what's cooking - smells great", he exclaimed, kicking off his shoes, backing off his coat and heading straight for the kitchen.
"Oh no you don't", Sienna rushed to head him off at the kitchen door. "Dinner is a surprise, so please don't come into the kitchen"
"So what's for dinner then?" Melvin asked trying to peek around Sienna.
"You have to keep guessing until it's served".
"Ooh"
"Go and take a seat Melvin", Sienna ordered.
"Okay but how long before dinner is served - I don't think I can wait too long", he said in a mock whiny voice.
"Shouldn't be too long - just waiting for Carlton and his girlfriend Becky", Sienna said placing accents upon "girlfriend" and "Becky".
"Wow - Carlton and Becky ehh - has a good ring to it don't you think?"
"Yeah", Sienna said but she was uncertain if she truly agreed.
"It will be great - I can't wait to see who has commandeered Carlton's full attention", Melvin chuckled, then continued - "I'll go and take a quick shower then".

"Good idea".

Sienna felt a tug upon her heart strings as she thought about moving away from her brothers - they truly were like siblings to her. Her mind strayed briefly to wonder what might have been if she had met either Carlton or Melvin in different circumstances. She conceded that she would most probably have found in them attractive suitors - Carlton moreso than Melvin, although Melvin was better looking by far, with his 5' 10" stature, flawless alabaster complexion, full hazel eyes, razor sharp cheekbones and well defined lips. He was classically handsome, with heartthrob movie star good looks that had women everywhere captivated, not just those in their University where he was hailed as amongst the most sought after bachelors. But Sienna had so much more in common with Carlton. They had the same taste in music which was wide ranging but with a preference for hip hop and reggae and Carlton told her that he enjoyed listening to her Gospel music when he overheard her playing them; they laughed loudest at the same jokes as they invariably found them funnier than others did; they liked the same food, films, colours, and more.

Sienna was aware of the curious vulnerability that had come to rule over her mind in past weeks, affecting her relationship with Carlton. She had involuntarily erected a barrier, an invisible wall that kept them from getting too close. It was obvious that he had done likewise. Now that Carlton had found himself a girlfriend, Sienna felt safer for there could be no chance of any romance developing between them now. That was just the way she wanted it - they were friends - brother and sister, family and they could never be anything else.

Confusingly, there was no mistaking that Melvin had grown funder of her by the day and now carried a flaming torch for Sienna - the only person that was oblivious to the fact was Sienna herself. All of Melvin's antics - his pleas of undying love - his constant pleadings for hugs, etc., were viewed by Sienna as mere frolics. She did not take him at all seriously, and he pretended that it was all a joke. But in his dreams he cherished her as more than just a friend - more than a mere sister.

Melvin could have almost any woman he pleased but Sienna was not aware that he ever dated - he had never brought a woman home before. She thought it was odd that a young man of 24 had never had even one girlfriend in the three years that she had known him. Sienna wondered why, for she had seen the way girls behaved towards Melvin - they often took the initiative, but he was incredibly efficient at rebuffing their advances.

Carlton had never brought a girl home since she was staying with them either but Sienna was aware that he dated girls from time to time. Becky was the very first of his girlfriends that Carlton would introduce to Sienna, which indicated how serious he must be about her.

Moments after Melvin had stepped under the shower Carlton arrived home.
"Hey" he called out.
"Hi Carlton" - Sienna called back.

After taking Becky's coat and showing her to the most comfortable corner of the lumpy sofa Carlton headed towards the kitchen. "Sienna - come and meet Becky - my girlfriend". He was headed off by Sienna at the kitchen door and stopped in his tracks.

"You are not allowed into the kitchen Carlton - dinner is a surprise", she commanded, as she dried her hands with a tea towel. She then escorted him back into the lounge.

"Hello Becky - I'm Sienna - sooo pleased to meet you", she spoke as she crossed the room. She took Becky by her right hand and reached down to give her a welcome hug. Becky felt instantly at ease in her presence.

"Pleased to meet you too", Becky's voice quivered betraying her nervousness.

"Dinner is almost ready - just putting the finishing touches and waiting for Melvin to come out of the shower", Sienna said as she made her way back into the kitchen, her warm inviting smile fixed, even as a twinge of jealousy tugged at her heart.

In ten minutes they were all crammed around the small kitchen table enjoying the fare. Sienna had stretched the £20 to a remarkable but cheap bottle of sauvignon blanc from Lidl which complimented the meal perfectly. Soon tongues, loosened by the wine, lavished compliments upon her between mouthfuls of food. Sienna lopped up the praise.

"Well thank you very much - glad you like it".

After dinner the boys volunteered to wash up while Sienna and Becky retired to the lounge with glasses of white. Small talk came easily to them as they reclined and relaxed. Becky did most of the talking - her main subject was her new relationship with Carlton. Sienna learned that they had met through a friend of Becky's who worked in the same office as Carlton. She became privy to their first date, their first kiss, and Becky's hopes and dreams for their glorious future together. By the time the boys joined them in the lounge, Sienna knew that Becky was a woman in love and she gathered that this love was for keeps.

As Carlton and Melvin re-entered the living room Sienna observed that Carlton's eyes were firmly on Becky and her gaze matched his own. Their eyes spoke their story - they were in love and although Sienna willed herself to wish them well, she struggled with her emotions.

"Guess what?" Sienna said stiffly but excitedly as they took their seats.
"What?" they replied in stereo.
"I've got a job - and guess what else?"
"That's great - what else", the three voices were unbelievably in sync.
"It comes with a flat", Sienna rose up to fetch her mobile. She had taken pictures of her new home when she was shown around by Linda following the impromptu interview and job offer.

"I'm going to live here", she announced showing the pictures first to Melvin and then to Carlton.
Melvin said nothing but looked contemplative.
"Wow", came the stunned response from Carlton. He then passed the snapshots to Becky.
"Whhhho - pooosh", Becky exclaimed then added "Looking for a flat mate?" before guffawing loudly at her own joke. Carlton roared with laughter too and Sienna joined in sniggering. She did not reply to the answer, however, she hoped that Becky was not serious because she could not invite someone she did not know to live with her at Mrs Addison's private residence.

Melvin was uncharacteristically quiet, prompting Sienna to enquire.
"So what do you think, Melvie".
"Yeah - it's great news", his reply lacked enthusiasm.
"That flat is absolutely beautiful", Becky enthused.
"It is isn't it?" Sienna said.

"Where is this place - it's really posh", Becky asked. Sienna was thankful for a feminine commentary.

"It's in Barnet - sooo beautiful - sooo opulent - it's unreal - I can't believe this is happening to me", she felt tears of joy threaten as she became overcome by the thought of her good fortune.

"You're really lucky - I hope you enjoy that job", Becky sounded sincere.

"You deserve a break Sienna", Carlton sounded earnest.

"What is the job doing, Sienna?" Melvin asked abruptly

"Gardening",   Sienna replied.

"Gardening - shouldn't you be spending your time trying to secure a Training Contract to qualify as a Solicitor?" Melvin said curtly.

Melvin's tone of voice surprised Sienna and it occurred to her that he was behaving like a big brother might (or was it like a possessive husband). She was careful not to react negatively.

"Yeah - apparently the job is just 12 hours a week - can you believe it - so I'll still have plenty of time to carry on looking for a Training Contract?"

"That sounds too good to be true", Carlton chimed in.

"Exactly - that's what I mean - too good to be true - so where is this place anyway?" Melvin asked, sounding convincingly like doubting Thomas.

"It's in Barnet - the lady that I saw, Mrs Addison, a Governess at the Wensley Grammar School (Mill Hill) for girls, the same school that granted me the Scholarship to come over from Jamaica and study here in London, she offered me the job and the flat too"

"You mean you got a scholarship to come over to London and study - wow - that sounds amazing in itself" Becky chirped.

"Ummmhh?" was all that Melvin said.

"Yes and guess what?"

"What", the three voices chorused.

"Mrs Addison has promised to use her contacts to try and secure me a Training Contract too".

"That's great", Carlton stated, then continued, "I would be happy for you if that happened - Training Contracts are too hard to get - it matters not how you come by one as long as you get one".

"Yes that's true - it is too hard to secure a Training Contract - hope it all works out Sienna - I sincerely do", Melvin conceded and continued. "Congratulations - it couldn't happen to a lovelier person - but I can't lie, I'll miss you around here though".

"Yeah - we'll miss you", Carlton concurred and his voice cracked.

"Don't worry - you won't get rid of me that easily". "It's only 5 miles up the road and I'll be back often - at least once a week - remember that you're my only family", Sienna said and as she chuckled they all joined in.

Carlton rose to his feet and encouraged Becky to do the same. Melvin followed suit.

"To Sienna - we wish you the very best with your new job and new home", he said and they all joined in disconnectedly "Cheers", lifting half empty glasses.

"Thank you so very much" Sienna responded, and as they all sat down again Carlton enthused.

"There's a Will Smith movie on at 9 o'clock". They laughed at the fact that Carlton was Will's biggest fan, then settled down to watch the movie. Will Smith's second biggest fan in the room was Sienna.

Chapter 13

October 2015

Sienna's meagre belongings fitted easily into Becky's Micra. Melvin sat in the passenger seat as his legs were too long to fit in the back and Sienna and Carlton sat in the back. Guided by the SatNav, Becky drove tentatively along the A406 before charting the course through New Southgate and Whetstone towards Barnet.

Upon arrival they were met by Linda. She opened the gate for them to drive through and handed Sienna the key to the flat through the car's open window.
"Can I have a private word?" Linda asked Sienna.
"Yes - of course", Sienna replied and alighted the vehicle.
Out of earshot Linda briefed Sienna as she provided her with the entry code and fob for the front gates, "Please make sure you don't share the code with anyone and keep the fob safely at all times," she cautioned and added, "You will appreciate that this is a private residence and the highest degree of security must be maintained to ensure the safety of Mrs Addison, her household and staff at all times".
"I understand", Sienna nodded her reassurance with a smile.

Linda briefly demonstrated how to operate the gates before saying goodbye.
"Well I'm going now - I should have finished work at 1 pm and my husband is waiting for me to go shopping" she headed to her car as she spoke.
"Oh I'm so sorry to have kept you waiting", Sienna apologised.
"No worries", Linda smiled warmly and added, "I hope you enjoy your new home - by the way, the dogs are in their pen", she entered her car and closed the door.

"Oh yeah - the dogs!" Sienna exclaimed - she liked dogs but was a little afraid of the ones she did not know, having been bitten by a dog some years before.

"A Great Dane and an Alsatian". "They are trained to guard the estate". " Miranda thought it best to lock them away today". "The dog trainer will be here later this afternoon to walk the dogs". "He may come to see you later to introduce you to them", Linda chortled then continued. "This arrangement will remain in place until the dogs get used to having you around".

"Aaah that's very thoughtful of Mrs Addison", Sienna smiled widely then added, "Thank you very much Linda".

"Don't mention it - bye then".

"By the way - is Mrs Addison at home?" Sienna enquired.

"No - she went out to a meeting - she should be back at around 8 pm".

"Bye then - I must dash", Linda said revving up the engine of her car.

"Bye Linda", they all chorused.

Linda waved goodbye to them, backed out of the parking space and drove out of the gate. She activated the gates electronically using the fob and as they began to close she drove off, leaving Sienna and her friends looking after her.

After Linda's departure, every hand was on deck to move Sienna's belongings into the flat. The flat was at odds with the rest of the house. Its decor was ultra modern in neutral colours and the furniture was also state of the art and "up to the minute". "Wow - it's absolutely beautiful", Becky exclaimed as she walked from room to room. "You are so lucky Sienna - wow".

"It's a bit unbelievable that you will not be paying any rent for this place". "I just hope that there is no hidden agenda - nobody does anything for nothing these days", Melvin commented.

"There are still some good people left in the world", Carlton commented and added, "you are almost as fortunate to have subsidized housing Melvin".

"Yes - I know, but good people are few and far between - just make sure you know what you are doing Sienna and if you ever encounter any problem remember that we are just a phone call away - okay", Melvin placed reassuring arms about Sienna's shoulders.

The comment from Melvin caused Sienna to wonder what Mrs Addison's motives might possibly be. But recalling the kind eyes and guileless smile of her benefactor, shooed all doubt aside. "Mrs Addison is simply an Angel on assignment from heaven", she stated.

"Yes - well I hope you are right", Melvin concluded as he walked into the bathroom.

The bathroom appeared never to have been used - everything looked brand new. It was the same in the kitchen. The white goods were brand new, evidenced by the fact that the operating manual was still inside the fridge freezer.

The four of them helped Sienna unpack and arrange her belongings. When they had settled her in, all were hungry so they ordered in pizza via "Just Eat". Melvin and Sienna went to collect it at the front gate.

They found the meal less than satisfying and Sienna made a mental note never to order from "Tony's Pizzas" ever again. Her guests left at 9 pm and her spirit dipped as she waved them off and activated the gate to close behind them. Sienna watched forlornly as they drove out of sight. As she made her way back to the flat she contemplated the change that the course of her life had taken in just 24 hours. She was overjoyed, yet apprehensive, for she had never before lived alone. How would she fare, she wondered? She wondered whether she should call on Mrs Addison as she could see that lights were still on in the big house, but Sienna thought better of it.

By 10 pm Sienna had showered and was ready for bed. But sleep would not come easily tonight - it evaded her overactive mind, not because she was in any way perturbed, but sheer excitement was responsible for her insomnia. She flicked through the hundreds of channels on the 42 inch wide screen HD Smart TV in the living room but of the hundreds of TV programmes, none of them had piqued her interest tonight. Now as she nestled down into the cosy quilt and extra deep duck feather filled topper and duck feather pillows she reached across to the bedside cabinet for her new laptop. She had found it during her exploration of the flat earlier in the smallest of the rooms which was furnished as a study. The computer was brand new and still boxed. A note that she found next to it informed that it was a gift from Mrs Addison.
"Oh no - this is too much Mrs Addison", Sienna had soliloquised. She had telephoned her benefactor as soon as she knew she would be home.
"Please just accept it Sienna - you will need it - whether you have passed your exams or not", Miranda's tone had been resolute.
"Oh Mrs Addison - I really don't know what to say - you have done so much for me already".
"I can do much more than this my dear and it is my absolute pleasure", came the reassuring voice.
"Ok - thank you very much Mrs Addison - I am most grateful", Sienna had conceded that her benefactor would never change her position. Melvin had remained sceptical - "Why is she doing all this?" he had repeated his mantra over and again, and he warned Sienna to be cautious of the true motives.

"You need to meet Mrs Addison, Melvin, then you too will realise that she is simply an Angel on assignment from heaven", Sienna had affirmed but Melvin remained an unyielding sceptic.

Becky, who works with computers and is technically savvy, had set the laptop up for Sienna, set up her email and installed various apps and programmes. Now Sienna was using it for the first time to surf the web. The king of laptops surpassed all her wildest dreams as she explored the web to her heart's content. Sleep finally came whilst she was still browsing. Moments later she was suddenly jolted awake just as she was about to drop her brand new treasured gadget onto the engineered hard wood floor. "Oh my goodness", she exclaimed then sighed with relief. "Phew - I must be more careful". Sienna got out of bed and placed the laptop safely upon the cabinet, then she stumbled back into bed and within a minute she was fast asleep and travelling through dreamland.

The next morning Sienna awoke refreshed. She grabbed her laptop and googled "places of worship in Barnet" - she wanted to go to church and give thanks for God's many blessings but wasn't ready to attend Born Again Church of God today. She knew there would be a barrage of questions from Bishop and Sister Gooden and she wasn't ready for that - not yet. She certainly did not relish the thought of running into Sister Newson. So she found an Evangelical church just two streets away and set about getting ready.

The congregation was comprised of around 30 individuals. All heads turned to observe Sienna as she entered and took a seat towards the rear of the small church hall.

The Pastor led praise and worship. He also doubled as the pianist and back up vocalist and his wife, the only other person on the small dais, sang lead vocals. All others worshiped in a far more subdued manner than Pastor and his wife's vibrant display.

As Sienna took her seat she made eye contact with a couple seated to her left. She smiled but the act of goodwill was blatantly rebuffed, leaving her feeling insulted. After two minutes or so the couple got up and moved away. Some others turned their heads to glare at her without a hint of a welcoming smile. Still Sienna sat fast - she had come to worship God and she would not be deterred from doing so.

The word was delivered in an animated fashion by the Pastor. Within 15 minutes the sermon was at an end and within a further 10 minutes the service was ended by pronouncement of an unconventional benediction - "Go forth and be a blessing", signalled the end of the meeting. Tea and biscuits were on offer after the service and Sienna was approached by Pastor Minns who introduced himself and asked her to say a little about herself. He then spoke up to introduce her to everyone else who had not already left the building.
"Hello everyone, this is Sienna Miller - she is a law student who has just moved into the area", he announced. He was ignored by everyone, including his wife. Sienna felt odium permeate the atmosphere. The Pastor looked apologetic but said nothing.
"Oh well I must get going now", Sienna said and quickly made her way towards the exit.
"Yes - bye then Sienna ... bye", the Pastor avoided eye contact, smiled weakly and hung his head.

A quick glance backwards as she exited the hall informed Sienna that all eyes were upon her departing back and if looks could kill.....

"Oh dear - what was that?" she exclaimed with a sigh, as she avowed that she would definitely not be coming back here again.

There was no doubt in Sienna's mind that the reaction toward her was simply due to the fact that she was black, which caused her to wonder how supposed followers of a loving God could flaunt His commandment so flagrantly by hating another human being simply because of the colour of their skin. And instead of feeling blessed, Sienna's spirit felt wounded as she made her way home.

The gloom was quickly lifted as Sienna stopped off at the local supermarket on her way home and purchased lunch. Shoving the ordeal to the back of her mind, she allowed anticipation to lift her spirit. She would be cooking in her new kitchen for the very first time and she could not wait.

Lunch/dinner was simple - scrambled eggs with beans on toast which was consumed with gratitude.

Chapter 14

October 2015

The next morning Sienna was awoken by the sound of a lawn mower. Grabbing her 'phone she saw that it was 7 am and it suddenly dawned upon her that she had not been briefed as to what her working hours would be. Having showered and dressed hurriedly she quickly made her way towards the sound of the lawnmower. As she approached the operative turned off the motor and stood watching her advancement.

"Good morning", he called out and waved.

"Good morning", Sienna replied.

"You must be Sienna - our new assistant gardener".

"Yes sir, that's right".

"I'm Bert the head gardener".

"Sorry I'm late", Sienna said as she reached out her hand.

"Late?" "I wasn't expecting you until 8 am at the very earliest", Bert shook her hand firmly as he chuckled jollily.

"Oh - really", Sienna said. A big smile graced her countenance - she was filled with the infectious joy that emanated from Bert.

"Well now that you're here I'd better find something for you to do for an hour or so", Bert said then continued. "I can do this job all by myself but Mrs Addison - God bless her - thinks I'm getting too old for it". "She's wrong though - I'm as fit as a fiddle".

"Yeah you certainly look fit enough", Sienna complimented.

"What would I do if I didn't do this - I'd only be at home getting under my wife's feet". "It keeps me active and I'm not about to give it up without a fight", Bert said and winked at Sienna cheekily.

Joy filled the air and wrapped Sienna in its warmth as she listened to Bert's adorable cockney lilt and appreciated his spirit.

"I understand that you have been doing this job for many years", Sienna encouraged Bert - she wanted him to talk some more - to cheer her heart on this gloomy overcast day. And he did not need much encouragement.

Bert spoke at length about his time working for the Addisons and filled Sienna in on the history of the family as he knew it. As he spoke she marvelled at his effortless ability to entertain with witty anecdotes.

"I've been working for the Addisons for nearly 50 years. "They put an advertisement on their front gate for a Gardener and I just happened to be walking past and was the first one to turn up and apply". "Mr Addison gave me the job on the spot - he didn't have any choice really - I wasn't going away", he chuckled and winked before continuing. "I could tell this was a cushy number you see - I've been working here ever since". "Me and my Mrs used to live in the flat where you're living now, but we moved out 25 years ago and bought our own house in Borehamwood". "Paid off our mortgage in 15 years, thanks to this job". "I like Mrs A a lot - I can't say the same for her dearly departed 'usband though". "Apart from the fact that he paid me very well, he was a mean old sod, he was - ooh he was a nasty one, I can tell you", Bert grimaced as he described Michael Addison. "An absolute monster to poor Mrs A". "Used to knock 'er about you know", Bert confided in a whisper, then reverted to speaking normally. "He wanted to sack me when he found out I had done the knowledge and was driving a black cab as well - till this day I don't know how he got wind of it". "But thanks to Mrs A - she tipped me off of his intention and told me to pretend that I was not driving the cab anymore, she did, bless her." Bert paused before continuing. "Anyway I know this sounds bad, but I'm glad he's *"brown bread"*. Sienna's brain ticked over as she tried to work out what the Cockney slang meant. She smiled as she surmised that it meant "dead". Burt continued his narration. "He kicked it 6 years ago - made my life easier I can tell you - he was truly an evil sod". "You wouldn't be here if he was around - I can tell you - he hated black people", Bert looked apologetic as he made this statement.

"He was a controlling monster, he was". "Poor Mrs A couldn't go anywhere or do anything without his say so - she couldn't even let him see her talking to me or he would freak out". "I knew he knocked her about - I've seen the bruises on her many times". "I was tempted to report him to the Police many a time", Bert paused, then continued. "She is a totally different person now that he's gone - good riddance to bad rubbish is what I say". "She has found her true self at last". "She was a virtual prisoner here until he became too sick - it was the best thing to happen for poor Mrs A".

As Sienna listened to Bert's narration, she felt sorry for Mrs Addison as she imagined how her gentle soul must have suffered at the hands of a cruel husband.

"Anyway love - enough of my *rabitting*. "I'm sure you don't want to hear my old crusty voice any more today".

"Don't say that - I really enjoy listening to you - you make me smile in spite of the weather".

"This job is a cushy number - if we do a bit everyday - stay on top of it, there's really no more than three hours' work a day - two hour some days, and when split between us only half of that", Bert winked and nudged Sienna and she understood that he was letting her into something secret.

"All you have to do today love is to water the plants - it will take you no more than half an hour and you don't even have to do that today if you don't want to - it's setting to rain anyway", Bert chuckled.

"I'll do it - sure, no problem", Sienna said excitedly and set about her task.

Within 15 minutes it started to rain. Bert found Sienna who was still watering the flowers, and told her to call it a day.

"I've finished half of the main lawn now". "I'll do the other half tomorrow, then it won't need doing again for another week - the grass grows really slow in winter", another chuckle then he continued "Get yourself inside love - there's no need to catch your death - the *currant bun* ain't coming out at all today, is it?" Bert said then chuckled. "No one will check on us - I'm in charge - off you go".

"Okay in a minute", Sienna replied as it began to pour.

"Get inside - off you go", Bert said more insistently. "I'm in charge, remember", a final chuckle.

Sienna obeyed, "Okay". Bert turned off the hose and walked with her to the door of her flat - he kept up his banter as he walked. "When I was younger I used to drive a black cab down the West End in the evenings - I know the whole of London like the back 'a me hand - all the little back streets". "That was my main job really but this gig was a good back up", another chuckle. "I don't do the taxi work no more - I retired when I turned 70". "I'm 80 now believe it or not - a pause - but I'm still strong and I can still do this job".

"You are never 80", Sienna said incredulously.

"Yes I am too - 80 and 4 months", Bert said and chuckled, then he continued. "But I'm as strong as an ox and as agile as a monkey so you will be my Assistant Gardener for a good while yet", then he guffawed loudly and joyfully. "See you tomorrow love".

"See you tomorrow Bert" "Thanks for showing me the job, and for the background history", Sienna smiled widely as she wondered how she would spend the rest of her day.

Back home from work far earlier than expected Sienna did not know what to do with herself. She telephoned Melvin but got voicemail, then Carlton and again she was put through to voicemail. So Sienna telephoned Marion and then Mimi and spent hours catching up with her girlfriends. They planned to meet up two weekends later and Sienna could not wait.

On the second day of work Sienna's working day lasted 1 hour and 10 minutes and on Wednesday she worked for no more than 55 minutes, and that was only because she stretched out raking of the lawn. She pinched herself several times a day to be sure that she was not in fact dreaming.

By Friday Sienna was getting bored. When she finished work which amounted to no more than 1 hour, there was nothing more for her to do but surf the net or watch TV. She did a daily job search and wrote to several law firms, seeking a Training Contract but she still had far too much time on her hands.

It occurred to Sienna that she did not spend nearly enough time praying so she fell into a daily routine of reading her Bible, meditating, praying and giving thanks. She tried to emulate the Goodens' daily routine and felt her spiritual life begin to blossom as the days passed by.

Each day Sienna spent a little time with the dog trainer and the dogs. Every afternoon she accompanied the dog trainer to take the dogs out walking and to exercise in the nearby common. These daily outings were good for her both physically and mentally, and caused her conscience to rest a little easier with the thought that she was actually doing something to earn her keeps. The weekly salary of two hundred pounds was unbelievably generous of itself, and in addition she had free accommodation. But as she checked her bank account at the end of her first week of work, excited to be receiving her first pay and that it would go some way to clearing her £300 overdraft, she found that she had a credit of £900 in her account. Upon checking further she found that not only had she been paid her weekly £200 salary, but another credit of £1000 which bore the reference "Bursary No.1" had also been deposited into her account. Sienna was certain that there had been an overpayment and not sure what to do about that money, she decided that she would not touch it until she had spoken with Mrs Addison. As far as she knew the bursary was £250 per month.

Sienna wanted to see Mrs Addison, for one she longed to see her benefactor and she also wanted to inform her of the overpayment into her account, but when she enquired of Linda, who had visited her several times earlier that week to obtain her signature to various documents, she learned that the older lady was in hospital. Sienna fretted that her benefactor was seriously ill and during her time of devotion, began to pray in earnest for her swift recovery.

On the second Wednesday after having moved to High Trees Sienna went to visit Melvin and Carlton. She arrived at 7.30 pm just as Melvin was returning home from work. "Good timing", he enthused and hugged her long and hard. Sienna felt the love.
"Hey sweet man", she pulled back from his embrace and looked into his face.
"How's it going?" he asked as he proceeded to unlock the door and usher her inside.
"Would you believe there is hardly anything to do - I'm really bored so I thought I'd come and pester you", Sienna said as she flung off her coat and flopped onto the sofa.

"Great - well I wish I was bored - they are absolutely getting their money's worth from me at work, so forgive me if I'm not much company", Melvin sounded drained.

"No problem - have you eaten yet?"

"No - I forgot to pick something up".

"Well, sit yourself down I'll go and rustle something up for you", Sienna headed into the kitchen. "Why don't you give Carlton a call and see if he's coming home and whether he will want something to eat when he gets home", she called out.

"Carlton always wants something to eat", Melvin said dryly.

"Innit", Sienna concurred as she busied herself checking what was in the refrigerator and kitchen cupboards. She found salmon fillets in refrigerator and frozen cod and prawns in the freezer. There were potatoes, baked beans and cheese too.

"You can have baked potato with chili beans and cheese in 10 minutes or you can have seafood curry with rice and salad in 30 minutes - take your pick", she announced what was on the menu.

"Seafood curry with rice and salad please - want a hand?"

"No it's okay I got this - you're tired remember and I'm definitely not tired".

Carlton promised to be home soon but had not turned up an hour later so they ate without him because Melvin was ravenous.

"Guess what - I'm rich", Sienna announced when they had finished eating.

"Rich - how do you mean?"

"I've got more money than I have ever had in my bank account in my whole entire life".

"Really - how much is that then?"

"£853", Sienna said smugly.

"Well that is a lot of money - I have not had much more than that at any one time either and I am working a full time job", for the first time this evening Melvin chuckled.

"But I can't touch it yet because I think it's an overpayment".

"An overpayment?"

"Yes - it's a long story".

They chatted easily as the News was read in the background, commenting variously upon the news items. Sienna felt so relaxed in Melvin's company - he felt so close. But suddenly it dawned upon her that apart from the surface details she did not really know that much about him. Involuntarily she opened her mouth and heard herself say.

"Melvin - tell me more about yourself".

"You know about me already - I'm incredibly handsome, nearly 25, single and eligible and madly in love with you - so what do you say", Melvin was ever trying his luck.

"You are like my brother, brother, so no way", Sienna showed Melvin her open palms in a playful manner. "I'll try and find someone for you to date though and that won't be hard". "I know some beautiful girls and most of them fancy you already", Sienna teased.

"Yeah really - like who?"

"Marion, Mimi.... shall I go on".

"Mimi - really - she's pretty".

"Yeah and she is sweet on you too".

"Ummph - I will bear that in mind".

"So tell me more about yourself ".

"Well you know that I'm the middle child of 5 children and that I was brought up by my grandparents but I didn't tell you the whole story so here goes".

"You must have wondered about my heritage", Melvin questioned.
"Well - maybe", Sienna replied.
"Well if so, I will put you out of your misery - I'm sort of mixed race.
"What do you mean "sort of" - either you are mixed race or you are not".
"Well - it's a long story - you see I was told that my dad may be sort of black or something - so I'm not sure what that makes me really - that's why I said "sort of" - get it?"

They both laughed and Sienna commented, "I must admit I did wonder whether you were mixed with a dash of something other than English blood because of your creamy Mediterranean complexion and curly hair that gets even curlier when its wet, but I wasn't sure and even though I thought that you might be of mixed heritage, I was not sure whether you would know, so that's why I never mentioned it," Sienna confessed.
"Funny you should say that - I didn't know for many years although a lot of people used to ask me whether I was or not - I only found out when I turned 18 that I am likely of mixed heritage". "And until then would you believe it - I thought that my grandparents were my parents," Melvin no longer seemed tired as he began to narrate his life story.
"No - are you serious?" Sienna asked - her expression, both sonically and visually, depicted complete surprise. This reaction spurred Melvin on.
"Yes - I'm serious". "It's a long story but I understand why mum had to do what she did".
"I was born in Richmond upon Thames where my mother, stepfather and two brothers lived before, and for up to a year after I was born".

"My birth was something of an accident", Melvin spoke matter-of-factly and Sienna was prompted to go and sit by him. She took his left hand into both own, "No one's birth is an accident, Melvin", she consoled him. "We are all born as purposed by God".

Melvin appreciated Sienna's caring gesture. As he continued to narrate his story she occasionally patted his hand, which he further appreciated.

"My mother and stepfather were childhood sweethearts - they met in junior school". "They were so much in love that when his family moved away to Richmond Upon Thames, he had begged her to go with them". "He had a job to go to down South and wanted to move with his family as there were no prospects for a young man like him in Dudley at the time". "At first she had declined. After only one month apart, he had returned to Dudley to be with her". "The situation in the job market had not changed and he was forced to return down South as he was finding it impossible to survive living alone in Dudley". "This time he convinced her to go with him back down South". "So they had a low key Registry Office wedding before leaving Dudley, intending to have a bigger church wedding when they could afford to". "They had both just turned 19 years old".

"The two of them survived on their love and handouts from my stepdad's family. They had two children, both boys but after 5 years of marriage they ran into serious financial difficulties and consequently cracks developed in their marriage. Their differences culminated in a separation". "At the time my two brothers Bill and Ken were 3 and 2 years old". "Then my stepfather and my mother separated for over 6 months" "During that time my mother met my father". "At the time she fully believed that her marriage was at an end and so she began to date my father with the full intent that they would become a serious item". "But when they had been together for three months, my stepfather re-entered my mother's life and begged for a second chance". "My mother agonised long and hard about it - she did not want to hurt my father because (she told me that) she knew that he was a good man, but because of the fact that she already had two young children with her husband and still loved him deeply, she decided that she wanted to give her marriage a second chance". "So she discussed it with my father and he was very understanding although he was hurt by her decision".

"Heartbroken, my father moved away from the area and mum never saw him again after that", Melvin paused and Sienna patted his hand. Then he continued his narrative.

"Mum and my stepdad got back together and after three months she found out that she was pregnant". "She did not know that the child - that's me - was my father's". "But when I was born my mother and stepfather fell out again - apparently he took one look at me and knew I was not his child". "My two brothers are very pale with straight platinum blonde hair and icy blue eyes and here I was with alabaster skin, olive green eyes and curly dark brown hair". "He demanded a paternity test and when the result came back he walked out again as he could not deal with the situation".

Another pause and another pat of his hand prompted Melvin to continue.

"When I turned 6 months, my stepfather came back begging my mother for another chance". "Loving him as much as she did, she took him back with open arms".

"The marriage was going along unsteadily - my stepfather just could not get used to having me around". "Each time he looked at me he was reminded that his love had known another man". "It got so bad that he did not allow mum to take me out of the house anymore and neither did he or anyone else take me out because he could not bear the shame of people knowing that his wife had been with another man". "I was their dirty little secret", another pause. Sienna placed her arms about Melvin's shoulders, "Do you want to go on?" she asked and he nodded.

"Yeah - I'm okay", then he continued. "When I turned 9 months old my stepdad gave mum an ultimatum - either she put me up for adoption or he was going to walk away again". "It was at that time that mum found herself pregnant with my sister Claire". "Coincidentally my stepfather got a new and lucrative job down in Portsmouth". "But while he did not want to leave my mother behind pregnant - he did not want to take me along either, so he presented her with a condition - he said that mum had to put me up for adoption with the Local Authority or make some other arrangements for my welfare". "Mother didn't want to be a single parent to four children as she had found it extremely difficult during the months when her husband had left her before". "She agonised over the situation and after many sleepless nights she discussed her dilemma with my grandparents, Maximilian and Audrey". "It was my grandparents that came up with the solution - they would take me as their own son and bring me up".

"And so I went to live in Dudley with my grandparents as my parents, leaving my mother and her husband free to get on with their marriage". "They moved away to Portsmouth with my brothers and a few months later my sister Claire was born". "They are still living there until this day". "It was thought best that I grow up believing that my grandparents were my parents, and so it was". "So I grew up calling my grandparents "mum" and "dad" and believing that my mum was my sister".

"The area that I grew up in was predominantly (around 98 per cent) white". "I realised that I was different somewhat because of my skin colour and my hair, but like everyone else, I assumed that my dark looks were a throw-back because my granddad (dad) was of Italian descent".

"Throughout my childhood, I met my mother only once". "I was 10 years old, when she and her family came to visit one Christmas". "Then just after my 18th birthday mum and her family came to visit again - up until then I thought that she was my elder sister and that my siblings were my nieces and nephews so it came as a complete shock when she told me the truth". "Her husband Ted was very apologetic and so was my mum". "They cried as they explained the dilemma that they had been faced with and I forgave them there and then". "You see I had enjoyed a privileged upbringing". "Nothing was too much for my grandparents to do for me". "I was petted but not spoilt and I had turned out well - strong emotionally, mentally, physically and spiritually because my parents, I mean grandparents, were   staunch Christians".

"I was in for an even bigger surprise - Mum told me of my mixed heritage - she said that because I had taken more after her white side and only the most discerning eye could tell that I was of mixed heritage, without knowing it as a fact, she had seen no reason to mention it before". "After finding out I spent many hours looking at myself in the mirror, noting my slightly flared nostrils, dark brown hair with curls that grew tighter (almost kinky) when it rained, hazel green/grey eyes and freckly skin that tanned efficiently with even a glimpse of the sun". "I walked about stunned for days - it was as if I was a completely different person, as if the person I was had died and had been re-born". "I felt as if I didn't know myself for a while". "It's strange really - now I feel that I have something in common with black people although I don't really feel black", Melvin freed his hand and gesticulated as he struggled to articulate his emotions.

"I think I know what you mean", Sienna said although she really didn't.

"I had so many questions for mum and she tried her best to answer them". "She was very cooperative and kept saying that she could imagine how I felt". "She kept on crying - I hated to see her so sorry". "She gave me all the information that she had about my father - his name, last known address, and the area from which he originated". "I kept all that information and now that my exams are at an end I intend to go searching for my father again", Melvin sounded whimsical.

"You tried to find him before?"

"Well - kind of - I had an ancestry DNA test carried out to see whether I had any unknown relatives out there", Melvin chuckled.

"Wow - that is so interesting - what was the result?" Sienna sat upright on the edge of her seat, belying her excitement.

"I didn't find any relatives but I did find out that I am 82% European, 16% Sub-Saharan African, 1% South Asian and 1% hunter gathers and 1% unknown, whatever that means", Melvin threw his hands into the air in an expression of confusion and added, "Who knew - the result came as a total surprise to me?"

"Imagine, you are 13% African - that is unbelievable", Sienna gushed.

"That's pretty amazing, isn't it", Melvin concurred.

So how do you intend to go about searching for your dad?"

"I really don't know right now - maybe I'll try and find an agency that specialises in tracking down missing relatives or something", Melvin sounded clueless.

"I know, why don't you ask Becky to help you - she's a computer whizz and you can find out so many things with electronic media", Sienna suggested.

"That's a good idea", Melvin looked thoughtful as he continued, "I'll ask her about it when they get here", Melvin replied.

"Wait - shouldn't they be here by now - its nearly 9.30 pm", Sienna checked her mobile

"Yeah, Carlton has not been staying here much since he and Becky got together". "Maybe he is not bothering to come home tonight after all".

"Looks like I will be spending another lonely night, unless you decide to stay over", Melvin said groggily and added a big yawn.

"No sorry I've got to get home - let me call a cab - I need to be up early for work". "I know it's not much work but I still need to show myself willing and able", Sienna sounded wise.

"OK - I see - when will you come around again?" Melvin hoped it would come across as a

casual question but could not disguise the needful tinge in his voice as it cracked.

"Don't worry you'll see me on Friday - I'm coming round to cook you up a feast next weekend".

"Can't wait".

They chatted generally until they heard the faint beep of the cab's horn.

"Ok Melvie - have a great night right - I'll speak to you tomorrow"

"Tomorrow?" "You mean tonight don't you - just make sure you either call me when you arrive home or send me a text - ok", Melvin ordered.

"Sure bro", Sienna obeyed and then she was gone, taking the sun with her. Melvin looked out of the window after her and as she closed the cab door behind her he yawned and forlornly headed off to bed, mobile in hand.

Later he lay in bed and mused over how much Sienna had come to mean to him. He truly loved her - so much it felt like his heart might burst with affection sometimes. He wondered how she really felt about him - was she in denial - was the feeling mutual? Only time would tell.

As the taxi drove away Sienna reflected upon the evening - she had enjoyed herself so very much although they had not done anything that exciting. Just being around Melvin was enough - she couldn't wait for Friday to come. Now that Carlton was barely ever around, she was growing closer to Melvin in a way but she still viewed him as a brother. Would her feelings toward him change? Only time would tell.

Chapter 15

Next morning Sienna awoke at 6.00 am. She was dressed and out the door by 6.30 am. It was her intention to be ready when Bert arrived for work. It was cold so Sienna pulled her small denim jacket up and took a seat by the small office which doubled as a store for the gardening tools. This was where Bert based himself and Sienna intended to ask him to show her how to operate the gardening equipment today. No-one would hinder her from pulling her weight and earning her keep.

Bert arrived 15 minutes later just as Sienna was contemplating that the cold was too much to bear. Her hands and feet were frozen due to sitting still in the cold. It occurred to her that she needed warmer clothing and could now afford to buy herself some with the money she had in her account. But first she needed to clarify the authenticity of the payment with Mrs Addison. If it was not an overpayment, she intended firstly to send most of the money to her parents. She knew that they were in dire need. She would keep back a little to buy some thermals.

"Mawning love", Bert chirped.

"Good morning Bert - how are you today - you're looking well", Sienna complimented.

"I thank the good Lord me love, I feel great - another day - another dollar is what I say".

"What are you doing here so early?

"I wanted to come early so that I can learn how to operate all the gardening machinery Bert".

"That's a good idea - but you know that is not necessary - not yet". "There is a lot of life left in this old dog yet", Bert said with an enormous chuckle.

"I have a living to earn Bert - just like you don't like to rest on your laurels, I'm the same", Sienna said, stealing one of Bert's favoured sayings, and continued, "I've got to earn my keep Bert", and they both laughed.

"Come inside love - out of the cold", Bert beckoned as he unlocked the office door and held it open for her. "It will soon get lovely and toastie in 'ere".

"Yes - it looks really nice and cosy" Sienna concurred.

Sienna was an avid and quick learner. In just one session she had learned how to operate all three lawnmowers and the electric scarifier. Bert also showed her the various supplies that he used. "I'll show you how to place re-orders later if we get time or tomorrow", Bert said. "All there is to do today is the side lawn and I need to get away by 9 am", he informed. "My missus has got to go to the 'ospital at 10 o'clock - she has to go for physiotherapy for her hip so I gotta take her", Bert explained.

"I'm sure I can do the side lawn by myself, Bert", Sienna volunteered. She was fed up of sitting around and watching or doing silly jobs that Bert made up to keep her busy. "Go on home - leave it to me and I will get it done, I promise", Sienna pleaded but Bert was not listening.

"Don't worry love - it'll only take half an hour or so to do the lawn", Bert said then continued. "But tell you what, you can tidy up the edges when I'm done".

"But Bert how am I supposed to learn if you won't allow me to do anything substantial". "Please let me do the lawn and you can tidy up the edges - just for today", Sienna tried again.

"Oh okay love - go on then", Bert conceded.

Sienna mowed the small area of lawn competently as Bert coached her on how to do strips. When she had finished Bert congratulated her, "You did a really good job - you're a natural, you are". "You'll be after my job before I know it", Bert said half seriously.

"Please don't worry about that Bert - Mrs Addison assured me that your job is safe for life". "Please just allow me to help you out a bit more - that is what I'm paid to do", Sienna said.

By 9.30 am Sienna had finished all the remaining small jobs that Bert had left for her to do and made her way back to her quarters. She decided to walk over to the main house to find out about Miranda. Linda was already seated at her desk when Sienna rang the doorbell.

"Hello Sienna - please come in and walk down to the door next to Mrs Addison's office".

"Okay", Sienna replied and obeyed Linda's direction. She knocked lightly upon the door on arrival.

"Come on in Sienna", Linda called out.

"Good morning Linda", Sienna smiled brightly as she entered the room. Linda's office was just as opulent as the rest of the building.

"Hi - is everything okay", Linda enquired.

"Yes - all is well - how is Mrs Addison doing?" Sienna sounded concerned.

"She is a lot better than before - she just needs a lot of rest but I anticipate that she will be home in the next day of two", Linda sounded hopeful.

"Please give her my best regards - I would like to go and visit her".

"I will pass on your good wishes - she should be home any day now so it's probably best to leave your visit until she gets home", Linda responded.

"I really wanted to ask her about the bursary payment that was paid into my account - whether it is an overpayment"? Sienna confirmed.

Linda reached across her desk, "I should be able to clarify that for you - let me see - the bursary payment was made on Wednesday - here it is £1,000", Linda stated.

"Yes - that's it", Sienna guided.

"That is correct - £1,000 per month - there has been no overpayment as far as I can see", Linda informed.

"Is it correct?", Sienna asked again.

"Yes - of course it is correct - it is only £1,000 per month", Linda stressed.

Sienna's mouth fell open as though she wanted to say something but no words were formed. After a long beat she said "Okay - thank you".

"Thanks Sienna - I hope that's alright", Linda sounded concerned.

"Yes - that's fine", Sienna replied.

Having ascertained from Linda that the bursary payment had not been an overpayment, Sienna returned to her flat where she gave thanks to God. Then, having located her Passport, she placed it into the secure section of her handbag and headed out again, on her way to the Post Office.

The Post Office was bustling with patrons. Sienna joined the queue that stretched outside the door and wound its way around the side of the building. The queue diminished quickly and soon Sienna was inside the hospitable warmth of the large building. The queue snaked around inside the building towards the 10-strong team of cashiers who provided relentless and efficient service.

Sienna smiled as she contemplated what she was doing today. For the first time since her departure from Jamaica she was in a position to send her parents a cash gift and this caused her heart to dance. The lion's share of the month's bursary that she had received would go to them, to provide her parents with much needed financial assistance and this was a gift of which they were so richly deserving. Sienna's smile grew wider as she imagined the sheer joy that this gift would bestow upon the whole extended family. She imagined them all gathering in the large dilapidated farmhouse where she was born, where she had spent her formative years. Family members and neighbours alike would be welcomed into the celebration and for many days a party atmosphere would pervade the entire village, and for once her family would be revered, albeit temporarily, for having enough money to meet their everyday needs instead of being the pariahs who often had to borrow in order to feed.

After she had made the transfer of £700, Sienna made her way to a business centre where she purchased a calling card. She would call Takema later on and send a message to her parents that there was money waiting for them to collect from the funds transfer agent.

Sienna hoped that her parents would sacrifice some of the money to buy a mobile telephone so that she could readily contact them as sometimes she wished she did not have to go through a "mediator".

As soon as Sienna entered her flat she made a beeline for the telephone. It had been so very long since she 'phoned home. Takema gushed with excitement. "Hey girl - how is everything - it's been a long time since I heard your voice". "If not for the texts I would not even know that you are still alive".

"Hi Takema - great to hear your voice too - how are things down there?" Sienna was suddenly overcome by an acute longing to return to Soursop Bay. "Everything still the same - you know nothing ever change in Soursop Bay", Takema replied then they both chuckled.

"How are mum and dad doing?"

"They are fine - not too long ago I saw your mother pass by on her donkey going to market - she looking well, man", Takema said, reminding Sienna that it must be around 7 am in Jamaica.

"And dad - when did you last see him?"

"I saw him last week sometime - he was busy as usual rushing to the piece of farming land up in the hills, you know". "He looked very well though", Takema reassured.

"And you - how you doing?"

"Well - I'm okay too - I have some good news too. "Last week Boris proposed to me".

"What - you mean Boris Fletcher - so when did that happen, Takema?" Sienna asked with the confidence of a best friend.

"Well, we have been talking to each other for a few months now - but I only just realised that he was interested in "that way" about a month ago".

"Wow - did you say yes?"

"But of course girl - this is "the" Boris Fletcher that we are talking about - the same Boris Fletcher that only dated the top girls in school, remember - the one whose father owns the banana farm over in Blue Tree - what would you expect me to say?" Takema said then chuckled.

"Congratulations girl - I'm so happy for you".

"I will keep you posted about the wedding - hope you can make it", Takema stated.

"Well you never can tell - I just might be able to come", Sienna replied, confident that she just might be.

The two conversed for many minutes before Sienna remembered the reason for her call. She passed on details of the remittance that she had made to

Takema and asked that she assist her parents in purchasing a suitable mobile 'phone.

"Please Takema - and make sure that you show them how to operate the 'phone". "You know what - can you get mum and dad to call me from their new mobile number?"

"Yes - no problem - I will take them to the shop tomorrow", Takema promised.

They talked until the credit expired and the familiar "peeps" signalled that the call was about to end. "Okay Takema - got to love you and leave you, but I will be calling you often now that my exams are over", Sienna promised.

"I look forward to that girl - tell you more about the wedding arrangements when you call again".

Chapter 16

November 2015

Next day, after Sienna had finished work and returned home, she noticed the flashing lights of the answering machine. Who could have called her, she wondered? None of her friends had her landline number. She hurried to check the message - it was from Linda.

"Hi Sienna - Mrs Addison would like to meet with you at around 1 pm in her office". Sienna was overjoyed that her benefactor had now been discharged from hospital but wondered what Miranda wanted to say to her. A pang of anxiety passed through her nervous system - she hoped all was well. After an anxious 10 minutes pondering, Sienna decided to call Linda to find out if she knew what the meeting was about.

"Hi Linda - how are you?"

"I'm very well, thank you for asking", Linda said warmly and continued. "I hope you are okay".

"Yes - I'm great thanks", Sienna replied nervously. "I...I.... just wondered what the meeting with Mrs Addison was about - that's all".

"You sound so worried - I don't think it's anything to be concerned about". "I overheard Mrs Addison talking to her son on the telephone earlier - I think she is planning to introduce him to you".

"Oh okay", Sienna breathed a sigh.

"Be warned though, he is ever so pompous - just because he works for one of the most well thought of Law Firms in London he thinks he's the bee's knees", Linda spoke in a near whisper as though she was imparting a secret.

"Oh, I see - I'm even more nervous now", Sienna said then sniggered affectedly. She was not joking either. It occurred to her that this must be the connection of which Mrs Addison spoke on their first meeting.

When she had replaced the receiver Sienna's anxiety level rose to fever pitch. After a few minutes her nerves calmed and her thoughts returned to normal. "I want to look smart for this meeting even though it is effectively in the place where I live - this could be a make or break encounter", Sienna soliloquised.

It took less than a minute for Sienna to check through her wardrobe. She quickly surmised that she did not have anything suitable to wear. "Oh no I haven't got much time or I would go and buy that lovely suit in the window of the boutique down the road", she mumbled her lament.

Making do with the best outfit she had, which turned out to be her baby blue crew necked top and black trousers, Sienna made a note to go shopping for some decent clothes as soon as she had checked that her second week's salary was in her account later that day.

Surveying her appearance as she walked back and forth in front of the mirror, Sienna detested what she saw. She straightened the trousers and readjusted the top but instead of making her feel better it caused her to despair further. If only she had a decent professional looking outfit. "Well there is no use crying over spilt milk", Sienna mumbled as she gave a final glance and headed out.

As she made her way towards the main building, Sienna espied a red Mercedes parked at the front of the building. A middle-aged distinguished looking gentleman of about 60 alighted the vehicle as Sienna approached the steps and their eyes met. They both negotiated the stairs towards the entrance of the house. As it was a natural inclination for Sienna to be friendly, she smiled and said "hello". She guessed that this must be Mrs

Addison's son. To her dismay, her affability was met with a scornful scowl and a look that caused her to feel like the dirt on someone's shoes. Taken aback by this blatant snob, Sienna stood stunned in her tracks, not knowing what to do. When the shock subsided and she could think clearly again, she contemplated what she should do. If this was, in fact, Mrs Addison's son whom she was scheduled to meet, it was obvious that he was none too impressed with her for whatever reason. Of one thing Sienna was certain, he had not inherited any of his mother's politeness, kindness or charm. "Some people can be so rude", Sienna muttered under her breath.

Good manners and commonsense prompted Sienna to follow the rude stranger into the house. She would not allow his behaviour to cause her to boycott the meeting that Mrs Addison had so kindly arranged.

The man walked with an arrogant stride through the front door, purposefully closing it loudly behind him right in Sienna's face. She took several deep breaths to stop from losing her composure, then she calmly opened the door and entered the house. The stranger's callous display further compounded the feeling of humiliation that pervaded Sienna's mind but still she determined that she would not be put off attending the meeting with Mrs Addison.

Linda was waiting at the door to Mrs Addison's office and Sienna heard her greet the stranger, "Hello Mr Addison". She observed that he responded with a cursory nod of his head as he walked past Linda. Just before Linda closed the door, she caught Sienna's eyes and gestured to her by casting her eyes heavenwards. This caused a surge of relief to course through Sienna's being - at least he wasn't a pig just to her, apparently.

Sienna walked slowly towards the door of Mrs Addison's office where she stood and waited to be ushered in by Linda. She could hear the conversation taking place inside.

"Who was that black girl that I saw at the front of the house, mother?" He exaggerated the "b" of black in a disdainful, sneering fashion.

"Oh that will be the delightful Sienna Miller, our new garden helper, or yard girl as she puts it", Mrs Addison replied cheerfully.

"What - do you mean you have actually employed her?

"Yes - of course I have - Bert needed an Assistant - he's getting old you know". "She lives on the premises too which is wonderful".

"What ... you can't be serious". "Have you lost your mind mother". "This latest hare-brained scheme of yours has gone way too far this time". "It's one thing to support AIDS orphans in Africa by sending them thousands if not millions of pounds, but it's quite another to bring strays and waifs to live in your own house". "Really mother how could you?".

"Be quiet Geoffrey - Sienna might hear you". "She is a wonderful girl so you'd better get used to seeing her around because she is not going anywhere". "Sienna is a highly educated and intelligent young lady - she is also obviously well brought up and cultured". "One does not always have to be born into money to have regal qualities you know Geoffrey".

"In my eyes and mind - she can never be cultured or regal, mother - never". "I certainly will be keeping a very wide berth from her as long as she remains here - and hopefully she won't be here for much longer". "Her sort does not belong in this neighbourhood, and certainly not in a home like ours", Geoffrey sneered. "What on earth will the neighbours think?"

"Oh shut up will you Geoffrey - Sienna won't be going anywhere - she is staying and anyway, you don't live here anymore - remember".

"I still have my quarters here and I have a right to come and go as I please".

"Well you barely ever come by here so why would you want to start doing that now - I am very much looking forward to Sienna's company actually". "She is a great conversationalist - so very interesting and exotic - I just love her to bits", Mrs Addison said then chuckled and continued as Geoffrey smarted.

"In fact Sienna is soon to be a law graduate and that is the reason why I invited you to come by today".

"Mother, the only reason that I came by today is to visit you - to see how you are keeping since you returned from the hospital".

As Sienna listened at the door she heard Mrs Addison address her Personal Assistant.

"Linda would you please get us some tea".

"Coffee for me, please, Linda", Geoffrey ordered then continued. "By the way how are you Linda?" in an *"I don't really care to know"* monotone. Without allowing Linda a chance to reply he continued "How is your husband and family?" "Good, I hope - great.....", he said dismissively without listening to what Linda had said in reply. Then he immediately continued to address his mother.

"So mother - how was your hospital visit?" Geoffrey sounded as though he was having a business discussion as opposed to enquiring about his mother's health.

"Linda - I take it Sienna has arrived", Mrs Addison called after Linda as she was about to exit the room, ignoring Geoffrey's feeble attempt to demonstrate concern.

"Yes maam", Linda said and closed the door behind her. Almost immediately she tapped on the door, opened it without waiting and stuck her head back into the room .

"Sienna is here, maam - shall I show her in now?"

"Yes - please do Linda". Linda held the door open and gestured to Sienna to enter. With much trepidation Sienna stepped into the room.

"Well hello my dear Sienna", Mrs Addison greeted jovially. "Please come in and take a seat".

"Thank you very much Mrs Addison", Sienna said as she walked nervously to an empty seat across the room from Geoffrey and her host.

"Sienna, this is my son Geoffrey - Geoffrey - Sienna - she is soon to graduate and I was thinking that she could come do her Training Contract at Addison and Lawson".

"Pleased to meet you Mr Addison", Sienna said cordially. Geoffrey ignored her and addressed his mother.

"Mother you know we only offer Training Contracts to the creme de la creme of law graduates - only first class personnel will do for Addison and Lawson - we can't afford to carry people".

"Geoffrey didn't you hear Sienna greet you?" "You were brought up better than this, you know", Mrs Addison sounded affronted.

"Hello", Geoffrey said without looking towards Sienna.

"You should not forget that I have some shares in Addison and Lawson too Geoffrey and I am certain at least one, if not both, of your partners will support my proposal for Sienna to do her Articles there". "They will surely have the good sense to recognise an outstanding candidate when they see one". Sienna said nothing for fear that she would undoubtedly say the wrong thing as far as Geoffrey was concerned. She felt very uncomfortable - the tension in the room was palpable.

"So mother are you feeling better now - you really should take it easy and stop worrying about other people's problems", Geoffrey sneered.

"Sienna dear - you can go now - I will speak with you tomorrow and let you know when you will begin your Training Contract once I have discussed with the other Partners at Addison and Lawson".

"Yes maam - thank you very much maam - goodbye". "Goodbye Mr Addison it was nice meeting you", Sienna lied - she spoke feebly as she made a hurried retreat. Geoffrey did not reply.

"Aren't you going to answer Sienna, Geoffrey?" his mother scolded adding, "you're so incredibly rude".

"Mother if you have nothing useful to say to me I'd better go", Geoffrey responded. Miranda said nothing further but her body language spoke loudly - she could care less if Geoffrey stayed or left.

"Really mother - I hope you come to your senses soon before the worse happens".

"What do you mean by that?"

"Well you know as well as I do that those people are bad news". "You can't have her living here - before you know it her whole tribe, clan, gang or whatever will move in". "It's just not safe mother - she has to go".

"Geoffrey, this is my house and I will have anyone I please living here". "Sienna is a wonderful young lady - she is going nowhere and that is final".

Linda waited until there was quiet in the room and then tapped at the door.

"Come in"

"Your tea and coffee Mrs Addison/Mr Addison".

"Thank you Linda", Miranda replied.

"Thank you", Geoffrey concurred.

Ten minutes later Geoffrey finished his coffee and bade his mother goodbye. "Goodbye mother - I will be coming around often to check upon you, especially since that... that.. creature is just a few yards away", he said.

"Goodbye Geoffrey", Miranda snapped loudly - she loved her son but disliked his prejudices. As she heard the powerful engine of the Mercedes stir and purr, her mind drifted back in time. Geoffrey was too much like his father, with the same narrow-minded thinking. Revelations like today's demonstrated that she had failed miserably. She had not ensured that her son was brought up with a broad perspective on life and society. Geoffrey displayed the same bigoted one-dimensional thinking that was sown into him from birth by a father who was an unapologetically racist white supremacist. But how could she have failed to influence her son even one iota. She knew the honest answer - it was because she did not know herself back when her son was a child. The real Miranda had been taken over by the evil doppelganger, the creation of which was begun firstly by her father, William, and later completed by her husband Michael. Back then she had been a "follower" - easily manipulated and controlled, and she had believed that she was just like her father and Michael. She had not been in touch with her true benevolent soul, the Miranda that possesses a cosmopolitan outlook, and she had not yet encountered the love of God, the agape love that she had spurned in her youth in order to feed upon the ugly ideology fed to her by her white supremacist father whose only real contribution to her life had been to feed her the dogma of white privilege and then disappear. And she had willingly gorged herself upon the grotesque carcass until her soul had become obese with evil, until it was not possible for anyone, even herself, to see the real Miranda - her beautiful self hidden beneath the odious folds of bigotry.

"But I know better now", Miranda whispered. "Now I know who I am - I am a benevolent philanthropist with a Christian world view". "I have been born again, reborn into God's holy family and His beautiful Spirit dwells within me and has full control over mind". But even such positive confessions did not fully reassure Miranda that she had been reformed.

As she regressed into the past, Miranda cringed at the memories. She had learned how to selectively forget some details of her past, and she had shunned dark truths from the light of her conscience, but tonight such memories had swam free from the depth to the surface of her psyche. And if she were to be truly forgiven, Miranda knew she had to face them - repulsive as they might be. For many years she had utilised the camouflage of charity as a shield for her soul from the bitter truth that she had once been a ranting racist with a rotten putrid heart. Her own father had passed that defective gene to her. Miranda had once believed that it was a congenital inheritance but in recent years she had woken up to the fact that it had been just an ideology, a parasite which had attached itself to her mind, instilling into her the abnormal love of self (which was in fact no love at all), that thrived upon the abominable detestation of others who bore a different skin colour or who were in some other way different.

They say that a child's formative years are from birth to 7 years old. Miranda's father had stayed in her life until she was 8 years of age - just long enough to ensure that the detestable seed that he had sown germinated, grew, matured and began to bear fruit. And that fetid fruit had reproduced and continued the cycle of hate.

For the first time in her life Miranda accepted that she was every bit as culpable as her husband in nurturing their son into the racist monster that he had grown up to be. She began to cry uncontrollably as she accepted that she could no longer hide behind the veil lie that her son had taken after his father, that due to her husband's controlling ways she had had no say in his upbringing, for the whole truth was that Geoffrey with his warped attitude was a re-incarnation of his deceased father but also a doppelganger of her youthful self.

"But I'm no longer like that - I detest the evil creature that once thrived in this now redeemed soul of mine", Miranda soliloquised as the tears flowed freely. "Oh my God - how ugly was my heart and so blind, for with impunity I embraced the vilest and basest standards". "But I know better now ...... I know better now ...... I know better now". "Lord God you know that I know better now"

Miranda rocked back and forth as she hugged herself. Suddenly she stopped sobbing. She rang through to Linda and, in her best *"I've not been crying voice"*, informed her that she did not want to be disturbed for the rest of the day. "Linda - no more calls for today, please and you may take the rest of the afternoon off when you have finished preparing dinner - I will serve myself when I am ready".

"Yes Mrs Addison - are you alright Maam?"

"Yes - of course I'm alright", Miranda replied - her *"I've not been crying voice"* had deserted her momentarily and Linda could hear that all may not be well.

"Are you sure that I can't be of any assistance to you, Mrs Addison?", Linda pressed her.

"I'm alright Linda - please go - thank you", Miranda replied abruptly.

"Thank you Mrs Addison - but if you do need me please give me a call".

Yes - of course - good day".

"Good day maam".

Having replaced the receiver Miranda entered her bedroom and sat in front of her dresser mirror staring at her reflection - she noted the tear stains on her face - the "perfection" face powder had been streaked by the tears, allowing a glimpse of her skin beneath - to her eyes she looked gross. After many more minutes Miranda rose up and walked into the en-suite where she washed and methodically cleansed all remaining traces of make-up from her face.

Back in front of the mirror Miranda noted the true state of her bare skin. But the wrinkles borne of old age did not cause her to baulk tonight. Suddenly they seemed friendlier than usual. In the past they had assaulted her eyes and she had viewed them with hostility, as enemies, hijackers of her youth and beauty. But tonight for the first time she appreciated that they came hand in hand with experience, hindsight and wisdom, attributes that only old age could boast of.

Life is the greatest teacher and Miranda had studied for much longer than most. Although she looked no older than 75 years old her true age was closer to 85. She was older now but blessed to still possess all her faculties, and she was so much wiser. During her lifetime she had experienced things that few human beings could speak of, that most could not even think of, and now with the benefit of hindsight she could see clearly where she had erred. Until she reached the age of 80 she had been a fool - had lived a life that she was not proud of. For she had despised humanity, had scorned God's own creation, had not only harboured racist thoughts but had been complicit with Michael in carrying them through, and she had many dark secrets, unspeakable disclosures that she could make but which she struggled to forget. Such horrible tales of devilish evils which not even the most understanding of souls would have a heart to forgive.

Until the light shone into her heart Miranda had lived each day as though she were superior and thought of people of different cultures, colours and creeds - and more particularly black people, as if she were their self-assigned god -

and as if they were nothing but filth. But when her husband Michael had become ill with cancer and later rapidly developing dementia, as his condition had deteriorated and she found herself alone even when in his company, she had sought comfort in the local Baptist church, something he would have strictly forbidden if affliction had not taken control of his mind. The church had offered her more than just solace, for while listening to the songs, Bible readings and uplifting messages, she had also undergone an awakening of her spirit. This new consciousness had come hand in hand with meekness and as the days went by she had grown more humble, shedding the tainted lenses that had coloured her vision.

With the departure of her husband's controlling influence, and the introduction to a new way, Miranda had been set free and having undergone some soul searching, she had found a love for humanity buried deep within herself. Over time she had come to appreciate more and more that she was no better than the next human being regardless of their colour, culture or creed. And her heart of iron had turned to one of purest gold.

Within a few months, by the time that Michael passed away 6 years ago, Miranda had become a new creature. It was with great sadness that she had said goodbye and buried him as an unrepentant racist. She wished that she could have gotten through to him to impart the grace that had sought and rescued her soul from darkness, but the terminal affliction had rendered him unreachable. So she prayed for his soul for many days, weeks and years, and embraced more fully the new path upon which she had embarked when Jesus Christ had entered the fray for her soul. In her mind the charitable acts that she did for others, were not simply acts of personal repentance and recompense, but were also done in order to make amends on behalf of

Michael. But no matter how great the act of charity that she did, her conscience was never fully pacified.

Geoffrey was not aware of the full extent of her benevolent ventures. Miranda had never made him privy to her deeds. Since her husband's passing, she had given away more than £1,000000 every year. What Geoffrey would never understand is that it was imperative for her to do good to the poor and needy. Each good deed demanded that she go one better the next time. If she failed, nightmares would hijack her dreams. Some nights she could not sleep at all. She felt some momentary peace after her philanthropic deeds, especially after having helped black people, the same folk that she had treated with such condescension in the past. Miranda was oblivious to the fact that her charitable actions were often so over the top that reasonable people interpreted them as pompous and showy. Consequently she did not have any real friends. The ones with a xenophobic world view she had abandoned and she had found it difficult to nurture new friendships at her time of life. Most people thought her altruistic ventures to be egotistical, not seeing that she had a genuine heart - one filled with love for those less fortunate than herself.

Afternoon turned to evening and evening gave way to night. The invading darkness did nothing to assuage the pain of guilt that still assaulted Miranda's soul. Up until recently the charitable giving and good works which she had undertaken, observing such activities religiously, had provided her conscience with some breathing space, but with the doctor's recent diagnosis, it had dawned upon her that charity alone could never go far enough. She might be getting closer to the imminent date of departure from the earth and the need to truly right the wrongs of her past had suddenly become pressingly urgent.

The news that her health was failing and that she could suffer a stroke or heart attack at any minute of any day had Miranda more worried than ever. Her doctor had tried to persuade her to stay in hospital for further treatment but had made no promises, so Miranda had opted to be discharged - she had things to do, things that could not be done from a hospital bed. Miranda had to go back to her past, for she had many wrongs to put right.

Chapter 17

November 2015

Jonathan had been sitting in his car outside his mother's home for over an hour. He was listening to his favourite music - reggae. He loved reggae, but not the sweet "Studio One" of Toots and the Maytals; not the lyrical genius of Bob Marley or the melodic strains of his Wailers; not the "Lovers Rock" of Berisford Hammond or the timeless air of Jimmy Cliff. No - he could not get satisfaction from listening to the beautiful, popular and preferred mainstream Artistes such as these.

Only the more rogue artistes specialising in rough, raw rhythms and discordant chords that many would argue do not deserve to be classified as reggae at all, appealed to his warped mind and only when accompanied by vice or violence filled lyrics or toasts - preferably both, could they appease, providing the darkness that his tortured soul craved. He had abandoned the morals taught to him by God-fearing parents and pious Sunday School teachers as soon as he had grown tall enough to intimidate those with authority over him into allowing him to do his own will. Now he could not remember even one of the orthodox ten commandments. Instead he adhered faithfully to opposite tenets such as thou shalt fornicate as much as possible, even to the point of violating others against their will; or thou shalt lie cheat and swindle, sometimes at knife point if necessary; or thou shalt hate thy neighbour as thyself, and plot their demise if they so much as look at you in the wrong way - and the list was in-exhaustive. On a daily basis Jonathan observed religiously an anarchic code of belief. Thou shalt blaspheme the name of the Lord thy God was amongst his daily favourites.   And occasionally he ventured to commit those deadly sins that even he wished to forget that he had done.

Goodness and purity are two of Jonathan's pet hates and he is passionate about sin, having embraced it in all its guises. He and the devil have close ties and Jonathan would have it no other way.

It was not that he particularly wanted to see his mother - no - Jonathan's visit today had been necessitated by her failure to answer any of the numerous telephone calls that he had made to her for over a week. He had been calling her to plead for a subsidy. Last week he had spoken to her and tabled his request, but she had informed him that she could not help. And since then she had been ignoring his calls. But he really needed help this month. There was no-one else that he could turn to and so he had come in person, hoping that his presence might prove more persuasive.

Jonathan knew how to manipulate his mother - he was certain that he could get her to change her mind - she would find some money from somewhere to give to him - she had never let him down before. Over the past two years she had been particularly flushed with cash, lavishing it upon him even without his asking, but in past couple of weeks she has become very tight-fisted indeed, pleading destitution.

The slack lyrics caused a stir in Jonathan's libido and his thoughts turned to Sienna - how he wished that he had acted faster, had pressured her more into submission. Now it seemed that he had lost his chance forever but she remained under his skin, like a very sharp needle. He wished that he could bump into her somewhere - preferably on a very dark night. Then he would show her how he really felt about her. He would make her scream - how he wished that he could hear her scream. And then he would shut her up - for good. His thoughts reverted back to the time when he had almost accomplished that goal - that night before Sienna had left his mother's home.

Suddenly it occurred to Jonathan that his mother was to blame for turning up at the wrong time, for spoiling his fun "silly old hag", he spat out his thoughts then repeated the refrain to the heavy beat thumping through the speakers "eeeh silly hag - silly silly hag". As he mused upon the fact that his mother was to blame for Sienna's departure from his life, he bopped his head to the beat and cursed her shamelessly - "silly silly hag" and "silly old bag", and he also interjects a word which speaks of a woman's licentious character and rhymes with "bag" and "hag". Then as the track ended he turned the music off, exited the vehicle and sauntered towards the house.

****

Having let himself in with his own set of keys Jonathan called out sweetly, "Hi mum - muuum".
"Jonathan - is that you?", Sister Newson exclaimed as if it could be anyone else. No other person visited her with their own key and without first letting her know that they would be coming and she had in fact had no visitors since Bishop and Sister Gooden had paid her a call over three weeks earlier.
"How are you son?" she asked caringly.
"I'm okay mum - but I could be better".
"Come and sit down, son - make you' self comfortable - I just finished cooking oxtail in brown stew, rice and peas - you want some?" Sister Newson twanged easily.
"Okay mum - you know I never say "no" to food", Jonathan took a seat and grabbed the remote. He flicked channels until he found "Nollywood

Movies". A movie about poverty was a sure way to twang at his mother's heart strings.

As he ate the sumptuous meal Jonathan made various comments about the storyline, "Oh dear - I really feel it for those people - look at their lives", he urged his mother to watch with him.

"Oh dear - it's really sad - I hope there is a turnaround in their situation soon".

"Me too - I feel so sorry for them", Sister Newson fully believed the story being played out and was moved to tears. She dabbed at her eyes as Jonathan delivered his trump card.

"You know mum, I find myself in almost a similar situation at the moment - I feel ashamed to keep asking you for money, I really do but the fact is that I don't have a choice". "If you stop giving me the help that you have been lending for the past 2 years, I just won't be able to survive", he pleaded his cause.

"If I don't pay my rent tomorrow, I might lose my flat", he continued.

"Then why don't you give up the flat and come and live here?" a pause followed before Jonathan replied.

"Mum - how could you even say that - I am a grown man you know - how could you even mention that".

"Oh - sorry son - it seems like a good solution to me", Sister Newson replied with a shrug, then continued. "I really wish I had it to give you but things "sour" at the moment". "You see the little money that they used to send me to pay for Sienna's upkeep has been stopped and so I can't help you any more - I don't know what you are going to do but that is the situation right now". "All I have is my little pension money and it cannot even cover all of my bills, food and so forth".

The colour drained from Jonathan's face when he realised that his own actions may have contributed to the slaughtering of the cash cow that had been providing him the proverbial milk and honey that his mother had freely and habitually doled out to him each month. He did wonder where all the money was coming from but he had surmised that she had cashed in some lucrative endowment or pension fund. He paused his chain of thought - maybe that was still the case. It was by no means certain that he believed all that his mother was saying. Jonathan made a mental note to come back one day when his mother was not at home, and have a good rummage around - see what he could find out about her financial affairs.

"So mum - you mean you can't even lend me £400?" Jonathan placed an accent upon the word "lend", although he had never before repaid any money "loaned" to him by his mother. That precedent would certainly not change now that his gambling habit had gotten significantly worse, his debts having double-eclipsed his assets.

"Son - believe me, I don't even have £10 to tide me over until my next pension pay day on Monday", Sister Newson said dejectedly, then added, "Luckily I have enough food to last until then".

"Oh - so when is Sienna coming back to live with you?"

"I don't know son - I haven't heard a word from her for months".

"Well don't you think you'd better call her and find out mum". "I thought you said that she didn't have any family at all in London".

"No - she doesn't".

"You should really look out for her more then you know mum - for all you know she could be in some trouble - you better call her mum and make her understand that you care for her and want her to come back home." Sister Newson said nothing - how could she begin to explain that her behaviour towards Sienna had broken a link that now looked to be irreparable.

"You are the only thing like family that she has - mum you really need to show her that you care", Jonathan said with his mouth full and wide open, a sight only a loving mother might not find repulsive.

After finishing his meal, Jonathan washed his hands and said a hasty "Goodbye mum - I've got to dash - since you can't help me I need to go and see one of my good friends who might be able to". "See you soon, mum", he lied as he barely glazed her cheek with his lips.
"Okay son - drive carefully - you hear", Sister Newson wished he would spend even an hour with her but did not verbalize her desire.

Through the bay window of her terraced house Sister Newson watched as Jonathan's car faded out of sight and the love she felt for her son warmed the cockles of her heart. However, this emotion was in pole opposite to that within the soul of her sinful offspring - his heart was as cold as ice towards her".

He had only just left and Sister Newson already longed for Jonathan's next visit. It occurred to her that for more reasons than one Jonathan's presence in her home and life would be more assured if Sienna came back to live with her. And by any means necessary she would get the girl to come back. Now all she had to do was to figure out how.

Chapter 18

December 2015

Sienna spent Saturday shopping for new clothes. She bought mostly casual separates for day-to-day wear, a dressy outfit for church but when she went to buy the beautiful suit that she had seen in the nearby boutique, she found out the shop closed early on Fridays and all day Saturday. She made a mental note to return on Monday.

On Monday morning after finishing work Sienna was once again summoned to Mrs Addison's office. The message sounded urgent and required her to attend as soon as she was free. Having freshened up with a shower and change of clothes she hastily made her way towards the main building. Linda was not around so Sienna approached the office door and knocked lightly.

"Please come in Sienna", Miranda had been looking out for her and saw her enter on the CCTV system secreted beneath her desk.

"Good morning Mrs Addison"

"Oh please do call me Miranda - after all you're not an employee in the true sense are you Sienna", Miranda said warmly. Sienna smiled and relaxed.

"Thank you, um Miranda", she felt uncomfortable being so familiar and resolved to revert to calling the lady maam.

"I must apologise for the behaviour of my son the other day, Sienna - please take no notice of him - you are more than welcome here. I truly appreciate your presence and hope you will stay at least until you have finished your Articles - I mean Training Contract - that's what they call it these days, isn't it?"

"Thank you maam - yes that's right".

"Speaking of Articles - I mean Training Contract, I spoke with Andrew Lawson, the Senior Partner of Addison and Lawson this morning and he has assured me that he will be happy to employ you". "I have made an appointment for you to meet him this afternoon - I suppose I should have checked with you first to find out whether you could make it". "But not to worry if you cannot make it - it can be re-scheduled".

"Thank you maam - this afternoon is fine - I can make it, but I need to go out and buy something appropriate to wear that's all", Sienna said - the slight tremor in her voice betrayed how nervous and anxious she had suddenly become.

"It's not exactly an interview dear - you have the position already - Andrew just wanted to meet you that's all".

"What time this afternoon, please maam?"

"Good question", Miranda said with a chuckle as she checked some written notes and continued. "He said anytime between 2 pm and 4 pm would be okay, dear".

"Okay - I'll be there", Sienna affirmed. "Maam, I was just wondering what will happen to my gardening job when I start working full-time?".

"Please don't worry about that Sienna - your legal career must rank first".

"Oh okay maam"

"Miranda dear".

"Okay Mmmiranda".

"I could always employ another Assistant Gardener if necessary but I don't really think that will be necessary".

"Mmmiranda - I could always help out on Saturdays if needed", Sienna volunteered.

"Yes - that would be absolutely perfect".

"Maam - there was something else I wanted to ask you"

"What's that Sienna?"

"I received £1,000 into my account last month which I assumed was 4 months scholarship money?" Sienna stated.

"Four months?" Miranda responded then continued. "Do you mean one month?"

"One month maam - yes that is what Linda said?"

"Yes Sienna, £1,000 is one month's bursary".

"Really?"

"Yes - do you mean you did not know that?" Miranda asked. Sienna did not reply - her mind began to whirl and she was rendered speechless. After a beat she found her voice.

"Thank you very much maam, I mean Miranda", now Sienna felt satisfied that what Linda had told her was a fact. She also appreciated that what Sister Newson had been telling her for years was a misrepresentation of the truth. But she opted to say nothing - it would serve no real purpose to bring this fact to light now.

"It's my pleasure Sienna - my absolute pleasure - I just hope it has been enough", the latter comment was rhetorical but Sienna just smiled and nodded in reply.

Fifteen minutes later Sienna stepped into the Paradisa.

"Can I help you?" the shop assistant came rushing towards her. The beautiful outfits that adorned various manikins strategically placed near the entrance of the shop commanded Sienna's attention momentarily. She forced her mind to focus and replied.

"Thank you - I know just what I am looking for ", and she made a beeline for the rack where the smart navy suit she had been eyeing ever since she had seen it in the window a couple of weeks before was hanging.

The shop assistant followed her and assisted in locating the correct size. "Would you like to try it on?"

"Yes, please but I must hurry", Sienna sounded frantic.

"Okay - the dressing room is free - come with me", and Sienna dutifully followed the tall slim blonde as she sashayed her way towards the rear of the shop.

"Thank you", Sienna said, grabbing the garment in her haste.

She was right to think that it would fit her perfectly - it was as if it had been tailored just for her figure. Sienna looked into the full length mirror at the transformation - a professional woman stood in her shoes - she was tempted to stand and daydream for a while, to retrace in her mind just how far she had come since her humble childhood, but reality gave her a nudge and she rushed back to the dressing room followed by the shop assistant.

"Any good?", the officious attendant called out through the closed door.

"Yes - I love it", Sienna called back.

"Okay - since you are in a hurry, please pass the suit to me and I will get it bagged up to go for you".

"Wow - thanks - that would be great.

It took Sienna just 10 minutes to get back home where she dropped her bags and headed straight into the bathroom. She took a four minute shower then dried and dressed in record time.

Sienna pulled her hair back into a neat bun and smoothed hair gel over for added shine. She surveyed the finished product in the bedroom mirror, "Perfect", she spoke her thought and nodded with satisfaction. "Sienna Girl - you are saying "one"". "Yes - you have made it girl - you are saying "A1", she did a jig and plastered a wide smile across her face.

For a few minutes Sienna reflected, looking back over her journey and then focusing upon where she was going with her life. Suddenly an irrational fear threatened her mind. What did the future hold in store - if only she could tell. What if things went terribly wrong for her at Addison and Lawson? What if it didn't work out? She fretted that Geoffrey might be a hindrance to her there and decided that she would avoid him as much as she possibly could. She would do the very best that she could to make it work out. She had to succeed - there was no way she wanted to fail. She would bend as far as was necessary but she would not break. Sienna vowed within herself that she would make her parents proud. If she was doing it just for herself she might not make it, but if she was doing it for them, she would surely succeed.

Miranda was out on the porch as Sienna headed off to her meeting.
"Bye dear - all the best", she called out and waved.
"Thanks a lot maaa, ... Miranda", Sienna replied. She was prompted to go over and hug her benefactor but resisted, smiled and continued on her way, looking back several times. Each time she looked back Miranda waved, until she was outside of the front gate and then out of sight.

Chapter 19

December 2015

"Mr Lawson is with a client at the moment - please take a seat", the receptionist instructed with a warm smile. Sienna was happy that she had arrived early for her appointment - she wanted to make a good first impression.

The reception area of "Addison and Lawson" was nothing like Sienna had imaged. In her imagination it would be state of the art in design and furnishings, but she was disappointed by what she saw. The drab blue grey walls, faded Axminster carpet and the lacklustre antique chairs set along one wall of the reception room all compounded to underwhelm. As she sat waiting to be called into the meeting Sienna surveyed the pictures hanging on the walls. They spoke of bygone days which was quaint in a way, but taken with the rest of the fittings they conjured in her mind images of past and faded grandeur. Here many years ago someone's dream had been born, had taken flight and soared over the years but now appeared to be in the throes of death. And Sienna knew then that she would push for change and upgrade if given the opportunity to do so in future.

After a 15 minute wait Mr Lawson's client left and a few minutes later, Sienna was ushered into his office.
"Hello Sienna - I'm very pleased to meet you - I'm Andrew", Mr Lawson's smile was warm and genuine. There was the distinct air of sagacity about him and while his engaging smile bade her to relax, his obvious superior knowledge persuaded her towards anxiety.
"I'm pleased to meet you too Mr Lawson", Sienna's voice was quieter than intended, as nerves got the better of her.

"You may call me Andrew - please take a seat", Sienna obeyed as she fretted whether her appearance was acceptable.

"You're looking very businesslike Sienna - that's excellent", Mr Lawson's words brought a degree of calm.

"Thank you Mr Lawson", Andrew seemed way too familiar to her - it was just too soon.

"So Miranda has told me a lot about you and on the strength of her recommendation we have decided to take you on as a Trainee", Mr Lawson wasted no time in getting down to business.

Sienna nodded her affirmation.

"Initially you will be working as my Assistant but later on you will be affiliated to other senior members of the firm".

Sienna wanted to say something but her nerves were winning the battle so she sat with a big silly smile on her face, unable to muster up the will to speak. Mr Lawson must have sensed her uneasiness as he spoke enough for two. He gave her a brief history of the firm which he had started with Michael Addison.

"It was 1964 when we started this firm. We had finished law school and articled at the same firm for five years when we decided to launch out in our own venture together". "I was 25 years old at the time and Michael was 40". "He had lived half his life already when he decided to study the law, and he brought to our firm a wealth of transferable skills and experience". "He had been the driving force behind the firm but when he fell ill, I had no choice but to take the reigns - I am not a natural manager though", Mr Lawson sounded candidly honest to Sienna's ears. She was surprised that he was being so open with her which caused her to relax a little.

"I'm a grafter - I love to knuckle down and work", Mr Lawson chuckled easily. "That's why at my age, I am still working a 3-day week, though mostly from home". "I can wade through the most complex of cases and come up with gold, but I am by no means at ease with management", his kind eyes regarded Sienna, inviting her to be perfectly at ease. "So I gladly handed the management over to Geoffrey". "I'm the Senior Partner though and retain the "last word"", he stressed, chuckled and continued "Geoffrey is a good Solicitor and Manager but his judgment in some other matters is not always what it ought to be", the last part of the sentence was mumbled under Andrew's breath. The words were intended to be an undecipherable aside but Sienna's keen hearing picked them up. She shuffled about not quite knowing how to react.

Sienna was relieved when the moment of silence was broken by Mr Lawson. "So Sienna, please tell me a little about yourself" It dawned on her that she would definitely need to say something now.

"We..ell - as you know I have just finished my exams and I feel confident that I have passed them all". "I enjoy Contract Law and I also like Civil Litigation a lot", Sienna said then smiled.

"Well most of my caseload is Property Law so there should be a good measure of Contract Law - hopefully you will be very happy working with me for the next few months", "I will try to come in most days for the first few weeks to get you settled in", another charming smile, then he continued. "Tell me a little about your family".

After a beat Sienna spoke again. "Well, I am an only child and I was born in Jamaica". "My mother and father still live there - in a place called Soursop Bay". "It's a little village where nothing much happens - there really isn't a lot to tell about my family", Sienna said. She did not want to divulge that her family were poor farmers who were at the mercy of the land to survive from day to day. She did not want to go into the fact that when the crops had failed they had been left to the mercy of neighbours and friends to get by. No - those were her secrets and she would never divulge them. She did not want others to judge her because of her poor background. For although her family were dirt poor, yet they had been highly respected in their village community - both her parents and grandparents had been the heads of wisdom to whom others in the village turned for guidance and the voices of integrity that enforced the common law amongst the people.

Andrew Lawson would like to have heard more about Sienna's background. He would like for the young lady to have told him more as she came across as intriguing to him, but she appeared either unwilling or unable to divulge. He did not press her though - no doubt he would get to know more about her in future. The main thing was that she appeared to have good manners and she was nice and intelligent enough - just a little nervous perhaps. Anyway Miranda had asked him for a favour and he had given his word - he would not renege on it.

"So Sienna - when shall we have you begin?"
"Oh I can start anytime you say Mr Lawson".
"How about the second week of the New Year - would that be acceptable?"
"Yes sir - that would be fine by me", Sienna responded immediately illustrating her keenness. "By the way sir, do you have a publication that I can read in order to prepare for the role?"
"Good question, Sienna" Mr Lawson's eyebrows shot up - he appreciated just how keen Sienna really was, then he continued, "I will see what I can do and will either send it through the post or deliver it personally to Miranda - great idea", he rose to his feet and proffered his right hand to her, signifying that the interview was at an end.

"Welcome on board Sienna", Mr Lawson said as he shook her hand heartily. "Thank you very much Mr Lawson - I won't disappoint you, sir", Sienna promised and Andrew knew she was good for the vow.

Floating on the highest cloud Sienna walked out of Mr Lawson's office. She felt more confident than she had at the beginning of their meeting and a new-found assurance made itself felt - everything would be alright. So she hummed a new tune as she walked. A hint of a smile graced her countenance, revealing the joy that bubbled over inside her soul:

"Everything will be alright, alright alright
Everything will be alright
No need to worry - no need for fright
Everything will be alright"

The simple song cheered her heart as she walked purposefully - she was headed towards the tube station on her way to visit Melvin and Carlton. She couldn't wait to share her good news with her brother/friends.

Along the way Sienna stopped at the nearby supermarket where she purchased items for a sumptuous meal. Today much of the meal would be ready cooked and only required reheating. She also purchased salad items and a bottle of white wine. As she walked towards the flat she telephoned Melvin and was put straight through to voicemail - she left a message informing him that she was visiting and would be at home when he arrived.

Sienna also telephoned Carlton and relayed the same message. She was hoping that he and Becky would be there this evening as she had not seen him for some time and was beginning to miss him.

Chapter 20

December 2015

Carlton was the first to call her back at 6 pm, "Hi Sienna - how are you?"

"I'm good - and you?"

"Yeah - not too bad - me and Becky are meeting up and then we will be there around 7.30 pm or so".

"Great - is Becky alright?

"Yeah - she's okay - it's our 2 months anniversary tomorrow".

"Congratulations"

"Thanks Sienna", there followed an awkward silent moment.

"Okay so I'm looking forward to seeing you two later then", Sienna broke the silence.

"Yeah - see you later then".

"Bye".

It was 7.15 pm before Melvin called back - he had been working later than planned due to his workload - the big Hearing of a huge case was due to begin on Monday. He would be home around 8.15 pm.

The salad had been prepared and placed into the refrigerator and now that she knew what time to expect the lads and Becky Sienna turned on the oven at 7.45 pm, just before she heard Carlton's key in the front door.

"Hiya" Carlton called out.

"Hi Carlton", Sienna called back

"Hi Sienna", Becky's gentle voice sounded strange to Sienna - she was accustomed to hearing only deep masculine voices in this flat.

"Hey Becky - how are you - be with you in a mo", Sienna was genuinely glad for some female presence.

When they were all present, before dinner, Sienna shared her good news, "Guess who got offered a Training Contract today?", she blurted out excitedly.

"Well done Sienna - I knew you would do it", Melvin said as he rushed over to hug her.

"Congratulations", chorused Carlton and Becky and they too went to hug Sienna.

"Let's celebrate", Sienna suggested and made her way to the kitchen where she had already laid out four glasses for the toast. Half filling them each with wine she carried them two at a time into the living room. Then they toasted her success.

"So can we eat now", Melvin whined.

"Yes - Melvin - your mind is always on food", Sienna joked. They all laughed then agreed that they were also famished.

The first course was jerk chicken strips with a pesto sauce dip. It was well received and devoured in gluttonous fashion. The same fate befell the main course of pork ribs with ginger and cheese mashed sweet potatoes, mange tout and a green side salad. Sienna was happy that her choices were on point as she listened to the comments from her friends.

"Pork ribs and ginger and cheese mashed sweet potatoes is so delicious - I didn't realise that you could cook like this Sienna", Melvin said as he patted his stomach.

"Oh shut up you - you know I bought it ready prepared", Sienna nudged Melvin playfully across the table as he laughed loudly.

"Yeah - just teasing you - it was a great choice though".

"I know - I knew they would be great together.

"You must tell me where you bought them from", said Becky and continued, "I'll definitely be getting that for us Carlton".

"Ummmh", Carlton said as he gobbled the last mouthful.

There was a choice of desserts, between apple crumble and custard or vanilla ice cream with tinned fruit salad. Three of them wanted apple crumble and cream while Melvin opted for vanilla ice cream - no one wanted the tinned fruit salad. As Sienna began to prepare dessert, Becky joined her in the kitchen. "Want a hand?"

"No - I'm okay thanks".

"You sure"

"Yeah - you've had a hard day at work so go and sit down and relax - I'll be in - in a mo".

"Okay but I insist on washing up, or at least on loading the dishwasher", Becky offered.

"Okay"

As they ate dessert Sienna broached the subject of Melvin's paternity search. "Melvin remember what we were talking about last time I was here - you said you would ask Becky if she could help."

"Oh yeah - Becky - I've been meaning to ask you something", Melvin took up the thread.

"What's that?" Becky sounded eager to help.

"I need to trace someone - do you know of any website that might be able to help me".

"Well I don't know of a website as such, but I know the best way to go about tracing people".

"How's that then?"

"I know a Private Investigator - he is very good". "I don't know quite how he works but he does it so very well - he gets excellent results".

"Really", Melvin was intrigued.

"Yeah - a friend of mine used him when she suspected her husband of cheating on her". "He found out so many sordid secrets about her husband and his numerous affairs - he had no less than three other women that he was juggling behind her back", Becky intimated in a hushed voice as though her friend were in the next room and might hear her divulging her secrets.

"Really?" Sienna exclaimed.

"Yes, really", Becky replied then continued. "Before that she only had suspicions that he was cheating, based upon the physical and mental abuse meted out to her and her two children by her husband".

"Oh dear - I really don't know why some men behave so badly", Melvin commented as Carlton concurred with a shake of his head.

"Anyway, that information helped her to decide to go for a divorce", Becky informed.

"So sad", Sienna hated the thought of a marriage breaking up especially when children were involved.

"How old were the children?" Melvin voiced the question posed in Sienna's mind.

"The boy was three and the girl was five years old at the time". "That was three years ago so they are six and eight now".

"So sad", Sienna repeated.

"Well anyway she got a divorce on the most favourable terms because of the information that Mike provided".

"Wow - he sounds really good", said Melvin - he paused for a beat then continued. "So do you know how much he charges?"

"He's a bit pricy - I think his starting price is around £500 a day".

"Whhoo", Carlton whistled.

"But I suppose it depends on what is involved", Becky tempered. "It took him about 5 days to dig the dirt on Pearl's ex husband but it might not take him nearly as long to find out your father's whereabouts".

"£500 a day - that is really expensive, but if he's good I don't mind paying him", Melvin was desperate to find his missing father. He had a little money put by - it had taken him several years to save it up but he was willing to use his nest egg for such a worthy cause.

"I would like to get a quote first though", he added after some thought.

"Ok - I'll send you his number and I'll tell him to expect a call from you", Becky said while grabbing her 'phone.

"Thanks Becky".

In a few seconds Melvin's 'phone buzzed with receipt of a text. "That's his number - his name is Mike Cotton".

"Thanks again ", he saved Mr Cotton's number to his contacts.

"So who are you trying to find then?" Carlton asked.

"My father - remember I told you about him a while back", Melvin replied.

"Yes - I remember - so are you ready now?"

"I think so - I've thought about it a lot and it is what I want". "I've got nothing to lose really - since I've never known him I won't miss him if he doesn't want to know me and if he does want to know me I might gain a new friend or even a father".

"Well you sound very level headed about it", Sienna observed, and added. "I hope it works out well for you bro". Then she walked over to Melvin and rubbed his back in a gesture of consolation. "And you know we have always got your back if you need us".

"Yes - we are always here for you bro", Carlton concurred.

After dinner Becky kept her word and washed up the dishes. Then she and Carlton retired to his bedroom - "We're tired - going to bed now", Carlton said.

"Yeah, I'm absolutely shattered - night", Becky said - then she yawned.

"Goodnight", Melvin sounded as tired as they did.

"Night you two", Sienna gave a little wave.

After Carlton and Becky had retired, conversation died down. The atmosphere was relaxed.

"Melvin - now that I will be working full-time, I can help you pay for the Private Investigator if you need me to", Sienna offered.

"Thanks Sienna - I think I can handle it though", Melvin was genuinely grateful for the show of support.

"Oh but I insist - it would be my absolute pleasure, in light of all that you have done for me, bro". Melvin nodded his assent and they both smiled easily.

As it began to grow late Sienna invited herself to stay the night, "Is it okay if I stay over here tonight?"

"Sure - you know you are always welcome", Melvin replied before heading off to the bathroom. Sienna reclined watching TV, musing upon how blessed she was to have this home from home and such wonderful friends as Carlton, Melvin and now Becky too.

"Sienna - you can have my room", Melvin called out from the bathroom.

"No that's okay - I can sleep on the sofa".

"I insist".

"But Melvin you are tired - you've been at work all day and need a good night's rest", Sienna whined and continued, "I'm not even tired - I'll be up watching TV for at least a couple of hours so if you want to get any sleep you better go to bed".

"Okay - but I'll stay up with you for a while though", Melvin conceded.

"Okay ".

"Brrrrr" "Nothing can stop you" "Brrr" "Nothing can stop you".

Sienna grabbed her 'phone to see who was calling her. "Miranda!", she voiced her thoughts.

"Hello", Sienna's voice sounded questioning.

"Hello dear - It's Miranda"

"Oh - hello Miranda - is everything alright?"

"Yes dear I was just a little concerned as you did not come home after the interview that's all". Sienna was suddenly touched that someone should be so concerned about her.

"Concerned?" "That is so thoughtful of you Miranda", Sienna gushed.

"It's just that I had a very unpleasant dream about you last night dear - please promise me you'll be careful".

Miranda sounded so caring - she reminded Sienna of her mother - it was just the way that she would admonish her. "Yes Miranda, I'll be careful", Sienna reassured - after a deep breath she spoke again. "Please don't worry about me Miranda - I do apologise I should have informed you that I was going to visit my friends this evening". "As it got late I decided to stay over until tomorrow - sorry I didn't say".

"Not to worry dear - as long as you are safe where you are". "I know you are a sensible girl - just make sure you're careful and remain vigilant", there she was again sounding just like her parents except that she spoke the Queen's English and not with a Jamaica lilt.

"I will be careful - thanks for your concern". "I will pop by to see you tomorrow when I get back".

"Alright Sienna - have a nice night then - God bless", Miranda then ended the call. "Good night Sienna"

"Good night Miranda - have a nice sleep and I'll see you tomorrow".

Just then Melvin returned to the living room, "Who were to talking to just now?" He asked.

"Miranda - my.... sponsor".

"Oh - is everything okay.

"Yes - she was just concerned because I did not go home after the interview".

"That's nice", Melvin smiled as he thought how nice Miranda sounded.

"Yeah - she is a lovely lady", Sienna replied then asked "Please can I borrow one of your pyjamas Melvin or a long tee shirt?".

"Sure - you know where they are".

"Thanks".

In the end Melvin fell asleep on the sofa and Sienna could not wake him so she lifted his feet and hauled them onto the sofa. She manoeuvred his body into the lying position, placed a pillow beneath his head and covered him with a blanket. Before going to bed she stood looking down on him. Overcome by a wave of emotion she bent down and kissed him upon his forehead - she loved him so much - he was her angel, her brother but romance was the further thing from her mind.

****

Christmas came and went in a festive haze as Sienna basked in the glory of her new blessings. She spent Christmas day with Melvin, cooking up a storm with him assisting her all the way. Later they played games, danced, sang, and later still a few friends dropped by and they had a small party. Sienna had invited her girlfriends Mimi and Marion and Melvin had invited 3 of his friends, Joe, Eric and Len. Joe and Eric brought their girlfriends. Len brought his sister, Frances. Before long it became evident that Frances was competing with Mimi for Melvin's attention. He was blissfully unaware that fur was about to fly in a catfight as he, as usual, only had eyes for Sienna. In the end both Mimi and Frances turned their animosity upon Sienna who was blissfully unaware that she was the object of jealousy. In the meantime Marion and Len started talking and by the end of the evening they were the newest couple in town.

Sienna had a ball oblivious to the fact that others left at the end of the night with ruffled feathers and backs raised. Mimi even snubbed her jovial wishes as she bade her goodbye. "Look - I just want to get home - I'm tired", she responded, pushing Sienna away as she tried to hug her.
"Okay", Sienna replied somewhat affronted. Marion overcompensated with her hug and next day informed Sienna why Mimi had behaved as she did.
"Take no notice of Mimi - she is just crazy about Melvin that's all", Marion had intimated. And Sienna decided that she would do her best to try and hook Mimi up with Melvin, if at all possible.

Sienna decided that she would have an intimate dinner party early in the New Year when Melvin returned from visiting his family. It was to be held at Melvin and Carlton's flat, her home from home. She scheduled it for the weekend after New Years and invited Mimi, Marion and her new beau and Carlton and Becky. Sienna thought it best to invite someone as her companion for the evening, even though she would be busy serving. So she asked Dalbert Green, a boy from uni who was every girl's good friend, to join her for the evening in the hope that Melvin and Mimi would be thrown together. However, Mimi did not show up, and did not even bother to contact her. But they had a great time in any case, albeit the main purpose was defeated.

Chapter 21

January to May 2016

Now that Sienna had started working full time, she had little time for anything else. She had fitted in straight away with the everyday hustle and bustle of the busy law firm's Property Department. Although she was initially terrified by the challenge, she had waded in with her "can do" attitude and sailed through the baptism by fire. The fact of having swotted up on Land Law, Conveyancing and Landlord and Tenant law had stood her in good stead and she was able to undertake what Mr Lawson termed "relatively simple tasks" effectively if not efficiently, and without any significant detrimental consequences. Instead of relying upon Mr Lawson to provide guidance at every turn, Sienna employed the independent approach, relying upon the law and practice manuals for direction. Mr Lawson appeared to appreciate that attitude, and commented at the end of her first week, "You have a great attitude Sienna - you will make a fine Solicitor".

Sienna was enjoying her job at Addison and Lawson. She got on well with others working there. Rosy, the Receptionist invited her to lunch on the first day of work, when she had filled her in on the office dynamics and warned her especially to steer clear of Geoffrey Addison.

"He's not a very nice man", Rosy cautioned before taking a huge bite of her BLT sandwich.

"I think I agree with you", Sienna had commented.

"His Secretary, Trudy is as bad as he is", Rosy spoke with her mouth half full. Usually Sienna would find such manners off-putting, but instead it had the effect of putting her at ease in Rosy's company.

"Rumour has it that they are having an affair", Rosy continued in hushed tones with a twinkle in her eye. Before stuffing the rest of her sandwich into her mouth Rosy solicited a promise, "Don't tell anyone you heard it from me".

"My lips are sealed", Sienna said as she passed her thumb and forefinger across her lips as though closing a zipper. And they both chuckled, sealing the bond of friendship,

Fortunately, both Geoffrey and Trudy worked in the Litigation Section of the firm that was situated in another office half a mile away and she had little to do with them initially. It was not until her third month of work that Sienna first encountered Trudy who had come over from the Litigation Section to prepare the meeting and reception rooms for a two day conference. She was using the photocopier when the tall blonde haired Amazonian woman approached and engaged her in conversation.

"So you are new here?" the statement was phrased rhetorically.

"Yes - I started two and a... no, three months ago", Sienna gave her signature bright smile as she proffered her hand for a friendly shake and added, "And you are?"

"Trudy Bainbridge", came the unfriendly reply as she ignored Sienna's gesture, "And as long as you keep out of my way you should survive". Sienna searched Trudy's face for a smile - surely she was joking, but she found not a trace of congeniality.

"Ohhhh - I see......" Sienna replied, withdrawing her unshaken hand. She felt insulted but took a deep breath and continued with her task.

Trudy paused for effect as she stared straight at Sienna, seeking eye contact but Sienna ignored her which seemed to irritate her. After a while she walked off, muttering under her breath, "primate". Sienna did not react, much as she wanted to. She wanted to retort that she would gladly be re-classified as a primate if every human being was as ugly on the inside and on the outside as Trudy was, for the offender was by no means a good looking woman, but Sienna bit and held her tongue. Humming a hymn always invited calmness over her spirit and so Sienna began to sing without opening her mouth as the words played out the ancient psalm in her mind.

"Peace of God embrace my soul - like a shelter from the storm
Save me from the raging torrents - keep me safe and warm
Like a strong and mighty armour, protect me from all harm
Peace of God embrace my soul - like a shelter from the storm"

After that encounter Sienna went out of her way to avoid both Trudy and Geoffrey. However, Trudy made it difficult for her. Each time Sienna saw her coming she would head in the opposite direction in an effort to avoid an encounter with her. Her colleagues tried to aid her escape in any way that they could, and where possible, provided her with prior warning. Rosy, the receptionist was her main ally. She would warn Sienna whenever Trudy would be coming over to use the meeting and reception rooms which was next to Sienna's office and if she gave an impromptu visit, an email or three rings of her mobile was the signal for Sienna to escape to the ladies room or other safe territory. But it was not always possible for Sienna to get away in time and each time she would be subjected to tongue in cheek derogatory slurs and on two occasions blatant racial abuse from Trudy.

It was obvious to the other members of staff that these encounters upset Sienna and they encouraged her to make a complaint to Mr Lawson. Rosy was the most vocal about this suggestion.
"Sienna - you shouldn't have to work in this sort of atmosphere - why should you have to run every time you see that ogre coming - you need to say

something to Mr Lawson", Rosy had suggested vehemently after overhearing Trudy deride Sienna once too many times.

"Do you want a bunch of bananas for your lunch dear - I know they are your favourite as I have seen how your cousins love to eat them as they swing through the trees", Trudy had said before laughing hysterically and alone at her own sick joke.
Sienna had not replied but started to hum the simple hymn in search of personal solace. And this time, as Trudy stood watching for her reaction she had vocalised the words of the song.

"Peace of God embrace my soul - like a shelter from the storm
Save me from the raging torrents - keep me safe and warm
Like a strong and mighty armour, protect me from all harm
Peace of God embrace my soul - like a shelter from the storm"

Trudy had waited as though listening until Sienna had sung the last word of the song before commenting, "Nice voice - shame its wasted on a "thing" like you". "Why is it that primates always have the sweetest voices", she had stated loudly before turning and walking off like a bull getting ready to charge at a matador holding a red flag.

"Sienna you cannot continue to put up with that crap", Rosy's cheeks reddened with indignation as she protested to Sienna when they sat at lunch later that day.
"I'll leave it - I can handle her - I know she is just an ignorant and unintelligent person so I won't sink down to her level", Sienna had informed Rosy before adding, "I won't allow her to put me off track - I want to qualify

as a Solicitor and if Bainbridge wants to stop me, she will need to try a lot harder than that".

"I understand", Rosy had replied then added, "but if she says anything remotely like that next time in my hearing, I won't let her get away with it".

"Thanks for your concern Rosy", Sienna replied, her faith in humankind fully restored.

Four months passed before Sienna had her first encounter with Geoffrey Addison. It was lunch time and her turn to provide relief to Rosy on the switchboard. As she walked along the corridor towards the front reception area she overheard a conversation between Rosy and a man she later realised was Geoffrey Addison.

"I'm just about to go to lunch I'm afraid - you will have to ask Sienna, the Trainee Solicitor to send that fax - she should be here any moment", Rosy had advised.

"Well where is the little chimp then?" Geoffrey had replied rudely.

"Don't call her that - she is a young lady and should be referred to as such".

"Are you challenging me, young lady", Geoffrey's sounded irate.

"Just call her by her name - Sienna - that's her name", Rosy had challenged.

"Never you talk back to me or you can kiss your job goodbye", Geoffrey had warned.

"You don't scare me - I have been working here for over 10 years now and I know my rights - I have more on you than you know so don't even threaten me", Rosy had countered.

"How dare you......" Geoffrey replied then turned and walked swiftly away as Sienna approached. He said nothing to her but if looks were lethal she would not have survived his glance.

"What was that all about", Sienna asked in a whisper before adding "sorry I'm late I had something urgent to finish".

"Oh nothing - that was about nothing at all", Rosy replied.

Rosy's warning must have worked because from that day Geoffrey avoided speaking to Sienna. However, he regarded her with glances, glares and glowers that spoke volumes of the hatred for Sienna harboured deep within his heart.

Later encounters with Trudy were at worst hostile and at best uncomfortable. Then suddenly they stopped, much to Sienna's relief. She settled comfortably into her role and began to enjoy her time working for Addison and Lawson. Unbeknownst to her, Rosy had taken it upon herself to make a complaint to Mr Lawson about the manner in which Trudy was treating her and a quiet word was had in Trudy's ear by the Senior Partner, after which she had fully understood her position - she was Geoffrey's secretary, but ultimately answerable to Mr Lawson as Senior Partner of the firm and it was stressed to her that racial intolerance would not be condoned or overlooked in any guise within the firm of Addison and Lawson.

Trudy now avoided Sienna where possible but when their paths occasionally crossed she too regarded the young lady with odious ogles and Sienna was in no doubt that she was surrounded by ravenous wolves that would plot her downfall if the opportunity ever arose, and so she developed eyes in the back of her head and the ability to write and keep copious notes and documentary records on a daily basis, fearing that she might need to rely upon them to defend her position sometime in the future.

Chapter 22

August to December 2016

Away from work Sienna's life had moved on too. She was now able to send money home to her parents on a regular monthly basis. Miranda continued to pay the Bursary, despite Sienna's confirmation to her that she could manage without it. For over six months Sienna did not use the Bursary funds, meaning to give it back to Miranda but her many offers of repayment were continuously rebuffed and Sienna learnt that there was no point in arguing with Miranda, who confirmed that the Bursary would be paid for a further year. Remonstrating against this decision had only amounted to wasted energy and Sienna had eventually given in and instead gave thanks to God for His abundant blessings and started to spend the money. When her monthly salary from her day job and her part time earnings for helping Bert out on Saturdays (for which her full Assistant Gardner's salary continued to be paid), were added to the bursary, Sienna's income amounted to £35,000 per annum.

Numerous offers to pay something in the way of rent, were strenuously refused time and time again, and despite Sienna's pleadings, Miranda would not relent.

After deducting enough to cover her expenses and a little to spend on her friends by way of recompense for their past kindness, and putting £500 a month into a savings account for a rainy day, Sienna sent the lion's share of her wages to her parents each month. She knew that they needed the money. Her parents owed money to almost everyone in their small village and Sienna wanted that to change. So she made herself a promise to send them all the money that she could during her first year of work in order to get them firmly back onto their feet.

To Sienna's heart's delight, her parents now owned mobile telephones and even a computer and were able to keep in constant touch with her. This simple development had brought her immense joy - more than could ever be put into words. She now spoke to her family daily, and when the network allowed, she was able to Skype call them. Her gratitude to Miranda grew and kept on growing - it knew no bounds and she made many personal vows to do her best to provide constant support and companionship to her generous host.

****

Although she saw very little of her friends, Sienna kept in constant telephone contact with Melvin and Carlton to a lesser extent. Carlton was not often available to speak with her when she called and Sienna gathered that Becky was a little concerned by their continued friendship, so she now limited their contact to the bare minimum.

****

The remarkable recovery of Miranda was a joy to Sienna. Her benefactor's recuperation was hailed a miracle by her doctors who had all expected her health to deteriorate rapidly. They had expected her to die within weeks of being sent home from hospital in November 2015. But it was now December 2016 and Miranda was exhibiting no further signs of an early demise.

Sienna saw Miranda most days as she came and went. Sometimes she observed a deep sadness within her host which Sienna could not interpret. It was as though Miranda carried a very heavy load sometimes and Sienna wished that her benefactor would trust her enough to share that burden. She would certainly listen at least - a problem shared is a burden halved. And she would also pray for that dear woman.

****

Sienna had spent last Christmas day with Melvin and her other friends. She was aware that he had only stayed in London to make sure that she was not alone on Christmas day. They had enjoyed the day and the memory was etched into their hearts. The rest of the Christmas season had been spent alone with her computer, the TV and her 'phone.

So tired of being a burden upon her friend at Christmas time, Sienna pretended to Melvin that she had been invited to go away with a friend over Christmas. Melvin had immediately made plans to go home to Dudley to spend Christmas with his grandparents. Sienna was happy that he would be with his family but she did not relish being all alone.

****

Miranda did not want to spend Christmas with Geoffrey and his wife. She had done so for many years and mostly had good memories. But last Christmas their marriage was on the rocks and their tumultuous relationship meant that Miranda's Christmas had been ruined by constant bickering and veiled threats passing from one to the other. So this year 2016 she decided to invite Sienna to spend the day with her as her guest.

Sienna was overjoyed to receive the invite from Miranda. She had accepted it without hesitation. Although she had had various invites from her university friends and work colleagues, she had declined them all because those parties' families were strangers to her. She could think of no-one in London that she would rather spend the day with than Miranda. The invitation had come just before she had booked a flight back to Jamaica which would not really have been feasible because she had only a week's holiday and when the travel to and from the airport both ends and the long haul flight times were factored into the equation, it would have meant spending only 4 days in Jamaica. She would no doubt have returned jet lagged and she needed to be rested due to the fact that she was dealing with several demanding transactions at work. In fact, she planned to go into work during the holiday to get on top of things while the office was quiet.

It came as a complete surprise to Sienna that on Christmas day a chauffeur-driven limousine whisked them to and from Born Again Church of God. There they enjoyed being beautifully serenaded by the Children Christmas Choir and the Christmas message was dramatized, which proved novel and refreshing. After the service Bishop and Sister Gooden had extended an invitation to Sienna to have dinner with them but she had gracefully declined and suggested they arrange something in the New Year.

It was a relief to Sienna that Sister Newson had not attended Christmas morning service. That would certainly have put a dampener on her day and reminded her of past unpleasant events.

Back home, Sienna was surprised to note that Miranda had ordered in a well catered fare and also paid two personal attendants top rates to pander to their every whim this Christmas day. They ate and drank like queens. The mood was jolly as could be as the two of them pulled crackers, told jokes and laughed over Christmas dinner. As evening turned to night the attendants tidied up and left. That was when the real party started. The night's festivities was marred only briefly by a dutiful telephone call from Geoffrey who stayed no longer on the line than he had to, which equated to 4 minutes. Then the two of them listened to music old and new, sang along to the songs old and new and danced the night away, forging a bond of friendship on the deepest possible level.

Their party finally ended after 11 pm when Sienna bade Miranda goodnight. They hugged goodnight and Miranda held on a little too long and far too tightly, as if she did not want to let go. Sienna felt embarrassed and it again occurred to her that Miranda might have an ulterior motive. As the older woman released her grip, Sienna sensed the profound melancholy that she so often discerned enfolded Miranda's spirit. "Sienna .....I... I... aaah... good night my dear", Miranda said. It seemed to Sienna that she had wanted to say something more, but had lost her nerve, and she believed that Miranda was fighting back tears. As she walked the short distance back to her flat, Sienna said a short prayer for Miranda.

Dependability directed Sienna's thoughts toward her family and as soon as she arrived home she reached for the telephone. Surprisingly the network allowed a Skype call to her parents who were just beginning their evening as she was about to end hers. Sienna longed to be home with them and partake of the exotic fare that was on offer but thanks to Miranda, she was not as homesick as she could have been.

Chapter 23

January - June 2017

The year 2017 arrived with the hope of a bright future for Sienna. She was upbeat about her life. New Year's resolutions included a promise to visit her parents in Jamaica - work permitting. Her days fell into a routine pattern now. The most conscientious of employees, she was never late for work and always gave more of her time than was required. Most evenings after work she popped by to visit with Miranda on her way home. They talked easily about the events of each day and also watched TV and discussed current affairs and the like. Miranda always had something ready for Sienna to eat which was shared with joy.

One evening in late January, Miranda had become emotional. She thanked Sienna for providing her with the companionship that a lonely old woman could only dream of and hugged her tightly as she said goodnight. Sienna pulled away when Miranda held on to her for a little too long and a little too tightly. The thought again crossed her mind as to whether Miranda could have an ulterior motive. Sienna shooed it away - surely Miranda's motives were nothing but pure.

It made Sienna very happy to know that she was providing comfort to this wonderful woman in her twilight years. But as the days passed by Miranda had become markedly older and frailer to Sienna's eyes. Her classic beauty was becoming less evident as the wrinkles became more dominant and Sienna wondered whether Miranda was keeping good health. However, she was too polite to broach the subject out of the blue and the opportunity to do so never arose, so Sienna left it that Miranda would say something about her health if she wanted to.

So fiercely independent was she that Miranda refused to have any live-in Assistant or Aide. Apart from Linda who worked Monday to Friday 9.30 am to 4 pm, she had no other regular staff and Sienna felt obliged to be there for her. Geoffrey did not visit his mother as often as he should do - once a week or less, and for invariably less than an hour.

On Saturday mornings Sienna pottered about in the garden - she did this to provide some ease to her conscience - to feel that she was doing something to earn the bed and board that came so freely.

Sienna's busy schedule did not leave her much time to keep in touch with her friends. Consequently she did not see Melvin as much or as often as she would have liked to. In fact, she saw him only about once a month and Carlton only about once every three months. Melvin was also constantly busy at work. He had now been admitted as a Solicitor and kept on as an employee by the firm where he Articled. Aside from work his lifestyle had also changed, leaving little time for interaction with Sienna, but they kept in constant contact by telephone and social media.

Carlton and Becky had moved in together and gotten engaged. They were planning a big party to celebrate and Sienna could not wait. The party was scheduled for Saturday 7 July and she had spent some of her limited time running up to that date shopping for something swanky to wear. It wasn't often that she got the chance to attend a party so she was so much looking forward to it and to catching up with everyone, especially Melvin - it had been far too long since she saw her brother.

****

For many months now Sienna had been meaning to visit Born Again Church of God - she had promised Bishop Gooden to return after their visit at Christmas and now it was June already and she had still not done so. She had started to attend the local Baptist church, which Miranda also attended occasionally. It was troubling her increasingly that she had not returned to Born Again Church to give thanks to God for all His undeniable blessings upon her life, which she believed had come upon her life due to the prayers of Bishop Gooden and the Born Again congregation. And there was no denying that praise and worship at Born Again Church of God was ultimate and unequalled.

Everything in Sienna's life was beautiful as she arose early, showered and dressed for church, she sang a new song.

"I sing an everlasting song
To pay obeisance to You
For all that You have done
Great things - so many great things You've done
My heart's in obedience before You
For all that You have done
Blessing and honour I bring
To You my Lord - my King
I bow to bless You Lord for all that You have done
I bless You Lord for all that You have done, ooh, ooh
I give You honour and praise
I give You honour and praise

I give You honour and praise.........

The sweet refrain buoyed her along as Sienna selected her outfit carefully, a navy jumpsuit accessorised in dusky pink jewellery and shoes and her light grey raincoat with a dusky pink scarf completed her attire.

As Sienna set out for church, Miranda was looking out. She espied her and called out. "Morning Sienna - you're looking absolutely lovely dear".

"Good morning Miranda - thank you very much - I'm off to Born Again this morning"

"That is wonderful - I don't go to church nearly as often as I should", Miranda looked whimsical as she continued, "I really should go more often - I would really love to go to Born Again sometime". She then said nothing more prompting Sienna to say something.

"Maybe you could come with me the next time I go - we could get a cab there and back".

"Really - why that would be superb", Miranda sounded excited, then added, "You'd better run along now dear or you'll be late".

"Okay thanks for reminding me", Sienna beamed, "Bye Miranda - see you later - I should be back by 3 pm".

The last person Sienna wanted to run into was the first person she saw as she entered the large edifice. Sister Newson stood larger than life just inside the entrance. Sienna did not know what to say or what to do. She had been avoiding Sister Newson's telephone calls. The calls had started at the beginning of 2016. She called several times a week but Sienna set her 'phone to divert those calls straight to voicemail.

"Sienna - you're looking beautiful", came the unexpectedly jovial greeting.

"Hello Sister Newson - thank you very much", Sienna replied politely.

"I'm so happy that you are obviously keeping well - you don't know how worried I have been about your welfare", Sister Newson stated. Sienna involuntarily cast her mind back to the night of her exodus from the Newson home, and the painful knife slashed at her heart. The wounds were still fresh even after over two years.

"I would love for you to pay me a visit - I would love to see you dear - how come you just left me up so?" Sister Newson's voice was as sweet as nectar. Sienna did not know what to say or feel. She tried to speak but the cat would not let go of her tongue. So Sister Newson continued. "I need to talk to you dear - some wrongs need to be made right", her voice was a conciliatory monotone and Sienna's heart was placated.

"Okay - I'll give you a call soon".

"Please Sienna - please - don't forget", Sister Newson pleaded.

"Okay - I won't", Sienna said then continued, "Okay I'll see you later then".

"Don't forget dear - don't forget", Sister Newson called after her.

At the end of the service Sienna caught up with long lost friends - she felt elated and a sense of belonging pervaded her psyche. It had been too long and she made an inner vow that she would not stay away so long ever again in her life.

Bishop and Mrs Gooden were overjoyed to see Sienna again.

"So good to see you Sienna - how are you? Bishop Gooden grabbed her hand and squeezed lightly indicating genuine warmth.

"I'm good Bishop - it's good to be here". "I've been meaning to come for a long time but I've been very busy, first with the exams, then with my new job as I informed you by text messages".

"Yes - yes - thanks for keeping me posted dear", Bishop Gooden said appreciative that Sienna kept them advised of her progress on a fairly regular basis.

"Let me formally congratulate you Sienna - you have done so very well", Mrs Gooden greeted Sienna from behind.

"Oh Sister Gooden - thank you - it's great to see you". The two women shared a loving embrace.

"You must come home with us for lunch dear - remember you promised at Christmas that you would", Sister Gooden said as she broke away from their hug.

"I would absolutely love to Sister Gooden but unfortunately I am expected back at home", Sienna replied. She knew that Miranda would be eagerly awaiting her return and felt obliged to get back as she had promised she would.

"I see, but you must keep in "personal" touch more often dear". "Don't leave it so long to visit us again and please make sure you arrange to come to dinner with us next time", Sister Gooden replied.

"Even though you are all grown up now, remember that we have some responsibility for you, Sienna". "Remember that we are always there if you need us", Bishop Gooden added.

"Yes, thank you Bishop - I promise to come and visit you very soon and I won't leave it so long next time. "I am thankful to you both for the interest that you have shown in my well-being by always calling me to check that I am okay". "Thank you both so much".

"It's our absolute pleasure Sienna - remember that we love you dearly", Sister Gooden said as she was pulled aside by another brethren.

"Excuse me Sienna - Mother Gooden, I need to talk to you", Sister Patricia announced her presence.

"Well Sienna - we'll see you soon", Sister Gooden said and air kissed Sienna before being dragged away.

"Yes - see you soon, Sienna", Bishop Gooden echoed as his attention was also commandeered elsewhere.

"Yes - see you soon", Sienna said and quickly made her escape as she espied Sister Newson headed in her direction.

Making a beeline for the door, Sienna was accosted by many well wishers who slowed her advance.

"Sienna, Sienna", Sister Newson called after her - she ignored the shouts and renewed her efforts to escape. But before long she was intercepted again, this time by Pearl, one of the most interfering of brethren.

"Sienna I think Sister Newson is calling you", Pearl stated unhelpfully.

"Oh really", Sienna replied. She turned and waved at Sister Newson, "I'll bell you", she said and mimed putting a receiver to her ear.

"Okay - I'll look forward to hearing from you then", Sister Newson replied. Her smile was warm and engaging, just like that of a saint, Sienna thought. Then the night of her exodus flashed across Sienna's mind again and she surmised that Sister Newson could never be a saint - definitely not. No saint could ever have behaved in such a heartless manner. But a still small voice whispered that no-one was beyond redemption.

Chapter 24

June 2017

Sienna hurried home as she knew that Miranda would be waiting for her. It had become apparent that Miranda worried about her a lot and Sienna did not want to give her any unnecessary cause to do so. Miranda was not a well woman and with a deep and growing affection for the older woman, Sienna gave priority to her wellbeing.

Each time Sienna stayed out longer than expected Miranda telephoned her to check up on her. It was rather annoying at first but Sienna had come to accept that Miranda truly cared about her and she now welcomed this show of concern. With sage-like wisdom flowing from her lips Miranda often warned her about the ever present dangers that lay-waited a beautiful woman in unexpected places, and backed up her admonitions with a story of a recurring dream that she kept on having. She did not divulge the content or context of the dream to Sienna, but warned her gravely, citing the recent rapes in their vicinity believed to have been carried out by the same man. One of the victims of the assailant dubbed the "Rampant Rapist" had died from the severe injuries sustained during the attack, meaning that the rascal was now also a murderer.

Today Sienna found Miranda sitting beneath the Leylandii, her head bowed. Sienna could tell that she had been crying. She slowed her approach and, not wishing to embarrass Miranda, backtracked, making sure that she was not seen. Sienna had seen Miranda here before. It was apparent that this was the place that she came when the burdens of life got too heavy for her to bear. Sienna breathed another prayer for her benefactor. "Lord please help

Miranda to deal with whatsoever burden it is that she is carrying" she said simply and Sienna believed that God would do just that.

Chapter 25

June 2017

The days passed quickly as Sienna settled into the monotonous yet enjoyable routine of work, rest and a little time for play. At work she excelled in practising the various elements of the law taught to her by the well learned Mr Lawson and other qualified Solicitors. She had become confident in the everyday routine tasks and relished the challenges of yet un-encountered ones. Emboldened by the words of accolade often showered upon her by Mr Lawson, she had taken the initiatives to introduce new ideas to make the office work more efficiently. And the more she contributed towards the positive growth of the company, the greater the unspoken animosity that developed and flowed from Geoffrey and Trudy towards her.

Whenever she was unlucky enough to encountered either of them they spoke asides of assorted insults, variously about her poor status and calculated to denigrate the colour of her skin. Sienna pretended that their comments did not concern or affect her. However, when she was alone she cried often and the voice of indignation was speaking louder every day in her mind. Why should she be subjected to such inhumane treatment by other human beings just because they were of a different colour? What is a colour? This question posed itself in Sienna's mind time and again and the only answer to it each time was "nothing". The mind of an individual is something for therein the thoughts, good or evil are formulated. So one could be justified for hating the mind that formulated evil thoughts. The character of a person is something. For characters came in classifications of good or bad. If someone's character were bad then they might be hate-worthy. But why hate someone because of their colour. A colour cannot make another cry; a colour cannot cause pain; a colour cannot make one happy or sad. So surely only a fool could hate another purely because of their colour.

Sienna was hurting but she vowed to herself that she would not repay Geoffrey and Trudy in kind, for then she would be no better than they were. Although she hated their characters, she would not allow her heart to accept that they were nasty to her because they are white. She drew contrast between their treatment of her and the unadulterated love poured upon her by Miranda, Rosy, Carlton and Mr Lawson to name but a few, all of whom are also white. The love of these dear ones aided her in the struggle against surrender to conform to the evil ideologies propagated by racists and calculated to cause division. Sienna refused to dance to the ugly tune that both Geoffrey and Trudy were fiddling. She refused to bend in the wind of their hostility, although she sometimes found it very hard not to, especially at times when Trudy went out of her way to denigrate her with asides, although anxiety rose to fever pitch about her mind at such times.

Most offensive to Sienna were the derogatory comments from Trudy about her personal hygiene or lack of it. Having showered and dressed herself immaculately, and having applied her favourite Christian Dior perfume, Trudy would loiter by the front reception desk some mornings, apparently waiting for Sienna's arrival. Then as she entered the reception area, Trudy would clasp her nostrils between her thumb and fore-finger as she walked past her, whilst commenting loudly for all within earshot to hear, that a foul smell had just contaminated the air. At times like those Sienna struggled not to give Trudy a piece of her mind or worse, a piece of her fist, and damn the consequences. But instead she took a deep breath, then two then three and the moment would pass and she would smile in spite of the anxiety. "I am bigger than you Trudy - I am bigger than you", Sienna would mumble and she drew strength from the smiles and greetings of her right thinking colleagues. At times like those Sienna thought about Miranda's beautiful heart, her benefactor, and her show of selfless love strengthened Sienna to go on.

Having resumed regular church attendances Sienna found herself more prone to praying. She also read the Bible a lot more and in order to motivate her to love and not to hate, every day she read the chapter containing the admonition of Jesus to pray for those who hates you. Fully obedient, she did just that, daily she prayed for Trudy and Geoffrey, that God would change their hearts of stone and open their eyes; that they would learn to love rather than to hate.

****

Geoffrey began to drop by more often to visit his mother. When he was there, Sienna avoided him as though he were a plague of ebola. Having become aware of Sienna's routine to visit his mother on her way home from work, Geoffrey started to arrive just before she did. Whenever she saw his car parked at the front of the house, Sienna would not bother to visit Miranda but walked on as quickly and quietly as possible, being careful not to make any noise in order to arouse Geoffrey's attention.

Sometimes Geoffrey locked her out by disabling the electronic entry system to the front entrance. Fortunately, soon after moving into High Trees, Bert had shown Sienna a back entrance to the estate situated at the far end of the vast grounds, in Forsythe Street. Bert always used that entrance - he was the only person who used that gate. He had given Sienna a key for the little used rear entrance, and whenever the front gate was inaccessible she trekked the quarter of a mile distance to enter her flat via Forsythe Street.

Miranda was none too pleased with this newfound attentiveness from her son. After he left most evenings, she telephoned Sienna to invite her over but often Sienna declined as she would be in the middle of doing something - usually cooking - or getting ready for an early night after a gruelling day at the office. Sometimes Miranda made her way over to Sienna's flat, plate of delicious food in hand after Geoffrey had left. She was always well received and thanked.

"Oh I do wish Geoffrey wouldn't drop by in the evenings so often - he's interrupting our little routine - I do so miss our little chit chats, don't you dear", Miranda would say on numerous occasions, to which Sienna provided only a wry smile in reply.

In spite of Geoffrey's attitude Sienna enjoyed living at High Trees. She loved her flat and had grown to love Miranda dearly. And she loved the dogs too - they had gotten used to her now and each time she arrived home they came running to greet her at the gate, tails wagging and only after she had patted their heads would they scamper off to their own business.

"Thank goodness he never stays for too long", Sienna mumbled often. Of a truth Geoffrey's visits hardly ever lasted for more than half an hour and as long as she could keep out of his way Sienna could tolerate the situation.

Chapter 26

June 2017

True to her word, Sienna called Sister Newson a couple of weeks after their encounter in the church foyer. It was an awkward conversation.

"Hello Sister Newson"

"Hello Darling - so good to hear from you"

"So how are you keeping Sister Newson?"

"I'm not too bad dear - just the arthritis plaguing me as usual". There then followed a long pause of up to 10 seconds as Sienna thought of something else to say. Then Sister Newson spoke again "The house is not the same without you Sienna - I really miss your company".

"Oh" was all that Sienna could muster.

"I have a lot to say to you but I would like you to come round so that we can sit down and talk", Sister Newson sounded penitent.

"Okay", Sienna replied quickly before giving due thought to the request.

"So when are to going to come - I am home every evening except Thursday as you know and Sundays, of course", Sister Newson said then chuckled.

"Okay - I'll let you know when I can make it then - as you know I am working full time now so I don't have that much time to spare", Sienna backtracked.

"Oh, I see - you can come anytime you like dear", Sister Newson reiterated.

"Okay - next week Friday evening should be okay but I'll let you know for certain next Thursday"

"Yes - yes, next Friday evening would be fine with me".

"Okay - I should be able to make it but if not I will let you know next Thursday", Sienna replied.

As soon as the conversation ended, Sister Newson called Jonathan. She had not seen her son for many months now. His visits had dropped off dramatically soon after she had had the break-in when someone had entered her home and ransacked it just before Christmas 2015. The Police had been of the opinion that the intruder may have been looking for something specific since nothing appeared to have been stolen, not that she possessed anything of any real value worth stealing in any case. Apart from Sienna who may have kept her key and returned for some reason, Sister Newson could not think who would want to break into her home. She did mention Sienna to the Police but they did not think that it was worth following up since nothing was taken and there was no proof to support this suspicion.

Jonathan called her from time to time and each time his main concern appeared to be Sienna - he just couldn't stop talking about the girl. Sister Newson gathered that he really cared about her and she surmised that Sienna must have misconstrued his interest when she had accused him of trying to molest her. She was convinced that her son had intended merely to show innocent affection. But if Sister Newson were thinking rationally, she would admit to herself that her son's interest in Sienna was nothing but an unhealthy one.

The call was put through to voicemail and Sister Newson left a message. "Hello darling - I hope you are well." "I just wanted to let you know that Sienna called me today". "She said that she is coming to see me next week". "Anyway, I just thought I should let you know as I remember that you were concerned about her".

In all honesty, Sister Newson's one true agenda was to ease her loneliness and heartache. She longed for a visit from her son and hoped that he would rush to visit her, thinking that he might bump into Sienna during his visit. She had been deliberately vague as to the day that Sienna would be visiting. Perhaps Jonathan would be so eager to see the object of his heart's desire that he would pay her a visit every evening next week. And suddenly a new agenda presented itself in Sister Newson's mind - it would not be a bad development if Sienna could somehow be persuaded to marry Jonathan. So beautiful and educated - apparently a Lawyer now - what a great catch.

Immediately Jonathan listened to his mother's voicemail message he rang her back. He had deliberately ignored her call, as he had been doing over past months, after all he had no time to spare - he was just too busy getting on with his life. There was no place in his life for an aging mother with her numerous physical ailments. The best place for her was a nursing home and he had been thinking about encouraging her to go into one soonest - she really shouldn't be living alone like that. It's too much for her to expect him to be visiting all the time. But he would make some time to go and see her. He wanted - no needed - to see Sienna again.

Jonathan wasn't happy that his mother had not ascertained the day that Sienna would be visiting - the silly old bag had omitted this important detail. He did not relish the thought of driving over to visit his mother's home on numerous occasions, let alone in the same week. Of course whatever it took to see Sienna again he would do - they were unfinished business after all and he would finish what he had started by hook or by crook. But he didn't have time to waste and so ended their conversation with a request, "Find out which day Sienna will be coming around will you mum - I am really busy at work at the moment and I don't want to miss seeing her again".

****

After work on Friday evening Sienna dutifully made her way to Sister Newson's home. She was very tired - it had been a challenging week and she would have very much preferred to head straight home to a hot bath and early night but she had always kept her promises. She did not notice the inconspicuous grey car with blacked out windows parked up the road from Sister Newson's home as she knocked at the front door on arrival at 7.00 pm and waited to be let in.

"Come in, come in my dear", Sister Newson stood back from the entrance to allow Sienna to enter. "Make yourself at home".

"Thank you Sister Newson", Sienna responded warmly, even as she struggled to exorcise the harsh memories of the last night spent living in Sister Newson's home. They talked for two hours as they drank lots of tea and consumed an assortment of biscuits and cakes. Sister Newson had baked especially for the occasion. Most of the conversation was carried on by Sister Newson and the words "sorry" and "apology" were used numerous times, almost as often as the phrases "please forgive me" and "I want to make it up to you". Even as she delivered her prepared repetitive spiel Sister Newson's mind was preoccupied with thoughts of her son.

On Sunday Jonathan had telephoned to ask which day Sienna would be visiting. Sister Newson had capitulated and informed him that she was coming on Friday. He had promised to drop by, but it was getting late and she wondered what was keeping him - perhaps he had been delayed in the traffic. As the short hand reached 9 and the long hand reached 12, she despaired that he would come after all, and when Sienna said goodbye at 9.15 pm Sister Newson's heart sank - Jonathan hadn't turned up after all.

****

Sienna walked briskly towards the high street. She had to get two buses home and it was getting late. She hurried past her old neighbours who had come out to put out their bins, waving at them but not stopping to talk. It was an 8 minute walk to the bus stop but Sienna made it in 6. So preoccupied was she with her quest that she did not notice the small innocuous looking grey motor vehicle that followed her at a distance.

The bus stop was crowded - apparently there had not been a bus for over 30 minutes. Sienna did not have to wait long - a bus arrived 2 minutes later. The little grey vehicle fell in three cars behind the bus. At each bus stop it drove idly allowing the bus time to let passengers on and off. Sometimes the little grey car caused other drivers to become enraged as it slowed down dramatically, lingering and failing to overtake the bus even when ample opportunity to do so presented itself. It waited as Sienna alighted the first bus and until she boarded the second bus, once more falling in line.

Sienna was oblivious to the fact not only that the bus was being tracked by the grey car, but also that its driver was a predator stalking her whose heartfelt emotions toed a very thin line between complete love and utter hate.

As though God were orchestrating her deliverance, essential unplanned road-works disrupted the journey of the cars while the buses sailed along in clear bus lanes. The bus that Sienna was on was second in a line of six buses that drove bumper to bumper and left no room for the little grey car to push through as the traffic light turned red. By the time the light turned green, the second bus, ferrying Sienna home was long gone.

The assailant cussed loudly as he realised that Sienna may have gotten away from him yet again. Then it occurred to him that he knew the route and he tracked the bus - soon he would certainly catch up.

****

"It's you again", the voice of the stranger sounded oddly familiar to Sienna.

"Do I know you?" she asked after a sizeable pause.

"Well yes .... and no", came the reply.

"Well either you know me or you don't - yes or no?" Sienna spoke in her best no nonsense voice.

"Yes - I know you", replied the stranger. He took a pause to contemplate, then continued "I'm not sure if you remember me though", he smiled disarmingly and Sienna softened her attitude as it occurred to her where she had met the man before.

"Oh - I know - you are the man at the bus stop", Sienna smiled.

"Ten out of ten - may I sit next to you?" the man did not wait for a reply before taking the vacant seat next to Sienna.

"Okay - it's a free country", Sienna replied rather abruptly. Her retort did not deter.

"So how have you been - it's two years since that fateful day and I have prayed for this day to come - to see your beautiful face again". "It's as though God has answered my prayer - this is not the bus that I usually take but I have been waiting so long that I decided to just jump on the first bus that came along".

As the man spoke he turned his head to the side and saw a number 97 bus draw level at the traffic lights in the lane turning right.

"Typical - see my bus there - it came just after this one - well I won't be able to catch it now even if I got off so you are stuck with me, I'm afraid", he said with a gleeful chuckle. Sienna shrugged dis-interestedly as the talker continued. "Maybe you will give me a chance to get to know you better this time". Still no reply. The conversationalist continued unfazed, "So what is a beautiful woman like you doing travelling on your own so late at night - you nah 'fraid people teef you?", he lapsed into thick Jamaican twang.

"I can take care of myself", Sienna replied involuntarily.

"Okay - but be careful", the talker was silent for a beat before changing tact. "My name is James and I am single and ready to mingle", James proffered his hand to be shaken. Sienna ignored it.

"That must be one of the corniest chat up lines I have ever heard", chimed in the woman sitting in front of them.

"Who said it's a chat up line, though?" the talker responded. "I am simply introducing myself to the young lady - nothing corny about that". "I'm truly single and ready to mingle, so baby what do you say - will you give me a chance to serenade you?" the talker said before bursting into song.

"Baby baby you make my heart go boom boom boom", he sang and as he continued to serenade Sienna, the bus passengers burst into applause.

By the time Sienna reached her stop, she had been won over and was happily conversing with James. As she stood up to alight the bus, James followed her. "Allow me to walk you home beautiful - I just want to see that you get home safely", he offered. Sienna smiled uncertainly. She felt somewhat vulnerable but James would not take "no" for an answer.

Sienna headed towards the Forsythe Street entrance. She did not want James to know where the front entrance to "High Trees" was.

As they walked along neither of them noticed the grey car that was cruising some distance behind them. James talked incessantly. He kept Sienna enthralled with stories about his life and past loves. Sienna learned that he had 3 babies with two different women but that he had refused to marry either of them. "All dem ooman want to do is have babies and tie me down but I'm a horse - I can't be fettered", James proclaimed as he flailed his arms in demonstration of breaking free. As Sienna thanked God that he had "fessed" up just as she was about to capitulate and exchange numbers with him, he continued, "I am still too young to get married - dem ooman get pregnant because they wanted to trap me, but the two of dem failed". "They are not in my league anyway".

"Well why did you sleep with them then James if you thought that they were beneath you?" Sienna asked - she was getting annoyed by James' denigration of his past female companions.

"Well they tempted me innit - they threw demself at me - seduce me, and I was too weak to resist", was his fragile excuse.

"Oh I see", Sienna replied - she breathed a sigh of relief as they reached the rear entrance of "High Trees". "Well let me say goodnight James - thank you for walking me home", Sienna's smile radiated warmth.

"So this is where you live then - can I have the digits so that we can meet up again sometime, sweet girl", James was in full flirting mode.

"I'm going to have to say "no" James - sorry". "The thing is - I have a swan's perspective - did you know that swans mate for life?"

"How do you mean?" "Baby you don't have to worry about that - I will love you forever, amen", James proclaimed.

"No James - I am not ready for anything right now but you give me your number and I will give you a call when I am", Sienna replied as she whistled. She knew that the dogs would arrive in a few moments. Less than a 30 seconds later her bodyguards showed up just as James was about to fall to his knees pleading for her number.

"No sorry James - goodnight - make sure you get home safely", Sienna said as she opened the gate walked through it and closed it behind her. James was tempted to follow her but had second thoughts when the Alsatian growled.

"Okay - good night - see you soon - make sure you give me a call", he sounded disappointed.

Jonathan watched from a distance as Sienna closed the gate and the young man walked away back the way they had come. He was peeved that he did not get a chance to talk with Sienna tonight but now he knew where she was living he would be back. The other man was not a concern to him - it was obvious that Sienna had no interest in him. So Jonathan set the little grey car in a different direction in search of the next victim of the Rampant Rapist as he vowed that Sienna would not get away the next time.

Chapter 27

June 2017

With little time to socialise Sienna still managed to keep in constant contact with her family and friends back in Jamaica by telephone and skype. It gladdened her heart each time she spoke with her family and especially when she received reports from them of how the money she was sending them was being used. The first project put in hand was repair of the house which had become dilapidated and leaked in several places each time it rained. Her parents had been confined to a single bedroom during the rainy season - it was the smallest bedroom in the large 5-bedroomed house into which all their worldly belongings had been crammed to keep them from getting wet and rotting or in the case of electrical equipment, becoming inoperable. The electrical system needed a complete re-wire. And to compound matters the roof space had apparently been infested by a plague of bats.

Each time they conversed Sienna got a blow by blow update on how the roof work was coming along. Because of the state of deterioration the work was very costly and stretched over several months. However, they were now almost complete and then the other works could begin. Sienna could imagine how joyful her parents were to be able to venture into the other parts of the house after many years of non-occupation. And her father would be overjoyed at not having to continuously patch up the roof and walls of the only useable bedroom. He had been undertaking that futile task for as long as Sienna could remember.

It was also wonderful to hear that her parents had been able to repay several long outstanding loans owed by them to various members of their small village community, thereby lifting their estimation to its rightful place in the minds of their fellow.

There were also reports of enterprise into farming in the case of her father and retailing which was her mother's chosen business venture. Her parents were industrious folk and Sienna was certain that they would strive to make a real go of the business undertakings. Failure was not envisaged.

Sienna was thankful to God and to Miranda for making it possible for her to provide the support that her parents now enjoyed. The monthly bursary continued to land into her account each month, which when added to her salary as a Trainee Solicitor (a paltry £1,000 per month), and the salary from her part time Saturday job as a gardener (£800 per month) meant that she earned over £3,500 per month, when free room and board was factored into the equation. Each time that Sienna reminded Miranda of the fact that the bursary was continuing to be paid her benefactor responded in the same way, "You've earned it Sienna - so just enjoy".
"Are you sure - it's a lot of money".
"Money is just money Sienna - don't worry about it dear - you need to get on your feet so we'll leave the bursary in place for now. I'm sure there are many things that you and your family can do with it".
"Yes - I guess there is a lot that we can do with that money - thank you Miranda".
"By the way - your birthday is coming up, isn't it?
A look of surprise crossed Sienna's face, "It's not until October, Miranda".
"Oh, I thought it was August - I want to spoil you my dear so I might give you an early birthday present"
"Maam ...?" Sienna's face was the picture of perplexity, as Melvin's warning echoed in her mind - did Miranda have an ulterior motive.

Each day brought new gratitude in Sienna's heart towards Miranda for her kindness, but hand in hand with appreciation came something else, a subtle voice whispering questions, "I wonder why Miranda is doing this?" or "Why would she want to be so kind to a black girl like me?" and latterly the voice had become more insistent and the questions had become statements "There must be something in it for her - why else would she do this" or "Nobody does anything for nothing these days" or even, "I need to find out why Miranda is being so kind to me" or "One of these days Miranda will shock me when she announces her true motive". But if Miranda had a secret intention, wouldn't she have tabled her true agenda by now?

The appreciative voice still spoke above the doubting ones. Sienna spent hours a day marvelling at how blessed she was to have won the bursary and now to have passed all her exams and to be well on her way to becoming a Solicitor. Her parents could never have afforded to support her through even one week's education in a Jamaican College, let alone paid for her airfare, her bed, board and fees during 4 years' of study. It was all thanks to Miranda - Sienna had come to realise, as she had suspected, that there was no board of Governors that had sanctioned the scholarship - it was all Miranda's idea from beginning to end. This was such a major blessing and Sienna thanked God that she was the chosen one to receive it even as she prayed for her benefactor every day. And there were times when she marvelled at the capacity of Miranda's heart to care.

Chapter 28

Miranda was growing more dependent upon Sienna as the days passed. She relied upon her for companionship and for strength. Sienna had become the rock upon which she leaned and she was sorely missed whenever she was away from home. Having accompanied Sienna to church one Sunday, Miranda had fallen in love with the animated form of worship and with the brethren. For the past two weeks she had returned alone to Born Again Church of God and was swiftly ingratiating herself with Bishop and Mrs Gooden. Having taken a personal decision to become one of the cornerstones of the church, she was ready to provide financial support to those in need and to back worthy community projects.

Although Miranda loved attending church services, the Word often provoked her conscience and got her thinking about her past sins. On Sundays she liked to be left alone to contemplate. For the past two Sundays she had been profoundly affected by Bishop Goodens' sermons and upon return from church she had sat beneath the Leylandiis, where she regressed until dusk when she slowly meandered back to the main house. This is the place to where Miranda always retreated when life got on top of her. Here she thought about those that she had loved and lost. Here she contemplated secrets that she had never before told a living soul.

The good deeds that she did were many and life changing for those in need, yet her past sins remained to taunt her. And the heavy weight which she carried needed to be lifted. There was only one way to secure this respite - through confession. She really wanted to share her secrets with Sienna. The prompting within her spirit to do so had become more and more urgent but so far Miranda had reined in the urge to offload her burden on Sienna. She needed so much to clear her conscience but she worried how Sienna would react - would she recoil - would she reject - would she retreat? Miranda did not want Sienna to ever leave her side now that she had fallen totally in love with her beautiful soul. And fear of losing Sienna kept Miranda's secrets hidden.

Still the prompting to confide in her beloved Sienna persisted to plague her. Perhaps she would divulge them just before she drew her last breath, for Miranda did not wish to go on living after her wicked secrets came out. She even contemplated suicide as often times the burden upon her mind became too heavy for any mortal to bear. And lately she heard voices coaxing her to "confess, confess, confess". She was on the verge of losing her sanity. Frequent migraines were apparently made more severe by Geoffrey's presence. Many a night sleep eluded her weeping eyes. When by happenstance she fell asleep, night horrors ruled her dreams and she sought refuge in waking up. Masked spectres laughed and chanted their constant mantra as she tossed and turned, fighting to wake from slumber ..... "confess, confess, confess".

Miranda had successfully camouflaged the ugliness of her past for so long but now it wanted to come out. Lately the voices also sang - "I'm coming out". This became the tune that played loudly in her mind's jukebox. She once loved that song but now she loathed its resounding familiarity as it pounded out the threat over and over - "let the world know - let it show". Miranda was losing control.

One evening when Geoffrey wasn't around, Sienna had stopped by on her way from work. Miranda had involuntarily opened up a window of disclosure. "Please don't take Geoffrey seriously - he will change - I am certain he will", she has spoken out of context as they conversed about Sienna's day at work. Sienna's response was to stare blankly. At a loss for words, Sienna did not know how she might respond to this statement. She breathed more easily as Miranda spoke again. "His father was a racist you know, so he really can't help it, but I am certain he will change one day". "He used to be much worse than he is now - in times past he could not even be in the same room as a person of colour". "His father was the poison - the disease that infected the whole family". "Sienna - believe it or not - I.... I...me .... I used to be prejudiced". Miranda spat the last words out as if they were scorching hot. She then fell silent and listened as Sienna reacted.

"Really - you... you... not you Miranda". "You.... you.... not you - no you could never be....", Sienna spoke as one who had received shocking news.

"Yes - Sienna I'm afraid I did despicable things at the behest of my dearly departed racist husband", Miranda said.

Sienna said nothing more - she could not believe what Miranda had just told her could it be true? The information failed to sink into her psyche, and hovered, rejected outside her mind's core.

Just as suddenly as she had broached the subject Miranda veered it into another direction.

"Tell me more about your day, dear", she said as Sienna took a deep breath and re-focused her mind. "My day - oh my day ... yeeesss of course.... as I was saying, it was productive", Sienna began and proceeded to recount the details.

It was easy for Sienna to pull herself together and narrate the day's events to Miranda. Most days her account was much the same as the next. But this evening she spoke as though in a trance - still under the influence of shock generated by Miranda's revelation. Could any true racist ever be reformed? The question posed itself in Sienna's mind. She looked deep into Miranda's eyes and saw the most beautiful of souls looking back at her. Surely Miranda was no racist - but could she ever have been - had she been reformed. Sienna really wanted to discuss the issue with Miranda but she bit her tongue and hoped that Miranda would one day broach the subject again - she would save her questions with bated breath.

Chapter 29

July 2017

Carlton and Becky's engagement party was a small but joyous affair to which Melvin escorted Sienna. Instantly they walked in, it had become obvious to Sienna that he was the focal point for almost every female in attendance at the small gathering of around 40 people, as all their eyes alighted upon his tall dark exceptionally handsome countenance. Sienna endured (or perhaps the more appropriate word is "survived") many a withering glance from over-amorous females who mistook her for Melvin's significant other. Several of the non-eligible women were also obviously smitten by Melvin and their interest did not go unnoticed by jealous suitors. It was evident that there were many broken hearts in attendance that night at Carlton and Becky's engagement party, nearly all down to Melvin, who was blissfully oblivious of the havoc he had reeked.

Sienna struggled with her own emotions also. She danced her cares away to every track - even the slow ones, laughing the loudest and drank two full glasses of wine, more than ever before in her life, which rendered her giggly and lighted-headed. She camouflaged her true feelings - profound sadness that the man she now realised that she was in love with, had just become betrothed to another woman. To compound her confusion, Sienna actually liked Becky. She felt cheated and could not understand why she had not faced up to the fact that she loved Carlton until now. Jealousy threatened to overwhelm as she observed Becky with Carlton - they made a radiant couple. All the years she had known him - even lived under the same roof with him, she had denied her feelings for him until now, and it was too late to admit them openly to anyone but herself.

It was not obvious to others but both Carlton and Sienna avoided getting too close. They were both aware of an invisible force at play between them - so strong, pulling them closer, tugging at their heart strings, inclining them to relent - to give in, and suggesting to them that they could no longer fight love.

When the party was at its hottest point Sienna was conversing with Melvin who only had eyes on her, when Becky pulled Carlton towards them.
Becky spoke first. "Hey you two - let's swap partners for this number".
"Yeah - sure", Melvin said enthusiastically
"Yeah .... sure", Carlton added hesitantly.
Sienna said nothing - her smile was fixed in place as Carlton held her about the waist and swung her into the centre of the room. Their hearts were in their mouths as they navigated through the uncomfortable closeness.
"Y...ou ll..ook wonderful, Sienna", Carlton said feigning that he was at ease.
"Thanks Carlton - you're looking great yourself - congratulations by the way"
"Thanks".
An uncomfortable silence followed, Carlton spoke first. As though providing an explanation he blurted out, "Becky's alright - she makes me happy". He sounded apologetic.
"So glad you found love, brother", Sienna feigned enthusiasm. Then their eyes met briefly and worry lines were quickly etched into each of their foreheads. No other words were spoken and both breathed a sigh of relief when the track came to an end.

As soon as the dance came to an end Sienna rushed off - apparently someone from university that she had not seen for ages was on the other side of the room and she just had to go and catch up. When she reached the other side of the room her old friend had inexplicably disappeared - perhaps her imagination was playing tricks on her.

Sienna looked around for Melvin but could not find him anywhere even though she walked all around the venue, including the grounds outside.

Unwanted attention from an over-enthusiastic, if not forceful party-goer who had stalked her to outside, drove Sienna back into the party hall. There she waited where she and Melvin had parted, for him to come and find her. Ten minutes later he returned. "Where have you been - I've been looking all over for you".
Melvin looked flustered, "Oh....I.... I was in the loo .... yes I was you know - in the loo". He smiled widely and hustled Sienna onto the dance floor before she could ask any more questions.

When the party ended it was 4 am. At the insistence of Sienna and Melvin, Becky and Carlton gratefully went home, leaving them in charge of the clearing up operation. When the catering crew had completed clearing up, Melvin called a cab before locking up the venue. They entered the cab and collapsed onto the back seats, blissfully exhausted. "Sienna where are we going", Melvin closed his eyes as he spoke.
"I'm coming home with you - you can make me breakfast in the morning".
"It's already morning though".
"Okay - afternoon then", Sienna said with a big Cheshire cat grim etched upon her pretty face. Great", Melvin feigned victimisation before informing the cab driver of his address.
"Sienna you know what - I will make you breakfast if you will agree to marry me", Melvin said playfully.
"Shut up, silly", Sienna responded with a chuckle.

Melvin strained to look her in the eye in the near darkness of the cab's back seat, "I'm serious Sienna - but I know what you will say - what you always say - you're my brother".

Sienna continued to smile, "That's right brother - that's who you are - so I can't marry you now, can I?"

"Well don't say I didn't ask you - and don't get upset when I decide to move on because I can't wait for you forever, Madam Beautiful", Melvin said groggily. Within seconds he was fast asleep. The next thing he knew he was being awoken by Sienna - they had arrived home.

Coffee enlivened them both and the two stayed up talking for the best part of an hour. Melvin filled Sienna in on the progress of his life generally. He had managed to locate his missing father with the help of the Enquiry Agent whom Becky had put him in touch with.

"It only took a couple of weeks for them to find dad".

"Really - only two weeks"

"Yeah - and guess how much it cost me"

"Let me guess - if it's £500 a day - uhm £2,000?"

"Guess again"

"£3,000"

"No lower - not higher"

"£1,500"

"Lower"

"Lower - £1,000"

"Lower"

"£500"

"Yes - can you believe it?"

"Wow - that's good

"So I found my dad - I'm soooo happy - I also found out that I have 4 half-siblings - a brother and 3 sisters.

"Wow - that's great - I owe you £250 remember - I'll give it to you when I see you next time".

"No - it's okay", Melvin assured. Sienna raised her palm in a "talk to the hand" gesture.

"I'll bring it next Friday - so have you met your siblings as yet?"

"Well I met one of them and guess what?"

"What?"

"They're all black - just like you"

"My sister is so beautiful - she looks just like Naomi Campbell".

"Wow - really", Sienna imagined how lovely Melvin's sister must be.

"So you have all black siblings on your father's side and all white siblings on your mother's side - that's variety for you", she continued then chuckled.

"Tell me about it", Melvin concurred enthusiastically, then continued, "Dad's cool - exactly what I dreamed he would be like". "His name is Julius Anderton". "We're so much alike - he said I look a lot like him when he was my age". "My sister is so beautiful but she looks nothing like me though". "She only lives 10 miles away - she is the oldest one from his first wife". "Her name is Ria and she has a little boy - so I'm an uncle as well - cool".

"Cool, uncle Melvin", Sienna teased.

"I can't believe it - I keep pinching myself", Melvin enthused. "I can't wait to meet my brother and other sisters too". "I keep wondering what they will be like". "They live in Birmingham so I'm planning to visit them over the Christmas and New Year Holiday". "It's the only time that I can take time off work". "I can't wait". "They're planning a big get together - wanna come?"

Sienna's eyes lit up - she loved family get-togethers, "Yeah, sure - I'd love to".

"Guess what?"

"What?"

"I've also re-connected with one of my siblings on mum's side".

"Wow"

"Yeah - Claire, my younger sister is studying law as well". "She attends the University of Law and I see her quite often as she lives in South London". "She's beautiful too - she looks just like Kylie Mynogue". They both chuckled at this statement.

"Really"

"Yeah - I feel so blessed". "All my life I have lived as an only child because my mum who I thought was my sister was so much older than me and lived so very far away, and now I am surrounded by siblings - it's great".

"When Carlton moves out this week Claire is coming to live here with me so that I can look after her".

Sienna shivered at the mention of Carlton's name, "Gr...great idea".

So excited was Melvin about his new found family, that he talked about little else until they both fell asleep through exertion on the sofa, as the long hand reached 12 and the short hand reached 6.

Later that day Sienna left before Melvin awoke and so her threat to make him prepare breakfast for her never came to fruition. As the bus meandered along its route, she mused over the developments in Melvin's life. While she was ecstatically happy for her brother/friend, now that he had located long lost relatives, she also felt strangely sad. The sadness threatened to eclipsed her joy for Melvin's positive life-change. Would there still be room in his life to accommodate her? Sienna hoped so. And she was also losing Carlton her brother/her love, to Becky. Suddenly Sienna felt incredibly alone and a tear traced its path down her left cheek, which was quickly wiped away with her trembling left hand.

Chapter 30

August to October 2017

The days passed quickly and uneventfully, then as Summer gave way to Autumn, three notable events rattled Sienna's world.

The first was that Carlton moved out of the flat he had shared with Melvin and into a new flat that he and Becky had rented together. Sienna secretly grieved his leaving during hours spent reminiscing. Tears were frequent but always in secret. Not even Melvin, with whom she shared her deepest thoughts, was privy to her feelings for Carlton. This was a cross that Sienna bore all alone.

Secondly, with Carlton's departure Claire moved into the vacant room. Sienna anticipated that this would be positive - she hoped that she would not in fact be losing a brother but gaining a friend at least and a sister at best. However, although Claire moved into the room alone, she had a friend, a constant visitor, one who developed a monster crush on Melvin. Her name was Amy and she had self-appointed herself as Melvin's jealous girlfriend. She followed him around like a tame puppy and watched him like a hawk. The girl could be forgiven for her endeavours to commandeer Melvin's attention, because of his incredibly handsome looks, debonair character and most eligible bachelor status. However, when it became apparent to Sienna that Melvin was no longer free to conduct their friendship in the manner that he had done hitherto due to Amy's relentless quest to cage and control her prey, clemency went out the door.

Each time Sienna and Melvin spoke on the phone, when Amy was within earshot, she would engage him in a side conversation, so loud that it became impossible to sustain their own dialogue. Once she even grabbed his 'phone and ran away with it before cutting the line. Sienna was at the least perturbed and at worst horrified by this intrusion. Who did this girl think she was? How dare she trespass upon the holy ground of their unbreakable friendship, without authority from Melvin? Due to Amy's behaviour Sienna was prompted to and asked Melvin to confirm categorically that he had no dealings with the girl, either currently or in the past.

"Absolutely not... I don't even know her - she is my sister's friend, not mine and I have no interest whatsoever in her...", was his immediate response and Sienna knew he was telling the truth.

One Friday in late August Melvin suggested that Sienna drop by to visit him. He wanted to introduce her to his sister Claire. Sienna arrived before Melvin and Amy answered the door. Immediately Sienna informed Amy that she was there to see Melvin vindictiveness manifested itself.

"Hi - Claire is it?" "I'm Melvin's friend".

"No, I'm Amy", came the abrupt response.

"Oh - I see", Sienna was taken aback by Amy's tone. "Is Melvin in?"

"No - who wants to know?"

"My name is Sienna", Sienna proffered her right hand for a shake.

Amy ignored her outstretched hand, "And who exactly are you?"

Sienna replied, "I beg your pardon?".

"Who are you to Melvin?"

Sienna wanted to reply that it was none of her business but instead said, "As I said, I'm his friend".

After a pause Amy asked, "What kind of friend - girlfriend or boyfriend"

Now this really got Sienna's back up, "I beg your pardon young lady - what exactly do you mean by that?"

"Well you can't always tell these days", Amy said insolently.

Now Sienna was livid, "How dare you".

"Sorry - just saying", Amy said then walked off into the bedroom.

Upon overhearing the commotion Claire came out of the kitchen, where she was busy baking. She smiled as her eyes alighted upon Sienna, "Hi, you must be Sienna".

Sienna breathed a sigh as she took Claire's outstretched right hand and shook it gently. "Yes - and you must be Claire - I'm very pleased to meet you".

"The pleasure is all mine - sorry about my friend's behaviour", Claire spoke quietly.

Sienna nodded as she wondered how such a sweet girl as Claire could be friends with the likes of Amy. Claire made tea and they ate biscuits and conversed generally until Melvin arrived home.

On hearing Melvin's voice Amy rushed from the bedroom into the living area, "Oh Melvin - I thought I heard your voice".

Melvin cast his eyes upwards as Amy propped herself close to him on the sofa, "Amy, hello".

"It's nice to meet your girlfriend, Melvin", Amy stated - the tone of her voice was rhetorical. Melvin ignored the unspoken question. He got up and walked over to the other side of the room where Sienna was sitting and sat down very close to her.

"So Sienna, what do you think of my beautiful sister?" he looked incredibly handsome in spite of the fact that he was tired after a hard day's work.

"She is lovely, Melvin", Sienna's smile was genuine.

"You're lovely yourself", Claire replied and added, "It's a real pleasure to meet you - I see why my brother is so crazy about you". All except Amy burst into laughter.

"Excuse me - I've got something in the oven", Claire said and left the room. Amy sat fast.
"So Sienna - what are we doing for your birthday next month?" Melvin asked.
"Well we can go out for a celebratory meal if you like, or you can come over and cook for me".
Faced with a choice Melvin quickly replied "Well the former sounds enticing", as he smiled broadly.
"It's a date then", Sienna said teasingly as Amy glared on.
"Maybe we can all go for a meal", Amy interjected - her suggestion was ignored.

Instead of getting the message and leaving the room when her frequent attempts to interject into the conversation were ignored, Amy, sat fast, glaring from Sienna to Melvin. They turned to discussion of plans for Christmas, as she seethed. Melvin appeared unperturbed by Amy's behaviour but Sienna became increasingly concerned, noting that Amy's stare had mutated into an ugly grimace. The girl looked crazed and Sienna made a note to raise the issue with Melvin later, in private. It occurred to her that she should raise it sooner rather than later as Amy commented loudly upon a programme being broadcast on the TV, "Some people better watch that they don't mess with the wrong man". "If anyone mess with my man, I will have to deal with them". Melvin and Sienna's eyes met and they shared a startled gaze as Amy added "I would kill for love, wouldn't you?".

"Melvin would you walk me to the bus stop, please?" Sienna arose to leave - she spoke pointedly.

"Okay", Melvin grabbed his coat and stood at the ready - he shouted to Claire, "Claire, Sienna is leaving now".

Claire rushed into the living room, "Leaving so soon?" "Why don't you stay for dinner?"

Sienna really felt bad about leaving - she had been looking forward to getting to know Claire but that would have to be some other time in the future, "Sorry I have some important research to do for tomorrow", then she hugged Claire and felt the same degree of warmth that she gave out emanating back to her. "I'll see you again soon".

"You bet", Claire said as she rushed back into the kitchen to check upon her baking.

"I'll come with you to the bus stop Melvin", Amy volunteered as she jumped to her feet.

"No - please don't", was the abrupt response from Melvin.

Before Amy could say anything else, Melvin hustled Sienna out of the door. They breathed a common sigh as they linked arms like lovers and walked briskly away.

As they walked to the bus stop, Sienna voiced her fears and Melvin concurred.

"I told my sister that I don't like her hanging around all the time but I don't think she can stand up to that girl - I don't really know what to do about the situation".

Sienna thought for a while, "Then you need to tell her yourself Melvin - I know people like that you have to be firm with them or they will just walk all over you".

Melvin nodded in agreement, "I think you're right Sienna - I have made hints but I will have to be firmer now and if that fails, I might have to move into your place". Melvin chuckled but he was serious. He hated confrontation and would much rather walk away, even from his own home for a quiet life.

Sienna smiled, "Yeah, I think I can sneak you in from time to time but I can't guarantee that you could stay with me on a permanent basis".

Days later Melvin informed Sienna that he had had words with Amy but instead of the situation improving, they had become markedly worse.

"Sienna - seriously, can I come and spend some time at yours?"

"Yeah sure - we'll have to be careful though".

****

It had been four weeks since Melvin moved in with Sienna when the third profound development happened. It began with a telephone call received from Sister Newson. Sienna's instincts had alerted her to exercise caution when dealing with Sister Newson and she had been screening calls from her since their last meeting. She had answered this call in error. Sister Newson sounded very distressed.

"Sienna, how are you - do you know how worried I have been about you", she gushed, and without allowing time for Sienna to answer she continued. "You said you would be coming back to see me soon but you haven't". "Why Sienna, why?"

Sister Newson paused and Sienna took the opportunity to speak. "Oh hello Sister Newson - sorry... sorry - I've just been really busy" "How are you keeping?"

"I'm not keeping good health at all Sienna - I'm getting old, you know - I'm not keeping well at all and there is no-one to take care of me".

"So sorry to hear that Sister Newson", Sienna wondered why Sister Newson was obviously trying to make her feel guilty - what about her own children? She said, "What about your son and your grandson Sister Newson - do they know you are not keeping well?" After another pause Sister Newson replied, "Yes, of course but Sienna that doesn't mean that you should leave me out of your life like this". Sienna felt pressure from Sister Newson and the temptation to stoke up the memories of how she was unceremoniously dismissed from her home niggled at the fringes of her mind, but she resisted those thoughts and made another fervent effort to forget and to forgive.

"Sister Newson, I know I haven't been to see you, but as I said I have been extremely busy", Sienna struggled to keep exasperation from her tone.

"I am getting very frail and I can't get out as much as I used to due to my rheumatoid arthritis - so please come and see me soon Sienna - surely you can make just a little time for an old lady, Sienna", Sister Newson pleaded.

"Okay Sister Newson, I will come and visit you soon", Sienna spoke in a soothing voice. A small voice in her mind warned that she should heed some of the advice that she had given to Melvin a few weeks earlier.

"When Sienna - when are you coming?" Sister Newson sounded anxious.

"Next week"

"What day - what time?"

Next Thursday after work - so around 7.30 pm, okay?"

"Okay dear - I look forward to seeing you". "Sienna - thank you", Sister Newson sounded grateful.

They chatted for a few minutes - well Sister Newson talked and Sienna listened. The older woman lamented about the woes of her daughter who was facing foreclosure and her daughter's husband who had been declared bankrupt. Sienna felt genuinely sorry to hear that Sister Newson's only successful offspring, upon who she boasted, had now fallen upon hard times.

****

"At last", Sister Newson exclaimed as she ended the call to Sienna. Immediately she dialled Jonathan's number. She genuinely liked and missed Sienna. But she loved her son unconditionally. She knew he wasn't perfect, but he was her son. The thought that Jonathan and Sienna could perhaps become an item one day had gathered momentum in Sister Newson's imagination. And this idea which would qualify as utter foolishness to right thinking people, was fully embraced as a distinct possibility by Sister Newson. "There could be nothing better than a union between the two", she soliloquised. And she surmised that she would no longer be as lonely as she has been, as she reminisced about the joy that she had known when Sienna lived with her. Sister Newson yearned for those days to return, so much so that she was rapidly losing touch with reality, or perhaps it was senility that had taken a firm grip upon her mind.

****

The call from his mother came as Jonathan sat patiently watching the rear entrance to "High Trees". He had been spending much of his time doing so, at varied times of the day and night over the past 3 months - since the night that he had followed Sienna home. Over past weeks he had seen a handsome young man entering and leaving the premises a few times but no sign of

Sienna. Jonathan surmised that the stranger must be Sienna's boyfriend and he sized him up. How would they fare during a confrontation? He concluded that he need not be concerned by the other man's 5' 10" stature and muscle toned build as compared to his 6' 2" muscle bound mass. He hated that man and each time he saw his incredibly handsome face the animosity grew, but it was nothing that a can of high strength acid could not take care of.

It had dawned upon Jonathan that there must be another entrance to the premises, but, not able to guess which of the imposing properties on the surrounding streets the front entrance was situated in, his only other option had been to keep on waiting and watching. Surely Sienna must emerge or arrive one day. In the meantime he had spent much of his watching and waiting time, plaguing his mother with numerous texts, asking her to arrange a further visit from Sienna.

As usual Sister Newson was put through to voicemail - Jonathan rarely took her calls. She proceeded to leave a message.
"Hello son - it's me mum - how are you?" "I wanted to let you know that Sienna is coming......."

In mid sentence Jonathan picked up and cut in.

"Mum - so you have spoken to Sienna then?
"Aahh... yes. Aahh..I spoke with her just now", Sister Newson was taken aback by her son's obvious lack of interest in her wellbeing. She felt injured - if he had enquired as to her situation, there was so much that she could tell, of the ailments that were worsening each passing day; of the lack of mobility that saw her trapped on the ground floor of her home without company for

days on end; of the difficulties in undertaking ordinary everyday chores like cooking and washing up and shopping. But Jonathan had not troubled to ask.

"So when is she coming to see you then?"

"Ar.....ah....", Sister Newson hesitated.

"Well mum - when is she coming?"

"I... she said next Thursday evening".

"What time - did she say what time?" Jonathan shouted. Sister Newson hesitated - wondering why her son was behaving so manically.

"Well?" he barked. "Speak woman".

Sister Newson felt affronted by Jonathan's attitude. He had shown little or no concern for her and as the conversation continued she became more hurt. So for the first time she allowed her mind an honest viewpoint and conceded that her son's interest in Sienna was not a healthy one.

"Are you sure you are not fixating on Sienna", she asked involuntarily.

"What do you mean?" "Now that is why I don't even bother to come and see you too often, mum". "You have an evil heart - what kinda thing is that for you to say to me?" Jonathan boomed.

"I'm not evil hearted but I wonder why you are so interested in Sienna", Sister Newson uncharacteristically stood up to her son.

"Yes mum - you are an old evil witch - only an evil mind could imagine anything sordid about my interest - Sienna is like my little sister". "I am interested in her welfare because I know that the streets are wicked". "It's like a jungle out there".

"Okay - sorry son - she is coming at 7.30 pm".

"Evil witch of a woman", Jonathan said before ending the call without so much as a "goodbye".

After the call ended, Sister Newson sat quietly, contemplating. She felt sadder than ever. She was unhappy not just because of the way that her son had spoken to her, but because his accusation had shone a light into her soul and there she had discerned a septic putrid mass of evil. And she now admitted that she was among the vilest of sinners not for the reason Jonathan had cited, but because of her duplicitous actions towards Sienna. Her honest personality gained momentary charge of her psyche, causing her to face up to the fact that her son was no good - she conceded that he had never been a good person. She thought about the initial accusation by Sienna which she had flagrantly ignored, and she allowed her mind to regress to her son's criminal history.

In light of this insight, how could she have ignored the innocent girl's cry for help - how could she have coldly turned a wilful deaf ear to her pleas. Yet she had done worst - a professing born again Christian she had betrayed her Saviour and instead of being Sienna's saviour she had been her betrayer, had ushered the blameless soul out of her home into potential peril and certain destitution.

The recollection of Jonathan's prior conviction for rape and sexual assault now stood firmly at the forefront of Sister Newson's psyche, and shame and guilt stood side by side, accusing her and causing her to tremble. And as the truth systematically bombarded her mind, Sister Newson began to weep uncontrollably. This was a very rare occasion for her - crying had never been a natural inclination. But tonight she did not hold back - tears flowed like a river. When she had no more tears, she hobbled into to the bathroom to wash her face. Then she hobbled back to her bedroom, picked up the receiver and dialled Sienna's number. From now on she would do the right thing.

Chapter 31

September to November 2017

When Melvin came to stay with her he accessed Sienna's flat via the back entrance while Sienna continued to use the front entrance. The only concern had been whether the dogs would cause any problem so Sienna had, with prior arrangement, met him as he entered the premises, and "introduced" him to the dogs. It did not take long for Melvin to get to know them - he loved animals and had an uncanny knack of seducing them. He tagged along that first Saturday and Sunday as Sienna took them out for their walks and their bond was forged then - soon they were literally eating out of his hands.

Sienna was overjoyed to have Melvin's company. He was equally happy to be living with his best friend, and in such luxurious surroundings but he missed his sister and visited her most evenings after work and over the weekend. His visits to Claire were often but short due to the fact that Amy continued to hang around.

****

Claire was becoming more and more fed up of Amy's intrusion into her home and family. Although Melvin still visited her almost every day she missed spending quality time bonding with her new found brother and was not best pleased that he had effectively been driven out of his own home by her friend's unwanted, persistent and vindictive behaviour. So she decided that she would bring their friendship to an end. She found the courage to do so a couple of weeks after Melvin had gone to stay with Sienna. Amy had turned up uninvited as usual, hoping to see Melvin. Claire took a deep breath before opening the door to her.

"Hi and bye - I don't want you coming around here anymore and anyway Melvin is not living here - he moved in with his girlfriend, Sienna".

"Sienna - his girlfriend?" Amy asked loudly as she forcibly held the door open.

"Yes - that's right", Claire attempted to close the door but Amy was stronger than she was.

"I thought she was just a friend of his", Amy declared.

"Well whatever - it's not important", Claire replied. She took another deep breath and continue, "Anyway, please consider me no longer a friend - you only wanted to befriend me because of my brother anyway".

Amy pushed against the door, trying to force her way in, "Why would you say that - of course I'm your friend".

Claire found strength she did not know she possessed and pushed the door shut as she replied, "Well it doesn't matter anyway - I don't want to be friends with you anymore so get the message and stay away". But she would come to learn that Amy was not that easy to get rid of.

****

Now that Claire had ended their friendship, Amy could no longer visit Melvin's home. But Melvin soon found out that Amy was not one to give up easily. Within three weeks of his move, she had tracked him from his flat when he went to collect a change of clothes, to where he was staying at Sienna's flat. She had also established where he worked and spent much of her time trailing him, to the neglect of her university studies which she looked certain to fail.

As Melvin went out for lunch one day, he was confronted by a nightmare - waiting at the front of his office was Amy.

"Hi Melvin - want to go to lunch?"

"What are you doing here?" Melvin walked briskly away as he spoke. What on earth did this woman want from him?

"I came to see you Melvin". "I miss you so much - I just want to be with you - I love you".

"You what?"

"I love you Melvin - I truly love you", Melvin stared into Amy's eyes and a deranged stalker stared back at him. He turned and walked briskly away. Amy ran after him. Melvin did not notice Gloria, one of his colleagues, who stood watching their exchange.

"Do me a favour and leave me alone, will you? Melvin shrugged off Amy's hand as she reached out to pull him back.

"No Melvin - I can't leave you alone - can't you see that I love you more than life".

"Leave me alone or I will not be responsible for my actions", Melvin was angry now. What made this woman think that she could keep interposing herself into his life without his consent? The expression on his face was thunderous - there was no mistaking that he was angry.

Gloria was intrigued. As Melvin marched quickly away in an angry rage, she quickened her pace to catch up with Amy. Everyone knew her to be the office busybody and today she would firmly cement that reputation.

"Are you okay - I couldn't help overhearing your conversation with Melvin - he's a colleague of mine?" Gloria sounded concerned.

"Yes - he's my boyfriend - it's just that we had an argument - it's nothing though - he's just angry but he will soon calm down".

"Do you want to talk about it? Gloria asked as her nose began to itch. "I'll buy you lunch - cheer you up a bit", she smiled warmly. And Amy, having all the time in the world, began to talk as they walked to the nearby fast food restaurant. She spoke of her long standing relationship with Melvin, of their ups and downs, of his callous disregard towards the love that she had so freely lavished upon him. And she told mostly of his duplicity with a cheap woman called Sienna. Following their conversation Gloria began to view Melvin in a much dimmer light.

****

It had been a few weeks since Claire ended her friendship with Amy. Melvin now spent much of his time back at home, although he continued to stay at Sienna's some days - he just loved being around her even though she remained resolutely just his friend. And anyway, the problem was not entirely resolved. Amy continued to stalk him. She seemed to know his every move. Every time he was at home she attempted to visit him there. But Claire was having none of that. Her resoluteness saw her build an impenetrable wall which Amy could not cross.

Undeterred, each day Amy spied on Melvin's flat from her car. Today she was babysitting and had her little sister, Selina, with her. She watched as Claire went out. This was her chance. With the hope and intent that her efforts would pay dividends today Amy left Babe in the car and went to knock at Melvin's door. When Melvin opened the door she immediately launched herself forward in an attempt to enter.
"You again - where do you think you're going? Melvin shoved her backwards but was surprised by her strength.
"I came to see you", Amy replied, getting a foothold inside the doorway.
"Look - how many times Amy?" "How many times do I have to ask you to leave me alone", Melvin was forced to manhandle her as he pushed her outside. "I am not interested in you so please leave me alone", he affirmed.

Appearing not to have heard a single word that Melvin said, Amy launched her whole body at him again in a concerted effort to re-enter his flat.

"Oh no you don't - you are not coming in here", Melvin used brute force and pushed the door shut.

Amy banged upon the door until her hands ached. Tears streaked her face as she fell to the ground crying. Selina, who watched everything that transpired, left the car, ran to Amy and tried to console her. "Never mind Amy - get up and let's go home", she entreated as Amy sobbed loudly.

"Never mind Amy - never mind - let's go home - lets go home and tell daddy - dad will sort him out". After a few minutes, Amy got to her feet and reluctantly walked back to her car where she sat for more than half an hour waiting and watching as her little sister encouraged. "Let's go now Amy - lets go home". And eventually she acquiesced.

"Selina, please don't tell dad about this", Amy knew that her parents would not understand or agree with her campaign of force to secure Melvin's love.

"Ok Amy, I won't".

"Promise?"

"Yeah - I promise".

Chapter 32

November 2017

It was a strange visit with Sister Newson. The elder lady had spent the entire 2 hour visit apologising to Sienna. Apparently her conscience had been troubling her, hence the reason why she had been trying to telephone Sienna several times a day in the past week but Sienna had ignored her calls. For one she had been far too busy for long chats over the 'phone and secondly, she knew that they would have plenty of time to talk when she visited tonight.

Sienna had stopped off at the local Caribbean bakery and purchased some staples for Sister Newson, including hard dough bread, fruit bun and cheese, some patties for her freezer and coconut cake. She had also bought various fruit that filled up the fruit dish to overspill. Sister Newson had accepted her gifts with a grateful smile and warm hug.

"Thank you very much Sienna - it's very nice of you to think of me like this", Sister Newson said with a distinct air of sincerity.
"It's no problem at all - I bought you a double portion of oranges - I remember how much you love them", Sienna replied and they both chuckled.
"Thank you my dear".

At the beginning of the evening Sienna found it difficult to shift the memory of the injustice to which Sister Newson had subjected her in that home over the years, firstly by working her like a slave, secondly by denying her the full benefit of her monthly allowance and causing her to exist like an urchin, and then by insulting her family and driving her out of her home unceremoniously.   Memories of those experiences triggered righteous indignation within Sienna's mind and she struggled.

Even as she had prepared for her visit Sienna had struggled. An ugly voice told her that she should not even have anything to do with Sister Newson let alone buy her stuff. But Sienna had overcome the insistent nag that told her she should not care for or think of looking after such an unworthy person no matter how old or frail they were.

As Sienna listened to Sister Newson's solemn apologies, another voice spoke louder from her heart, suggesting that she should do good, even to those that had used her and Sienna became repentant. She made a fresh promise to forget and to truly forgive.

Sienna left Sister Newson's home feeling as light as air. It was as though she had shed the weight of un-forgiveness that had beset her for too long. The light drizzle that began to fall felt refreshing, as though it was renewing and reviving her. She did not use her umbrella but allowed it to sprinkle over her.

So engrossed was she in her graceful thoughts that Sienna did not notice the shadowy figure in dark trousers and a mid-grey duffle coat with the hood pulled up and over that followed her at a distance. When she boarded the first bus the figure followed and sat at the back. He followed her as she got off the bus half way through her journey and waited; as she met the incredibly handsome young man with whom she got onto the next bus and continued her journey; as they chatted excitedly, obviously comfortable in each other's company. The stalker began to shake uncontrollably, whether with anger or fear one could not tell but the quivering became gradually worse until it was noticeable to passengers seated nearby who began to move away. Taking deep breaths helped to calm the shadowy figure but his eyes remained wild.

Engrossed in laughter and good companionship, Sienna and Melvin failed to notice the shadowy figure that alighted the bus at their stop and followed them at a distance until they entered the gate and locked it behind them. He loitered about outside the high brick walls topped with razor wire which spelt certain death to anyone who should attempt to scale them. The man was so consumed by jealousy - he felt invincible - he could break through the wrought iron gate locked with a dead lock with his bare hands. He approached the gate and shook it with all his might but it stood fast. He continued to shake the gate. Within a minute, two vicious dogs appeared and yapped loudly at his hands. He withdrew from the gate and began to walk away.

It began to pour with rain and as though looking about for shelter, the man suddenly noticed a car parked in the shadows of the dead-end street - the person inside appeared to be a lone female. What could this young lady be doing here alone at 11 o'clock on this dismal night? There was nothing here in this dead-end street - no houses, just the side wall of a large warehouse building that was opposite to the two entrance gates and the walls of garden grounds. As Jonathan walked towards the car he studied the woman and noted the crazed expression. He recognised a fellow stalker and surmised that there was only one explanation for her presence her - she was watching and waiting too.

Jonathan approached the car and knocked on the window. The watcher looked out at him startled.

****

"Hi, who are you looking for? Mr Handsome?" the man asked.

Amy ignored the stranger at first. He repeated the questions. She reacted only to say, "Go away, you old f**t".   This mildly infuriated the man, who reigned in his emotion well. As he stood by contemplating his next move, Amy suddenly changed her mind - it occurred to her that this man must be interested in Sienna. So she changed tack and wound her window down".

"So why are you here - for her?" The man did not reply - he stared coldly as Amy burst into laughter, "I'm right aren't I - you're after Sienna".

"What is it to you? he replied as he sidled up to her window.

"Did she ditch you for my boyfriend - can't say as I blame her", Amy added insolently as she gave Jonathan a derisive glance. She chuckled again but he did not get the joke.

"You want him and I want her - maybe we should work together", he said coldly.

Just then it started to pour down heavily.

"Can I sit inside the car so that we can talk?" the stranger asked. Amy studied him, contemplating his request. She decided that he seemed harmless enough, so she opened the passenger door to let him in.

"So who are you looking for then Sienna - that s..g?", Amy said the four letter word that described a woman of ill repute as if it were indeed filthy, then she laughed again, a dirty if not filthy laugh. She looked over at the man but he still failed to see what was so funny. He turned his head to gaze at her with a strange vacant stare as she wondered what he might be thinking.

"You look just like my ex girlfriend", he said. "She was the most dishonest, unfaithful cow that ever lived - that's why she had to die".

Suddenly Amy felt unease bear down upon her, "Anyway I've got to get home now so please can you get out of my car", she said in a tiny voice.

"I'm going your way so DRIVE", came the thunderous reply.

"Okay"

"And don't say anything else b...h", the man called Amy a female dog. No one spoke to her like that.

"Don't you dare speak to me like that", Amy said and before she finished speaking her head was knocked backwards by his huge fist, leaving her seeing stars.

As Amy tried to recover her chain of thoughts and focus her mind Jonathan commanded again, "Now DRIVE - I said".

"Yes okay". Amy got the feeling that this was going to be a very bad night.

Chapter 33

November to December 2017

Life meandered along uneventfully for a time, then in early November Geoffrey came to stay. Day after day Sienna looked forward to him leaving again - he had never stayed for more than a few hours before, but to her dismay, he did not look to be leaving anytime soon. Since his coming Sienna had experienced a couple of unpleasant occurrences which were questionable. She had found excrement at the front door of the flat. On both occasions Bert had helped her to clean it away, blaming the dogs. However, it occurred to Sienna that the dogs had never done anything like that before. They were well trained to defecate only in the designated areas and it looked very much like human faeces to her, if she was not mistaken. The question in her mind remained unanswered - would Geoffrey really sink that low? Did he hate her that much?

Rosy informed Sienna that Geoffrey's wife had found out about his affair with Trudy and kicked him out and there was no reason to disbelieve that that was the truth.

As Christmas drew near the air of merriment that usually pervaded the High Trees Estate during this season of goodwill was noticeably absent. Sienna put it down to Geoffrey's presence. All hopes that he would leave were dashed and he ended up staying for the entire Christmas period. A heavy cloud had come to rest over High Trees Estate and a wedge divided the usually close relationship between Sienna and Miranda.

At mid-afternoon on Christmas Eve Sienna approached the great house with trepidation - she rang the buzzer to Miranda's living quarters and hoped that she did not bump into Geoffrey. Miranda buzzed her in almost immediately. The house was eerily quiet as Sienna stole into the building and crept down the long corridor that led to her benefactor's living quarters - her heart was in her mouth and she felt as though she was a burglar afraid of getting caught.

Once inside Miranda's apartment Sienna breathed easily again.

"Sienna darling - it's so nice to see you", Miranda's face beamed as she hobbled towards her. Sienna rushed to meet her and they air kissed on both sides and hugged momentarily. The older woman was obviously experiencing great challenge in her mobility.

"Are you okay, Miranda?" Sienna asked with genuine concern.

"Yes dear - it's just that my body can't keep up these days, but my spirit and mind are intact", Miranda chuckled - no one would suspect the degree of pain that she was experiencing at that very moment.

"Sorry I have not been to see you for over a week, it's just that I've been sooo very busy with Christmas preparations," Sienna fibbed. She had not been to see Miranda because of Geoffrey's constant presence in the big house.

"That's okay my dear - sit down and make yourself comfortable". Sienna helped Miranda back to her seat and settled her before taking a seat in the armchair by the window.

"I know that Geoffrey's presence probably deterred you", Miranda said matter-of-factly. "But I have missed you so very much". A tear sprung up in the corner of her left eye and her voice cracked. Sienna was touched by this show of genuine affection.

"I have really missed our little chats too Miranda", she said.

"Well we have a lot of catching up to do then, don't we dear?", Miranda said in her distinctive old English parlance.

"Happy Christmas", Sienna got up and walked over to Miranda and handed her a small silver envelope.

"Thank you dear", a smiling Miranda quickly opened the envelope.

The card was tasteful and classically beautiful, with a winter scene depicted on the front and a message of hope on the inside.

"That's so beautiful", Miranda cooed, then took a deep breath and continued, "Yours is on the mantle and your present is inside the envelope too - but you are not allowed to open it until tomorrow, please", the gentle order carried tremendous force.

"Thank you Miranda - I promise I won't open it until Christmas day", Sienna smiled gleefully as she picked up the large A4 brown envelope and wondered what was inside.

"And here is your present Miranda", she beamed. She loved to give far more than she liked receiving and hoped that Miranda would enjoy the Ipod that she had bought her. Her smile broadened with excitement as she imagined how her patron would fare when trying to operate the gadget. Then trepidation set in - new technology was an enigma to Miranda which caused Sienna no end of amusement. She had pondered long and hard before purchasing the Ipod and was suddenly uncertain as to whether she had done the right thing. She was hoping against hope that it would not be too much like hard work for Miranda to navigate her way around the new adult toy, especially now that Geoffrey was around all the time preventing their previously cohesive existence. A sobering thought caused Sienna to stop fretting - Linda was technically savvy and would no doubt be able to guide Miranda - she was reassured that she had bought the right present. Miranda loved music and the Ipod would liberate her into mobile listening.

****

Since Geoffrey had moved back into his old living quarters upstairs in the great house, his presence had stirred up a lot of memories for Miranda. Although she loved her son, she did not like him very much because he reminded her too much of his father. He possessed the same ugly personality.

Although Geoffrey had moved back into his quarters at High Trees, Miranda felt lonelier than ever. She now spent much of her time alone which afforded her the chance to think. Thinking meant regression and the load that she had been carrying for far too many years had become heavier than ever before. She needed to off-load the burden. It was just too heavy for her now. She felt that her mind would explode if she did not open up. The prompting from her conscience was growing stronger each day and she had no more time to waste in sharing her haunting secrets with the world - she would begin to jettison the debris today - she had to tell some of her secrets to Sienna.

Only half of Miranda's psyche was engaged as Sienna updated her about her work life. The other half was trying to decide how she should broach the subject of her confession - she had to tell the secrets that she had kept hidden in her heart for so many years. The only other person who knew them had been Michael her husband. When he was alive he would constantly remind her of the secrets that they shared, threatening that she keep her mouth shut or suffer the consequence of his wrath, but even that release was better than having none at all. If she did not talk to someone, the dam was sure to burst - she might just go crazy.

"I really hope that you like your present Miranda", Sienna gushed.

"Any hint as to what it is dear", Miranda replied.

"Now, now - no peeking - make sure you don't open it until tomorrow".

When Sienna finished speaking, the room fell quiet. A faraway look glazed Miranda's eyes. Sienna sensed that she should say nothing more.

Miranda took a deep breath and looked across the room. Finding Sienna's eyes, she looked meaningfully into them and said. "Sienna my dear I need to share something with you".

"Well share away", Sienna shrugged and chuckled in an effort to lighten the atmosphere. Miranda did not laugh back. Instead the expression on her face became sombre. Her look was a precursor, a warning that she was about to regress back into her shameful past - back to the time when she had been a racist. Sienna's smile faded and she listened in anticipation. Whatever Miranda would say, she was ready to hear - she would listen without prejudice to her benefactor's story and she would not judge her.

Obviously Miranda needed to off-load a burden and Sienna would help her to do that because she knew in her heart of hearts that her patron was truly remorseful for any past sins that she may have committed, no matter how heinous they might have been. If the almighty and holy God could forgive sins, who was she to enforce guilt upon someone who was truly repentant.

"My husband Michael was a racist as you know", Miranda regarded Sienna with an apologetic glance. Sienna concurred with a sympathising nod of her head.

"I married him without really knowing him at all". "I mean, I knew that he didn't like black people he made that clear from the start, and truth be told at

that time I shared that interest - I too hated". "It was learned behaviour you see - my father had taught me to hate". "He had been a diligent teacher and I an attentive student". "My father and my husband were of the very same ilk", Miranda spat out the words as though they were offending her mouth, demonstrating her fervour to off-load. A short pause followed. Sienna said nothing although she wanted to speak, to reassure Miranda that she believed that she was a changed person now. But words did not form in her mouth.

"I was not aware of the degree to which Michael would go to demonstrate that devilish passion". "I was to learn that his heart's capacity for hatred knew no bounds" "It was as if Michael's obsession to hate another race was bequeathed to him from the very depth of the heart of Satan". "It was as though he had studied to the highest level and had passed every devilish exam with flying colours, on how to hate men and women of other colours and ethnicities".

"But in truth, what I now know and hate about my late husband and father was what I had admired in them both, then". "I was blind you see, but now I can see that the good Lord created us all as equals - whether we be black, white, brown, yellow, red or somewhere in between". "But what God meant for variety, mankind has misinterpreted - the evil one has filled hearts with pompous pride so that we hate instead of love, where there should be empathy he has substituted misunderstanding and where unity should reign the heinous face of segregation now holds court". "The minds of men and women have been effectively warped by the evil one so that the things that should be considered beautiful are viewed as ugly and those that should be revered as wholesome, are regarded as deficient" "Instead of celebrating our differences as the good Lord had meant for us to do, mankind has used those very differences to entertain the ugliest hatred and to disdainfully *degrade those who are different".* *"We have no right to taint the things created from the loving and beautiful heart of God - no right whatsoever and I am so, so very sorry, so ashamed for the part that I have played in doing so".*

"No man is more supreme than the other based upon the colour of the skin or some other physical difference". *"For there is only one supreme being to whom we must all answer, whether we be black, white, yellow, brown, red or somewhere in between".* Sounding like a preacher delivering a particular poignant sermon Miranda continued. *"For which one of us can keep alive our own bodies or yet breathe life into any soul".* Straining her eyes to see in the near darkness, she kept eye contact with Sienna as though drawing strength to carry on as she delivered her discourse. At times she wrestled with shame that threaten to silence her.

"We had only known each other for 4 months when we got married". *"Michael proposed to me three months after we met and I said yes".* *"Truth be told, I was afraid to say no, because Michael was a dictator, a controller too - he was a manipulating monster".* *"Oh he wore the trousers and the crown as king in our relationship - nothing I did or said was ever good enough for him".* Pause. *"He didn't like women either - not really".* Another pause as the wheels of retrogression turned slowly.

"I became aware that I was pregnant before Michael and I got married" *"That was why he insisted that we get married".* *"Five months after we got married, I went into premature labour - at least I thought it was premature labour but I later realised that the baby was in fact full term".* Pause.

I gave birth at the Garston Hospital for Women that was close to where we lived in those days. I was in labour for 25 hours - it had been a hard fought battle". "I nearly died as the baby was turned. The midwife said that it was a miracle that I lived". "The baby lived too and was very healthy in spite of his ordeal". "He was a boy - a beautiful boy". "But he must have known that he would suffer in this cruel world". "I always thought that that was why he had turned an awkward way - he didn't want to be born into this wicked world where a man can be judged purely based upon his skin tone - not by his capacity for integrity or by his inclination towards uprightness but purely by his colour" "He did not want to face the struggles associated with being born black in England back in 1949".

"But what's a colour I now ask?" Miranda shouted this sentence vehemently. *"What is a colour when you fight side by side against a common enemy and need the help of your fellow man?". "What is a colour when death comes to call upon the white man, and also pays a visit to his neighbour who happens to be black". "What then is a colour - can either by his hue keep alive his mortal soul?" "Does sickness and disease distinguish between colours". "Is true love not colour blind - yes - for surely it is". "And so I ask again - what is a colour?"*

The gasp involuntarily escaped from Sienna's lips, as her eyes popped wide open. Well she certainly was not expecting that revelation. Miranda must have been with a black man to have given birth to a black baby. Sienna's mind could not picture such circumstances - no image would form for it was impossible to envisage Miranda with a black man in the liberal 21st century, yet alone way back in 1949.

Miranda caste her eyes downwards as she continued and the gathering darkness as the evening rolled in became a cover for her to hide behind from the shame of her past conviction. *"It was a time when, although not enshrined in law, being black was a crime in this country and for a white woman to give birth to a black child was regarded as a cardinal sin by most people - black and white ".* Miranda appeared distressed so Sienna walked over to the water dispenser, poured a cup of water and handed it to her. The cup was accepted gratefully by trembling hands. Sienna returned to the water dispenser and poured herself a much needed cup too. To say that she was shaken by Miranda's disclosure would be to state the truth.

*"When I saw my son my eyes filled with tears". "I was shocked to see that he was definitely black". "I strained my neck to look at him as the midwife cleaned him up - I was willing him to become whiter, but there was no questioning the fact that he was black". "And denying the undeniable love that tugged at my heart strings, I cursed my own child with my tongue under my breath". "Black *******"".*
"Pardon?", the midwife had asked.
"Nothing, it was nothing", I had replied

"Then I pretended not to notice that the child to whom I had just given birth was black - I thought if I pretended that nothing was wrong, the midwife would not notice, but I was wrong". "Luckily it was just the one midwife that attended to me during the birth". "I could see her demeanour change as she cleaned the baby up and noted its curly hair, dark thick lips and dark skin". "But she was not unkind to me". "She complimented upon the beauty of my child and suggested that she would vouch that the child was stillborn if I wanted to keep the live birth a secret from my husband". "She told me that

she could arrange for an orphanage to take him in but I refused to listen and she left...".

At that point Miranda grew quiet again for a very long time. Sienna wondered where her mind had gone to. After a full 5 minutes had passed without another word from Miranda, Sienna walked over and sat beside her, placing her hand across her shoulders. The divulgence had obviously proved too harrowing for the elderly woman, and it became evident that her mind had collapsed when she replied in gibberish."Caaaacou.." It was then that Sienna found her voice.
"Shall I turn on the lights now Miranda - it's gotten very dark in here", her tone was light as she sought to inject buoyancy into the atmosphere.
"Yeesss, please do ... that ", Miranda replied absentmindedly.

When the lights were switched on Sienna saw that Miranda's face was tear stained. Sitting down close to her, she placed her arm about her shoulders once again and tried to console her gently.
"Never mind Miranda", she said. She wanted to ask her to carry on her narration because she was dying to find out what had happened to her matriarch's black son, but she somehow restrained herself, *"Not now Sienna"*, her psyche whispered, and she reluctantly obeyed.
"Miranda, I think you ought to try and get some rest now".
"Yes dear - that's a good idea", came the frail response.

After helping Miranda to bed and sitting with her a while, Sienna bade her a good night. As she was about to leave Miranda mumbled a request through tired lips.
"Will you please help me to find my son Simon - Simon ... yes Simon was his name". "I never saw him after that night when he was born you know,

my Simon". "It was January 27 1949. He'll be around 69 now, Simon". "I often wondered what had become of my beautiful boy Simon", a far-away look glazed her eyes, signalling that Miranda had left the building yet again. "Okay Miranda - we'll talk more about it when I see you tomorrow", Sienna said, aware that she had almost certainly not been heard.

Chapter 34

December 2017

Christmas morning dawned a crispy cold and bright day which lightened Sienna's mood. As sanguinity moved in to seize control of her mind she looked forward to enjoying Christmas, albeit alone.   She had been sorely tempted to travel back to Jamaica to be with her family this Christmas, but once again, her work demanded that she could not. She would be going into work over the holidays, to deal with pressingly urgent matters.

Now that Geoffrey was present in the great house, there was no way that Sienna would be invited over for Christmas dinner as she had been last year and in any case Miranda was definitely not in the mood for any kind of celebration. So she was prepared to cook herself a sumptuous and befitting Christmas meal.

Melvin was going to spend this Christmas with his father and newly discovered siblings and she would miss him terribly. He had invited Sienna to join him, but when she telephoned him a couple of weeks before Christmas to firm up arrangements she had received no reply and a message that she left had gone unanswered.   She was mildly perturbed but she surmised that he was perhaps busy with his new found family and not wishing to pester him, she had not called again.

Several people had invited Sienna for Christmas dinner but she had turned them all down because she was not sure whether Geoffrey would be going away or not and she had to anticipate that he would be. Sienna did not want to leave Miranda all alone on Christmas day if Geoffrey did decide to go away.

Not being one to see the glass half empty, Sienna planned to have a royal ball all by herself. She was going to "Skype" or "What sap" her parents and friends across the miles and no doubt at some point during the day she would also speak with Melvin, hopefully Carlton too, and her other friends here in London. She prayed that Geoffrey would go out at some point during the day to enable her a free pass to pop over and see Miranda. Concern briefly clouded her thoughts as she recalled her benefactor's disclosure last evening, but she shook off those worries. After Christmas day was over with she would make it a priority to sit down with Miranda and talk, for Sienna had a feeling that her benefactor had more on her mind to share.

Sienna cooked like never before - there was no way she could eat even a quarter of what she had prepared but she intended that nothing would go to waste. The food prepared today would see her well into the New Year. "Waste not, want not" was a motto that she had grown up reciting and with it in mind, as soon as the fare cooled, she began to transfer what she anticipated would be surplus into containers for the freezer.

When she had finished in the kitchen, Sienna sat down and made the round of Skype, What sap and telephone calls. She also posted on Facebook best wishes to all her friends and family. When she called Melvin, he sounded so happy - they spoke briefly and the joy emanating from him, flowed to her, lifting her mood even higher than before. She also called Carlton and was put through to voicemail. Sienna guessed that he must be so busy with Becky that they did not want to be disturbed on this special day so she did not bother to leave a message. They would probably catch up in the New Year sometime.

The table was set for one at 3 pm. She began her meal with a prawn cocktail starter. The sauce was ready prepared and the prawns were also "ready to eat". All that had been required of the lettuce was a quick wash, shake dry and chop. Perfectly ripe avocado was scooped onto the bed of lettuce with the prawns languishing on top covered by a cladding of sauce. Sienna gave thanks and ate slowly, luxuriating in the blend of flavours which complimented each other perfectly.

As she prepared to begin her main course, Sienna's 'phone began to buzz. She had placed it on vibrate because she did not really want to speak to anyone while she ate. But whoever was trying to get her did not seem to get the message as her 'phone proceeded to buzz every few minutes.

Main course was a Turkey breast roast. She had seasoned the Turkey breast with sage, onion and thyme, layered it in bacon and placed mini sausages all around its perimeter before covering it with butter the double foil and placing it into the oven. She had also purchased a collection of prepared vegetables ready to be steamed.

A touch of Jamaica was added by spicy jerked leg of lamb and roasted sweet potato with a cheese side sauce. These dishes she had prepared from scratch - she had never cooked like this before but the resultant success proved that she had learnt more from watching her mother cook than she realised.

When Sienna had force fed herself the last spoonful of Christmas pudding with brandy sauce and cream, she felt like the proverbial stuffed turkey. Having loaded the dishwasher, she made her way into the living room where she reclined on the sofa in front of the TV. Just then her 'phone began to buzz again. "Who is that?", she soliloquised as she pressed the button to answer.

"Hello"

"Hi Sienna"

"Carlton?"

"Yeah - it's me".

"Oh, I didn't recognise your number".

"Sorry - I recently changed my 'phone and there is a mix up with transferring my number - I need to sort it out in the New Year".

"Oh - I see".

"Anyway Sienna, I was just ringing to wish you a Merry Christmas".

"Merry Christmas to you too bro - and to Becky".

"Thanks", a deep breath then Carlton added, "..but me and Becky have split up".

"What", Sienna almost shouted.

"Yeah - it was a shock to me too".

"What .... how comes ..... what happened", Sienna stuttered.

"Well it's a long story but the crux of it is that it wasn't really working out between us". "We kept on arguing a lot and eventually other people ... well one other person got involved and we decided to call it quits".

"Really"

"Yes - just like that". "I hasten to add that the other person that got involved was nothing to do with me - I was faithful even through the arguments". "I never looked at another woman".

At that point the conversation became strained as both Sienna and Carlton appreciated that although he may not have looked wilfully at another woman, his heart had strayed. Sienna had felt it - his heart belonged to her and hers to him.

****

Carlton had not been perfectly honest to Sienna - they had not called it quits but Becky had in fact left him. He would let her know the truth in time but right now it was painful to admit it - it was a man thing. Since Becky had walked out on him two days earlier, he had been thinking. He thought of the many times that he had overlooked Becky's shortcomings, had turned a blind eye to her overt flirting, had swallowed her derogatory comments about his prowess in and out of the bedroom. It was important that he satisfy himself that he had in no way engineered or contributed to the break-up, and it was only when he had dissected the circumstances and inspected the depth of his heart that he had allowed his mind to embrace the future prospects for him and Sienna now that he was definitely a free man.

From now on Carlton intended to follow his heart and Becky had done him nothing but a favour, pushing him towards his true destiny. He would embrace his love as the friend that she was and bide his time until it was right to move closer to Sienna, to become more than just her bro. For he knew that she was his only true love - she had always been, although he had initially not realised it and latterly had tried to deny it. He accepted that it was because of the differences between them - she being black and he white. It was the anxiety and worry about his family and other friends - how would they react to him being with a black girl. There were no other black people in his family. That was the reason why Carlton had never pursued the love that made him feel whole, but now he had decided that Sienna would be in his life regardless of who or what he may lose in the process. He would never let her go - she was his life, she would be his wife. It never occurred to him that Sienna might not want to marry him. He instinctively knew that she felt the same way.

"So how is your Christmas day celebration going?" Sienna asked.

"Well I'm here all alone - Becky moved out two days ago".

"Oh really?" "So when did you break up then?"

"Well we went to a party last Saturday night - we had a row during the night and Becky went off and snogged some other bloke". "Then she came back into the party hand in hand with this bloke - stood and danced with him for an hour and completely ignored me across the room". "When I got fed up, I went over and asked her what she thought she was doing and she just exploded". "The other bloke tried to interject into the argument and that's when I thought "this is silly" and walked out". "So she followed me outside and shouted after me that we were finished anyway". "Then she came back to the flat an hour later and collected some clothes and left, saying that she would come and get her other things before the New Year".

The full and true story of the break-up had tumbled out without restraint.

"So Becky was the one who ended it then", Sienna asked. It was equally important to her to know what really transpired.

"Yes - I guess so - that is truly what happened", Carlton admitted.

"Ahhh I'm sooo - sorry", and Sienna was being honest in spite of the fact that in the back of her mind was a smaller voice, shouting jubilation, reminding her that she would perhaps get a chance with Carlton now with Becky out of the way.

"Never mind Carlton - I'm sure you two will sort this all out".

"I don't care to sort it out - I'm done - that's life", Carlton said far too quickly. Sienna did not know what to say in reply and her breath caught in her throat.

"Well I'm not too sorry though - I knew things weren't 100% what they should or could be", Carlton continued pointedly.

"Uhhm", Sienna concurred.

"So you're on your own and so am I so why don't we get together - it will be just like old times".

"Yeah it will be like old times, except that Melvin won't be around", Sienna observed.

"Instead of the three musketeers it will be just the two musketeers", Carlton chuckled.

Sienna chuckled a little too hard at what was just a basic joke - if it was a joke at all. Her heart was doing somersaults and twerks as she tried to grasp the fact that the man that meant so very much to her was almost certainly free and was now openly petitioning her, albeit in the name of their long friendship. She would take that for now.

"Yeah I guess it would be great to have some company - it is Christmas day after all".

When the conversation had ended Sienna texted the address for the back entrance to Carlton, adding that he should telephone her on arrival and then wait for five minutes for her to let him in.

After mulling the development over in her mind Sienna was overcome by many emotions, fear, doubt, love and joy wrestled for pride of place within her psyche. Fear prevailed momentarily as she questioned whether she was ready to launch into a different direction with Carlton. Having decided that she was indeed ready, doubt took the reins. What would her family say about her being with a white man - it would certainly be something of a shock to them. Sienna knew that her family loved her and wanted her happiness above all - they would come around to accepting her choice in time.

"But what if he doesn't actually feel the same way that I do - what if I am only imagining that he does?" Sienna verbalised the doubtful statement. But the doubts were soon allayed as unassailable love took control of her mind.

"Of course he does", responded her ego.

"You know he does", the final word on the issue was uttered with conviction and a smile.

Sienna knew that the feelings were mutual between Carlton and herself. They were not just feelings but electrical charges - some kind of unusual chemical reaction that was undeniable. As she concluded that what they had was extraordinarily special, Sienna's heart began to sing as joy entered the fray.

Joy increased to fever pitch when Sienna began to open her presents - an oil painting from Melvin delighted her - she recalled when they had admired the painting together at an exhibition at the local library and was deeply touched by the fact that he had remembered and gone back to purchase it.

Various tokens and trinkets from her other friends and brethren filled her with glee and kept a fixed smile upon Sienna's face, cementing her joy.

"Oh my goodness", Sienna gasped as she opened the envelope from Miranda. *"Oh wow - this is too much"* , the soliloquy continued for several minutes as Sienna tried to take in the enormity of Miranda's kind gesture - she had purchased her a brand new car as a Christmas gift.

"This is too much - how can I ever repay this lady? how could she stop the tears that began to flow freely down her cheeks. They were tears of pure joy. The happiness that embraced her soul was surpassed only by that felt at past

Christmases spent with her parents and family. Sienna dialled Miranda's number and waited for an answer

"Miranda - this is too much - you really shouldn't have done this", Sienna gushed as soon as Miranda picked up.

"Happy Christmas to you too dear - I absolutely should have - no regrets". "You deserve the best", Miranda chuckled.

"But....t...t" Sienna stuttered.

"Please don't say another word Sienna - there is a serial rapist on the loose and no young girl should walk the streets alone after dark". "You absolutely need a car - do you like the colour?".

"Red and black", Sienna read from the log book that was also enclosed in the brown envelope. "Yes I love red although I haven't seen it as yet - I'm going to have a look now".

"Okay dear - its parked next to the Mini".

Sienna entered the vehicle and sat in the front seat of the brand new red MXLX Brogue. She breathed in the smell of brand new textiles and thought that she must be dreaming. *"Who does this?"* she questioned. *"This is crazy"*. Then Sienna recalled the sermon preached last Sunday entitled *"Be thankful"*. Bishop Gooden had taught that we should give thanks for all gifts received and not question the generosity of others. He had stated that God often prompted the heart of others to give gifts to His people and that we should therefore treat each gift received as one from the very heart of God.

"Thank you God - I remember that I did ask you for a car but I did not expect you to answer me is such a grand fashion - thank you so very, very much for using Miranda to bless me", Sienna prayed in earnest. She inserted the key into the ignition and listened to the sound as the engine was ignited and purred.

Although Sienna had not yet passed her driving test, she did know how to drive a little. The gift also included a complete course of driving lessons which she intended to book up as soon as the holiday was over. Until then, she would settle for sitting in the driver's seat and imagining when she would at last be able to drive it legally.

As she walked past the great house, Sienna was sorely prompted to call in on Miranda - she wanted to give her a big hug to say thank you. Geoffrey's car parked up on the other side of the forecourt deterred her, but she found herself involuntarily approaching the front door and buzzing Miranda's suite. "Come in dear".

The corridors were once again dark and eerie as though Geoffrey's negative spirit haunted them. Sienna had never noticed how dark this house was until Geoffrey moved into it. With relief she entered Miranda's suite.
"I just had to come and say "thank you" in person Miranda - you are a good person". God bless you".
"Thank you my dear Sienna - you have brought me so much joy". "The car is only a little thing - it gives me great pleasure to be able to do this for you my dear". "I have wanted to do this for a long time but I did not know what you or others might think but now it does not matter to me what anyone thinks - it is what I wanted to do and I have done it", Miranda stated emphatically.

They hugged then stood back and admired each other fondly with smiles of promise for a long and blessed friendship.

"I can't stay long I'm afraid Miranda - I'm expecting a friend but I promise to stop by and see you tomorrow, alright".

It had been almost an hour since Carlton telephoned and Sienna was expecting him imminently.

"Okay my dear - enjoy the remainder of the day with your friend".

Neither of them realised that Geoffrey was eavesdropping on their conversation. After Sienna left he confronted his mother.

"You bought her a car - mother have you lost your mind?" "You bought her a car - not just any car but a Broque - a £40,000 car?" "I thought that you had bought the car for yourself even though you no longer drive?"

"It's none of your business what I do - it's my money and I will spend it in any way that I like". "That young lady brings me a lot of happiness and this is only a small gesture for me".

"It's my money too mother - half of your wealth belongs to dad, remember".

"You're wrong - your dad was a penniless seaman when I met him". "He had nothing but the shirt on his back, so please leave me alone to spend my money in any way I please". "I am getting old and nearing my end - when I'm gone you can do as you please with what I bequeath to you but while I am alive, I will spend my money as I please".

"You silly old crowe......", Geoffrey shouted then quickly backtracked.

"Sorry mum - I didn't mean to say that - I'm sorry".

"You are just a selfish egotistical man, Geoffrey". "You are a great disappointment to me - will you ever change?"

This exchange affected Miranda more than either of them realised.

It had been nearly two hours since Sienna spoke to Carlton when she received the call announcing his arrival. She lost her chain of thought and struggled to regain it. The key to the gate was nowhere to be found and Sienna searched frantically for them. "Oh where are the keys - I knew they were on the key hanger", she scratched about for more than 5 minutes becoming more frantic with each passing minute and finally located them in her jacket pocket she now recalled she had placed them there as she made ready for Carlton's arrival.

Running as fast as she could, Sienna made her way to the gate in less than half the time it would normally take. When she saw Carlton, her eyes fixed upon his face where they remained. He spoke first.

"Hey - you took your time - I was beginning to think you weren't coming anymore"

"Sorry Carlton - I misplaced the keys".

"Oh - I see - Merry Christmas", a bunch of yellow roses and a bottle of red wine were proffered along with this greeting.

"Thanks", Sienna said then lost her voice.

Carlton had taken a taxi cab over at the cost of £40 - four times what it would usually cost. This sum was significant to him - his Assistant Solicitor's salary was not enough to get by on even with shared expenditure. He was glad that he would be starting a new job in January, paying him three times his present salary.

"It's so expensive to travel around on Christmas day", he commented involuntarily. A stroke of anxiety threatened to crash his party but euphoria at seeing Sienna shooed it away efficiently. "I can't wait to start my the new job in the New Year", Carlton chuckled mirthfully and Sienna joined in, becoming more relaxed.

The moment of relaxation soon passed and Sienna felt herself becoming more affected by Carlton's presence. Conversation was disabled as her tongue tied up securely against her will. Vainly she tried to speak but the words wouldn't come out as she gazed up into sea blue/green eyes. Standing 6' tall, his gel spiked blonde hair made him look much taller. He had never looked more handsome to Sienna's eyes, although others might think him just a tad above average.

Conversely Carlton's nervousness affected him in the opposite way - he just could not stop talking. One futile statement after another tumbled from his mouth.

"I wish I could have gotten a bus but they aren't running today". Great now she's going to think that I am a real skinflint. Carlton smiled in spite of the daunting thought.

"I wonder what time the buses will start running in the morning". Now he was digging the hole even deeper by inviting himself to stay the night. "I mean - I hope I can sleep in your guest room tonight - if that's okay", he listened anxiously for Sienna's reply.

"Oh ssssure", she didn't sound too enthusiastic.

"Are you sure cos I can always walk home - no problem". "It would only take me two hours or so", another chuckle.

Carlton's voice carried far and wide and the dogs came running and as they approached they began to growl. "Stop... stop......STOP", Sienna found her lost voice. The dogs recognised her immediately and obeyed even as they continued to eye Carlton suspiciously and whine.

"Woo Sienna - you've got the power".

Sienna smiled, "Yeah - they're harmless unless I say so, so you better behave yourself", they both laughed as the dogs scampered off.

"So how's your Christmas day going then Sienna?"

"Oh - reeery goodb", Sienna's tongue tied up again and she uttered gobbedy gook. Her heart was doing somersaults, back flips and twerks and her palms became sweaty in spite of the extreme cold of the deep mid-Winter evening.

As they arrived at the flat and she opened the door and invited him in, it suddenly dawned upon Sienna that she should not be alone with Carlton. It was just tempting fate as the attraction between them was just too strong.

"Come in from the cold", Sienna's warm smile melted Carlton heart to mush. "Thank you Lady Sienna". As she closed the door behind him suddenly their eyes met and they switched reactions. Sienna began to chatter. "What can I get you to drink - I've got almost everything - juice, wine, pop, squash, water.

Carlton responded with a shrug of his shoulders as the will to say anything other than to profess undying love for Sienna defeated him. The desire to pull her close was overwhelming - yet he resisted, for the fear of alienating her was even stronger. "And you should see what's on the menu", Sienna said rushing towards the kitchen as though in a bid to escape.

After the initial kafuffle Sienna served up the fare to a ravenous Carlton who chomped as if he had not eaten good food for a very long time. When he was fit to burst they settled on opposite sides of the lounge - he with a cava filled glass and hers filled with tropical juice. They talked late into the night as the TV and gospel music provided background ambiance. Sienna had deliberately selected gospel tracks in the hope of injecting holiness into the atmosphere for fear that she or Carlton could be overcome by ungodly thoughts.

Their points of interest were shared and seamless as they commented variously on what was on TV, current affairs and life in general.

Conscientiously Carlton resisted the continuous urge to walk over and sit next to Sienna. He wanted to cradle her in his arms - he wanted to kiss her beautiful lips - to take her to paradise, but he was well aware of Sienna's stance on intimacy and although he did not agree that even the simplest show of intimacy should be reserved only for interaction between husband and wife, he was happy to put her interest before his own. He would wait - that was settled in his mind - wherever she led he would follow - however she wanted it to be he would acquiesce. All he wanted from now on was her total happiness and he would give his life to secure that. And Carlton began to look forward to the day when he would love her totally as his wife, for he knew that was their destiny.

For her part Sienna became more relaxed in Carlton's company. She basked in the comfort and security of his presence and smiled so much and so widely that her face began to ache, but even the pain was a pleasure. She was at the beginning of her ultimate destiny - Carlton would soon be her husband. Everything would wait for she was answerable to a higher authority than her desires. And as she looked deeply into the windows of Carlton's soul, she knew there would never be a problem that they could not surmount together. Their love was built upon the solid foundation of true friendship.

As it grew later Sienna had an idea, "You can borrow my car to get home if you like as long as you bring it back", she chuckled.
"You've got a car?"

"Yes - I do", the excitement at seeing Carlton had overshadowed her excitement at receiving the gift of a car from Miranda but it now came gushing to the surface as she told him about her good fortune.

"Are you serious?"

"Yes - guess how"

"How come?"

"Miranda - my proverbial Angel got me a car for Christmas"

"Get outta here - she never did"

"Yes she did - honest - and you can borrow it until buses start running again".

"Are you sure", Carlton looked at Sienna with tenderness as he contemplated how beautiful and selfless she truly was.

"Yes - of course - I would let you keep it for days but Miranda might wonder where it is". Carlton nodded in acquiescence.

As midnight approached Sienna suggested that Carlton take her out in the new car. He couldn't wait to see and test drive it and jumped up like a shot without further prompting.

"You're kidding", Carlton exclaimed upon seeing Sienna's car. Sienna just smiled as her heart swelled with gratitude.

"Miranda bought you this car?" Carlton questioned as Sienna nodded.

"Wow, wow", the dogs came running to see what was causing the little noise in the usually deathly quiet courtyard. Upon seeing Sienna they quickly scampered away about their business. Geoffrey also looked out and fumed as he realised that Sienna and her friend were the cause of the activity in the courtyard.

"What's going on out there?" he shouted from his first floor window.

"It's me Sienna". This response was met with an abrupt slamming of the window and in a few minutes, a switching off of all the automatic courtyard lights.

When they arrived at the gates, Sienna tried to input the code to open the gates on the fob but for some reason it did not work, so she alighted the car and went to input the code manually. However, the gate still did not open. She tried and tried over and again before giving up. Unbeknownst to them Geoffrey had also switched off and disabled the front gates.

They returned to the flat where they talked some more until the wee small hours. Carlton fell asleep on the sofa. Sienna fetched a blanket and pillows and made him comfortable before going to bed herself. Before falling to sleep, she thought about their future together and when she fell asleep her fairytale unfolded more gloriously in visions of the night.

Chapter 35

December 2017 to January 2018

The ring of the telephone aroused Sienna from sleep. As she was aroused from sleep she realised that it was not her 'phone after all but the sirens of an ambulance. As she became more conscious it dawned upon her that the noise was coming from the courtyard. Grabbing her dressing gown, Sienna rushed to the door. Still wearing just her slippers she ran towards the courtyard where she saw Geoffrey standing on the veranda. He looked worried but upon catching sight of her the usual venomous glare crossed his face.

"What do you want here - go away", he shouted to her. A look of dismay crossed the ambulance driver's face as he observed Geoffrey's behaviour.

"No - I will not go away", Sienna stood up for herself to Geoffrey for the first time. He opened his mouth as though to speak but no further words were uttered.

"Is it Miranda - what's the matter with her?" The driver shook his head indicating that he did not know anything, "They're inside", he replied.

It was Miranda, she had apparently suffered a stroke. As she was wheeled out on a stretcher, Sienna got a look at her benefactor and tears streamed down her face. "Be strong Miranda - hang on in there", was all she could think of saying. "Please stand back", the paramedics fussed frantically.

"Can I come along with her to the hospital?

"Only family members are permitted to accompany the patient - are you family?" the over officious paramedic exerted an authoritative air that Sienna found annoying. Geoffrey piped up, "I'm her son and I will be driving behind the ambulance - no one else will be coming along", he announced commandingly.

He wore an expression that said he was the cat that got the cream. This made Sienna's gut boil. "Anyone would think you cared", she muttered.
"Did you say something?" the paramedic asked.
"Nothing - I just wanted to know what hospital you are taking her to, please".
"Royal Park Hospital in Kingsmere".

Sienna stood watching as the ambulance drove away. "It's as well I wasn't able to go with Miranda", she mumbled upon realising that she was still wearing her dressing gown and PJs. Then she ambled forlornly back to her flat.

"What's the matter Sienna", Carlton stretched and rubbed sleep from his eyes. He stared into Sienna's eyes - yes, she was definitely crying - but why?
"Sienna - what's wrong", he got up and followed her into the kitchen.
"It's Miranda - she's had a stroke".
"Oh no"
"They've taken her to the hospital - I wanted to go but Geoffrey.....Geoffrey...."
"Never mind Sienna - come on sit down - I'll make you a nice cup of tea", Carlton took charge. "Did you find out which hospital she went to"
"Yes".
"I'll call them later to find out about her condition - don't worry Sienna - I'm sure she will be alright", he reassured. But Sienna would not be consoled.

"Thank you Carlton", Sienna was glad that she was not facing this by herself. She wanted to cry on Carlton's shoulder but remained aware that the chemistry between them was at fever pitch - that would just be asking for trouble so she kept some distance between them. For Carlton, it was a real struggle not to draw her into his arms and comfort her but he too allowed commonsense to prevail.

****

The rest of the holiday period passed in episodes of highs and lows. One moment Sienna was wafting on a cloud of ecstasy in the knowledge that Carlton was now her very own and the next she was wallowing in sorrow about Miranda's illness.

Miranda remained in a coma for four days and Sienna spent many hours sitting by her bedside talking to her, willing her to wake up. She talked as though Miranda was listening, as when they had had their daily tete-a-tete in the past, in the happy times before Geoffrey came to stay. Sienna also read Bible verses and discussed the readings as though Miranda were a party to the discussion. In spite of the sad situation, peace embraced her spirit.

On the fifth day after the stroke, on New Year's eve afternoon, as Sienna read Psalms 23 to her, Miranda's eyes flickered open.
"Nurse - she's awake - she's out of the coma", Sienna's shouting brought several nurses running into the private ward. They fussed around carrying out several tests until they were satisfied that the patient was stable.
"I'm afraid you'll have to leave now to allow the patient to get some rest", the nurse spoke softly as though not to cause any disturbance.
"Okay - is it okay for me to just say goodbye to her?" Sienna's tone mimicked the nurse's.

"Yes - of course, but please don't be too long".

"Thank you ".

To Sienna's disappointment Miranda did not recognise her at all. It was apparent that even though she had woken up from the coma she was not herself.

"You're still lost in a world of your own, eh Miranda", Sienna kissed Miranda and stroked her cheek. Then she left the ward quietly.

The New Year celebration was bitter sweet - Carlton did his best to cheer, but in spite of the joy that he brought her, Sienna had frequent moments of sadness.

Sienna had put off going in to work over the holidays after all due to the fact that she spent most of her time with Miranda. On the first working day in 2018 she was glad to be returning to work. She had now completed her Training Contract and, having been offered full time employment as a Solicitor with Addison and Lawson, she was to begin her new job in the Private Clients department today. Moving into her new role was less challenging than anticipated as Sienna took the helm like a seasoned professional. The greater challenge was presented by the fact that there were various matters that she had to finish off in her last role which she had intended to do over the holidays but which she now had to fit into her daily schedule.

Sienna soon fell into a routine, visiting Miranda at least three evenings a week and also on Sunday afternoons after church. Saturdays were reserved for Carlton who had fallen into the routine and played the part of her beau proficiently. On Saturday afternoons Carlton gave Sienna driving lessons.

She also had once a week driving lessons with a professional during her lunch break on Wednesdays.

The agreement between them, that Carlton should drive Sienna's car until she passed her driving test, further cemented their bond. They quickly became inseparable.

****

January was cold and the Brexit negotiations and uncertainty regarding the future cast its gloom over the City of London. Conversations were dominated by the what, why and how regarding the divorce of Britain from the European Union?
Sienna was cocooned in her own world and routine of work and hospital visits. Only the joy brought by Carlton and the sunshine that briefly warmed her heart when she spoke to her parents aided her struggle to ward off the cloud of depression that threatened to engulf her mind.

The end of January brought a sense of relief and as February approached two notable events brightened Sienna's life.

The first took place the last Sunday in January. She had been to Sunday morning service where she had prayed earnestly for Miranda and during her visit that afternoon, as she sat telling her benefactor what had transpired at church, Miranda spoke for the first time since she had suffered the stroke. The sentence was slurred but Sienna deciphered it "Weeee es Simooooon?".
"Simon - you mean your son?"
"Wweee es Simooon - aass anyone seeeen him".
"Simooooon....."

"Asss ....seen Simooon"

Miranda was in a zone and repeated the same questions over again and again more than twenty times. At first Sienna tried to engage in meaningful conversation but to no avail so she stopped trying and simply listened. As Miranda began the sentence again, a tear trickled from her left eye and touched Sienna's heart. She lifted Miranda's right hand and held it tightly.

"Okay Miranda - I promise I will find Simon for you - I will do my best to find him - I promise". Sienna said gently as she looked into Miranda's eyes. She saw a glint of remote hope registered there.

"Simooon", Miranda repeated over and over, signifying to Sienna that she understood the promise. And Sienna made an inward vow to leave no stone unturned in order to keep it. If she failed it would not be for want of trying.

Later when Carlton came to collect her, Sienna told him what had transpired.

"Miranda spoke today - she kept on asking for Simon - over and over again, all she said was "Where is Simon - has anyone seen Simon". "So I promised her that I would find her son Simon for her".

"Her son Simon? "I thought he was called Geoffrey".

"Didn't I mentioned to you before about her missing son?" "Well it's a very long story - she apparently has another son called Simon".

"Oh - I don't recall you mentioning it before - so what happened to him"?

"Well, like I said it's a long story". "Just before she suffered the stroke she told me a story about a son that she had". "She said that he is black - can you believe that?"

"Really - I can't imagine that", Carlton sniggered.

"Well apparently she has an interesting past - she had a son who is black".

"What before she got married", Carlton's eyes flicked between the road ahead and to look at Sienna sitting in the passenger seat.

"Well she was married to her husband at the time apparently".

"It gets juicier by the minute", Carlton said then sniggered. Sienna nudged him, "Stop it you", she said then continued. "She told me that they put the boy up for adoption". "Now she wants me to help in locating him".

"So how are you going to do that?"

"Well she told me the hospital that he was born at so I guess we can start there". "I remember the date that she said he was born on as well, 27 January 1949".

"Okay, well that is a good start - if you need any help I'm available", Carlton reached over and squeezed Sienna's hand in a show of support as they waited at a red light.

"Thanks baby", she reciprocated his affection with a warm kiss intended for his cheek. He turned just in time for it to land on the side of his mouth and both shared a deep intimate moment.

"Love you Sienna"

"Love you more Carlton".

"No - I love you more"

"Okay you win - for now", they both shared a moment of ecstatic joy as they laughed loudly. It felt so good to be in love.

That evening Sienna began her quest. She "Googled" the name of the Garston Hospital and learned that it had closed down sometime in the 90s. The rest of her evening was spent in contemplation of what her next step should be. She decided to ask Melvin for the private investigator's details. But first she wanted to carry out some preliminary investigation by herself before briefing the professional.

"I'm going to begin at the library nearest to the site of the old hospital", she informed Carlton. "They must have some useful information, records or something that could assist in the investigation", Carlton listened - what he heard did not please him much. They already had limited time together due to the fact that Sienna spent every minute that she could at Miranda's hospital bedside and now this.

"Well if you need any help let me know", anyone within earshot of this comment would think that Carlton's heart was in it.

"Oh you're so sweet - that is why I love you so much", Sienna pressed all the right buttons in Carlton's heart without even knowing that she was doing so.

"You know you can count on me sweetheart", he would say anything just to hear her say she loved him again.

"Ahh I'll hold you to that though", Sienna replied then continued, "Are you sure you don't mind Carlton?" Sienna's voice sounded like a tuneful chime - Carlton was captivated. He replied.

"Of course I don't mind - I said I would help". "That's what husbands are for", Carlton said then winked cheekily at Sienna.

"Husband eh", Sienna said as she blushed in unexpected places. Carlton's smile was fixed.

"You're taking a lot for granted Carlton Haines - I mean you haven't even asked me".

"Just you wait and see", Carlton's comment was loaded with promise.

Carlton agreed to Sienna's suggestion that he attend the library closest to where the hospital had been situated and begin his research the very next day.

"It's not that far from my office - I'll go straight after work before I pick you up from the hospital", he reassured.

"Great - love you lots"

"Love you too".

The search was made significantly less difficult by the fact that the library had computerised all its records and Carlton was able to search much quicker than anticipated. Having searched extensively over and again, he was unable to find any baby with the name of "Simon" born at the Garston hospital in 1949 and none at all born there on 27 January 1949.

There was something that caught his attention though, a note that one baby boy had been left as unwanted at the entrance to that hospital. The child's name was given as "Moses", but there was no further information.

It occurred to Carlton that there might be some corresponding news in the local newspapers and so he searched using the weekly local newspapers for the whole month of January 1949 for any entry about "Moses". He waded through various headlines in the Islington Standard, flicked through "Factory Closure - hundreds lose their jobs", skim read "Murder Most Foul", glanced over "Protest at Strip Club Opening", before hitting upon the report "Coloured Baby Abandoned". The news was sketchy but concluded that the baby was to be put into care with the hope that suitable adoptive parents could be found. The report stated that the parents of the baby were unknown - there was no further information.

A search of the record of births rendered no result for a baby boy born on 27 January 1949 in Islington. Only two babies, both girls, were born on that day.

After only an hour and a half Carlton felt he had found out all that he could and called it a day. He headed off to the hospital to meet Sienna, as he telephoned her to let her know what progress he had made in his search.

Having gone as far as they could hope to with their search, Sienna decided that it was time to hand the matter over to a professional. So she telephoned Melvin to obtain the Private Investigator's details, Mike Cotton who had assisted him in the search for his father.

It had been over a month since either Sienna or Carlton had spoken to Melvin. Since they had exchanged New Years greetings with him, Sienna and Carlton had had little time for anything or anyone else but each other and the various events of their lives. They were engrossed in the novelty of their new relationship. They slotted in quality time together between work and visits to and from the hospital, in Sienna's case to visit Miranda and in Carlton's case either to drop her off, to collect her or to accompany her.

After Sienna had conveyed numerous apologies for not having been in touch for so long, she and Melvin talked, catching up on what each had been up to.
"Well I have been dealing with my own dilemma", Melvin reported. Guilt tugged at Sienna's heartstrings as Melvin narrated the adversity he had faced alone.
"I was arrested by the Police on suspicion of murder".
"Murder?"
"Yes - Amy was murdered and they brought me in for questioning and subsequently charged me with murder - I was there for over a week". "I almost lost my job over it. It was fortunate that they found DNA at the crime scene which matched to someone else and they released me straight away with a written apology". "It was lucky for me that none of my bosses or colleagues took any notice of the malicious gossip being spread around about me and Amy having been an item by Gloria, the office busybody". "It was

down to their persistence that the Police were placed under pressure to find real evidence that vindicated me". "In fact my employers are also backing me in a complaint against the Police in the way that they handled my arrest and detention because they apparently acted on a tip off from someone with absolutely no physical or other evidence whatsoever. I suspect that it was Gloria who tipped them off - that awful woman.

"Oh my goodness - Melvie I am so so very sorry - you should have called me - or Carlton - why didn't you let us know?"

"Oh I was just in my own zone - I didn't want to get you two involved with this mess - I knew I was innocent and I hoped that I would be proven to be so - sooner or later".

"But Melvin - you should have called us".

"But you could have called me too, Sienna".

"If I had known that you were going through that I would certainly have been there for you, Melvie - you know that". "Yes - I'm sorry that I haven't been in touch". "I feel hurt that you did not see fit to call on me..... and Carlton... in your hour of dire need". "That's what friends are for Melvie". "Promise me that you will never do anything like that again".

"Ok - yeah I guess I should have let you two know and I promise I would never leave you out again".

Sienna proceeded to explain to Melvin how much of her time had been monopolised by the Miranda's illness. "She needs me and I have been there for her but I admit that I should have made more time for others too - sorry Melvie".

"Oh yeah - I remember you telling me that she had a stroke but I didn't realise that it was that serious". "Sorry I have not been in touch to ask how she was doing....".

"No need to apologise - like you say you had your own plate of tripe to eat", Sienna interjected, then continued.

"Her son Geoffrey hardly ever visits her and I have felt it incumbent upon me to go that extra mile".

"Umh - I hear you Sienna - I love you for your caring heart", this comment absolve some of the guilt that Sienna felt for not having been there for Melvie in his hour of need.

"Carlton has been my rock.... he's been going through everything with me so please forgive him too for not having been in touch"

"So you guys are tight now, huh?"

"Yeah - we are close", Sienna admitted. She did not realise that her and Carlton being together was partly the reason why Melvin had not been in touch. It took him time to deal with his emotions and was now at a place where he could wish them the best and mean it from the heart.

"I guess I always knew you two were meant to be together", Melvin divulged.

"What do you mean?" Sienna questioned.

"The way you looked at each other sometimes - I knew there was something unspoken between you ", Melvin teased and continued, "And what was also obvious was that Becky did not love Carlton so I'm glad he found out before he tied the big knot".

"Do divulge your meaning Melvin - as far as I knew Becky was madly in love with Carlton?"

"No - she wasn't - would you believe that she came on to me on several occasions".

"What... really - are you serious?"

"Yes - even at their engagement party she cornered me outside in the car park and tried to snog me".

"What - never - you're joking right", Sienna gasped then chuckled disbelievingly.

"No I'm not - you remember when I disappeared for a long time - well I was outside with Becky, trying to fight her off".

"No...."

"Yes - she was coming on to me big time - said that I was the one she really wanted - said she would gladly call off the engagement if I would agree to go away with her somewhere", Melvin took a deep breath then launched on with his narration, "She said she was in love with me". "In fact she has been belling my 'phone almost every day for the past month, but I know her number so I don't answer". "Claire told me that she even called at the flat twice looking for me but I am hardly ever home these days due to work, family and a certain new lady in my life, Sandra", Melvin sounded excited.

"You're dating now?" Sienna chimed.

"Yes - I am indeed - we must get together sometime so I can introduce you".

"Sure thing - that will be great - just let us know when and where you want to meet and we will pull out the stops to show up".

"I'll give Carlton a call later - I haven't spoken to him in way too long".

"By the way Melvin - you know the Private Investigator who helped you to find your dad - do you think you could let me have his details?" "There is a job that I need him to do".

"I knew you had to have a reason to call me these days", Melvin teased.

"No - don't say that - you know you are always on my mind". "We all must do better in keeping in touch in future", Sienna concluded.

"I guess so", Melvin said and added "I'll text you the details".

Sienna instructed the Private Investigator immediately she had received the text from Melvin. With Miranda's prognosis uncertain she wanted to do all that she could to reunite her with her son before she either suffered another stroke or worse - it was the least that she could do for this selfless woman who had done so much for her and consequently, for the betterment of her entire family.

Mike Cotton was very confident that it would be possible to trace Simon.
"Yes - since you have a date and place of birth, it should be relatively easy to trace him", he had reassured.
"That's great news - I certainly hope that you can - it's very important", Sienna gushed excitedly. "How long do you think it will take?"
"Hopefully not too long - a month or two perhaps"
"I would so much appreciate it if you could expedite".
"Okay - I'll do my best".
"Thanks a lot Mr Cotton".

The following week Mr Cotton telephoned Sienna - he thought he might be on to something, or someone but he was not certain. He said that he needed the DNA from Miranda so that a test could be carried out to ascertain whether the individual that he had located was her biological son.

Sienna was able to gather the DNA from Miranda easily. The next time that she visited, that very evening, she brought with her some cotton buds which she was able to insert into Miranda's mouth when the nurses were out of the room. She rubbed it against Miranda's inner cheek, ensuring that it was soaked through with saliva. Next morning on her way to work, Sienna delivered the DNA sample to Mr Cotton's office. She felt excitement build with anticipation that the DNAs would match and that Simon, or whatever he was now called, would be proven to Miranda's long lost son.

Chapter 36

February 2018

The second amazing thing that happened was that Carlton proposed to Sienna - in draft. They had just eaten Sunday dinner on 25 February - Sienna would never forget that date, when Carlton went down on one knee and asked her.

"Sienna - you must know you mean the world to me - I want us to get married as soon as possible - if you'll have me, I'd love to become your husband".

"You mean all it took for you to propose was a beautifully cooked meal, eh Carlton?", Sienna said as she chuckled.

"Technically it is a draft proposal, actually, as I haven't brought the ring as yet - so what do you say?"

"Well, I say yes, but of course it is a draft reply", Sienna replied and they both fell about laughing until they cried.

Bursting with joy Sienna had shared this draft news, as though it was the real thing with her family the next time they spoke - she wanted to gauge their response.

"Dad, I've met this amazing English man and he wants to marry me", Sienna held her breath unsure of the reaction that she would receive to this news.

"Marriage - how long have you known this man for Sienna - can he be trusted".

"Yes daddy - I have known him for 5 years now".

Alexander was the typical daughter's daddy. When Sienna was born he had vowed to fight off every unwanted man that came around his baby. And he had always lived up to that promise. Now she was talking about marriage and the first thing he knew he had to do was meet this culprit and vet him thoroughly.

"You must bring him to Jamaica - we have to meet him before any talk of marriage", Alexander said commandingly.

"Marriage - Sienna - what she getting married?" Sienna heard Myra, her mother say in the background.

"It has been nearly 7 years now since we waved you goodbye at Montego Bay Airport and high time that you paid us a visit", Alexander spoke gently, tempering his initial knee-jerk response.

"Dad I would love to - it would be so wonderful to see you all but I can't come at the moment due to work and other commitments".

"Oh - I see", regret was registered in Alexander's baritone.

"But why don't you and mummy come over here instead", Sienna heard herself say. She knew her parents could not afford the fare and that if they decided to come it would be all on her.

"We would love to come if we could", Alexander said whimsically.

"You can dad - you and mum can come", Sienna said, settling the uncertainty. "I will send you a letter of invitation which I believe you need to take to the British High Commissioner in Kingston so that they can grant you a visitor's visa.

"Okay", Alexander replied uncertainly.

"Okay what - Sienna coming to Jamaica?" Myra asked in the background.

"No she wants us to go to London", Alexander answered his wife.

"Us - go to London? Myra continued the inquisition.

"Yes".

"So dad - I will arrange to send a letter of invitation - can I speak to mum now, please?".

Next day Sienna sent off the letter of invitation to her parents, asking them to come and visit her in London for the Easter holidays. As she posted it, her excitement reached past fever pitch. Later that day she also sent them £2,500 to cover their air fare and other expenses. Miranda had never cancelled the bursary payments despite the fact that she was no longer a student but was now a full-time worker and Sienna had amassed a substantial nest egg as a result. Sienna had reminded her several times to do so but all she ever said was, "It is not a problem, dear, relax and enjoy". Sienna could not be happier as anticipation and excitement buoyed her through each day.

Between them, Sienna and Carlton had also managed to save £3,000 towards their wedding which they intended to keep low key and she had not touched that money.

Carlton had started his new job and was earning an excellent salary. In an endeavour to save money for the engagement and wedding rings, for the wedding and also towards a deposit on their matrimonial home, he had moved out of the flat that he had shared with Becky and into a one-room flat share.

Chapter 37

January to February 2018

The Police had been in touch with Sister Newson - they said they were looking for her son Jonathan in relation to a very serious incident. She had overheard two of the officers as they left her home. They were discussing the murder of a young lady called Amy Warren which they believed had taken place last November. And Sister Newson gathered that they were looking for Jonathan as he was the main suspect in the murder of that young lady. "Murder - murder - Jonathan - a murderer - God forbid - oh no - not the son that I suckled - that I nurtured - brought him up to fear God and have manners - to respect human life", Sister Newson soliloquised. "No not Jonathan - it could never have been Jonathan". Yet even as she denied it verbally, her heart pounded out a doubt.

The recollection of the supposedly accidental death of Jonathan's ex girlfriend, who had been found dead in a deserted supermarket car park sprung to the forefront of Sister Newson's mind. The cause of death had been blunt force trauma to the head. Initially the Police had believed her death to be a homicide and had suspected and questioned Jonathan extensively, as the only one with a motive to see her dead, as they had recently had an acrimonious break-up, but without any evidence to prove his guilt they had dropped the case against him and her death had instead been ruled a hit and run incident. In all honesty Sister Newson too had inwardly questioned her son's behaviour following Genny's death, especially in light of his comments variously that "it couldn't have happened to a better person" or "rest in peace gold-digger" and such the like, following which he would snigger. She had pushed her concerns tidily to the back of her mind then, but now it occurred to her that one could not continue to ignore the roar of a lion at an open door or they would do so to their own peril.

Sister Newson pondered - was Jonathan truly an ogre? She conceded that she had good reason to believe that he was. And if so what steps should she take now that she strongly suspected that he had Sienna in sight as his next target. Depression clouded in upon Sister Newson's mind as she regretted that she had treated the beautiful Sienna the way that she had, all because of her misplaced and flawed loyalty, and blind love for her delinquent son. She had chosen to disbelieve what she knew to be the truth. And now she could no longer continue to bury her head in the sand for she believed there was a real and imminent danger to Sienna.

Completely out of character, Jonathan telephoned her often of late, always asking her to invite Sienna around. Sister Newson recalled that the last time that she had done so she had seen Jonathan following Sienna. She had wondered then what her son was up to, had watched as he left his car to follow the young lady. Yet she had kept her mouth firmly shut, had kept her fears buried deep inside. But now her conscience was working overtime - she was losing sleep and her nerves were frayed. She recalled the date that Jonathan had followed Sienna - it was the same night that the girl Amy Warren had apparently met her death.

With the benefit of loneliness and solitude Sister Newson had had time to think. She reminisced about the time when Sienna lived with her. Since the passing of her husband and departure of her children, those were in truth the happiest days for her. She missed Sienna - that innocent and humble young lady. She had to face up to the fact that to say that she had been grossly unfair to Sienna was a huge understatement. Jonathan's obvious obsession with Sienna was gnawing at her conscience too. The truth stared her in the face - she had known her son to be a rapist for many years, having discovered his trophies and diary entries secreted away beneath his bed when he was but a teenager. She had kept his secrets buried to the back of her psyche and lied to herself. Unbeknownst to her Jonathan was not only a convicted rapist but a violent offender too. She was only beginning to appreciate the true extent and proliferation of his crimes.

Over past months she had been watching the news reports of rapes in Hertfordshire and London, and the mention of a grey coloured motor vehicle and the description of a tall, well built black male, and she had questioned whether Jonathan was involved, yet still she had cradled the ghastly secrets and shooed the voice of suspicion into silence. But the revelation from the Police and constant effort of denial since then was becoming too much for her senile mind to handle and she was relenting. While she might have been able to live with the thought that her son was a rapist, murder was another category of crime entirely which demanded a completely different reaction. How would she appease her conscience if she discovered that the Police were right, that she was shielding a murderer? The Police did not usually get things that wrong and even if they were wrong, the situation had to be investigated further to reach the right conclusion - what if they were right and Jonathan's next victim turned out to be Sienna? Would she be able to live out her few remaining days in peace - and what would transpire after death - would the Court of heaven pardon her actions? Could she face her God as an aider and abetter of a murderer. "Thou shalt not kill" resounded constantly in her mind and Sister Newson knew that the answer was "No - she could not shield a murderer - not even one who had suckled upon her own breasts".

Sister Newson wasted no time in telephoning Jonathan. Her intention was to get him to visit by saying that Sienna was coming. As usual she was put through to voicemail and she begun to leave a message.

"Hi, Jonathan - it's me mum - Sienna .... ".

"Mum what's up", came the brusque salute as Jonathan picked up the receiver.

"Hello son - how are you - are you okay?"

"Yeah - I'm alive but I could be much better". "I really need some money that is my main problem", Jonathan sounded on edge and in a hurry.

"Money?", the questioning word hung in the air for a few seconds until Jonathan spoke again.

"Yes mum money - I need some money - m...o...n...e...y, Jonathan spelt out the word insolently. "So can you help me out?"

"Well all I have is £25 to last me for the rest of the week so I guess the answer is "No - I can't help you out this time son", Sister Newson's tone betrayed her growing exasperation with her son.

"What kind of mother are you anyway - you've never got anything to give your children".

"I am the kind of mother who brought you up single-handedly after your father died", indignation stung the back of Sister Newson's eyes as she recalled her struggle.

"And ... so what .... that was what you were supposed to do". "After all I didn't bring myself into the world - did I?" This statement further irritated Sister Newson and she let rip as tears spilt from her eyes.

"Look Jonathan - you are a grown man and it is about time you were standing on your own two feet", She had never spoken to her son in this manner before but it was high time she did. Why should she keep subbing this middle-aged delinquent fellow who no longer cared about her or anyone else but himself.

Sister Newson was just about to end the call abruptly when it occurred to her that she was straying from her agenda, which was to lure Jonathan to her home, so she quickly changed her tone. "Anyway, I have a little savings put aside - it was for a rainy day but you can have it, okay son".

"How much?"

"£250".

"Is that all - well it will have to do I guess", Jonathan's tone was thankless.

"What time are you coming round to get it?

"About 6.30 - bye"

"See you later then", Sister Newson replied before realising that she was talking to herself - Jonathan had cut the line.

The hardest thing that Sister Newson had ever done in her life was to shop out her own son, but she realised that she had no other reasonable option.

As soon as the conversation with Jonathan ended, Sister Newson dialled the number that the Police had left with her. "Hello is that Inspector Pratt...."

When she had finished speaking with the Police, Sister Newson set about preparing her sons favourite meal. She did so with love and care - it would be the last time she cooked for her son if the allegations being levied against him proved to be true.

Just as she had finished cooking Sister Newson heard someone at her front door. She thought it was the Police and prayed that Jonathan did not see them entering. But it wasn't the Police - Jonathan had arrived earlier than expected - it was just 6 pm.

"Hello son", Sister Newson's voice cracked nervously. How would she explain to Jonathan that she did not in fact have the money that he had come for.

"So where is the dosh?" he looked every bit the classic fugitive. Sweat bathed his forehead and his eyes darted constantly in every direction as though seeking out adversaries lying in wait.

"Son come and sit down - I just finished preparing your favourite red peas soup", Sister Newson was buying time.

Against his better judgment Jonathan reluctantly obeyed - he never could resist his mother's red peas soup. His mouth began to water, "Well I'm in a hurry but I will have a little soup", he said abruptly.

"Okay son - I'll be very quick", Sister Newson said and darted off to the kitchen. She shouted conversation as she prepared her son's meal. "So how is the traffic this evening?"

"Look mum - just hurry up with the food - I'm not in the mood for talking"

"Okay son - I won't be a minute - just coming", Sister Newson began to fret - what if the Police didn't come in good time? What would she do. She continued to play for time.

"What's taking you so long to prepare the food".

"I'm just heating it up son".

"I thought you just finish cooking it"

"Yes son, but I know you like it nice and hot so just a couple of minutes in the microwave, that's all".

"Well hurry up - I've got to get going soon.

The sound of chaos emanated from the kitchen "What's going on?" Jonathan shouted as he rushed to see.

"Oh no - I dropped your basin of soup - let me mop up the floor".

"You know what I'll get my own food", Jonathan shouted, adding "You're just useless- look at you - you're hopeless".

He proceeded to walk across the kitchen to get a basin and then to the cooker where he began to ladle soup into it, presenting a challenge to his mother's efforts to mop up. Then he marched across the kitchen floor, distributing the soup wherever he tread, including on the living room carpet.

Jonathan ate hastily as Sister Newson cleaned up the kitchen floor slowly. Soon he was finished.

"Mom I want to go now - can you get me the money", he shouted.

"Yes son - I'm just coming", Sister Newson looked at the digital clock on the microwave - 6.18 pm. She continued cleaning up as she counted the minutes - 6.19 pm. The microwave clock was always 2 minutes slow so it was really 6.21 pm, she thought which provided some comfort. She hoped that the Police would come early. "Coming son", she prayed that the Police would come now.

"Look - tell me where the money is and I will get it myself", Jonathan boomed irately.

"Hang on son - I'm just coming". She heard footsteps going up the stairs and rushed after them. As she did so, she slipped on the wet floor and landed with a thump, hitting her head against the corner of the old cast iron kitchen sink and then again on the stone floor.

Jonathan searched the bedroom, ransacking it efficiently. He knew all his mother's usual hiding places. After 2 minutes, he knew that there was no money in the bedroom.

"Look mum - you better come and give me the money you promised", he shouted. Upon receiving no response he ran down the stairs two at a time and headed into the kitchen.

"Mum - where's the ******money", he demanded. "Mum - mum". Jonathan stood over his mother as she lay semi-conscious on the kitchen floor. "Stupid useless cow", he cussed. "What's the matter with you - get up", he reached down and grabbed her by the arm.

Sister Newson tried to get up but her feet failed her. Jonathan released her arm and it flopped down to her side. She tried to crawl over to the chair to lever herself to her feet but the effort was proving too much. Grunting loudly Sister Newson kept on trying to get to her feet.

Instead of investigating his mother's condition further, Jonathan turned and walked back into the living room where he located her bag and sought for her purse. Having extracted £25 and emptied all the loose change which he placed into his pocket, Jonathan headed towards the front door. As he closed the front door behind him, he walked straight into two Policemen as they entered the front garden.

"Well, well, if it isn't Jonathan Newson", Inspector Pratt announced for the whole neighbourhood to hear.
"The very man that we are looking for", the second Policeman emulated his superior.
"Hello officers - so why are you looking for me then?" Jonathan replied innocently.
"You tell us Jonathan - we're listening", Inspector Pratt gestured towards the door, "shall we go inside for a little chat".
"I was just leaving", Jonathan replied.
"Well it's up to you - we can do this inside or out here for all the neighbours to observe - it will only take a couple of minutes and its far more private behind closed doors, wouldn't you say, Jonathan?"

Jonathan was in a hurry. He needed to get a smoke so he re-opened the door and let the Policemen in. Hopefully they didn't have anything on him in which case it wouldn't take long. Inspector Pratt entered the living room and plumped himself down in the armchair. He invited Jonathan to take a seat as though he were the proprietor of the home. "Take a seat Jonathan".

Jonathan obeyed. "So what's this all about officers?".

The second Policeman paced about the living room, observing. He was annoying Jonathan whose eyes flashed anger when he looked over at him.

"Well Jonathan it appears that you have been a naughty boy - no let me re-phrase that, a very naughty boy", Inspector Pratt stated. He looked intently into Jonathan's eyes, gauging his reaction.

"I don't know what you're talking about", Jonathan replied, becoming agitated.

"Yes you do - does the name "Amy" ring any bells?", Inspector Pratt pulled his glasses down to look over the top of them.

"Amy - I don't know anyone called Amy I'm afraid officer".

"You see that causes me some concern Jonathan because we have sound information that suggests otherwise - you knew Amy alright - it appears to us that you knew her very well indeed".

Jonathan began to shuffle from side to side in his seat. He did not know what else to say as he wasn't aware what they had on him so he thought it best to say nothing more.

Meanwhile the second Policeman peeked through the crack in the kitchen door. "Inspector come and have a look at this", he proclaimed as he pushed the door open. As Inspector Pratt headed towards the kitchen, Jonathan saw his opportunity to escape and bolted for the door.

"Get him Stanley", Inspector Pratt shouted and the second Police officer gave chase. Within a few strides Jonathan was rugby tackled to the floor "Got you", the officer announced triumphantly as Inspector Pratt caught up and placed the handcuffs on him.

With Jonathan safely handcuffed, Inspector Pratt rang for an ambulance but by the time they arrived it was too late for Sister Newson. Now Jonathan was charged with the murder of two people. He continued to deny both charges. Eventually he accepted the murder plea for Amy but continued to deny that he had murdered his mother, but no-one believed him.

Chapter 38

February - April 2018

Each day that passed saw Sienna's expectancy grow - she could not wait to see her parents. But added to her incredibly busy schedule was the task of preparing for their imminent arrival. Without any difficulty whatsoever they were granted leave to travel to London. The flights were booked and they were due to arrive on the Easter Sunday. They would be staying for 2 months and Sienna and Carlton were hoping they would get to know him in that time and give their blessings to them getting married.

****

Miranda's condition continued to improve and by mid-March, in the face of pressure from his mother and her personal physician who felt it was in her best interest, Geoffrey had reluctantly arranged for her to return home with a nurse employed to live in and provide 24 hour nursing care. Her doctor would also be on call around the clock. Sienna breathed a sigh of relief - it would prove easier to juggle her responsibilities for work, and that she had assumed for Miranda, when she was back at home.

Sienna no longer felt intimidated by Geoffrey who lately hung his head down each time he encountered her. It was apparent that he did have some form of conscience after all. Each time Sienna bumped into him she felt empowered by his reaction. He could not make eye contact with her. This she put down to the fact that he had treated his mother in a most appalling manner since her hospitalisation, his visits to her having been sporadic and fleeting - never more than once a week for less than an hour at a time.

The contempt that Sienna felt towards Geoffrey with each passing day had built a bonfire of rebellion that was kindled within her heart. She defied him and entered Miranda's living quarters at will, ignoring his sneers and snorts which had diminished to de minim. There was no way she would allow his bad attitude to deny this dear woman of her genuine love and care, just because he was related to her by blood.

A day after her return home, Miranda had enjoyed a visitation from Mr Lawson. Following that visit, Mr Lawson had intimated to Sienna that they had discussed Miranda's affairs, including the drawing up of a new Will. He also told her in confidence that Miranda had asked him to ensure that Sienna had the right to remain living at High Trees and to come and go as she pleased no matter what happened in future. Buoyed by that revelation Sienna started to do just that. Having asked Andrew's opinion, he confirmed to Sienna that she would be at liberty to live in the flat with an invitee such as a partner or husband if she so pleased. This news was music to Sienna's ear. She and Carlton could get married sooner than anticipated now that they had somewhere to live.

On occasions when she passed Geoffrey in the hallways Sienna held her head high, nose in the air and walked on boldly. For his part Geoffrey had adopted an attitude of tolerance.

Although she had never voiced this concern to anyone, Sienna questioned within herself whether Geoffrey really loved his mother at all. Each time she contemplated the question, his actions provided food to nurture the growing doubt. She felt that by standing up to him she was also standing up for Miranda against an egotistical man whose reckless attitude was doing nothing to better his mother's health.

****

Geoffrey tolerated Sienna - she was doing what he should be - she was doing him a big favour so he could put up with her - for now. But he hoped and dreamed of the day when he became king of the castle, as soon as his mother breathed her last he had every intention of changing things for good. And the first thing that would change is that Sienna and her invitees would no longer be welcomed to stay.

Some nights Geoffrey prayed, and whichever god he prayed to knew that one of his constant requests was for Miranda to go to rest for good and soonest. Geoffrey felt no pang of remorse in wishing his mother dead - after all, with her alive he was being denied his rightful position. She was almost 90 years old, for goodness' sake, it was about time she gave up the ghost. He had waited for long enough and was now getting old himself. How much longer would he have to wait to get his hands on the fortune that she still controlled. All hope that the stroke would have finished her off were now fading as the old battle axe looked to be making a fast and full recovery.

After she had suffered the stroke, every day he anticipated receiving the call to tell him that she had kicked the proverbial bucket, but that call had never come and now she was back home, recovering fast and he was still waiting, waiting and longing for the day when he could get his hands on all her assets, the day when her Will was revealed by Lawson, who was her confidante.

Geoffrey regarded Lawson with some animosity since although he was his partner, Lawson was more loyal to his mother than he was to him.

Lawson had his mother's Will hidden away somewhere - only he knew where it was and now Geoffrey wished that the old sod would drop dead too because Lawson had also begun to stand up for Sienna. He had become aware, through Trudy's snooping around the office, of a document that Lawson had drawn up at Miranda's behest, giving the black ***** a right to remain at High Trees after her death. And Geoffrey was convinced that although his mother appeared sane, she had in fact lost her marbles a long time ago. What on earth was she thinking - accommodating strays at High Trees in the first place. Doing so during her lifetime was one thing but allowing them the right to remain after her death was quite another. Geoffrey certainly had no intention of honouring that wish. Miranda, Lawson and Sienna would pay any price he liked, even the ultimate price, to allow him full control. It was his time and he so rightfully deserved to rule now as an only son. And he would reign by any means necessary. He would find a way to quash any legal arrangement that allowed any kind of concession to anyone else, especially some black stray from the streets. He knew what he had to - he would begin by searching through Lawson's files while he was on holiday in a couple of weeks' time.

Chapter 39

March 2018

The week before Easter brought good news. Mr Connor telephoned Sienna and changed her day from bright to celestial. "I have great news", he announced.

"Let me guess - you have found Simon".

"Yes".

"Wow - that's so great", Sienna enthused.

"Yes - we found him, and he was just as excited to be found by his mother as you sound right now", Mr Connor chuckled. It always made him feel so fulfilled when he was able to help a client resolve a problem. And today he was buoyed by the obvious joy of the parties on either side of this transaction. This was a favourite part of his job, bringing long lost relatives together and he could not be happier as he conveyed the news to Sienna. "He is called Julius Anderton".

"Julius Anderton - that name rings a bell".

"Funny you should say that, I tracked that gentleman before a few months ago for another client".

"It was a strange and wonderful coincidence. I could not find any record of a baby boy having been born on 27 January 1949". "So I decided to search the local newspapers". "I came across the story of a baby boy that was found abandoned on the front steps of the Garston hospital on the following day, 28 January 1949". "As I read the story, I immediately recalled that another gentleman I had traced a few months ago had told me a similar story about his nativity". "He had narrated his story with the intent of instructing me to find his biological parents". "He told me all he knew, but in the end he never formally instructed me to proceed after the initial consultation". "It is as though God himself has orchestrated this chain of events", Sienna listened and she found this story fascinating.

"So that was why I needed the DNA from Miranda". "I also contacted Mr Anderton for his DNA sample, and to my pleasant surprise it came back as a perfect match - mother to son", Mr Connor continued, then said, "The hardest thing I had to do was wait for the DNA test result to come back", he laughed heartily at what he considered to be a very funny joke.

"Wow - what an amazing happenstance", Sienna spoke at last as she surmised that God's divine hand may truly have intervened. "Thank God", she concluded.

"Amen - such a twist of fate", Mr Connor concurred then continued, "Hold the line a moment - I need to take an urgent call on the other line".

Excitement mounted as Sienna waited for Mr Connor to return and speak with her. She couldn't wait to deliver the good news to Miranda. At last she would be reunited with her son. Carlton would be just as happy as she was to hear this news too.

"Sorry about that", Mr Connor apologised for the break in conversation then launched on. "Okay so Mr Anderton is very excited - he cannot wait to meet his mother". "Would it be in order to pass on her details to him?" "Apparently he has been hoping to find his real parents for many years but without success due to the fact that he had very limited information". "DNA was his last resort".

"Oh that is truly amazing", Sienna felt so good she could burst. She had kept her word and Miranda was going to get the chance to be reunited with her long lost son.

"Mr Anderton seems well adjusted - I don't think there will be any danger in passing on his mother's details, but it would be a good idea to have someone else present when they meet for the first time - just in case", Mr Harris cautioned.

"Okay - I will arrange that", Sienna promised then confirmed Miranda's details could be released to Julius Anderton.

Thirty minutes later when Sienna told Miranda that Simon had been found, tears rolled down the elderly woman's face, as a lopped-sided smile revealed her joy.

"My Simon", Miranda repeated time and time again.

"Miranda - there is something that I need to ask you - did you abandon Simon at the hospital?"

As Miranda's mind processed the question her smile slowly faded, then she nodded, "Buutt - he was in d...danger - great ... danger". And as her memories peeled back time Miranda began to weep.

Miranda gestured that she wanted to go outside, so Sienna helped her into her wheelchair and wheeled her to the spot where she was accustomed to sitting for many hours, beneath the leylandii. The unusually warm Spring air soothed the spirit and calmed the soul. Both Miranda and Sienna breathed deeply and a relaxed atmosphere engulfed them. Miranda lolled her head to one side and began to narrate the story of Simon's birth and abandonment.

I met my husband Michael when I was just 18 years old. I was young, naive and impressionable. Michael became everything to me. I hung upon his every word. I was his willing slave and he was my commanding master. Four months after we met Michael and I got married. I didn't really want to marry Michael - he had shown me a side to him that I didn't like - I was scared of him sometimes and I didn't feel ready for marriage, but I was pregnant and even more scared of being alone with a baby. Michael said it was the right thing for us to do - I didn't have any real say in the matter, and did not remonstrate.

After we got married, Michael became even more oppressive than before. He added domestic violence into the equation. Now if I did not obey his every command, he would not only verbally abuse me but would also settle the matter with his fists or his feet - whichever took his fancy. Not a week went by that Michael did not lay his hand upon one part or other of my body. Bruises littered my whole body. At first Michael hit me only where the bruises could not be seen with my clothes on, but later it didn't worry him quite so much. A black eye became my constant accessory - two black eyes sometimes. Michael commanded that I should never leave the house and I was so conditioned that I became his willing prisoner. At first I planned my escape, but fear stopped me from running away. I had nowhere to go you see - I had no family, having been orphaned as a young child.

When I was 8 months pregnant, I went into labour, that is I thought that I was 8 months pregnant, but it was in truth a full term pregnancy. It wasn't Michael's baby you see. The baby was a black man's that I had known a long time ago.

Miranda became quiet for a time, as the wheels of regression turned.

Sienna wanted to ask Miranda to explain how she came to be pregnant by a black man, but she thought better of it. Miranda seemed to be in a zone - a world apart and she did not wish to interrupt her.

Because I was battered and bruised, Michael did not want me to go out in public and so he had engaged a private Midwife to deliver my baby at home. I know I told you that Simon was born in the hospital before but that was not the truth - he was in fact born at home. We were living in Islington at the time. The Midwife was called as soon as my waters broke and it was 25 hours before Simon came - it was a difficult labour (pause). The wheels of time appeared to slow as Miranda forced her mind to open up its vault and release the hidden memories.

When I saw my son for the first time, I felt love tug at the strings of my heart as I beheld his beauty. But then love was overshadowed when it dawned upon me that I had given birth to a black child. And I cursed my child. The Midwife scolded me - she said that my baby was beautiful and that if I did not want him she knew other people who would have him. I listened to her and my heart softened. She was getting through the solus of racial prejudice that covered my humanness - that hung as a cloud above the true heart of me. She said that she could vouch that the baby was stillborn - that she could take him away and have him placed in an orphanage and later adopted. But I went into my shell and refused to discuss it further.

After the birth the Midwife left the room - but she was still in the house. Michael thought that she had left the house. He came in to see me and the baby and when he saw that the baby was black he began to cuss and proceeded to batter me black and blue. Then he walked over to the Moses basket where my son laid - he took a pillow and began to suffocate my baby. Just then the Midwife entered the room. Miranda spoke as though she was in a trance. Her speech became laboured.

As Michael ..murdered my child the Midwife ...she ran over ...challenged him to stop. Then Miranda continued her narrative more fluently. *She jumped onto his back and began to fight him. She was a big woman but still proved no match for Michael's well muscled arms and physique. He shook her off as though she were a mere ant and then turned his murderous rage upon her, sitting astride her body he squeezed her neck as she struggled to free herself from his deadly grasp. After a while she ceased struggling and relented limply under his grip. I was crippled by fear and pain. It haunts me that I did nothing to try and help that poor soul.*

As if she were filth, Michael spat upon her, "That's what you get for meddling into other people's affairs", he said then he spat upon her again and again. He cussed her until he was lost for cuss words. My baby was eerily quiet and I thought that he had died at Michael's hand. But as the door closed behind Michael who had dragged the body of the Midwife from the room and announced "I've got to clear this mess up", I heard a whimper from the Moses basket. My baby lived - I was overcome with love - love overpowered hate. I listened as Michael left the house. He went into the back garden where I heard him digging - I assumed it was a grave to bury the Midwife in. It was then that I wrapped my baby up snugly and sneaked out of the house with him in the Moses basket. It was the dead of night. I was weak and my body was in severe pain but I dragged my tortured body through it all. I covered my face with a scarf to hide its grotesqueness after the beating at the hand of my husband. It was pouring with rain and thankfully there were not many people about. I walked around trying to decide the best place to leave my child - where he would be found. We did not live too far from the Garston Hospital and as I walked past I saw people inside through the windows. I knew it was just a matter of time before someone came out and so I kissed my baby and left him in a sheltered place by the front entrance in his

Moses basket. I walked across the road where I found some small stones and threw them with as much force as I could at the door of the hospital. I then hobbled off as quickly as I could, and hid in a stairwell. I prayed that he would be discovered soon as I feared that he might be at risk to the adverse weather conditions. I watched as someone came to the door to investigate and from a distance I saw my son being found.

I didn't know what else to do so I went back home. I had nowhere else to go - no money, no job, nobody - nothing. I don't know what I was thinking - it would have been better for me to have remained on the street. It must have been a fear of the unknown that propelled me to go back. I returned to another beating. My husband wanted to know what had happened to the baby. I lied that the baby died where I had left him. He stopped the beating short of killing me. Luckily he had bigger fish to fry - because the back garden was too stony he was not able to dig a grave deep enough to accommodate the corpulent Midwife's body. So he went off to load her onto his wheelbarrow. He took her away and dumped her in the square around the corner from our home. No-one saw him in the wee small hours. I wanted to run away before he returned, but he had locked me in and in any case I would not have gotten far because I was in such a state after a very difficult labour and the beatings. It was months before I recovered. From that night on Michael kept me as a virtual prisoner in my own home. It was a miserable existence.

When Miranda had ended her exposure she looked drained.
Sienna was speechless - so many questions hovered in her mind but did not form - she was stunned by the revelation. Whilst she could accept that Miranda was misguided in her youth, Sienna was not sure how she felt about her benefactor having concealed a murder and shielded a murderer from

justice for all those years. She could certainly be viewed as complicit. Sienna was unsure what to think but there was no doubt about one thing, Miranda had acted in love in taking her baby to a place of safety in the face of imminent danger to herself.

"I need to rest now", Miranda announced.

And Sienna concurred - after carrying such a load for so many years, Miranda certainly deserved to rest.

Later Sienna intimated to Carlton the secret that Miranda had divulged to her. She faced a dilemma - what should she do about Miranda's disclosure that she had been complicit in covering up a murder all these years. Carlton was unsure what to make of it himself but his opinion was that it all sounded so far- fetched that Miranda could have been mistaken. After all she had recently suffered a stroke and at her age senility was probably a threat to clear recollection.

"Even if she is telling the truth, would the Police be interested in listening to events that took place nearly 70 years ago?" Carlton questioned.

"I don't know - probably not", Sienna replied.

They left it that they would discuss the matter further after the reunion and when they had the visit of Sienna's parents on an even keel. Right now they were far too busy to give it full attention.

Chapter 40

March 2018

Since learning that her son Simon had been located, Miranda seemed to have taken on a new lease of life. She was sitting up and talking again, more like her old self. Sienna was happy that she had also began to take an interest in her appearance. Although she had a way to go before she was fully restored, she was improving by leaps and bounds.

"So when is Simon coming to see me?" Miranda asked for the fourth time. Each day when Sienna visited her she asked the same question.

"He said that he would come at the weekend - Saturday or Sunday", Sienna explained. "He was not certain but said he would let me know on Friday - so as soon as I hear from him I will be able to say which day it is likely to be".

Miranda had instructed Linda to prepare a veritable feast to celebrate Simon's visit and the PA had in turn briefed reputable caterers who were waiting at the ready to get to work.

On Good Friday morning Sienna received two telephone calls. The first was from her father. It came in the wee small hours of the morning.

"Hi Sienna - it's dad", Sienna thought she was dreaming but as she looked at the clock on the wall she began to focus.

"Hi ..hi dad", she said rubbing her eyes and stretching.

"Sorry for calling you so late or early", he said with a chuckle.

"It's okay dad - you know you can call me at anytime, but it's unusual that you would call me at this time - what's happening?"

"I just had to call and tell you that Myra did get the date wrong for our trip so we are not arriving on Sunday as we thought but tomorrow, Saturday, we will be landing at Gatwick Airport at 1.15 pm". Alexander proceeded to give Sienna the flight number and she promised that she would be there to meet them.

"Dad, please make sure you text me the details as well so that there is no mix-up", Sienna cautioned.

The second call came at 8 am from Julius Anderton.

"Hello - is that Sienna Miller?"

"Hello, Sienna Miller speaking"

"Miss Miller, it's Julius Anderton - I hope I haven't called you too early"

"You can call me Sienna, Mr Anderton - it's great to hear from you and "no" you have not called too early", Sienna said.

"Call me Julius please".

They both laughed and Sienna decided that he sounded really nice.

As she spoke to Julius she imagined how Miranda would feel when she finally got to meet her long lost son.

Julius informed Sienna that he would be visiting Miranda the next day, Saturday, at 3 pm in the afternoon and they double checked address details.

"Miranda is so excited to see you - I can't wait to meet you in person too Julius"

"I reciprocate Sienna - I can't wait to meet my mother - oh and you, of course"

"She has been longing to meet you for so long Julius - your mother is a truly wonderful woman". "Whatever has transpired in the past, please find it in your heart to forgive her". "We all make mistakes and Miranda truly regrets hers", Sienna pleaded.

"I have had the most wonderful upbringing Sienna - my adoptive parents were exemplary - angels without wings". "They gave me all the love, grounding and everything else that I could have ever dreamed of so I lacked for nothing". "I hold no grudges against my biological parents regardless of the circumstances of my birth and adoption".

"That's good to know Julius, because Miranda just needs a blank slate - so although I am sure that you will be interested to know about the circumstances of your birth and adoption, please listen without prejudice when you meet her". "Please take no note about the past - give her a new page to write on from here on". There was a small pause before Julius spoke again.

"I hear what you're saying Sienna - but right now all that I have in mind is meeting my mother and giving her the biggest hug ever - I have dreamed of doing that ever since I was 10 years old, when I learned that I was adopted".

"Ahhh", a lump arose in Sienna's throat and she swallowed hard to try and dislodge it.

"I want to tell her thanks for giving me life - there is no bitterness whatsoever - really".

"I'm so glad to hear you say that Julius", a tear escaped from Sienna's left eye and meandered down her cheek. She scolded herself inwardly - why was she so affected by this? The answer readily presented itself - it was because she had grown to love Miranda so very deeply.

"Trust me Sienna - there is no animosity - just a lot of joy and glorious anticipation".

"You sound like a wonderful person Julius "

"I can hardly wait - this is long overdue", Julius stated.

"Yes, it is", Sienna concurred.

"Yeah - wow - thanks for finding me, Sienna", as Julius chuckled, he reminded her of someone - Miranda?

"It was the least that I could do for Miranda - she asked me to find you", Sienna said then added "Your mother is the kindest and least selfish person that I have ever encountered in my life".

"Wow - really?"

"Yes - see you tomorrow then Julius".

"Bye Sienna - see you tomorrow - bye"

When Sienna had ended the conversation it dawned upon her that she could not be in two places at the same time. She was meant to be collecting her father from the Airport at about the same time that Julius would be coming to meet Miranda and she had a promise to keep - she had to make sure that Miranda was not alone when she met Julius for the first time. She could not rely upon the nurse to oversee the meeting - that was not a part of her duties. Sienna would have to ask someone she knew, someone she could trust and if she could not find a suitable deputy, she would have to be there herself.

"Oh no - what shall I do?" Sienna verbalised her thoughts.

Carlton had to drive to the Airport so he could not be with Miranda at the same time. And she certainly could not ask Geoffrey - for one they did not even speak to each other and secondly, he would be certain to refuse any request that she could make of him. Sienna was not sure if he even knew that his mother had given birth to another son, let alone a mixed race son and in light of the racist tendencies he had exhibited to date, it was best if he did not know about Julius' proposed visit at all or he might not even allow him to enter the gates.

Linda was not able to help out due to childcare issues, and there was only one other person that Sienna could trust to help her out - Melvin. So she telephoned to ask him.

"Hi Melvin - how's it going".

"Great - good to hear from you - I've been meaning to call you".

"Yeah right - you hardly ever call me these days Sienna bemoaned - now that you have a girlfriend you don't have time for your friends anymore".

"Sorry Sienna - it's just that I've been so busy - I promise to do better in future".

"Well you can start to make it up to me right now - I really need you to bail me out tomorrow".

"What.....?" Melvin sounded apprehensive.

"Can you come over here and sit in with Miranda for three to four of hours or so tomorrow afternoon?" "I promise it won't be for any longer than that". "Just between 1.00 and 4.00 pm".

"Oh I'm sorry again Sienna - I can't do tomorrow - I already promised Dad that I would meet him tomorrow". "I wish I could help but I can't".

"Oh never mind - I know you would help me out if you could - not to worry, I'll have to resort to plan B".

Plan B meant that Sienna had to send Carlton alone to collect her parents at the airport while she stayed at home with Miranda. So she immediately sent her parents a What Sap.

"Sorry mum - dad - I really would love to come and collect you in person at the Airport tomorrow, but due to unexpected circumstances I will not be able to". "I am sending Carlton". "I'll explain later - sorry again".

Having attached a clear close-up photo of Carlton Sienna pressed "send" with a silent prayer that her parents would be understanding.

Miranda could hardly contain her excitement when Sienna told her that Julius was coming the next day. She began to fuss about what she should wear and also got Sienna to call the caterers to make sure that they put Linda's earlier instructions into action.

****

When Carlton visited her later that evening Sienna explained her dilemma to him - there was no way she could go to the Airport and oversee Miranda's meeting with her son.

"No worries", he assured.

"Thanks Carlton - I love you ".

"I love you more", .

"No - I love you more".

"No you don't I love you more".

"Okay - I believe you", Sienna said and they both chuckled.

So it was settled - Carlton would go alone to collect her parents at the Airport. Sienna shared the clearest photo of her parents with him and prepared a name sign for him to hold up as he waited in "Arrivals". Although she was longing to see her parents more than words could tell, after not having seen them in so many years, she had to make this small sacrifice for Miranda and Sienna determined that she would have to wait just a little longer.

Saturday dawned cloudless but cold. Rain was forecast for later in the day. Sienna awoke early and lay still in bed as she mused over, with anticipation, the imminent joy that the day promised.

Carlton was also excited - today he would be meeting the parents of his future wife. Regardless of what his family thought, Carlton was taking control of his own life. A few weeks ago he had informed his parents that he was dating a black girl and that he intended to marry Sienna. His mother, who wore the proverbial pants in the family, had baulked at the very suggestion and his father had promptly followed suit, delivering their verdict. "You marry that girl and you can forget that we are your parents". This comment cut a swath through the middle of Carlton's heart. He loved his parents so very much - they had been almost perfect parents, having nurtured him from birth and he would be eternally grateful to them for his life - for their sacrifices - for everything.

Although Carlton had always known of his parents' negative attitude towards people of other races, he was not prepared for their reaction which amounted to blatant racism. It took days for him to come to terms with their indictment. And after mulling over their rejection, he had come to his decision. Sienna would be a part of his future, regardless of whoever else was or was not in his life. The door of his heart and mind would remain open to his parents eternally if they cared to return to his life in future, but he had made his choice - he had chosen Sienna over them and from that day forward her people would be his - he only hoped and prayed that he would get along with her parents when they met. Like Ruth and Naomi in the Bible, he had also accepted her God as his God recently and was learning new ways of love.

****

Having already received her draft reply, Carlton's nervousness in officially asking for Sienna's hand was somewhat alleviated. In anticipation that her answer would be "yes", Carlton sought out a single diamond set in a cradle of 22 carat yellow gold and when he had found it, he smiled. He knew Sienna would just love this ring and imagined how her countenance would radiate light when she saw it for the first time. He planned to propose to her at the Airport. It had been his intention to ask the Airport administrators to grant him the favour of broadcasting his proposal over the "intercom". But now that Sienna would not be accompanying him, that plan had been scuppered. He wracked his brain for a unique way in which to pop the question and present his token of love. He could not come up with one so settled upon plan B. The main thing is that he would be taking that most important step. He reached for his mobile.

****

Sienna spent the morning cleaning, preparing for the imminent arrival of her parents. High on the adrenalin of excitement, she danced and sang as she worked, laughing at intervals as though she had just heard the funniest joke ever told. It dawned upon her that if others were to see her they might think that she were mad and that thought elicited the biggest chuckle of all.

"Who cares - mum and dad are coming", Sienna said. The proclamation sounded foreign to her ears and so she repeated the sentence, "mum and dad are coming", then she repeated it a third time, "mum and dad are coming", and she danced a peculiar jig around the living room.

The very best bed linen had been purchased, along with new kitchen utensils and toiletries. No expense had been spared in an effort to impress her royal highnesses. Corners left untouched for months were meticulously scrubbed clean and particular care was given to her bedroom - she would be relinquishing occupation of it to her parents during their stay as it was the most spacious and best situated room - it overlooked Bert's immaculately coiffured lawn and border hedges and lovingly cared for bed of Spring bulbs that had bloomed in a colourfully riotous splendour.

Trepidation set in momentarily - would everything be to her parent's liking and comfort? This thought dissipate as quickly as it had formed, as Sienna recalled how humble her parents were. They would not mind if they were put up in a stable, after all it was good enough for "Baby Jesus", her mother would be sure to reason.

A smile crossed Sienna's lips as she anticipated the loving arms into which she would shortly fall - how on earth had she survived for so long without those comforting embraces and voices of consolation? Sienna reflected briefly upon the blessings that she had encountered over the past six and a half years that she had lived in London. Right at the top of her list were Carlton, Melvin and Miranda. Sienna could not say which of the three she was more thankful for on a friendship level. They had each played their own unequalled part in her journey. So she thanked God for each of them. And gave a separate thanks that Carlton was no longer just a friend but the man with whom she was contemplating sharing her future.

Sadness clouded her thoughts as she thought about Sister Newson's demise. She did not like to think of the fact that the elderly lady had met her death at the hands of her own son - the very son who had caused the insurmountable rift between them. Although things had not worked out in the end, she had Sister Newson to thank for guiding and directing her when she had first arrived in London and she said a prayer for her soul to rest in perfect peace.

****

Having booked the Plaza Place restaurant for 8 pm on Saturday evening, Carlton telephoned Sienna to relay his plan to her. He did not tell her that he would be getting down on one knee, but that he had planned a celebratory dinner for her parents' arrival.

"Oh baby - that is soooo sweet", Sienna cooed. She wondered what she had done to earn the love of this veritable angel.

"I thought it would be good to take them out - drive around London and show them some of the sights before going on to the restaurant", Carlton said. He sounded so excited and Sienna hated to burst his bubble.

"Sweetie - that is such a lovely thought.... ", she then hesitated and Carlton could tell that there was a "but" coming so he coaxed it out.

"But?"

"B...but... but, well I think we should do that another day". "You see, mum and dad will be jetlagged and they will probably need to rest after their long flight".

"Oh yes, of course, I hadn't thought about that", Carlton said sheepishly. He was disappointed that his plan would have to be pushed back but he perfectly understood where Sienna was coming from.

"No worries - I'll cancel then".

"Yes I think that's best and anyway that place is "hexpensive", Sienna joked.

"Yeah - yeah - I know but I just wanted to treat you and your parents"

"Ahh you're such a sweetheart ".

"Yeah - anything for you babes".

" I tell you what though, Miranda has ordered up a feast to celebrate finding her long lost son and its lucky that mum and dad are coming today or I really don't know who would be eating it all", Sienna said and they both chuckled.

And Carlton had another idea - he would propose to her at church tomorrow. As he ended the call to Sienna he dialled Bishop Gooden's number - time to put plan C into place.

Chapter 41

March 2018

Within 30 minutes of meeting Carlton, Myra and Alexander had become fully acquainted. Carlton wooed them with his disarming smile, impeccable manners, wit and charm while they fascinated him with their Caribbean effervescence, ready laughter and natural warmth. Conversation flowed freely inside the vehicle as though between family who had known each other for donkeys years. Alexander's resolve to strenuously vet the young Englishman who had his sights on his daughter's hand had thawed within the first 5 minutes of meeting Carlton and Myra had asked him to "call me mum" in a record 10 minutes. Although no invitation to call him dad had yet been forthcoming from Alexander, Carlton took Myra's invitation to mean them both. Alexander, having warmed to being called "dad", reciprocated by calling Carlton "son" and as they arrived within 10 miles of Sienna's home, first names had been forgotten and substituted for "mum", "dad" and "son".

Chapter 42

Sienna approached the front of the main house at 2.00 pm - she was surprised to see that the porch and front entrance were decked in a sea of baby blue and white - balloons and streamers. A baby blue and white banner across the top of the main entrance bore the legend "Welcome".

"Hello there - I'm Sienna Miller - I live in the flat in the grounds", she greeted the butler stationed by the front entrance. He appeared to be aware of her as he smiled dutifully and nodded, "Thank you kindly Miss Miller - I believe Mrs Addison is expecting you".

In contrast to the fuss that had obviously been made by the entrance, the hall was untouched. Sienna walked briskly along the corridor's now familiar grandeur, as she headed towards the living room in search of Miranda. There she was, sitting demurely, hands folded across her lap, looking expectantly towards the door. Baby blue and white dominated the scene throughout the room.

Miranda's hair had been styled immaculately. Her mobile hairstylist had tweaked the thinning platinum locks, which had been ravaged by her recent illness, to give an illusion of a fuller head of curls. This feat was accomplished with the aid of a "fascinator" that provided a covering for the nearly bare crown. The style framed her face beautifully. An artist had also done a splendid job of her make-up - the degree of her infirmity less evident beneath layers of foundation, fixing powder, rouge, lipstick and eye-shadow.

Looking elegant in a well-cut but understated Jacque Vert suit in dusky pink, no-one could doubt Miranda's impeccable taste upon seeing the pearl stud earrings and matching 3-stringed pearl necklace that completed her attire. She looked healthier than Sienna had seen her since she suffered the stroke, the rouge on her cheeks aiding the figment of youth and imaginary health .

A large banner in baby blue and white spanned an entire wall and proclaimed "Welcome ". Helium balloons in baby blue and white hovered about the room. Sienna thought what a great job Linda had done. Walking across the room toward Miranda, she commented. "Miranda it looks great". She approached the elderly lady and bent down to engage her in a warm hug. A watery kiss left a ring of saliva on her cheek which Sienna wiped away surreptitiously. "You look lovely darling", Miranda complimented.
"And you look absolutely beautiful yourself Miranda", Sienna responded. She was happy that Miranda was almost like her old herself again. Their smiles revealed that they were each comforted by the other's presence.

After a few minutes of pleasantries Sienna excused herself and, leaving Miranda in her nurse's care, made her way towards the dining room to check out the arrangements. Her first reaction was one of total surprise as she walked into the hospitality area and observed the fuss. "Why on earth has Miranda gone to such lengths - this is just over the top", she murmured. "Who's going to eat all this food?" Sienna gestured to the head chef who stood observing her. He smiled amiably and shrugged.
"Maybe she is expecting more people than you know".
"Well I don't think so", Sienna gave him a questioning glance.
"I was asked to cater for 50 attendees", the chef stated and continued "and champagne is on tap".
 "Really?"

Each platter of finger food looked delicious, from the prawn toasties to the aubergine and cheese slips to the turmeric chicken strips to the lamb kebabs to the avocado and spinach dips with sweet potato wedges to the asparagus wrapped in prosciutto to the apple, brie and prosciutto crostini bites, to the mini meat and vegetable patties, each plateful looked as delicious as the next. The mingled aromas of well cooked food saturated the air.

Ten round tables, each seating five, were adorned in baby blue and white silken tablecloths and each chair had a matching back cover and helium balloon attached proclaiming "Welcome". A matching banner spanned an entire wall of the room.

"What else is on the menu?" Sienna asked as she looked across the room and observed three servers kitted out in theme colours, standing at the ready holding trays laden with filled champagne glasses.

"Well there is a choice between roast lamb, roast chicken, jerk chicken or pork and roasted halibut with either roast potatoes, fries, rice and peas, pasta bake or sweet potato fries and sides include green beans, carrots, mushrooms and there is also a choice between a Caesar salad or a green salad. Various sauces are also on the menu", proclaimed the head chef who walked by her side.

"Umm", Sienna exclaimed as she suddenly remembered that she had not eaten all day. "Well I think I will start the party right now", she announced, grabbing a plate.

Don't forget to leave some room for afters, the chef called after her with a chuckle in his voice.

"Don't tempt me", Sienna replied with a beaming smile.

Sienna sighed. She was glad that she had dressed up a little or she would have looked out of place amid the grandeur. She wanted to look good for her parents, so she had chosen a purple designer sample above the calf dress with intricate detail around the neckline, which she had complemented with a silver belt and matching silver shoes. She had coaxed her hair into an attractive roll at the back and piled it towards the left front of her head, where it was secured with a bejewelled pin. Sienna looked sophisticated and beautiful and oozed confidence.

Her plate piled high with the sumptuous finger food, Sienna returned to the living room to find out whether Miranda wanted anything to eat.
"No thank you dear - l..laater", Miranda sounded nervous.
"Okay just let me know when you're ready then", Sienna sat down next to her and began to eat, making small talk between mouthfuls.

Several minutes later the door opened and Linda entered with a tall silver-haired gentleman. Sienna guessed it must be her father. She was dressed much the same as she was any other day in a calf length black skirt and pink pullover with no embellishments, while her dad looked to have made a special effort in a black dress shirt and smart black slacks that looked like a designer cut. Silver cufflinks and a silver chain around his neck completed his attire. His tall elegant form drew credit to the designer's creation.

Sienna got up and walked towards Linda, "Hi Linda - I didn't know you would be here today".
"I was able to get a baby sitter after all - so glad, I didn't want to miss Miranda's birthday party", she replied then gestured to the man by her side, "Meet my husband, Robert".

"Birthday party?", Sienna exclaimed - surprise caused her to ignore Robert's outstretched hand. "What do you mean birthday party?"

"It's Miranda's birthday, didn't you know?"

"Oh my goodness - I forgot - oh no - I didn't even get her a card or wish her happy birthday or anything - oh no", Sienna was beside herself with discontent, not to mention her surprise that Robert, was a spouse and not a dad.

"Well I wouldn't worry too much anyway - I don't think Miranda will mind", Linda consoled her. "I think the main reason for the party is not her birthday but the fact that she is going to meet her long lost son". "Robert this is Sienna the young lady who lives in the flat annexe", Linda incorporated Robert into the conversation.

"So very pleased to meet you, Robert", Sienna hid her surprise well as she greeted Robert and added, "sorry I didn't mean to ignore you", then they chuckled and shook hands.

"Pleased to meet you too Sienna".

Sienna stared at Robert for far too long trying to work out how old he was. She surmised that he must be nearer 70 than 60. But his smile and youthful spirit belied his true age. It now became apparent that Linda, who was much older than her 29 years, both in the way that she dressed, her conversation and general outlook, was a perfect match for her husband. They communed generally as they ambled casually towards where Miranda was sitting.

"Oh Miranda - I'm so very sorry - I didn't realise that it is your birthday today - I didn't even get you a card, but I promise I will make it up to you - happy birthday dear Miranda", Sienna bent down to hug and kiss the matriarch with evident affection.

"Thank you", Miranda's voice sounded frail. Pulling away from her Sienna patted her lightly on the back. It was obvious that Miranda was making a valiant effort today and she silently applauded her as she asked again.

"Would you like me to get anything for you Miranda?"

"No dear - I'm alright", came the faint reply.

Linda proffered a card and gift to Miranda, accompanied by a duet of "Happy Birthday" from her and Robert, which exacerbated Sienna's feeling of guilt at having forgotten the day's significance. She skulked away in embarrassment towards the hallway just as Bert arrived in the company of his daughter and son in law. He was well turned out in a dark grey suit, light blue shirt and navy tie. His guests were more casually attired but did not look too out of place.

Sienna rushed towards Bert and engaged him in a hug - he looked equally glad to see her.

"Hi Bert - how are you?"

"Oh I'm okay - can't complain - I'm better than most people my age I suppose", Bert replied and continued, "This is my daughter Christine and her husband Sasha". "Sasha is an Accountant", Bert boasted.

"Pleased to meet you Christine - Sasha", Sienna shook hands with both and commented, "Oooh an Accountant eh?"

Bert beamed proudly, "Yeah .... didn't 'e do well", he replied. Sienna understood only too well how Bert felt, having hailed from humble beginnings herself. She knew how much it meant to her parents that she had done so well in qualifying as a Solicitor.

Both Sasha and Christine returned Sienna's warmth and exuded the same charisma as Bert. They all three engaged Sienna in conversation as she walked with them over to greet Miranda and later into the dining room where they proceeded to pile their plates high with finger food. They sat down at a corner table and with gusto began to chump heartily whilst maintaining a steady stream of banter, keeping Sienna enthralled. As the room began to fill with more guests, Sienna noted that theirs was definitely the corner to be in as they laughed, joked and had a good time.

Whilst Sasha and Christine went off to the be served with main courses, Bert gave a humorous account of his efforts at cooking during his wife's absence in hospital, causing Sienna to laugh until tears sprung to her eyes. Through tear filled eyes, she espied Mr Lawson across the room and reluctantly made her excuses and left Bert, to resume the role of hostess which she had neglected for over 20 minutes.

Mr Lawson was with his wife Nina. They made an odd looking couple, Sienna thought - he 5' 5" and she not an inch below 6'. She felt no anxiety in relating to her boss outside of the office for she knew Mr Lawson to be a wonderful human being, one that she would gladly call a friend in any circumstances, and she was happy to learn that Mrs Lawson was of a similar ilk to her husband. They conversed easily as she enjoyed Mr Lawson's knowledgeable wit complemented by Nina's dry humour.

As more guests arrived, tables filled up and a happy ambiance flowed throughout the dining room. But only too soon the atmosphere was clouded as Geoffrey entered the room. He was with a woman that Sienna did not recognise. They paused by the entrance and surveyed the guests before making a beeline for Mr Lawson and his wife. As he approached, Sienna made her excuses and walked away. She knew only too well that he would totally ignore her if she remained standing there and she did not want to have to deal with his attitude - not today. Lately she had been standing up to Geoffrey when he behaved in an unacceptable manner towards her and she did not wish to banter words with him and potentially mar Miranda's big day in any way.

Exiting the dining room, Sienna returned to the lounge to check on Miranda, although her nurse was seated next to her on standby. "Miranda - are you okay?" Sienna bent down to speak quietly to Miranda.

"Yes - Sienna, where's Simon?

"He hasn't arrived as yet". "I'll go out front so that I can be there to welcome him when he gets here - it's best that I wait out there as I am also expecting my parents to arrive from the Airport at any moment", Sienna stated.

"Your pa..arents..? Miranda stuttered, sounding surprised.

"Yes - oh - sorry Miranda - I should have told you - I totally forgot to mention that my mum and dad are visiting me from Jamaica - they arrive today". "Is it okay for them to stay with me?" "If not I can arrange a hotel for them".

"Of course... of course - they can stay - but ... you should have told me they were coming ...todaay?" Miranda looked somewhat distressed and Sienna wondered whether she was not overdoing things.

"So sorry - you're right I should have told you but there was so much happening that it totally slipped my mind". "Sorry", Sienna took Miranda's hand and squeezed it lightly.

"It's perfectly alright Sienna - I just wish I had known, that's all".

"I'll wait out front for Simon then", another reassuring squeeze of Miranda's hand.

Sienna made her way out of the living room through the milling guests and headed towards the front entrance. As she arrived at the front door she stood aside to allow a group of new guests to enter, noting that the Butler was executing his duty efficiently.

"Well done - you're doing a great job", she complimented.

"Thank you", he replied and beamed a winning smile.

As the group of four guests entered, Sienna smiled warmly and directed. "The dining room is that way - second door on the right", she added, "Miranda is in the living room if you want to say hello to her - first door on the left". One of the guests engaged her in conversation and she walked a few steps back into the house as they conversed. After a few moments she heard a familiar voice call out her name.

"Sienna", the last person that Sienna expected to see stood by the entrance. Forgetting that she was in mid conversation with someone else she turned and walked towards the speaker standing by the entrance.

"Melvin - what are you doing here?" "I thought you said you couldn't make it.

"I couldn't but you'll never guess what?"

"What?"

"My dad is Julius Anderton - he forgot his 'phone in the car and went back to get it".

"That is where I heard the name before - I thought it was familiar", Sienna had an "aha" moment.

Sienna and Melvin stepped outside away from the door as two further guests arrived and were ushered in.

"So your dad is Julius - what... really?" Sienna tried to process the coincidence.

"Yeah - can you believe it?" Melvin appeared more animated than usual, demonstrating his excitement.

"That means.... that... means that", Sienna stuttered.

"He is Miranda's son - unbelievable isn't it", Melvin beamed.

"So that means you must be related to Miranda", Sienna surmised.

"Yeah - I suppose I am", Melvin said as he contemplated the circumstances, "Miranda must be my grandmother - whoa".

"Oh my goodness", was all that Sienna could say.

"You know I told you that I was going somewhere with dad today, well I didn't realise that he was coming here", Melvin explained.

"Wow - what a coincidence", Sienna said as she reached over and engage her friend in a hug. As they pulled apart Melvin continued his account.

"He did not tell me that he was in fact meeting his birth mother today until I met him this afternoon, and even then I didn't realise that he was referring to Miranda". "It wasn't until the SatNav told him to turn into this road and announced "you have reached your destination" that the penny finally dropped, as I realised that I had been here before. It was only then that I put two and two together as I recalled that you told me that Miranda was going to meet her long lost son today". "I couldn't believe it ......".

As Melvin chattered away enthusiastically, Sienna's attention became diverted - she had just caught sight of her father who was climbing the stairs and walking towards them. She was surprised to see him - he appeared to have lost a significant amount of weight though and she hoped that he was not ill.

"Dad, dad - where's mum?" Sienna exclaimed as she ran to embrace her father. Tears filled her eyes as she reached out to him - it had been over seven years since she last saw her father - far too long. She hugged him tightly but he appeared to be holding back his embrace somewhat. Sienna was surprised that her father did not react in the usual warm manner that he was accustomed to doing.

"Sienna - are you okay?", Melvin asked.

"Yes - of course I'm okay - come and meet my dad".

"Sienna - that's my dad", Melvin looked perplexed.

"Oh.......", Sienna said and added "What did you just say".

"You're hugging my dad".

"Are you okay, young lady?" Julius sounded concerned.

"What.... ", Sienna sounded confused and Melvin worried that she was ill or had had too much to drink.

"Have you been drinking, Sienna", Melvin chuckled.

"I was just about to ask you the same thing, Melvin".

Sienna did not laugh though - she took a step back and stood very still, confusion etched across her beautiful face.

Melvin fell silent too when he realised that Sienna was not laughing - something was wrong - he did not really believe that she was drunk either because Sienna never over indulged. They stood in silence for a beat, confusion etched upon their faces. Then Sienna heard another familiar voice call out her name. Turning to look towards the parking area, she saw Carlton, and alighting from the back of the car were her parents.

Sienna stared at her father then turned to look questioningly into the eyes of Julius Anderton who bore an uncanny resemblance. At the same time, Melvin looked towards Alexander and then back at his own father.

"I see why you mistook my dad for yours", he said and chuckled. "Looks like you've got a doppelganger dad".

Julius was not sure what to make of it all. He had thought the young lady who embraced him to be a relative who had known of his coming today.

Now it suddenly dawned upon him that there was some sort of mix up. As he looked at Alexander, he felt a connection and knew that the same blood ran through their veins but clearly the look of perplexity that was fixed upon this man's face told that he did not know anything about him.

As Alexander approached the entrance steps he looked up curiously at Julius. Who was this fellow that looked so much like him?. Then Myra voiced his thoughts.

"But what a man look like you een Alex - 'im is almost the dead stamp a you", she exclaimed in pronounced Jamaican lingo.

"Uhmm - a so me a tink too", Alexander replied.

Coincidences or otherwise momentarily forgotten, Sienna ran and fell into the arms of her loving parents and they each hugged and kissed and cried as Melvin, Carlton and Julius looked on.

Eventually they broke apart and made their way into the living room where Miranda was sitting. She was beginning to show distinct signs of fatigue after having met so many people in one day and having sat for so long in an upright position, but she visibly perked up as they entered the room and walked towards her. Sienna was still in a fog about the strange resemblance of her father to Melvin's. However, she pulled herself together and took charge.

"Miranda - this is Julius Anderton, your long lost son".

Julius stepped forward and tears immediately filled his eyes. Tears also flowed freely down Miranda's cheeks.

"My son - my de..a.r Simo...on", she called him by the name she had given to him as a newborn baby. They embraced long and hard.

When they finally broke apart, Sienna noticed that Miranda was looking intently towards her father. She gestured to Sienna to come over and asked, "Sienna - is that your father over there?"

"Yes Miranda - my mum and dad have arrived and my father looks very much like Julius, your son".

"Al..e..ex ......Alex ... my darling first son".

"What.....what?"

"I'm so sorry - I wanted so much to tell you Sienna", Miranda said apologetically.

"What.... you mean..?" Sienna felt faint. She stumbled over to a chair and sat down.

Alexander and Myra immediately went to their daughter's side, "What is the matter with you Sienna - you feeling okay?" Myra fussed.

"Sienna ..... what's the matter?" Alexander bent down to cradle Sienna in his arms.

"Dad I'm just confused - Miranda just said that you are her son - her first son - how comes you never told me - how comes nobody told me?"

Alexander felt as if he had received a knock-out punch. He was in a daze - what on earth was happening? Was he dreaming. How could this be? His first instinct was to call his father and ask him to provide some clarification. As far as he knew, he had buried his mother over 5 years ago and as far as he remembered, she had been a dark shade of black. This woman who was now purporting to be his mother was a light shade of white. Questions filled Alexander's mind as he took each faltering step towards the woman who beckoned him with her eyes. He could not deny the uncanny resemblance to this other man whom she was also calling her son. And he gathered that

Julius too had been estranged from the woman he now approached and involuntarily hugged as his mother. As Alexander succumbed to the frail arms that embraced him, he experienced an emotional attachment, felt a love that he had known fleetingly a very long time ago, that had been buried somewhere in the deep recesses of his mind, the true love of his real mother.

The unbelievable scene unfurled before Sienna's eyes. Miranda just referred to her father as her first son? But how could that be? Sienna crossed her arms and gently pinched herself. She was definitely wide awake - wide awake in a dream.

Linda watched the development in astonishment. In all the years that she had worked for Miranda, although she knew there were secrets to tell, she could never have guessed at the revelation that had just unfolded before her eyes today. Miranda had welcomed not one but two long lost sons.

****

Miranda should have collapsed with exhaustion hours ago, but adrenalin was holding her upright.
She wanted to speak to Sienna, but how could she begin to explain.
"Alex..aanderr, please call Sienna for me".
"Okay", Alexander walked over to Sienna and took her hand. He led her over to where Miranda was seated.
"Sit next to me please - dearest Sienna", Miranda's voice was now all but a whisper.
"I wan..ted so much to tell you Sienna - I tried to tell you many, many times b..b..but. - I just couldn't divulge my terrible secrets". "So, so, sorry dear - please forgive me?"

As Sienna looked into Miranda's eyes she viewed a tortured soul, a soul that she had grown to love very deeply. "I wish so much that you had told me" - a pause then she added - "I love you Miranda".

"I love you too, my dear", Miranda's eyes refilled with tears.

"You have shown me nothing but love and care Miranda - as far as I am concerned, there is nothing that I have to forgive you for", Sienna added.

"Thank you so much - you don't know what it means to me to hear you say that, Sienna".

"Miranda you are my grandma - that means so very much to me", Sienna smiled through tears of joy.

As Miranda smiled back gently, Sienna realised for the first time that her cheeks resembled her own.

As Sienna and Miranda hugged, Julius walked over to Alexander and looked into eyes that mirrored his own. He engaged him in a big brotherly hug. "Pleased to meet you brother", he said and Alexander replied, "Glad to make your acquaintance too brother", even as the questions that needed answers played about his mind. Together they walked over to their newly found mother and sat down, one on either side of her as Sienna moved away to allow them to get closer.

Some guests began to cheer as they learned about the family reunion that was taking place. Others cried emotional tears while others still laughed and everybody in the room celebrated with Miranda who had found her long lost sons.

The commotion carried through to the dining room, bringing most of the other guests into the living room to find out what was happening. Amongst the last guests to arrive were Geoffrey, his companion and Mr and Mrs Lawson. As Geoffrey entered the room he noticed Alexander and Julius seated next to his mother and became immediately incensed. As far as he was concerned his mother had gone too far now. Why on earth had she invited all these black people and not only that, she was openly fraternizing with them. It was bad enough that that stupid black girl Sienna was here, hob-nobbing in circles way above her station, but now his mother was bringing black men in as well.

Geoffrey marched intently over to where Miranda was seated. She had left him no choice, he would have to confront her - here and now.
"Mother, just what do you think you are doing?" "What are all these B-L-A-C-K people doing here?" Geoffrey placed an emphasis on the word "black" as though it were a dirty word.

Miranda tried to speak but words failed her. It was obvious that she was not up to the stress of this confrontation. Sienna involuntarily stood up and faced Geoffrey. "Would you mind not shouting at Miranda - she is too frail to take this sort of treatment?"
"Just you shut your dirty mouth young woman - I can't believe I almost said "young lady"". "The likes of you should never be called a lady", Geoffrey proclaimed as several guests gasped at the insult.
"Clearly you have no concern for your mother's health and well being, but let me tell you something - I will not stand by and allow you to send my grandmother to an early grave - you get that?" Sienna countered as Mr Lawson smiled - he whispered into his wife's ear, "That's my brilliant Assistant talking". He felt proud of Sienna's response and ashamed of Geoffrey's behaviour. Mr Lawson made a mental note to give full consideration to splitting up the partnership. He had been meaning to do so

for some years and this repulsive display today was the straw that broke the back of a very long suffering camel. He was tired of covering up for Geoffrey's incompetence. Over the years his partner had proven to be far less than an average Solicitor and Mr Lawson had taken to scrutinizing his files to see that he was "toeing the line". He had tolerated him because what Geoffrey lacked in legal intelligence he made up for in business acumen and ran the practice quite well. But Mr Lawson detested hateful people and he had had a gutful of Geoffrey's particular brand of nastiness, especially the unacceptable manner in which he treated Sienna, whom he had come to revere highly.

"Grandmother - how dare you refer to my mother as your grandmother - point of correction mother is white..W H I T E and you are B L A C K", Geoffrey spelt out the colours insolently, then he continued. "I think you should also be put away, but into a different kind of institution to the one I will be placing mother into AS SOON AS POSSIBLE". Geoffrey shouted the last four words of the sentence for emphasis.

As Geoffrey finished speaking, Julius joined in the conversation, "Actually I have DNA evidence that proves that I am the true son of your mother, Miranda Addison", Julius withdrew a letter from the inside pocket of his jacket and handed it to Geoffrey. He continued to speak, "And as you can plainly see from our uncanny resemblance, Sienna's father is my brother - your mother has confirmed that to be a fact, which makes Sienna the granddaughter of Miranda".

As Geoffrey looked at the DNA letter he became even more irate. He grabbed it out of Julius' outstretched hand and proceeded to rip it into tiny pieces as he laughed loudly at a joke only he had heard. All the guests stood around gaping at him as he sneered.

"I want all of you (the "n" word) and gold-diggers out of my house now before I call the Police". "I am counting to 10 and then I will be calling the Police".

Miranda looked helpless but spoke authoritatively, although in a near whisper - "It's my house - not yours and I say they stay and if you don't like it - you can leave".

"You stupid, stupid whore.....", Geoffrey shouted at Miranda. And as the final word was uttered he looked aghast when he realised what he had said, but it was too late - like an egg once cracked cannot be put back together so the offensive word once uttered could not be retracted and the apologetic look that crossed his face did not convince anyone present that he had not meant to say it.

"You have gone too far Geoffrey - apologise to your mother, now", Mr Lawson interjected brusquely. Geoffrey looked shamefaced but did not apologise.

"Well - of course I did not mean to say that", his tone was conciliatory.

"But you did say it - you should not even have thought it", Mr Lawson was livid and the red glow that rose from his neck upwards through his face testified of that fact.

"You disgust me Geoffrey - how dare you speak to your mother like that and especially in the presence of all her guests", Mr Lawson said. He then stomped over to where Miranda sat. His wife following closely behind. He took Miranda's hand and spoke the apology that Geoffrey had declined to, "So so sorry Miranda - try not to be too troubled - Geoffrey just lost it somewhat", he said as his wife cooed her concurrence.

Geoffrey's girlfriend skulked away quietly as he ended his rant. He looked about the room as though seeking some complicit smile, but found none. Most looked at him with varying degrees of disgust although one or two looked pitifully upon him as he shuffled about in shame.

One by one the guests quickly made their excuses and left and within 5 minutes only Miranda, her nurse, the family members, Carlton, Linda and her husband remained. Geoffrey went to sit in a corner by himself where he swigged from a large bottle of brandy like a commoner on a park bench, directly contradicting his ethos of superiority to other races when juxtaposed against Julius' and Alexander's staid posture seated next to Miranda. Conversation was limited to soothing remarks trying to comfort Miranda. After a few minutes the nurse, assisted by Sienna and Linda took Miranda back to her quarters to put her to bed.

When only the men remained, Julius walked over to talk to Geoffrey, willing to put first impressions aside and to embrace him as a brother.
Proffering his hand, Julius offered, "Why don't we start over.....",
"Get away from me", the response was loud and uncalled-for.
"Okay - if that is how you feel", Julius laughed heartily as Geoffrey left the room with his nose held high in the air haughtily and headed to his quarters. He thought about calling the Police and reporting a break-in but his phone battery had died. Getting more intoxicated by the moment as his earlier over-indulgence kicked in, he began to stagger. When he arrived at his rooms, he collapsed in a drunken stupor upon the floor.

And so ended Miranda's birthday and reunion party. After having tucked her new found grandmother into bed Sienna bent over and kissed her upon the forehead.

"Goodnight grandma".

"Goodnight granddaughter", Miranda took hold of Sienna's hand and squeezed it lightly. "I love you so very much".

"I love you too", and they both smiled as hope of a bright tomorrow filled their hearts.

Miranda asked for her sons to come and say goodnight to her. As they stood by her bedside she whispered "I love you" to them. Then she continued, "Of course you want to know the whole story - there is a lot to tell - I will tell you tomorrow".

"I'm just happy to have found you at last" Julius said, finding his long lost birth mother was more than he could ever have hoped for.

"Oh I look forward to hearing your story", Alexander replied and he truly would wait with baited breath, for he needed to know, to unravel the thread of his past. He needed answers to the questions that he had asked all his life. Questions like, "Why do I have hazel green/grey eyes whilst my other siblings' eyes are brown"; or "Why is my complexion so much lighter than my brothers and sisters". Alexander needed answers. Those unspoken questions had only ever been answered by scoffers who had so often accused the lady he thought to be his birth mother all his life, as an adulteress who had given his father a "jacket" for a son. And he had believed those lies without raising questions of his mother or his father. But now that he knew the truth - he wanted to know the whole truth. For as the Bible rightly says "...the truth shall set you free", and Alexander needed to be liberated.

Alexander wondered why Beryl, whom until tonight he had thought to be his mother, had borne the scorn poured upon her all those years without revealing the truth. The answer immediately sprung to his mind - she must have made a promise to his father never to divulge his maternity to anyone. Yet he now recalled that on occasions one or other elderly village resident would give one hint or another which he had then thought to be spoken in jest but now he knew that they were based upon truth. He distinctively recalled a couple of discourses with Mr Morse, the local shopkeeper, whose comments he had found very strange. These notable remarks had never shifted from his memory. On the first occasion, he had paid for his flour and milk and was leaving the shop when Mr Morse had called after him.

"Say hello to your father and Beryl for me".

"Okay - I will tell mummy and daddy "how de do for you sah",

"Who is you mummy?"

"I beg your pardon sah?"

"Ask you papa who you mummy is".

"Sah - what you mean...?"

"Nothing - Is a joke me a run", Mr Morse had replied and laughed loudly.

On another occasion Mr Morse had commented, "You don't realise that Beryl is too dark to be your mother?". This remark had caused Alexander to feel somewhat confused, but when he had sought clarification from Mr Morse he had received the same reply.

"A joke me a run, son". And as Mr Morse was always "running joke pon other people", Alexander had taken his word for it. But now he knew that Mr Morse must have known this secret all along.

****

Sienna needed to know the whole truth too, especially in light of Miranda's earlier revelation that she had witnessed her husband commit murder. But come what may she would never cease to love Miranda. And joy filled her heart now that she knew that Miranda was her grandmother she could demonstrate her deep love with unbridled fervour. But trepidation also simmered on the back burner of her psyche.

****

The caterers, supervised by Linda, finished clearing up. They all left at the same time as the day nurse. When the night nurse arrived, Sienna, accompanied by Carlton, took her parents, uncle and cousin back to the flat.

Julius and Alexander were enamoured with each other. They sat around the kitchen table where they drank never ending cups of strong coffee and talked. They conversed about their lives, each fascinated by the other's adventures and accents. But the greater fascination and repeated discussion was reserved for the unexpected revelation that had taken place in the last few hours.

Sienna and her mother took to the main bedroom where they chatted and giggled like schoolgirls as opposed to mother and daughter.

Carlton and Melvin caught up on the past few months and also discussed their plans for the future in the living room.

By midnight the flat had quietened down. Her mother had fallen asleep after having taken a long hot bath, Carlton and Melvin had crashed in the living room where Sienna made them comfortable with pillows and blankets. Now, she sat up in bed in silent contemplation, where she had been for the last half an hour. It occurred to her that the men had also fallen silent in the kitchen so Sienna went to investigate. She found them both asleep, heads resting upon the table.

"Daddy - why don't you go to bed", she asked.

"Yes - A tink I should do dat", Alexander replied and arose. Sienna led him towards the master bedroom.

"I need to take a shower first". Sienna pointed out where the bathroom was.

"We'd better get going now", Julius called out as he made his way into the living room. He loped clumsily over to Melvin and attempted to rouse him from sleep. "Let's go man".

"Oh dad - I'm too tired to drive and you have been drinking far too much - let's just stay the night".

"How do you mean - we can't just stay the night....". He was just about to add that they could not possibly encroach on strangers when he recalled that he was with family.

"Yeah - why not just stay the night - you can sleep in my bed - I'll sleep in with mum and dad - I've got a sleeping bag", Sienna volunteered.

"No - its better if you sleep with your mum and I can share with Julius - we still have a lot of catching up to do", Alexander called from the bathroom.

"Yes - okay dad", Sienna said and they all laughed.

For Carlton and Melvin it was just like old times.

Chapter 43

April 2018

Next morning Sienna arose bright and early with the intention of attending Easter Sunday service. She tip-toed around so as not to awaken the others who were all still fast asleep. Carlton awoke just as she was about to steal out the front door.

"Morning babes - where are you off to?"

"Shooo - sorry I woke you up - I'm going to church".

"Let me drop you off on my way home".

"Okay - that would be good".

"Yeah - I'll go home, have a shower and change. Give me a buzz and I will come back to pick you up after church".

"Okay darling", Sienna felt so blessed.

Sienna arrived early for church thanks to Carlton. She waited a full half an hour before praise and worship began. Thanks to God flowed freely from her lips, heart and spirit during praise and worship. The prolonged Easter Sunday morning programme included a dramatisation of the crucifixion and resurrection and the Mass Choir was the highlight of the day. By the time Bishop Gooden took to the dais to bring the Word two hours had flown by and Sienna was experiencing a spiritual high.

Before bringing the Word Bishop Gooden informed the congregation that he had a special announcement to make.

"Good afternoon brethren - it is with great pleasure that I announce that wedding bells are ringing again here at Born Again Church of God". Ooohs and Ahhhs rang throughout the sanctuary as Bishop Gooden gestured with a nod of his head to someone near the back of the large auditorium. Applauds arose and built to a crescendo as someone began to make their way towards the front of the sanctuary. As the person walked past Sienna's pew she glanced at him then glanced again. Her mouth fell open - it was Carlton. To say that she was surprised was an understatement.

Smiles beamed and eyes darted from Carlton now standing at the front of the sanctuary, to Sienna who was still riveted in her seat.

"And who is the blessed lady whose hand Bro Carlton wants in holy matrimony?", Bishop Gooden asked with a large grin plastered across his face. "Does anyone know who she is?"
"Sister Sienna", the congregation chanted.
"Did you say Sister Sienna", Bishop Gooden was enjoying this game.
"Yes - Sister Sienna", all eyes now turned to where Sienna was sitting, including Carlton's who gave a mischievous smirk and wink.

Sienna stood up gingerly, nerves causing her to tremble. She walked quickly to join Carlton where she wagged a forefinger at him, "You - I should have guessed that you were up to something", she said as she laughed joyfully.

A mike was held up to Carlton's mouth so he could be heard. "Thank you very much - I feel incredibly blessed to have met this beautiful lady and I would like firstly to request the consent of her wonderful parents to propose to Sienna".

Suddenly Sienna became aware of her father walking quickly up the aisle towards them and her mother walked a few paces behind him, next to

Melvin. It became apparent to Sienna that they had all been a privy to this surprise. She wagged a playful finger at them as they laughed happily.

The mike was placed to Alexander's mouth and he spoke his consent, "I have only known Carlton for a very short time, but in spite of that I have no hesitation in consenting to him proposing to my dear daughter Sienna". Rapturous applaud greeted this statement.

Upon receiving consent Carlton did not hesitate in getting down upon one knee "Sienna Miller will you do me the honour of becoming my wife?"

Without hesitation Sienna replied "I will". A joyous atmosphere filled the sanctuary, as the family hugged and well wishers approached to convey congratulations and good wishes,

It is unfortunate that not everyone shared in the merriment, notably two gentlemen who had been seated on either side of the building and a lady that was seated at the front of the middle section, who had walked out as Sienna gleefully accepted Carlton's proposal. One of the men was heard to comment, "....these white men have stolen everything from us and now even wants to steal our beautiful women". And the other two culprits had variously caste daggers, hissed and held noses high as a mark of their disapproval to the coming union.

Bishop Gooden was sensitive to the Holy Spirit who dictated to him there and then that he should forsake his pre-prepared sermon and instead orate about the sin of racial prejudice. He obeyed, entitling his sermon "Colour Doesn't Matter - racial prejudice in the church". He quoted Acts 10 vs 34-35:

"So Peter opened his mouth and said "Truly I understand that God shows no partiality but in every nation anyone who fears Him and does what is right is acceptable to Him"."

He defined prejudice as preconceived preferences or biases.

Bishop Gooden explained the definition of racial prejudice as irrational suspicion, hatred of a particular race, group or religion, also passing judgment or forming an opinion about a person before you know them. He went on further to explain that racial prejudice is played out by individuals believing that race or skin colour accounts for differences in human character, intelligence or ability, resulting in the person harbouring racially prejudiced views showing partiality towards one race over the other. He invited the congregation to evaluate themselves critically, to ask themselves whether, taking into account the definitions, they were in fact racially prejudiced.

A pin dropping would resound throughout the auditorium as they hung upon Bishop Gooden's words. He then went on to divide up prejudice into four categories - generational prejudice; environmental prejudice; reaction generated prejudice and institutional prejudice. Elucidating on each kind before concluding that the church as a body are in denial. For although Christians - black, white brown or other - maintain that they are not racially prejudice, there is no other body where segregation is more prevalent and evident.

Bishop Gooden concluded that all racial prejudice, including reaction generated prejudice amounts to sin, that we must purge our hearts with the love of God because the commandment is to love one another regardless of race, colour or creed. There was not qualification in respect of race or skin colour in the Bible he taught.

"Brother Carlton and Sister Sienna are fine examples for all of us to follow". "They have looked beyond colour, beyond differences and discovered the beauty of true love - a love that will no doubt sustain their union and guarantee a beautiful married life together", Bishop Gooden smiled towards the happy couple as he brought his message to a close.

"God is no respecter of persons, brothers and sisters". "God loves us all unconditionally and we must emulate Him. It is only then that we will experience the full and true joy that the love of God brings". Ask yourself this "What is a colour?" I am proud of Sister Sienna and Brother Carlton today who can say that a colour to them is nothing except beautiful in their eyes because their hearts are full of unbending love for each other.

To the true Christian the only answer should be that intended by God - variety". "Let us celebrate our differences brothers and sisters".

****

After church Sienna paid Miranda a visit. She found her propped up in bed and in good spirits.
"Sienna darling, I'm so happy to see that you have not deserted me".
Of course I would never abandon you Miranda"
"Please call me grandma - I have waited so long to hear you say that". Sienna said nothing for a beat - Miranda spoke again, "I understand that it may be a lot to ask of you so if you don't want to - I won't force it upon you".
"No - I do want to - grandma - it's just strange that's all - I'm still in shock".

"I understand - I will try and explain later - have you been to church?".

"Yes Mi...... I mean grandma", they both chuckled.

"I hope you said a prayer for me"

"You know I did" - another chuckle in stereo. "You are looking very well today Mi.. grandma".

"Thank you dear - I feel marvellous". "So did you go to church alone?"

"Yes - that is, I thought I had gone alone, then Carlton turned up and proposed to me in front of the whole church". "And guess what, mum, dad and Melvin were there too". "They all knew except me".

"Really - Carlton proposed?" Miranda sounded like an excited schoolgirl. "Let's see the ring darling". Sienna proffered her hand, shaking the third finger of her left for emphasis. The solitary diamond twinkled her happiness.

"Ta da - isn't it beautiful?" Sienna enthused.

"It certainly is gorgeous", Miranda agreed and continued "I'm so happy for you darling - we must celebrate", she said with a twinkle in her eyes.

"Yes - we will", Sienna concurred.

Suddenly Miranda became solemn, "You know dear - I owe you all a full explanation". It is good that you are all still here, so I can talk to you all at once". "Why don't you all come over and join me for dinner at 4 pm".

"Sure - I will tell the others when I get over to the flat and let you know what they say then", Sienna said as she turned towards the door.

"The refrigerators are fully stocked with all kinds of goodies from yesterday", Miranda enticed.

"Great idea - I'll go and tell them then".

That afternoon they gathered once again in Miranda's dining room. Alexander and Julius had now fully bonded to the extent that Julius wore a Caribbean themed shirt loaned to him by his elder brother who was similarly attired. Melvin was happy to find that he had a change of clothes that he had left at Sienna's flat when he was staying there temporarily.

After they had eaten heartily and enjoyed joviality and frivolity with their meal, they retired to the living room. Carlton, having been made aware of the nature of their gathering, thought it a good time to leave the family members alone and kissed Sienna as he left, "See you all later".

Miranda sat in the centre of the room, holding court. She had invited Geoffrey to join them for dinner but he had not turned up and it was evident that he would not be putting in an appearance. Geoffrey's slighting caused her sadness but she had to proceed with or without his presence. Unbeknown to her, Geoffrey had taken somewhat of an interest in the gathering - he had activated the monitoring system that was fitted to every room in the building. It had not been used to full effect since it was installed several years previously but he had been pleasantly surprised to find it in perfect working order. Being convinced that the black people in his home had brainwashed his mother and had sinister fraudulent intentions, he wanted to ensnare them, so when his mother had informed him that they would be dining with her, Geoffrey had wasted no time. He would bring these fraudsters to justice - he would record their every move and then he would throw the book at them.

****

Like a miracle, Miranda seemed to have gained divine strength overnight. Sienna made her comfortable and sat close by her to attend to her every need. And as Miranda began to narrate her history the room fell deathly silent.

Look out for The Yard Girl - Miranda's Story - available March 2020.

In the meantime, if you have enjoyed this novel and would like to read more of Eugenie Laverne Mitchell's works, please check out "Washed", "Philanthropic Ways" and "Rebel Seed". Happy reading.